THREE PATHS TO GLORY

"It's apparent the author did much research before putting words to
paper."
Stan Roeser, *Litchfield Independent Review*.

"Every high school student should read *Uprising*."
Alice Seagren, former Minnesota Commissioner of Education

"No one knows or better appreciates the significance of events associ-
ated with what is known as the 'Great Sioux Uprising' of 1862 as told
by Dean Urdahl in his critically acclaimed book, *Uprising* and its
sequel, *Retribution*."
Edwin C. Bearss, Chief Historian Emeritis, National Park Service.

T0099252

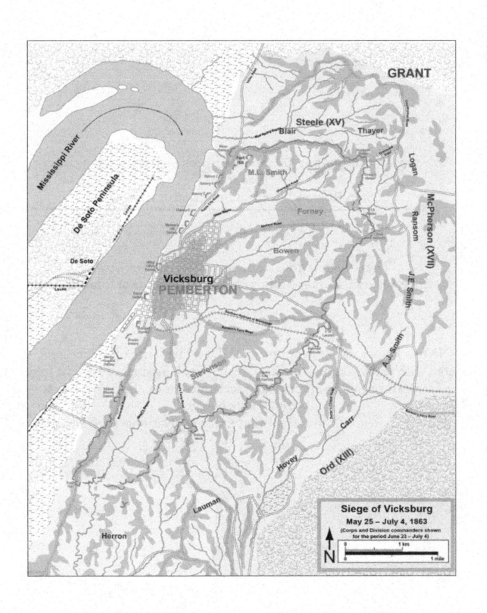

GRANT

Steele (XV)
Blair   Thayer

Mississippi River

De Soto Peninsula

Fort Hill

M.L. Smith

Forney

Logan

McPherson (XVII)

Ransom

Bowen

J.E. Smith

De Soto

Vicksburg
PEMBERTON

A.J. Smith

Stevenson

Carr

Hovey

Ord (XIII)

Lauman

Herron

Siege of Vicksburg
May 25 – July 4, 1863
(Corps and Division commanders shown
for the period June 23 – July 4)

N

1 km

0   1 mile

Three Paths
to Glory

Dean Urdahl

NORTH STAR PRESS OF ST. CLOUD, INC.
St. Cloud, Minnesota

Front cover images: © iStock Getty Images.

Author photo: Joe McDonald

Printed in the United States of America

Published by
North Star Press of St. Cloud, Inc.
Saint Cloud, Minnesota

www.northstarpress.com

DEDICATION

To my wife and editor, Karen,
for her countless contributions to my multitudinous projects
and
to the memories of Clinton Cilley, Jimmy Dunn, and Sam Davis.
May courage and commitment always be a part of our nation's story.

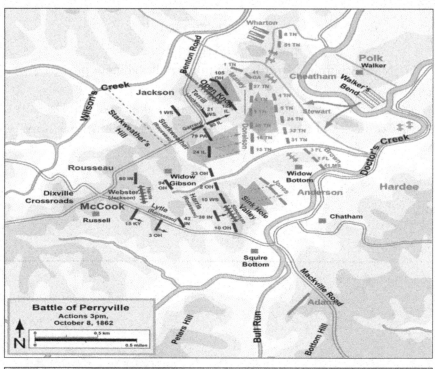

Battle of Perryville
Actions 3pm,
October 8, 1862

0.5 km
0.5 miles

N

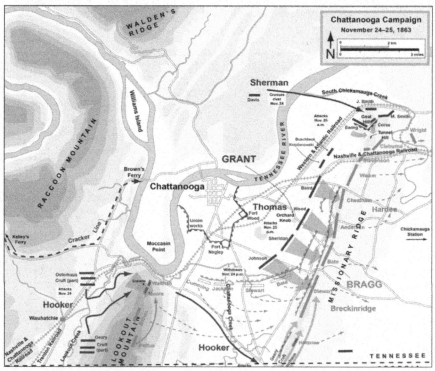

Chattanooga Campaign
November 24–25, 1863

2 km
2 miles

N

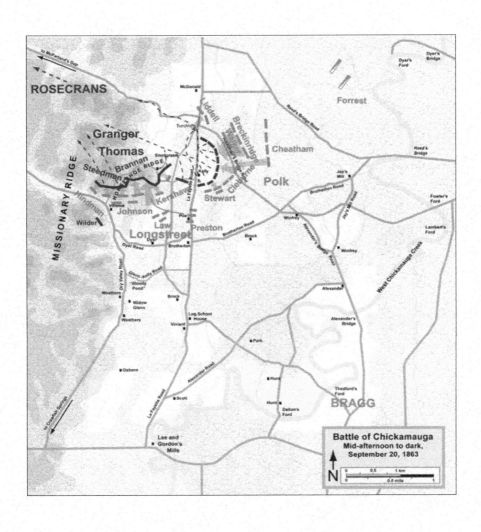

ROSECRANS

to McFarland's Gap

McDonald

Dyer's
Ford

Dyer's
Bridge

Reed's Bridge Road

Forrest

Turchin

Liddell

Granger

Thomas

Brannan

Steedman

SNODGRASS HILL

HORSESHOE RIDGE

Kelly

Breckinridge
Hill-Walker-Adams

Cheatham

Reed's
Bridge

MISSIONARY RIDGE

Hindman

Vittetoe

Johnson

Kershaw

La Fayette Road

Cleburne

Stewart

Polk

Jay's
Mill

Brotherton Road

Fowler's
Ford

Wilder

Law

Longstreet

Poe

Pioneer

Preston

Brock

Brotherton Road

Winfrey

Jay's Mill Road

Lambert's
Ford

West Chickamauga Creek

Dyer Road

Brotherton

Glenn-Kelly Road

Bloody
Pond

Dry Valley Road

Weathers

Widow
Glenn

Brock

Winfrey

Alexander

Weathers

Log School
House

Viniard

Alexander's
Bridge

Park

Osborn

Alexander Road

Scott

La Fayette Road

Hunt

Hunt

Thedford's
Ford

Dalton's
Ford

BRAGG

Lee and
Gordon's
Mills

to Crawfish Springs

Battle of Chickamauga
Mid-afternoon to dark,
September 20, 1863

N

0   0.5   1 km

0   0.5 mile   1

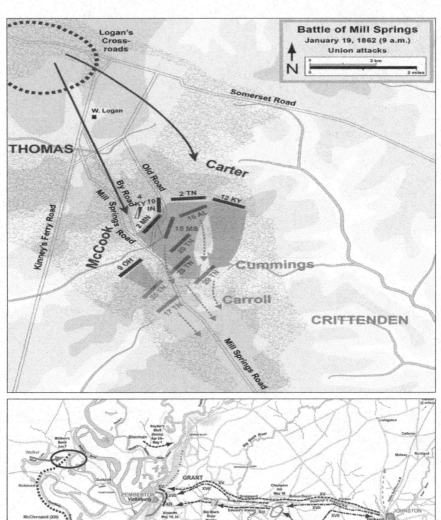

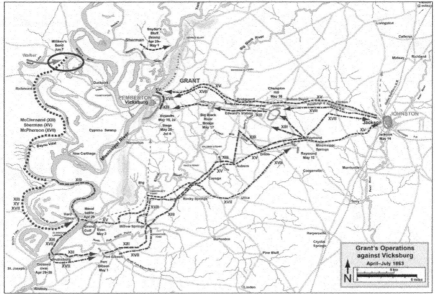

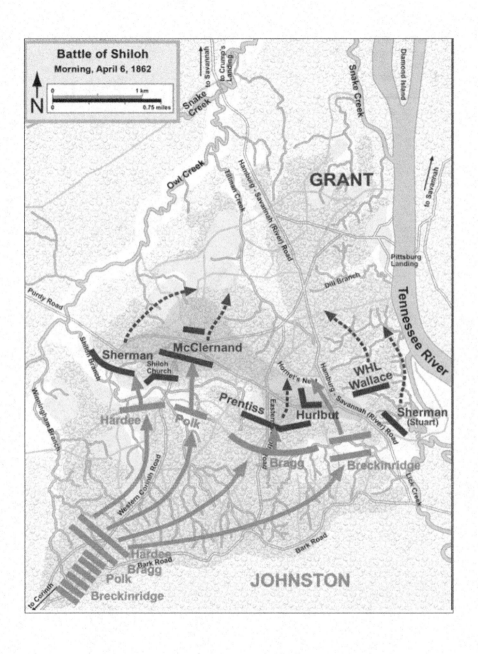

Battle of Shiloh
Morning, April 6, 1862

N

0 ____ 1 km
0 ____ 0.75 miles

to Savannah
to Crump's Landing
Snake Creek
Snake Creek
Diamond Island

Owl Creek
Tillman Creek
Hamburg - Savannah (River) Road

GRANT

to Savannah

Purdy Road

Pittsburg Landing

Dill Branch

Tennessee River

Shiloh Branch

Winningham Branch

Sherman

McClernand

Shiloh Church

Hornet's Nest

Hamburg - Savannah (River) Road

WHL Wallace

Hardee

Polk

Prentiss

Eastern Corinth Road

Hurlbut

Sherman (Stuart)

Western Corinth Road

Bragg

Breckinridge

Lick Creek

Hardee
Bragg
Polk
Breckinridge

Bark Road

Bark Road

JOHNSTON

to Corinth

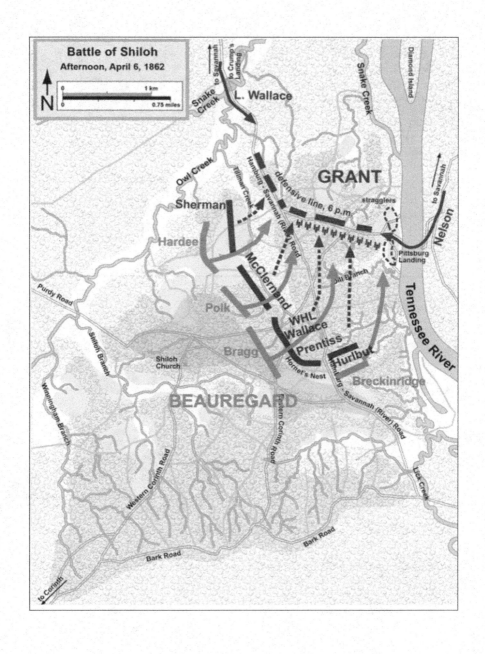

Battle of Shiloh
Afternoon, April 6, 1862

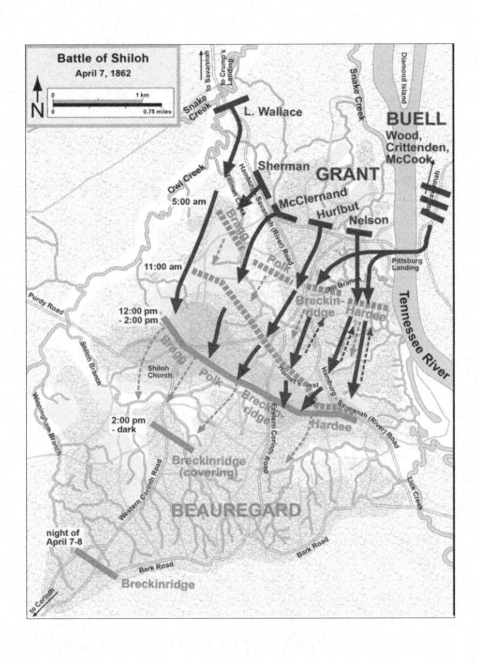

Battle of Shiloh
April 7, 1862

N

0   1 km

0   0.75 miles

to Savannah

to Crump's Landing

Snake Creek

Snake Creek

Diamond Island

L. Wallace

Sherman

GRANT

BUELL

Wood,
Crittenden,
McCook

Owl Creek

5:00 am

Hamburg-Purdy Road

Gilbert Creek

Savannah (River) Road

McClernand

Hurlbut

Nelson

Bragg

Polk

Pittsburg
Landing

11:00 am

Tilghman Branch

Breckin-
ridge

Hardee

Tennessee River

Purdy Road

12:00 pm
- 2:00 pm

Bragg

Polk

Shiloh Branch

Shiloh
Church

Hornet's Nest

Breck-
ridge

Hamburg - Savannah (River) Road

Hardee

Eastern Corinth Road

2:00 pm
- dark

Waninngham Branch

Breckinridge
(covering)

Western Corinth Road

Lick Creek

BEAUREGARD

night of
April 7-8

Bark Road

Bark Road

to Corinth

Breckinridge

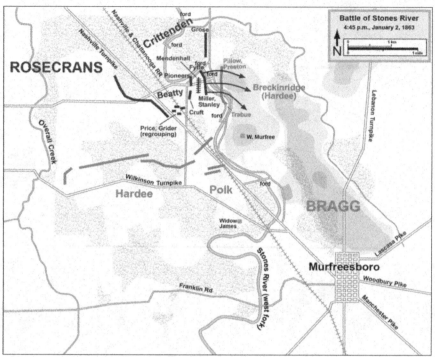

Battle of Stones River
4:45 p.m., January 2, 1863

ROSECRANS

Nashville & Chattanooga RR
Nashville Turnpike
Crittenden
ford
Grose
ford
Mendenhall
Pioneers
ford
Fyffe
ford
Pillow, Preston
Beatty
Miller, Stanley
Cruft
ford
Breckinridge
(Hardee)
Trabue
Price, Grider
(regrouping)
W. Murfree
Overall Creek
Wilkinson Turnpike
Polk
ford
Hardee
BRAGG
Widow
James
Lebanon Turnpike
Stones River (west fork)
Lascasa Pike
Murfreesboro
Woodbury Pike
Franklin Rd
Manchester Pike

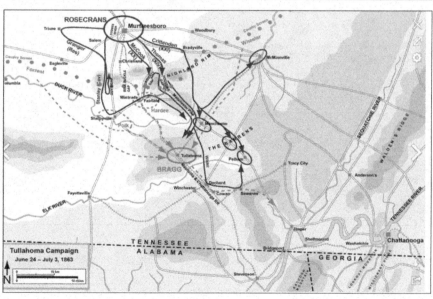

ROSECRANS
Triune
Murfreesboro
Woodbury
Wheeler
Granger
(Rsv)
Salem
Crittenden (XXI)
Bradyville
McMinnville
Cavalry Screen
Forrest
Eagleville
McCook
Thomas
HIGHLAND RIM
Christiana
Columbia
DUCK RIVER
Stanley (Cav)
Liberty Gap
Wartrace
Fairfield
Hardee
Manchester
Shelbyville
Polk
THE BARRENS
Pelham
Tullahoma
Hillsboro
Tracy City
Anderson's
WALDEN'S RIDGE
BRAGG
Fayetteville
Winchester
Decherd
Cowan
Sewanee
ELK RIVER
TENNESSEE
ALABAMA
Jasper
Shellmound
Whiteside
Chattanooga
SEQUATCHIE RIVER
TENNESSEE RIVER
GEORGIA
Stevenson
Bridgeport

Tullahoma Campaign
June 24 – July 3, 1863

Foreword

THIS IS THE STORY of three regiments in the American Civil War: the Second and Fifth Minnesota and the First Tennessee. I've followed these regiments through the major battles each participated in from the beginning of the war to the winter of 1863.

I've tried to depict the lives of common soldiers and the uncommon valor that followed them throughout the conflict. The book traces the wartime lives of three men: Clinton Cilley, Jimmy Dunn, and Sam Davis. It became my goal to intersperse the experiences of these three men with the great battles that made up the Western Theater of the Civil War. I have tried to explain in plain terms how these great battles were fought and the roles of regular soldiers in them. Technically, the U.S. Dakota War of 1862 contains battles classified as Civil War battles. This will, I hope, give you a real sense of what happened in the west during the first two years of the Civil War.

This is a work of historical fiction. Most of the fiction lies in the dialogue. Wherever possible I've used the actual words of those speaking. I also tried to be as accurate as possible in my depiction of the battles and events.

I found that while researching I was set off on side trips. For example, the 2nd Minnesota's attendance at a church service in Florence, Alabama, led me to contact the church to find out what had happened to the pastor.

In researching Sam Davis, I discovered Mary Kate Patterson was an espionage agent herself. I might add there's no record of a romance between Kate and Sam, save one source that suggested the possibility. I chose to elaborate.

My original intent was to cover the whole of the Western Theater in one volume. As I wrote this story I realized I couldn't do justice to what happened in the constraints of one book. Therefore, there'll be a volume two that finishes up the war through the campaigns of 1864 to the end in 1865.

Many more adventures and experiences await my characters and the three regiments along their paths to glory.

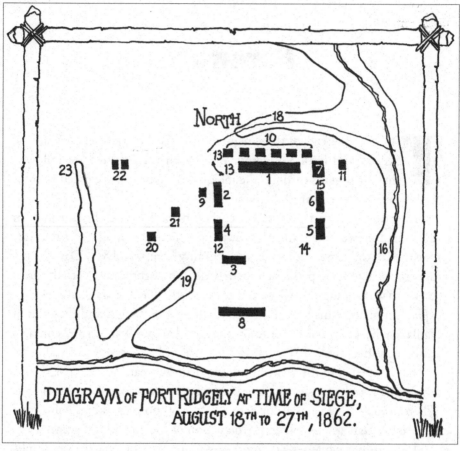

DIAGRAM OF FORT RIDGELY AT TIME OF SIEGE,
AUGUST 18TH TO 27TH, 1862.

1. Barracks	13. Position of McGrew
2. Commissary	14. Position of Bishop and Nathan
3. Headquarters	15. Position of Gere and Whipple
4. Officers' Quarters	16. Fort Creek in Wooded Ravine
5. Officers' Quarters	17. Minnesota River
6. Officers' Quarters	18. St. Peter Road down Ravine
7. Laundry	19. Depressed Ground
8. Large Barn	20. Sutler Store
9. Blacksmith Shop	21. Guardhouse
10. Old Log Quarters	22. Powder Magazines
11. Building Wipple Fired	23. Timbered Ravine to West
12. Position of Jones and Renville Rangers	

Illustration by Bill Gabbert

Wasioja

WASIOJA WAS A GROWING, bustling southeastern Minnesota town in April of 1861. The future seemed as bright as a gloriously sunny, spring morning. A dozen storefronts framed the main street, including a hotel. A flour mill ground wheat on the river. Wasioja even boasted a small, one-room brick law office with a shingle out front proclaiming, "James George, Attorney at Law." But the pride of Wasioja was a brand-spanking-new two-story brick building at the edge of town—a school, founded by the Free Will Baptists. Northwestern College had been established for primary grades through college. Opened the previous fall, it boasted nearly 300 students.

On this beautiful spring day, people streamed along the road to the school. They weren't just students, and a sense of urgency hurried everyone's steps. This was an important day. There was news to hear.

A large downstairs room, furnished with benches on either side of a center aisle, was quickly filling with men and a few women. The front benches were already occupied by college-aged boys. The final seats filled as a hush enveloped the room. A young, suit-clad man strode to a lectern at the front of the room. The professor had no notes; for what he had to say he didn't require them.

Clearing his throat, he brushed his dark hair alongside his head. The mane hid the tops of his ears and draped below his collar in back. A pair of wire-rimmed glasses rested on his straight nose. Although he tried to appear calm, sweat beaded his forehead that already showed a receding tide.

The young man began to speak. "First off, for those of you who don't know me, I'm Clinton Cilley, a professor of mathematics here at Northwestern. Our country faces a great turning point. The bombardment of Fort Sumter has plunged our nation into a great crisis.

"When President Lincoln called for 75,000 troops, our governor, Alexander Ramsey, happened to be in Washington City and immediately

offered President Lincoln 1,000 Minnesota troops to help preserve our
union. He was the first in the nation to offer troops. At the first call, Minnesota men stepped forward to enlist. Nearby Chatfield formed the Chatfield
Guards, electing Judson Bishop captain. They're prepared to go to Fort
Snelling to join the 1st Minnesota Regiment.

"However," Cilley continued, "word reached Captain Bishop that the
1st had already filled its contingent of ten companies containing 780 men.
The men of Chatfield were instructed to wait until the need arouse for more
troops and the formation of a second regiment. That regiment is now being
formed. That's why we gather here today.

"We're fortunate to have a veteran of the Mexican War, James George, in
our midst. He's using his law office as a recruiting station, signing up new soldiers. Mr. George asked me to speak to Northwestern students today."

Cilley paused a moment, glancing at the back of the crowded room. A
young man silhouetted the open doorway, looking for an open seat. Finding
none, he leaned against the door frame and listened.

Cilley continued. "We are faced with a most monumental decision. Will
we allow our great nation to be torn apart simply because one group doesn't
like how something is, or may be done?"

A chorus of "No!" and "Never!" reverberated off the brick interior.

"Mr. George has made a generous offer. For those who wish to stand up
and fight to hold our country together and put down the rebels forever, his
law office is open for all to sign on to join the Union army. I pray our time
away from Wasioja will be short. But be it weeks, months, or years, we have
a sacred and glorious task before us.

"Would it were God's will that peace prevailed, but now we can do no
other than serve our Union cause. Are you with me! If you are, follow me to
Mr. George's office!"

As Cilley strode quickly down the center aisle. Young men in the first rows
sprang to their feet and followed their professor. The young man in the doorway waited for the procession to pass, then joined the march down the street.

A queue of sixteen students formed in front of the law office. A desk
had been set up outside for signing up. Inside a doctor thumped the boys in
turn on their chests, looked into their eyes and asked a quick series of questions, "Age." Enlistees had to be eighteen. "Any sickness?" "Got good feet?
Walk around in a circle for me. Turn around slowly."

For each he signed a slip of paper, handed it to the recruit and pointed him out the door with, "Good luck, see the fella again out front. He'll sign ya up."

The line moved quickly. After the doctor's inspection, the men signed an enlistment paper handed to them by the man at the table.

Cilley shouted to them, "After you've signed up, gather on the street in front of the hotel! We've got some company business to attend to."

Eighty men gathered down the street, including many students and some from Chatfield in Fillmore County, boys who had hurried to Wasioja. The last to stand before the doc for his physical inspection was the young man who had watched from the seminary doorway.

The portly, white-haired doctor looked up from his chair as the boy entered.

"Last one?" he questioned, his glasses slipping to the edge of his nose.

"Yes, sir."

"What's yer name, son? I don't recall seeing you around here."

"I'm James Dunn, from Chatfield. Folks call me Jimmy."

The older man looked over the youth. Slender, with a full head of unruly dark brown hair, Jimmy was dressed in dark woolen pants and a white cotton shirt. His face was pleasant, smooth, like it had never seen a razor.

"Mr. Jimmy, how tall are you?"

The boy straightened his back and threw back his shoulders. Doc looked down and smiled as he saw Jimmy's heels raise ever so slightly off the floor boards. "I'm five-foot-ten, sir."

"I think five-foot-six would be stretching it. And, by the way, that's what you're doing, stretching it."

The boy's face creased into a wide grin that lit up his whole countenance. "Ya got me, Doc, I'm five-foot-six and three-quarters. And that's in my stockin' feet."

"How old are you, Jimmy?"

"Nineteen."

Doc stood up from his chair and walked over to the youth, placing his hand on the boy's shoulder. "Sorry, son. I don't believe you're nineteen. Hell, I don't even think you're seventeen. Do you have a note from your parents authorizing under-age enlistment?"

"No, sir," the boy mumbled.

"Go back to Chatfield, Jimmy. Grow a little and git older."

"The war'll be over by then."

"Maybe. I don't think so. I got a feeling this is gonna take a lot longer than folks think. It isn't a picnic. I think you'll git all the war you want. Now git outta here and go home. The war'll wait for you."

The disappointed young man left the law office/recruiting station and stood on the edge of the new recruits gathered in front of the hotel. They included Chatfield men. He knew Judson Bishop, the newspaperman. He was standing out front with Clinton Cilley and James George, the lawyer.

It was Bishop who spoke. He brushed a hand through his full head of wavy, dark hair and began, "Welcome, men, I'm Judson Bishop of Chatfield. I commend you for your courage and commitment to saving our nation. We will be mustered in at Fort Snelling and become the 2nd Minnesota Volunteer Infantry Regiment before heading south. We formed Company A in Chatfield. I was elected as captain. More men are being recruited in Fillmore and other counties under the efforts of Josiah Marsh of Preston."

"What 'bout his brother, John?" a voice cried. "He fought the Mexicans."

"John couldn't wait. After the 1st was filled and he heard the 2nd wouldn't be mustered until we have enough men, he crossed the river and joined up in Wisconsin. He's in their 2nd Regiment now. But a spot's reserved for him in Minnesota. I'm sure when the time comes, John Marsh will be leading Minnesota troops. For now, he's a private in Wisconsin."

"The item of business we need to attend to is the election of your officers."

"That's easy!" a voice shouted. "They're standin' in front of us."

The man's words were true. The new soldiers voted and elected their first company commander: James George as captain and Clinton Cilley as Sergeant Major. As the group dispersed, Dunn approached Cilley.

"Sir," Jimmy began, "I wuz turned down by the doc. He don't believe I'm nineteen."

Cilley looked the boy up and down. "Well, I think I agree with Doc, but I believe that quite of few of our boys managed to fool him by adding a year or two to their birth dates. For some reason you didn't get by with it."

"What can I do? I wanna be with this company!"

"I'm afraid you'll have to wait. What's your name, boy?"

"Jimmy Dunn, from Chatfield."

"Look, Jimmy, things will change. We've got two regiments now, but I think Minnesota will have ten or eleven, maybe more before this is over.

What I'm saying is that the regiments aren't set yet. We elected officers, but that might change, too. Go home and wait. I'm sure a company of more Chatfield boys will be formed, and you'll be able to hook up with them."

"It might all be over by the time all this shakes out."

"It might be longer than we think. I hope not."

"I wanna fight."

"What do you want to fight for, boy?"

"To save our country. Them rebs wanna rip it apart."

"What about the slaves? Don't you want to free them?"

"Sure," Jimmy grinned, "we'll take care of that, too."

Cilley slowly shook his head. "I think you'll get your chance. We just formed the 2nd. There'll be more. I guarantee it. Now go back to Chatfield.'

Jimmy turned to leave, then stopped. A small smile flashed across his face. "Seventeen," he said.

"What?" Cilley asked.

"I'm seventeen."

"Then you don't have long to wait."

Sam Davis

EIGHTEEN-YEAR-OLD SAM DAVIS glanced at the glass window of his classroom. Rain splattered against it and ran in rivulets down the pane. But Sam didn't care about the rain this day. He quickly refocused his attention as the headmaster/professor of Western Military Institute took his place before them.

It was May 8, 1861, and Sam had entered the school just ten weeks before. The air at the institute was electric with conversation about secession, the firing on Fort Sumter and Tennessee's reaction. Since the day of Lincoln's election, Tennessee had ridden a tumultuous roller coaster of public opinion with demonstrations and votes reflecting the ebb and flow of the Volunteer State's support of the new southern Confederacy. On May 2nd boys from Sam's home county of Rutherford had arrived in Nashville after forming a company supporting the Confederate cause. On May 7th the state legislature had voted to remove Tennessee from the Union.

Professor Bushrod Johnson stood before his crowded classroom. He noticed some weren't registered for this class. Many had come because they expected something more than an engineering lecture from their headmaster.

Johnson tugged at his mustache, then ran his hand over his wide forehead before clearing his throat. "Gentlemen," he began, "this is a monumental day for the State of Tennessee. We are leaving the Union. Forces are gathering here in Nashville to support the new Confederate States of America.

"We know Tennessee has its reservations. An early vote blocked a convention to consider secession. Eastern Tennessee still has strong opposition. But that should all be behind us now. It became our duty to fight for our rights after the Union aggression called for 100,000 men to fight against the Confederacy and end our rights here in Tennessee. Governor Isham Harris stood his ground when the call came for two regiments of our militia to help put down a rebellion. He told Lincoln's Secretary of War Cameron, 'Tennessee will not furnish a single man for purpose of coercion, but fifty thousand, if necessary, for defense of our rights and those of our Southern Brothers.'"

Applause broke out in the crowded, stuffy room. Johnson held up his hand to silence them and continued. "It won't be easy, and I'm from the North. I know those people. Take nothing for granted."

A young man in the front raised his hand, still following classroom decorum. "Mr. Wilson," Johnson acknowledged.

"Sir, you were born in Ohio, trained at West Point. You're a Yankee, but you sound like you're going to fight for the Confederacy."

"I've been in the South since 1848 ever since I left the military after the Mexican War. I've taught at two southern schools including this one in Nashville. I've married a southern lady. My family is now rooted in the South. Yes, I'll offer myself to fight for Tennessee and the Confederacy."

Once again the room erupted in applause as the young men rose to their feet whistling and loudly clapping. Johnson gestured downward with his palms.

As the room silenced, Sam, sitting near the back, raised his hand.

"Mr. Davis," Johnson called.

His classmates looked back at Sam with expectation. The young man was quiet and deferential. He didn't speak often, but when he did his thoughtful observations had earned esteem and respect.

"Professor Johnson," Sam commented, "I don't know how many realize what a hard decision this must have been for you. You weren't just from Ohio. You were a pacifist Quaker and helped escaped slaves on the Underground Railroad. It must have been a great sacrifice to leave your family in the North behind and transform your life."

Johnson smiled grimly. "Mr. Davis, your observations are quite prescient. Life changes one's opinions of things. Pacifism wasn't the proper course in dealing with Indians or Mexicans. I came to see that slaves in the South often lived better lives than millions of immigrants who live in squalor in crowded cities. Most importantly, I came to believe it's beyond the rightful power of the federal government to dictate the rights of sovereign states who voluntary joined the Union of states and should be able to leave it in the same way."

"What should we do?" a voice shouted.

"As headmaster, I declare this term now ended. Each of you is free to do what you wish." His calm voice rose as he concluded by shouting, "But if you're true sons of the South, you'll join me tomorrow and begin our great crusade!"

Cheers and applause drowned the crack of thunder from outside. Students crowded around Johnson, thanking him and shaking the professor's hand. Sam hung back and approached Johnson when he was alone.

"Sam," Johnson smiled, "I'm glad you waited. I did want to talk to you. You're going to enlist, I expect?"

"Yes, sir. I am."

"Will your family stand with you?"

"I have no doubt. Smyrna is only twenty miles south of here. Our farm is our way of life. The Yankees would destroy all my family has built."

"We need men like you. Oh, there'll be hundreds of thousands ready to fight. But I've noticed things about you, Sam. You're special. The boys look up to you, even older ones. We'll both be in the same army. I'll keep you in mind for duties that might benefit from the skills I believe you have."

"Will Professor Smith join us?" Sam wondered.

"I'm sure Kirby Smith will be an officer in our army. He's a West Point man, too."

Johnson extended his hand. Sam matched it with a firm grip. The boy was slightly taller than the five-foot-ten professor, but his build was slight. Sam's curly dark hair flopped over his ears, framing a slender, handsome face.

Sam smiled at Johnson and responded, "Thank you, sir. You'll know where to find me when the need for something special comes up. I'll be ready."

"You've got a little time. Will you be going home first?"

"Regiments are enlisted by county. I'll go to Murfreesboro in Rutherford County, enlist, get some things and tend to some personal business."

Johnson laughed, "No girl involved is there?"

Sam reddened and then smiled. "Maybe."

"How will you get home?"

"The train stops at Smyrna. I'll have a few hours with my family before heading on to Murfreesboro."

"And a young lady, no doubt. With luck," Johnson concluded, "the war will end quickly and nothing more will be needed from you. But I don't think that likely. May God bless us all."

Sam soberly added, "And may He bless the Confederate States of America."

* * *

SAM DIDN'T HAVE TO GO home to see his young lady. Mary Kate Patterson lived just nine miles from his father's plantation. But she wasn't there. At present she was in Nashville as well, attending the Elliot School.

He hoped his message had reached her and Kate would be waiting in their accustomed meeting place, a grove of trees near her school. The rain had stopped. Blue sky peeked through streaks of lead-gray clouds. Sam picked up his pace to reach the school.

She was there. In a green clearing with trees all around, Sam saw her trim, straight figure. A hooded cloak shrouded her features, but Sam had no doubt it was Kate. She ran to Sam when he appeared and embraced him.

Sam reached down and drew her hood onto her shoulders, revealing Kate's beautiful face and flashing brown eyes framed by a cascade of bouncing brown curls.

"Oh, Sam," she cried as they eagerly embraced, "what will you do?"

"I'm going home to enlist. What about you?"

"I can't stay here in school, not with Tennessee fighting for our glorious cause of freedom. I'll go home, too, to LaVergne."

"What will you do there?"

A mischievous smile flashed across Kate's face. "My father's a doctor and a Mason. He has contacts and entrée to people and places others don't. Through him I believe I can find ways to be of service to the Confederacy."

"Your father won't let you be exposed to danger. I'm against that, too."

Kate gazed up at Sam and set her mouth. "I'll find ways to help. This war isn't just all about men."

"Yes, Kate, nurses will be needed and your father is a doctor."

She reached up and kissed Sam, then smiled again. "Maybe a nurse, maybe something else. Time will tell."

"When will you leave school?"

"I'll finish the term to the end of May."

"I expect only to be gone a few days. The Rutherford boys are already camped in Nashville. After I enlist, I'll be back here."

Kate kissed him again. "Don't forget me."

* * *

SAM DEPARTED the next day on a twenty-mile train ride to Smyrna. By noon he was in his home town and only a few miles from the Davis Farm. He rented a horse and trotted down the trail to home, two miles east of town.

Charles Davis, Sam's father, had moved to the farm on Stewart's Creek in 1847. Charles had come to Rutherford County from Virginia. Margaret, his wife, had borne three children. Through hard work, speculation in real estate and gambling, Charles had prospered. A four-room log cabin and a few dozen acres had grown to a nine-room, white clapboard house with a classic Greek four-column portico across the front and over eight hundred acres of farmland.

Fifty-two slaves grew corn, sweet potatoes, and cotton. But the prosperity had come at a price. Margaret had died in 1840. Charles married Jane, a woman with coal-black eyes and a kind, gentle and loving nature. They had their first child together in 1842 and named him Sam.

The boy grew up surrounded by a large, active family as six more followed him, with another on the way. They would total eleven Davis children from both of Charles's marriages. But Sam's closest friend was Coleman Smith, a young slave four years younger than he.

Sam prodded his horse to quicken its pace as his impatience grew in anticipation of home. The neat rows of corn signaled Davis land and promised a fine crop. Sam swatted his steed into a canter as the neat farmstead came into view. The barns, outbuildings and slave quarters and the simple, yet majestic white house brought joy to the young man.

He passed black men and women at various tasks and grinned as he waved a greeting to them.

"Mastah, Sam's back!" a young man shouted. "Somebody git da mastah!"

But Charles Davis didn't need to be notified. The ramrod-straight sixty-one-year-old wiped a handkerchief over his broad forehead and brushed back his shaggy, white hair as he strode down the porch to greet his son. Jane, thirty-nine, and obviously pregnant, burst through the front door and raced past her husband to welcome their son. She wrapped her arms around Sam and exclaimed, "You're home! It's so wonderful to see you! Are you hungry?"

Then she stopped and her face sobered. "Why are you home? School isn't over. No," she considered, "you mean to join the army, don't you. Sam, you can't. You're just a boy."

Charles walked beside them. "Jane, Sam's a man. He'll do what he thinks is right and we'll support him in that."

"I have to, Mother," Sam explained. "Rutherford County already has a company. They're at Nashville. I'm going to sign up and join them there."

"Your brother John's already joined. I suppose Alfred and William will too. Will I have no children left?"

"Mother, Oscar's only fifteen. The war'll be over and we'll be free before he's old enough to fight."

Jane's eyes filled with tears. "God save you. God save us all."

"I'll be careful, Mother. Don't worry."

"She has a right to worry, boy. We all do. We're all in God's hands. He'll decide everyone's fate. How long do you have here?"

"Just a few hours. I have to take the next train out of Smyrna for Murfreesboro to enlist."

"Get some food going, Jane. Sam can't leave here on an empty belly."

Soon they were seated at the end of a large table in the dining room. Sam chewed a slice of cornbread and stuck a piece of ham with a fork, ready to follow the bread with a bite of pork.

"Did you tell Kate?" Jane asked.

"Yes, she'll leave school when the term's up."

"That's what you should have done."

"I don't know who'd be teaching us. Professor Johnson and Professor Smith left the school. I'm sure others will follow them."

"It won't be easy, Sam," Charles advised. "War's a nasty business. You'll have friends who'll die. People will try to kill you, and you'll try to kill them."

"Maybe," Sam considered, "or maybe they'll just let us be. We don't have to fight."

"The Yankees won't let us go. Lincoln made it clear he'll fight a war to hold us in the Union. For there to be a war, they'll have to come south to try to force us back into the United States, and they will come."

"Then I'll be standing with the other boys from Rutherford County. We'll be waiting for them to come and try. Where's Coleman?"

"He's off with Joe. They took some corn to town."

"I'm sorry I missed him. Greet him for me."

"Your teacher, Mr. Sharpe, inquired after you. He said you were a very fine student."

"Greet him for me, Father. I'm sure our paths will cross again."

A few hours later Sam was in a train car heading for Murfreesboro. He would soon become a member of Company I of the 1st Tennessee and would be returning to Nashville to join them.

2nd Minnesota Regiment
THE ROAD TO WAR

War seldom happens according to plan or accommodates men's timetables or expectations. The men who signed up at Wasioja and other Minnesota towns expected to head east immediately, put down the rebellion and be home in three months.

The United States Army had other plans. Companies A-K mustered in at Fort Snelling during the last week of June. There was no Company J because the letter was too easily confused with others. As was common in the Union army in the war's early days, companies were mainly made up by county. Fillmore, Olmstead, Dodge, Ramsey, Nicollet, Washington, Brown, Goodhue, and Blue Earth counties were organized in companies from A through I. Company K was recruited at large.

Early in July, instead of going south, six companies were sent to garrison Minnesota frontier posts previously maintained by regular army troops already fighting rebels. Companies A and F went to Fort Ripley, B and C to Fort Abercrombie, and D and E to Fort Ridgely. The rest of the 2nd Minnesota stayed at Fort Snelling. All the companies devoted their time to drill and instruction.

On July 22nd Horatio Van Cleve was appointed colonel of the 2nd Minnesota by Governor Ramsey. He named James George as lieutenant colonel. Both had served in the Mexican War. To soothe or inspire, depending upon the circumstances, a band of twenty musicians were enlisted with Michael Esch as bandleader. The State of Minnesota paid for the instruments and music. Judson Bishop was elected captain of Company A; Clinton Cilley, Sergeant-Major of Company C.

On the 20th of September, orders were sent out from regimental headquarters to bring the frontier companies back to Fort Snelling. The whole regiment was given instructions to prepare for the front. For a few days the men went through instruction, drill, guard mounts, and dress parades. They were issued clothing and equipment. When munitions were handed out, there was general concern and disappointment.

"Tarnation!" Private Dan Black was confounded. "Where are the new Springfields? This here musket's as old as the hills, prob'ly used in Mexico."

"Right you are," agreed Private Aaron Doty. "The calibers ain't even the same. Some guns is .58. Some ain't."

Clint Cilley shook his head and smiled. "Don't worry, men. Better muskets will be had later. For now, look pretty marching with them. That's all you'll be doing for a while."

Cilley was right. On the morning of October 14th a large river steamboat docked on the river flats below Fort Snelling. Nearly 1,000 men boarded and began their journey. It was a short one. An hour later they docked at the upper levee in St. Paul, disembarked and paraded through the city.

Throngs of people lined the dusty streets as the 2nd Minnesota filed past. Flag bearers proudly led the way with the regimental band stepping out behind them. The rhythmic stomp of feet at times was drowned out by drumbeats and gay music.

The citizens of St. Paul displayed a gamut of emotions. Some cheered, some cried. Smiles mixed with sobs as people waved flags, hats, and handkerchiefs.

"Look at them!" a pretty young woman cried. "Their uniforms are so blue, their swords and rifles so shiny. I've never seen anything so grand!"

An old man nearby wiped his rheumy eyes and answered, "Grand they is, but the bands won't be playin' if they come back. And those that do come back won't look so pretty. The buttons won't be shinin'. Neither will nothin' else. War ain't no party. It's a killin' business. I know, I bin there, Mexico in '46."

The girl turned to the old man with disgust. "Don't be such a spoil sport! It is a grand day!"

The old man slowly shook his head.

* * *

THE PARADE ENDED at the lower levee. The regiment climbed onboard the steamboat again and set off downriver. It was time for the boys from Minnesota to finally do what they had signed up for: go south and fight rebels.

But the road to war was a long one, both in time and travel. At LaCrosse the regiment switched over to the railroad, where they herded into box cars. On the morning of October 16th, they arrived in Chicago and spent the night in the Wigwam, a cavernous building constructed the year before to house the Republican National Convention that nominated Abraham Lincoln for the presidency.

Then came a march to the Pittsburgh and Fort Wayne Railroad depot and off on another train to Pittsburgh, where the 2nd arrived in the afternoon of October 18th. In a large community hall, a sumptuous hot supper was provided for the soldiers. Bands played as young ladies sang and served the men their feast.

Rincie DeGrave smiled at a pretty blonde girl as she heaped dumplings onto his plate. He brushed a curly thatch of black hair from his forehead and flirted, "Thanks, missy. I'll come back through here when it's all over. Will you have something for me then, too?"

The girl smiled back, "More dumplings then, but how's this for now?" She removed a blue kerchief from her hair and handed it to him. "Something to remember Jenny Murphy by," she grinned as she moved down the table.

Rincie held it to his nose and breathed deeply in a mock swoon as nearby soldiers laughed and called out. The young man waved the kerchief high and then stuffed it into his pocket.

The next morning the city's populace lined the wharves as the regiment boarded three small steamers that would take them down the Ohio River to Louisville, Kentucky. Jenny Murphy was there to wave goodbye.

Once in Louisville, Colonel Van Cleve and Captain Bishop reported to the headquarters of General William Tecumseh Sherman, commander of the Army of the Cumberland. "Cump" Sherman stood just under six feet and weighed about 170 with a close-cut red beard and matching hair.

The general had taken over a law office in the center of town as his headquarters. His bright eyes flashed recognition as Van Cleve entered, followed by Bishop. The two presented a contrast before Sherman. The colonel was tall, bespectacled and professorial-looking with a chin beard and gray receding hair. Judson Bishop was much younger, a little shorter with wavy dark hair and a handsome chiseled face.

"Colonel," Sherman stood, "it's good to see that Minnesota finally got here. Things are going to heat up and we need you."

"This is Captain Bishop," Van Cleve said.

"Fine, fine," Sherman replied with curt dismissal as he paced to the window and peered out at a steady rainfall.

"When did you leave Minnesota?" He didn't wait for an answer. "Secretary of War Cameron was just here. Seems Kentucky's a key to holding the country together. Can't let 'em out of the Union. There'll be Hell to pay here."

Sherman began to pace across the small room, speaking as if to himself with occasional glances at his visitors. "I didn't ask for this, you know. I was an abject failure at Bull Run. Lincoln promised he wouldn't give me a major command. He lied. Politicians do that, you know. My brother's one, I know all about politicians. You hungry?"

"Volunteers! They give me volunteers. I need real soldiers and more of them. Hell, I shouldn't be here, either." Sherman paused, wiping his sweaty forehead. "I shouldn't be anywhere.

"Here." He bent over and quickly scribbled on a scrap of paper. "Your orders. I expect the rebels to take a stand east of here. They've got to shore up Kentucky and Tennessee, too. East Tennessee is filled with union sympathizers. Jeff Davis can't let another of his states split. West Virginia was bad enough for him. Take a train to Lebanon Junction. Ride the flat cars. Leave tonight."

"Sir," Van Cleve responded, "it's raining. The flat cars are open."

"This is war, Colonel," Sherman rejoined, "not a picnic. Get on the train."

As Van Cleve and Bishop left Sherman, the captain spoke softly to his colonel. "Well, that was interesting. Have you known him long?"

"Yes, Captain, I have. There's something wrong. His head's usually as clear as his eyes. Not today. He was a banker, you know, after the Mexican War he left the army. Maybe he shouldn't have come back."

The 2nd Minnesota climbed aboard flatbeds, huddled under blanket, tarps or whatever covering they could find and endured thirty miles in a cold, hard rainstorm. Traveling at six miles an hour, it took most of the night to reach Lebanon Junction.

The regiment established camp there with anticipation of coming action. They were soon disappointed. For several weeks they were subject to tedium, misery or both. Cold rain proved to be commonplace, and the ground became a morass until deep ditches were dug to drain off the water between tents. Sick call rates mounted.

Each day an hour before sunrise, reveille sounded and the men stood at arms to guard against a surprise attack by the rebels. Detachments were sent out to guard nearby railroad bridges. Others continued a monotonous round of picket duty drill and instruction.

On an early November morning, Company C gathered on a damp open area near their camp. Fog hung over the men like a soggy blanket. A cup of coffee and hardtack sufficed until a breakfast of salt pork. The hot coffee in tin cups was heaven sent as it also warmed their hands.

Sergeant-Major Cilley relentlessly drilled the men of Company C in the manual of arms and every maneuver.

During a pause one of the men called out, "Sergeant-Major, ain't we done this enough yet? We all know right oblique, left oblique, wheel, prepare for cavalry charge, double quick, and every other order we bin doin' 'bout a hundred times each. Can't we do somethin' else?"

As sergeant-major, Cilley had not attained the rank of officer, but his bearing bespoke one. "Private Kline, success in battle depends upon companies and all army units moving as precisely as possible. You must be able to move into position without thinking about it. Your feet need to move without your head, or you may surely lose your head in battle.

"The 2nd Minnesota must move as one and with precision. These drills are for that outcome. You shall learn until you can do these in your sleep.

"Now, attention! Right shoulder arms! Forward march! Right oblique!"

Van Cleve watched the company with Lieutenant Dan Heaney and Captain Bishop. "Lieutenant," Van Cleve relayed, "I've received word that Captain Mantor has resigned. You are now the captain of Company C. Who would you suggest to replace you as first lieutenant?"

Heaney briefly considered and replied, "Cilley, sir. The man drilling the troops down there. He'd be a great officer."

"Done, and here's another important bit of news. General Sherman has been replaced as our commander by Don Carlos Buell."

"Sherman, replaced?" Heaney questioned, "Why?"

"Something about mental instability."

"That doesn't surprise me," Bishop noted.

Van Cleve eyed his two officers. "The 3rd Minnesota is coming to relieve us. We're going back to Lebanon where division commander Thomas is headquartered. I think we'll be headed east soon. Word has it that the rebs are moving up the Cumberland. We might be in for a fight."

"I'm ready," Heaney replied.

Bishop looked down at the marching soldiers. "I think we all are."

Jimmy Dunn

CHATFIELD

S UMMER AND FALL OF 1861 brought an ebb and flow of emotions for Jimmy Dunn as if he rode a river raft that alternated between raging rapids and dead calm pools. Excitement and anticipation gripped him and the town of Chatfield with every scrap of news that came from the East.

Jimmy clerked at his father's hotel, but his thoughts were with the fifty Chatfield Guards of the 2nd Minnesota and Judson Bishop. Word from those around town who had received letters from loved ones was that the men were in Kentucky, stuck in the mud and waiting for something to happen.

He sat on a wooden bench on the hotel porch and watched people coming and going on the busy, dusty main street of Chatfield. Another young man plopped down beside Jimmy on the bench.

Jimmy was pulled from his thoughts and greeted Marty Wilson, the eighteen-year-old son of Chatfield's other hotel keeper. "Any word from your brother, Marty?"

"Naw, Danny's still sittin' in Kentucky with the rest o' the 2nd."

"Maybe the war won't be over by the time we get there."

"Well, Jimmy, at least we both got old enough to enlist."

"If we were better liars, we woulda been in before. Beecher Gere recruited all able-bodied men between eighteen and forty-five. Seems like everyone either tacked a year or two onto their ages or reported they were forty-four—more patriotic than honest."

Marty chuckled. "Isaac Lindsey even got gray hair." Marty paused. "Ten Chatfield boys are with Company C of the 3rd Minnesota, and Beecher Gere's got near fifty more Chatfield boys signed up with the 2nd. Soon as the call comes for another regiment to report, we go."

"I hear Gere's got fifty-five. William Beecher Gere, the pride of Fillmore County," Jimmy intoned. "The ladies hereabout'll miss him, that's for sure."

"He is a fine man, Jimmy. That's why he got elected captain."

"Norm Culver will make a good lieutenant."

"His kid, little Charley, is in, too. Barely twelve years old, and I swear he don't make the five-foot minimum. They made all kinds of 'ceptions for drummer boys."

"He stood on his tiptoes," Marty chuckled, "plus his dad told Doc Mayo he'd be watchin' over him."

Jimmy laughed. "Charlie's a drummer boy. Zeke Rose heads the musicians. He stands way over six feet. He's the one that'll be overlooking Charlie."

"Way over," Marty nodded. "And we got other dad and son combinations. Gilbert and Oscar Wall and the Frenches. I hear Preston's lining up men, too. Fella over there called Josiah Marsh. He's the one whose kid brother couldn't even wait for Bishop and crossed over to join a Wisconsin Regiment. John Marsh is already fightin'. I wouldn't be surprised if he winds up with us. I hear a spot is being held for him."

"I swear," Jimmy shook his head, "it seems like half the company is related to somebody else in the company. Beecher Gere's brother Tom is a sergeant. Judson Bishop's brother John is another sergeant."

"Sure," Marty continued, "how about the Parsley boys, John and Tom, the Parks brothers."

"Yep," Jimmy remarked, "it's a regular rolling family reunion, and they all came from some other state. 'Cept Andy Williamson, only one Minnesota-born, his dad is a missionary at Lower Sioux. Then ya got the Gardners from Lake City, and ya throw in other family combinations like Bill Perrington and his brother-in-law Willie Blodgett."

"I heard his dad, Franklin Blodgett, tried to get Willie discharged, said he lied about his age and that Perrington helped him. But Willie wanted to stay put and said," now Marty tried to sound official, "'I, Willie Blodgett, do not want to leave the army without an honorable discharge.' Then his brother-in-law did his duty and argued to let Willie go, but they told him they ain't in the business of letting people *outta* the company. They're in the business of signing men up. 'Sides, they said, Willie's a damn good soldier."

"I bet there ain't a dozen that didn't come from Chatfield or Preston."

Marty frowned in thought as he considered, then replied, "I believe you're right. It's prob'ly less than a dozen, maybe eleven."

"What about Greg Davids?"

"He's from Preston."

Jimmy wondered, "Do you know 'im?"

Marty nodded emphatically. "I know him and I trust him."

Jimmy picked up a small stone from the porch and flicked it onto the street. "I sure hope we get goin' soon. I hear it's a lot warmer down South in the winter. Let's get there, fight some rebs, enjoy the warmth and come back heroes. I hear that pretty girls really like soldier blue heroes."

Marty chuckled. "A good plan. I'll let Beecher Gere know what you think."

But fall stretched into winter as Jimmy, Marty, and the rest of the men and boys of Chatfield and Preston waited for the order that would put them on the march to the fight to save the union.

Middle Tennessee
SUMMER 1861

THE 1ST TENNESSEE INFANTRY Regiment was mustered into Confederate service on August 1, 1861. Fifty thousand young Tennesseans had answered the call for troops. The original ten companies were sent first to Camp Harris for a short time and then to Camp Cheatham in Robertson County to receive instruction in drill and tactics. Nearly one hundred and fifty young men from Rutherford County reported. They had named themselves the Rutherford Rifles and were led by Captain William Ledbetter.

Camp Cheatham was located in Robertson County just north of Nashville, which was in Davidson County between Robertson and Rutherford counties. Sam Davis rode into camp astride a bay mare. He wore a clean, new gray uniform. A little smear of brown fuzz adorned his upper lip. It was early evening, with the setting sun beginning to cast an orange glow to the west.

Sam rode up to an overzealous young picket who held up his musket and demanded, "Who are you and what do you want?"

"I'm Sam Davis reporting for duty."

"Duty with who?"

"The Rutherford County boys. I think they're Company I."

The young man peered through the smoky haze of campfires and gestured with his gun. "Over there, they's 'round that reg'mental flag with the one on it."

Sam turned. "Nice flag."

"It was just gived to 'em. The guy that use ta be gov'ner, Campbell, his daughter herself gived it to the boys."

"Thanks," Sam replied, "I'll go get a better look at it."

As Sam grew closer he recognized friends he'd grown up with around Smyrna. Half a dozen crowded around a smoky fire, holding their rifle ramrods over the flames. Cornbread dough was impaled around the end of each rod.

"Supper time?" Sam called as he rode up.

"Sam Davis!" A young soldier squatting before the fire called out. "So ya finally decided ta leave school and jine us." He grinned. "Didja bring yer books?"

"No, Joe," Sam replied as he dismounted, "left them at the farm in Smyrna. What's ta eat?"

"Sloosh!" Several called out as they crowded around Sam to shake hands. The soldiers were all tall, each one an inch or so either side of six feet.

"Sloosh?"

A man with two stripes on his shoulders smiled and held a ramrod out to Sam. "Cornmeal, lard, water, and eggs all mixed tagether and baked over the fire. Best we got on short notice."

"Fine with me. Johnny, you've got stripes."

Joe Cates poked Sam and explained, "He's Corporal John Beesley now. He gets ta boss us around some."

"Wait'll ya see Jim Becton," Bob Jones said excitedly," he's got three stripes."

"Becton a sergeant! Good for him," Sam replied.

"What's that fuzz on yer lip?" Bob teased. "Ya kiss a cat?"

They laughed as Sam said, "Thought it might make me look a little older."

"And catch a girl or two," Joe chided. "Ya got one yet?"

A shy smile tugged at the corners of Sam's mouth. "Maybe."

"Sit yerself down." Marion McFarlin gestured expansively at the ground around the fire. "We got plenty o' room. Here, take some sloosh."

Sam slid the six-inch roll of baked dough from the rod and sat cross-legged on the ground. The others joined him around the flickering fire. Sam bit into the concoction and chomped slowly as he considered his friends. They were all about his age; a couple, Beesley and Cates, a few years older.

McFarlin and Charlie Miller had helped out Sam's father on their farm. Bill Searcy was a storekeeper's son from Smyrna. None of their families owned slaves. Just the Davis family did.

"How long have you been here?" Sam asked.

"Lemme see," Charlie Miller thoughtfully rubbed his forehead as if to force memories into it, "we left Murfreesboro on a train on May 2nd. Got ta Nashville where they made us the First Tennessee Volunteer Regiment, George Maney commanding."

"Spent 'bout a week camped at the Nashville Fairgrounds," Joe added, "then by rail to Camp Harris in Franklin Coun'y."

"Camp Harris?"

"Yep, Sam," Joe continued, "named afta Isham Harris, guv'nor o' Tennessee. Afta another week we took a train here to Camp Cheatham. This is where we bin doin' all our trainin'. Got the 3rd and 11th Tennessee here, too."

"William Ledbetter's our captain?" Sam questioned.

Joe Cates responded, "Oldest and shortest captain in the 1st Tennessee. Still, he's got the largest company in the reg'ment. Most is over six feet tall."

"A true soldier and an honest gentleman," Beesley added solemnly, "even at thirty years old and five-foot-six. I guess he must o' bin drinkin' somethin' different than the rest o' us. Rutherford County's got some big boys."

"So, what've you been doing?" Sam wondered as he waved a hand to clear away smoke.

"Jest larnin' ta be soldiers," Joe Cates answered. "March this way, march that way. Turn right oblique, turn left."

"Right shoulder arm," Beesley continued, "prepare for cavalry attack, load in nine times."

"Sergeant says we gotta be able ta march in our sleep," Charlie Miller added. "I don' see how that's poss'ble."

Corporal Beesley stretched straight and tall. "What you youngsters don't seem to understand," he proclaimed while pointing at his stripes, "is that a private soldier's jest a machine. You—hell all of us—work by command. The higher-ups don't 'spect us to know anything at all 'bout what's goin' on. We're here ta load and shoot and ta obey the commands we git—good or bad."

"If it helps me shoot Yankees better, I'm all fer it," McFarlin countered.

"Me, too," Cates echoed. "We gotta show them Yanks we'll stand up fer our rights. They wanna make us like them, but I ain't gonna work in no factory."

"None of us here even got slaves, 'cept Sam," Joe continued, "so that ain't why we're ready ta fight."

Sam considered the exchange. "This isn't about slaves for me, either. Sure, we have about fifty, and they've helped make our place prosper. But if we had to, we could do without 'em. The North wants to change how we live in Tennessee, and that I will not stand by and let happen."

"And ya git eleven good Confederate dollars a month," Marion added.

Sam ripped off another chunk of sloosh and inquired, "What do I do next?"

Beesley explained. "First we'll bring ya up ta Sergeant Becton. Then we'll git ya fixed up with ordinance and t'other supplies. Every soldier gits blankets, shirts, pants, and old boots that's supposed ta last a year. Then ya git a gun, car-tridge-box, knapsack, and three days' rations, a pistol and a long Bowie knife."

"William Wood of Columbia's a rich guy," Charlie explained. "He gave us all the knives."

As the men finished their meal, Corporal Beesley rose to address the group. "Gentleman, I think it's time ta welcome Private Davis officially."

The rest rose to their feet, stood at attention in a relatively straight line and raised their right hands in salute.

Sam straightened his lanky body and responded with his own salute.

"Now, private," Beesley said, "let's get ya to meet the sergeant."

Sam already knew Jim Becton from back home, so the meeting was more of a reunion.

"How's your father?" the red-haired, muscular man asked.

"Just fine. Crops are in."

"I knew your mother. She was a fine lady. I'm glad your father found another fine lady and remarried."

"Thank you, Sergeant."

"How's your older brother doing?"

"He's joined another regiment. I expect to hear from him soon."

"Get settled in, Sam. You're a bright boy. Still there's much to learn."

Learning was a steep curve for the new recruit. Learning to perform commands by rote was necessary but time consuming and boring. In mid-July the 1st Tennessee was deemed ready to depart Camp Cheatham. The regiment voted to go to Virginia.

A long line of railroad cars stretched along the tracks near the camp. Bugles sounded and orders flew to strike camp and load everything into the box cars. Soldiers crammed into and on top of the cars. As the engine slowly picked up speed and chugged south, hundreds waved hats, kerchiefs, and flags in farewell.

The reception was similar when the train reached Nashville. The city turned out in large numbers to greet the soldiers, who stepped from the boxcars to the cheers of thousands and a band blaring, "The Girl I Left Behind Me."

Many of the girls being left behind acted as servers at a meal spread out for the men in a grove near the college. Sam Davis wistfully looked out at his former college classrooms. But there was no regret in his heart. He had left behind a college life to begin a great adventure and a crusade to save a way of life in which he steadfastly believed.

Kentucky

January 1862

LINT CILLEY SAT ASTRIDE his horse alongside Captain Dan Heaney. The captain's mount snorted softly in the early morning mist. Before them Company C and the rest of the brigade struck their camp.

Like a nest of ants, all were busy at a task. In the distance the 2nd Minnesota's band played martial music as men folded tents packed and jammed their baggage into the thirteen overloaded wagons allotted to each regiment.

"They sound better," Cilley commented as he nodded at the band.

"Fort Snelling and Lebanon Junction gave them plenty of time to practice," Heaney rejoined.

"It's a pretty sight," Cilley said, "clean uniforms and the colors unfurled."

Heaney scratched his chin as he watched. "It'll all change. Won't be so pretty once we find the rebs."

"We're part of a great thing, Captain. It makes me proud."

"Not quite like a classroom, is it?" Heaney said.

"No, but we still have order. It all follows. General Buell heads the Army of the Ohio. General Thomas is given the First Division with the First, Second and Third brigades."

Heaney said, "And we fit in under Colonel McCrook in the Third Brigade."

"Through the Eighteenth Regiment under Carrington to us, Second Minnesota Volunteers, Colonel H.P. Van Cleve commanding."

"It's a fine system, Lieutenant. Van Cleve even has the look of one of your school superiors."

Cilley laughed. "Maybe a little. We all have round spectacles."

"It does all fit nicely," Heaney said. "A hundred men to a company, ten companies to a regiment, three regiments to a brigade. Three, sometimes four, brigades to a division, two to three divisions to a corps, and more than one corps makes up an army, and here we are."

"Just a little piece of a real big pie."

"Right down to platoons and squads."

"Where the heart of the army beats, Captain."

"It's time to lead 'em to the fighting. Let's go, Lieutenant Cilley."

The two officers spurred their horses and trotted onto the road beside their company. With flags snapping in a sudden breeze and a tune following them down the Columbia Pike, the men of Company C shouldered their equipment and marched with anticipation. Private Charlie Orline marched smartly, a smile on his face. "Well, Mike, I know we'll git action now!"

Mike Rohan shifted his haversack and grimaced. "You may be right, Charlie. I wish we could've loaded more in the wagons. I hate luggin' all this around."

Charlie laughed. "C'mon, Mike, it's not that tough. You're a big, tough farm boy. Can't ya carry a few pounds on yer back?"

"We got a rifle, forty rounds of ball cartridges, a knapsack filled with personals. We got overcoats, blankets, canteens, and a haversack with three days' rations. Charlie, we're haulin' forty-fifty pounds. I'm not a soldier. I'm a mule."

"Mike, the wagons're already packed to the top. Even if they let us, there's no place to put our stuff."

"So we march with it," Rohan concluded.

The sky brightened as the army marched. They covered fourteen miles on January 1, twelve miles the next day. At Campbellsville the regiment camped and sent the wagons back to Lebanon for more supplies.

Eight days into January, the 2nd Minnesota passed through Columbia, Kentucky, and turned east, off the pike and onto a dirt road. Here rain dumped down in buckets, turning the road into a slush of mud deep enough to make a herd of swine happy.

When General Thomas called a halt late in the day, the soggy, muddy, exhausted troops stumbled out of the sucking morass of the road and crawled off into woods, fields, and roadsides to rest. Two soldiers huddled under a tree.

"When're the wagons comin', Rincie?" Bobby Dearmin wondered.

"Judgin' by the road, sometime tomorrow," Rincie DeGrave answered.

"They got our tents, Rincie."

"So pull a coat over yer head."

Dearmin winced. "At least the mules seemed ta be workin' all right."

"Bobby, I never thought they'd git those teams broke in. Six mules to a wagon and one muleskinner. They was buckin' and kickin' all over."

"Rincie, didja ever hear such words as them drivers used? Billy Bacon's mother would o' twisted his ears off if she heard 'im."

"I heard Chaplin Chessey offer a hundred dollars to any muleskinner who could go thirty days without cussin'."

"Well," Dearmin drawled, "he ain't had ta pay nothin' out yet."

"I don't think he ever will, Bobby."

DeGrave blew warm breath into the frosty air. "Not quite cold enough ta see it."

"You would back home. It's freezin' and snow there."

"I'd rather that than this wet chill that goes right through yer bones."

"Bobby, didja hear that? Somebody's callin' out somethin'."

"It's Sergeant Burnell."

In a moment Sam Burnell approached the cluster of soldiers near Bobby and Rincie. "Good news, fellas. Gen'ral Buell's announced a little change in his order that no private property be disturbed. We need dry wood fer fires, and the top rail of the three-rail fence is now fair game. Warm yerselves up, boys."

In short order bonfires flared up all around. Men huddled around them, palms out, and basked in the warmth. Steam from evaporating water on damp clothing rose above the soldiers.

Bobby Dearmin wondered aloud, "This is great, but when the top rails are gone, we'll be cold again."

"Seems ta me," Private John Acker reasoned, "that once the top rail's gone the second rail becomes the top rail."

Using that logic, the entire three-rail fence disappeared by morning. For another week the Third Brigade of the Army of Ohio slogged its way into middle Kentucky. The men passed farmsteads populated by old men, women and children who sullenly paused to watch the men in blue march by.

Charlie Orline called out to his friend Mike Roher, "Where's the young folks, they jest have old men and kids here?"

"Charlie, I 'spect we'll see them soon enough. I'd be surprised if they ain't waitin' for us down the road."

On January 17th the 2nd Minnesota and their compatriots arrived near the Cumberland River at a spot call Logan's Crossroads.

* * *

General Thomas established his headquarters near Logan's Crossroads, a tiny hamlet with a few rough houses and a post office on the east-west Columbia-Somerset Road. In the sitting room of an old farm house the division commander met with his brigade commanders. Colonel Mahlon Dickerson of the Second Brigade sat across a small table from Robert McCook, Colonel of the Third, and Samuel Carter of the Twelfth.

Thomas tugged on his thick, bushy beard as he stood at the head of the table. "Gentlemen, the war's been on almost a year and we've been on our heels most of it. Albert Sidney Johnson has a line of defense from Arkansas to the Cumberland Gap. But it's a thin line, only about 40,000 men. Polk on the left has about 12,000 at Columbus. Tilghman in the center has roughly 4,000 at Henry and Donelson on the Tennessee and Cumberland Rivers in Tennessee just south of the Kentucky border.

"Our concern is here, Johnston's right flank in Kentucky. Crittenden guards the Cumberland Gap, the gateway for entering pro-Union East Tennessee. He has General Felix Zollicoffer commanding the 1st Brigade to keep the gap closed. He's camped on the north bank of the Cumberland about ten miles away."

"Sir," McCook interrupted, "my scouts tell me the southern bank's a bluff and a strong defensive position. What's he doing on flat land on the other side?"

"I don't know, Colonel. We need to capitalize on his poor judgment. I intend to wait for General Schoepf's troops to get here from Somerset before we attack. In the meantime, I want you to move into position. There's a road leading down to Beech Grove and Mill Springs. Get control of it. We can't lose Kentucky and we can't lose our opportunity in East Tennessee."

"So much for Kentucky being neutral," Dickerson commented.

"It couldn't last. Once Polk ordered Pillow into Columbus for the rebs and Grant took over Paducah for us, neutrality was doomed. A neutral Kentucky was supposed to be a shield allowing Tennessee to send men into Virginia and the Mississippi River Valley. But Kentucky's a battleground, and we have to win it. We must drive the Confederates over the Cumberland River and break up Crittenden's army. See to your men, gentlemen."

Mill Springs

A FEW MILES AWAY Major General George Crittenden stood in a wall tent alongside General Felix Zollicoffer and General William Carroll. Heavy plops of rain battered the canvas. Crittenden pulled a flask from his pocket and took a quick swallow of fiery amber liquid. He offered the flask to Zollicoffer, who shook his head. Zollie, as his men called him, had a full head of dark unruly hair that contrasted with a neatly trimmed mustache and goatee.

Carroll accepted the flask, took a quick swallow, wincing as he passed it back to Crittenden. "Powerful stuff, sir."

"Hard trip from Knoxville, General. This picks me up a little. Zollie, General Johnston and I want to know why you're here on the north bank. You were ordered to the south bluffs."

"I believed the north was more defensible. When I received the order to cross the river to the south, I didn't have enough boats to move over the river quickly. It's unfordable. I couldn't risk my brigade being caught halfway across by the river or by the enemy."

"Well, it's too late now to worry about that. You're on the horseshoe bend of a river. This isn't a fortress. It's a trap. I recall a similar situation in the Mexican War. You have nowhere to run and an unfordable river in the rear. You're in a bad spot, and we have to take the offensive. Thomas has three brigades at Logan's Crossroads, Schoepf's brigade's at Somerset with Fishing Creek between them. The creek's rain swollen and dangerous. It'll keep Schoepf from moving quickly to help Thomas."

"What do you want me to do, General?"

Crittenden took another pull from his flask. "I want you to attack the Union camp at Logan's Crossroads at dawn. I can give you eight regiments, three battalions, and two artillery batteries. Thomas's army is in two parts. Smash 'em at Logan's before they can get together."

28

"General, it's midnight. The men are asleep in their tents. It'll take us hours to get into position. With all this cold rain and mud, our boys'll be miserable. I can't ask them to fight in this."

"The decision's been made, General Zollicoffer. The Yankees will be just as cold and miserable as your men. Guard the gap that leads into Tennessee. It must not be opened. You'll attack them at dawn, and you must prevail."

Zollicoffer stood at attention and snapped a brisk salute. "My brigade will do its utmost. They're fine boys. But for the record, sir, I think we should wait."

"Your request is noted. General Carroll, any questions?"

"Just one. How's your brother doing?"

Crittenden grimaced. "Thomas is doing just fine, from what I'm told. He's a general, too, you know, in the Union army. I guess it really is brother against brother. Anything else?"

"No, sir. I understand what we must do."

"Good, now move to the attack!"

* * *

CLINTON CILLEY AND DAN HEANEY marched alongside Company C as it slogged through rain and mud toward the Mill Springs Road.

"By God, Cilley, it's so dark I can't see my hand in front of my face."

"Company A has it lucky, Dan. Picket duty."

"I don't know if I'd call that lucky. Standing guard duty in an inkwell doesn't appeal to me. Besides, we're going into a fight without Bishop."

Unseen in the blackness, Cilley shook his head. "They took one of our best out of the fight. It doesn't figure."

"Well, Lieutenant, the other nine companies of the 2nd Minnesota will have to take up the slack."

"Along with the Ninth Ohio," Cilley noted. "There's more than just the Third Brigade here. Up ahead are the 10th Indiana and 4th Kentucky, 2nd Brigade and the 12th Kentucky from the 12th Brigade."

"Captain, why do we have to march tonight?"

"The general thinks the rebs are on the move. We have to head 'em off."

"What difference does it make who's moving? We can't see them anyway."

"It'll be dawn soon."

* * *

HALFWAY DOWN THE COLUMN from the officers, Charlie Orline and Rincie DeGrave endured the misery and considered their enemy's position.

"Think, Rincie, here we are and them rebs is toasty warm in their beds. It ain't right."

"Prob'ly got full bellies, too. Warm food and hot coffee."

"We can't even think 'bout warm food—no way to start a fire in this."

"Well, Charlie, just gnaw off another chunk of hardtack."

"At least it's not so hard it can break yer teeth, the rain made it soggy."

"Small comfort, Charlie."

* * *

IN THE CONFEDERATE CAMP, known as Camp Zollicoffer, a solitary figure approached a rough wood shelter. He knocked on it softly.

A voice cried, "Unless you be an officer, git the Hell outa here!"

"I *am* an officer," came the reply, "Colonel Moscow Carter, I'd like to see my brothers."

An instant later the door opened. Two men, in uniforms they'd slept in, stepped out. Both were young and looked it. At twenty-one, Tod was nine years younger than Moscow. Wad, the youngest of the three, was eighteen.

They stood together in the drizzling darkness while Moscow spoke. "Boys, the fight is coming and the 20th Tennessee will be in the forefront. It's your first fight. Look out for each other. Don't try to be heroes.

"I promised Ma and Pa I'd watch out for you. But the fact is, you're pretty much on your own. Just use your heads."

"You be careful, too," Tod cautioned. "Just because you fought in Mexico doesn't make you bullet-proof. Remember, we're going to be law partners someday, Carter and Carter."

Moscow chuckled. "You're already the best lawyer in Franklin, Tennessee, and you're only twenty-one. Wad, you can join in, too."

The boy's smile was tight. "Let's just get through the war first."

A light glow, like a dying candle, cast a faint pink light through the mist on the eastern horizon. The Carter brothers went to their respective duties knowing the battle was near.

* * *

AS THE COMING DAWN struggled with the stubborn night, the 2nd Minnesota neared the Mill Springs Road. Mike Rohan, Christian Sebilt, and John Cartwright, all privates, stood together and peered into the distance.

Cartwright tried to reckon their position. "Brush, then woods, all in this pea-soup fog. How're we supposed to fight in this?"

"We can leave it up to the Indiana and Kentucky boys," Rohan replied. "They're already up by the woods."

* * *

FELIX ZOLLICOFFER, in his white slicker, rode at the head of his brigade with his aides, Captain Fogg and Lieutenant Shields. The general stroked his clean-shaven chin. "This is going to take some getting used to. I had the beard most of my adult life."

"Why'd you shave it, sir?" Fogg asked.

Zollicoffer chuckled. "Just trying to confuse folks some. Some of those Yanks know me. Running a newspaper and being a Whig congressman got me known in the North."

"You opposed secession and now you're fighting for it."

"Lieutenant, things have a way of changing. I did oppose secession. Fiercely. But I'm also for a state's right to determine its own future. When Tennessee voted to leave the Union, I was honor bound to support her."

A gunshot from ahead sliced through the muffled quiet of the misty morning. Then a cry echoed from the woods. "Rebs comin'! Rebs comin'!" The shouts were followed by a few more ragged shots.

"Keep steady, men!" Zollicoffer ordered. "Lieutenant Shields, bring word back to prepare to charge."

* * *

THE UNION OUTPOST PICKETS who had spotted the advancing Confederates raced back to their main line and reformed with the 10th Indiana. Colonel Mahlon Manson quickly recognized he was outmanned and dashed through the nearby camp of the 4th Kentucky, where he encountered Colonel Speed Fry, who was garbed in a rain slicker.

"Fry," he shouted, "get your men to the front! Hell's breakin' loose! The rebs are about on us!"

Fry looked around for his drummer. "Billy, beat the long roll! Lieutenant," he turned to a subordinate, "get the men out of their tents. Move 'em up!"

As groggy soldiers of the 4th Kentucky stumbled from their tents, Fry and Manson hurried ahead. Where the Indiana troops waited, the two colonels surveyed the field—open and bordered on all sides by a woodland. Through the fog and mist materialized a mass of Confederate soldiers.

Then, like the unleashing of a maelstrom, the woods erupted in gunfire, thick and fast. In the distance a man in a white raincoat, swinging a saber high above his head, charged at the head of gray-clad men who appeared like specters out of the mist. The screech of defiance known as the "rebel yell" sounded as if an army of banshees were racing toward them.

* * *

A RAVINE RAN IN FRONT of and parallel to the position of the 10th Indiana. Zollicoffer's men gained control of the depression before Fry's men could get there and poured murderous fire into the Union line.

* * *

FRY STOOD IN THE MIDST of the hailstorm of lead and cried, "Get up and fight like men, you rebel cowards!"

A sergeant pulled him down. "That's a brave thing to do, but being brave and dead ain't gonna help us. You make a good target in your raincoat."

The men of the 4th Kentucky and 10th Indiana broke and ran back toward the road. They reformed in the woods and turned. After a few minutes, all shooting stopped. The eerie quiet was broken by a long drum roll from behind the 2nd Minnesota, as other troops raced into formation.

* * *

FIRING BROKE OUT AGAIN. Zollicoffer led his men into the breach once more. They slammed into stiff resistance. Zollicoffer, his white raincoat shimmering in the mist, shouted to an aide, "Get Carroll up here with his brigade! We need to concentrate our forces to drive the Yankees back!"

"Sir," Lieutenant Shields screamed above the roar of battle, "we sent word to Carroll. On the left it looks like we're facing fire from our own men."

"Damnation! Take Fogg and stop it!"

The shooting stopped again. "Wait," Zollicoffer cried, "I'll go with you!"

* * *

SPEED FRY TURNED to his officers. "We've gotta take advantage of this quiet. There must be a way to flank that ravine. I'm gonna find it. Let's go!"

The Union officers rode off to the right through gunsmoke mixed with fog that formed a translucent curtain. As they trotted down a hill, Fry spotted a lone figure in a white raincoat riding through the distant mist.

"Who's that, Colonel?"

Fry squinted, peering intently. "I don't know. Must be one of ours."

Another rider trotted up beside the solitary rider. Fry and his men continued on toward them.

* * *

FOGG, RIDING BESIDE Zollicoffer, asked, "Who are they?"

"Mississippi, I think. Hard to see." Being nearsighted didn't help. "The fellow out front seems to have a raincoat on."

"Or a gray uniform."

A minute later the two parties halted a few feet of each other. Zollicoffer admonished Fry, "Sir, this is hard enough. We must not fire on our own men." He nodded to the left. "Those are our men."

Fry nodded.

"We must try to not let our men be cut up more than can be helped."

"I agree, I'll prevent it as much as possible," Fry replied.

Fry rode twenty yards beyond Zollicoffer to investigate further where the shots were coming from.

As the two men separated, Lieutenant Shields, pistol in hand, bounded out of the brush on his horse. "General, they're Yankees. Get out fast!" Shields fired a shot at Fry, hitting his horse.

"They're rebels!" Fry's aide yelled leaping from his wounded horse. Zollicoffer drew his pistol and emptied it at Fry.

The Union officer yelled, "That's your game, is it!" as he drew his Navy Colt .36 and fixed his aim on Zollicoffer. The general, somewhat confused, looked back. An instant later Zollicoffer rocked back from the impact of a bullet in his chest. He murmured to Fogg, "Keep the men fighting, I'm killed." Then he tumbled to the ground.

As Fry watched, the two rebel horsemen disappeared into the woods. The Union colonel walked over to the man he had shot and looked down at his still form.

"He's dead," Fry pronounced.

"That rider," an officer pronounced, "he called him 'general.'"

"Unless I'm mistaken," Fry continued, "I've just shot General Felix Zollicoffer, commander of Crittenden's First Brigade."

* * *

AS FRY'S WORDS hung in the air, the sepia-toned world exploded again as Fry's regiment renewed heavy fire on the Confederates before them. Fogg and Shields raced back to General Crittenden to inform him that Zollicoffer was dead. For a moment confusion reigned as the Confederate center was pushed back.

Crittenden took a hard pull from his flask, found the courage he needed and rallied his men. "Come on, boys!" he urged. "Follow me and take the road." To an aide he shouted, "With my compliments tell General Caroll to bring up his men. We must hit them hard!"

* * *

THE REBELS CRESTED forward like a long gray wave through the fog, bursting through the woods and across the open field. The men of the 4th Kentucky and 10th Indiana fired at will. Fry had returned to the front to lead his men when General Thomas arrived.

"You've got a hot time of it, Colonel. We need to shore up your right."

"Yes, sir, and I've been told the men are running low on ammunition. We need to replenish from the rear."

Thomas looked back over his shoulder. "I've got McCook behind you with the 2nd Minnesota and the 9th Ohio. Fall back. They'll take your place."

Colonel Van Cleve's staff major, Simeon Smith, wrenched his horse to a stop in front of Company C. "Captain," he called to Dan Heaney, "the regiment's to move up, all nine companies, head through the woods, guiding on the road. The rebs are trying to bust through. Attack from the left. Ohio's on the right."

Heaney saluted. "Company C is ready."

As Smith rode off to alert other companies, Heaney turned to Cilley. "Move 'em out, Lieutenant. It's time to do what we joined up for."

General Thomas, himself, rode to the front, stood tall in his stirrups and hollered, "Attention, Creation! By kingdoms, right wheel!"

Charlie Orline shouted to his comrades, "We got old Pap, hisself, with us! Let's make them rebs pay!"

The line of blue from Minnesota advanced through the woods and brush. The rain finally stopped, but the air remained thick with smoke and mist. Rincie DeGrave pushed through the dense undergrowth of vegetation. "Charlie," he called to Orline, "I can barely see past the end of my musket."

"We just keep movin' 'til somebody says stop," Orline answered.

"Where's our artillery?" DeGrave wondered.

"Artillery won't do no good shootin' in pea soup."

The forward push came to a halt when they came against a rail fence. Cilley called a halt as Heaney joined him at the barricade. The two men searched intently, seeking any color or movement.

"Confound it," Heaney muttered, "gray mist and a gray army coming."

"Look! There!" Cilley called as he pointed at a dim apparition in the distance. "About a hundred yards out. Here they come!"

An instant later the line of Union muskets at the fence line blasted a volley of fire and lead. Bullets fired with unerring accuracy from Union muskets and ripped into the bodies of charging rebels. Miraculously, in a few minutes the distant line of gray disappeared.

Fry jumped on top of the fence, shook his fist and yelled, "Come forward like men!"

The cheers and huzzahs of the Minnesota soldiers were cut short when a Confederate volley erupted, not from one hundred yards away, but literally from the other side of the fence. The 20th Tennessee was the first line of Crittenden's attack. They had gained a position on the other side of the rail fence just before the 2nd Minnesota arrived and were lying in the low fog.

"Shoot, boys, shoot!" Cilley yelled. "They're here, right under our noses!"

* * *

BOBBY DEARMIN LOOKED down the fence line at muskets protruding in both directions from either side of the fence. He grabbed a rebel gun sticking between rails to his left and wrenched it from the hands of a rebel soldier. When the man jumped to his feet, Dearmin slammed his musket butt into the man's face, sending him crashing to the soggy earth.

All down the fence line muskets blasted in both directions and men struggled hand to hand. The ferocity of the Minnesota and Ohio men drove the rebels back from the fence. They raced to the rear, leaving dead and wounded behind and losing more men in the retreat.

Company I and Lieutenant John Stout were aligned next to Company C. They joined in huzzahs claiming victory. Then through the smoky haze a soldier stood to face them, his men having run off to the rear.

Clint Cilley moved over to Stout to shout at the single combatant before them. "He's an officer," Cilley informed Stout before calling, "Surrender, sir! You will be treated fairly!"

The Confederate remained silent. He raised his pistol and took deliberate aim before firing. John Stout crumbled, a bullet through his body.

"Fire!" Cilley shouted. An instant later the lone rebel was slammed to the earth, his body riddled with lead.

Heaney called to Cilley, "The Ohio boys are stuck, they need us!"

A stubborn band of rebel soldiers sheltered by buildings and fences stubbornly held their position in front of the 9th Ohio. Joined by the 2nd Minnesota in a bayonet charge, the rebels were dislodged and the battle ended.

* * *

Thomas returned to his headquarters at Logan's Crossroads for debriefing. In his mid-forties with a thick, bear-like physique, he stood before a dozen men and summarized, "We have a great victory. The stopper has been pulled out of the gap. Eastern Tennessee is open to us. Our losses were slight, thirty-nine dead, just over 200 wounded. The Confederates lost several times that."

"I wish we could have stopped them, General," Van Cleve said. "They got south of the Cumberland."

"That's because they're no longer an army. They're a disorderly mob that crossed the river in frantic rout, leaving behind twelve cannon, 150 wagons, 1,000 horses and mules, and all their dead and wounded."

Colonel Fry added, "That includes General Zollicoffer."

"Where's McCook?" Thomas inquired.

"Shot leading a bayonet charge," Fry replied. "The doctor thinks he'll pull through all right, though."

"I pray to God he does. McCook's a fighter. We need more like him."

"Also," Colonel Van Cleve continued, "a young man of some note. A young lieutenant, Balie Peyton of New Orleans, was shot dead by my Minnesota boys. But not before he put a bullet through Lieutenant Stout. Fortunately, he'll survive."

Thomas ran his hand over his bushy, dark beard. "Peyton's father was one of the foremost Union men in Tennessee. New Orleans gave him a sword in recognition of his Mexican War service."

"The sword was found on his body," Van Cleve noted.

"Send it back to his father."

Malon Manson cleared his throat. "General, there's a rumor Crittenden was drunk on the field of battle and incapable of leading his men."

"We outnumbered them and outfought them. I don't think anyone could have stopped us from running them into Tennessee, drunk or not."

* * *

ON THE OTHER SIDE of the river, Tod and Wad Carter searched for their colonel in the retreating mass of gray clad refugees. Ahead they saw him.

Tod ran up. "My brother, Lieutenant Colonel Carter, have you seen him?"

The officer looked down from his horse and nodded sadly. "They caught him. Your brother Moscow has become a Yankee prisoner of war."

The Adventure Begins

JIMMY DUNN BENT over the hotel register, making notes with the stub of a pencil. He gazed out the frosty window at the snow-packed street and rooftops laden with white fluffy flakes. *Too much snow for January*, he thought silently. *Makes for a long winter.* Then Jimmy walked to a round iron stove in the center of the small lobby, opened the door, welcomed a blast of warmth and tossed a log into it.

The door flew open. Marty Wilson and Will Sutherland burst into the room.

"Did ya hear the news, Jimmy?" Will cried excitedly.

"Did ya?" Marty echoed.

"What? That we won at Mill Springs? That's old news."

"No, Jimmy!" Will corrected. "The order came! We gotta report next week ta move out. We're goin' ta Fort Snelling. We're the last of Father Abraham's first call for Minnesota troops!"

Marty cried through a wide grin, "Then we go south ta fight rebs!"

"I can't believe it!" Jimmy said, bursting with excitement. "Are you sure?"

"No doubt about it. Beecher Gere hisself told me."

Jimmy turned giddy. "It's about time! You ready to go?"

Will Sutherland clapped Jimmy on the back. "Six months ago."

It took three and a half days for the Chatfield men to march overland through Rochester and Cannon Falls to Fort Snelling. Once there, they found they had hurried to wait. More men were being recruited to fill out the new 5th Regiment. Training became the routine.

Each day on the frosty parade ground of Fort Snelling, the men marched and learned how to fight as an army. Repetition led to boredom but also a sense of confidence and mostly unwarranted feelings of expertise. At night, guard duty was regularly assigned as Jimmy and others patrolled the walkways of the stone-walled fort. Jimmy paused upon a round rock tower that stood like a lonely sentinel above the rest of the fort.

He looked down where the Mississippi and Minnesota rivers converged and longed for the day a steamboat would take him down the river to where the action was. He knew the time was coming soon.

March came, and the stronger sun began to win against the still-deep snow. The Chatfield men, fifty-five of them, housed in a long barracks, played cards after mess and talked about their prospects and the war.

First Sergeant Tom Gere entered the building and shook snowflakes from his blue heavy coat. Gere, nineteen, had enlisted with his brother, William "Beecher" Gere on January 17th. Beecher was the captain of Company B.

"Men," Tom said forcefully, "I need your attention. I have announcements."

The soldiers put down cards, stopped conversations and turned to the young sergeant.

"Captain Gere has been promoted to major. He'll become a staff officer for the regiment. Our new captain will be John Marsh. He'll join us next month, and Second Lieutenant Culver will be first lieutenant and become quartermaster. I'll be promoted to second lieutenant and adjutant."

The men, actually boys mostly eighteen to nineteen, broke into a loud cheer.

Gere was relieved at the acceptance and grateful not many were older than he. He held his hand up for silence and shouted, "Quiet, please, I have another announcement."

The troop quieted and looked expectantly at Gere.

"This is hard for me to tell you, because I know you'll be disappointed. As you know, the regular army has been garrisoned on the frontier at Forts Ripley, Abercrombie and Ridgely. All regular army soldiers are being sent south. To take their place, Company C of the 5th Minnesota is being sent on garrison duty to Fort Ripley; Company D, to Abercrombie, and," he paused, "Company B will man Fort Ridgely. The other seven companies of the 5th Regiment will go south."

A chorus of no's and curses followed Gere's words. He raised his hand again for silence. "You're still soldiers. You'll accept your duty! Come to order!"

"Why, Sergeant?" Oscar Wall cried. "Why us?"

"I don't know, Private, luck of the draw? This is the hand we've been dealt. I'm assured this is only for a limited time, and we'll go south soon."

Edwin Cole, another private, wondered, "What do they need us out there for? There's nothing to do. The Indians are peaceful. There's never been a bit of trouble with them. It's a waste of time when we'll be needed to fight rebs."

"There are immigrants on the frontier who expect the presence of the government. It's been promised to them, and we're to provide it."

"It's not fair!" someone in back called.

Jimmy Dunn's face flushed red like a ripe tomato as he angrily shouted, "This isn't what we signed up fer."

"We are soldiers and we do what is expected of us," Gere concluded. Then he turned and exited, welcoming the frosty air outside as heated words from the barracks echoed behind him.

At noon on March 22nd the eighty-six men of Company B, including fifty-five from Chatfield and twenty-three from Preston, loaded into eight sleighs at Fort Snelling to slice through the deep snow of the Minnesota River Valley and traverse the one hundred ten miles to Fort Ridgely. The first night the cold, tired soldiers welcomed the warmth and hospitality of the people of Shakopee, who opened up the Scott County Courthouse to them. On the 23rd, the journey entailed a fifty-mile run from Shakopee to St. Peter, passing through Belle Plaine and Le Sueur on the way.

Jimmy Dunn, seated on a bench on the side of the sleigh, tugged his blue wool coat around his body and turned to his Chatfield friend, Marty Wilson.

"Gettin' dark, Marty. Do ya 'spose we'll get to another courthouse soon? I sure could use another warm meal."

"I don't know. I'll ask. Lieutenant Gere," he called to Tom at the front of the sleigh, "when we gonna camp?"

"Not 'til we cross the Minnesota, men."

"But it's gittin' dark, Sergeant."

"Full moon tonight." Gere gestured to the white globe rising in the east. "We cross on the ice at Traverse des Sioux. Then we bivouac at St. Peter."

Marty turned to Jimmy. "You were born in Canada. If your folks hadn't o' moved here when you were little, you wouldn't be goin' ta war. Yer whole life would be different."

"Like we've said, almost everybody came from someplace else. It'd be different for everyone. I guess this is where God wanted us ta be."

The men in the sleigh stifled groans as they hunkered down in their heavy coats. In the middle of the night the troop glided into St. Peter. To their delight and surprise, a delegation from St. Peter welcomed them into the cozy, warm glow of the Nicollet County Courthouse. A long table was set and loaded with a bounty of warm food.

The soldiers attacked the feast with fervor and then, bellies full, bedded down on the floor. On the morning of the 24th, Gere stood his men in formation at attention in front of the sleighs. "Gentlemen, we owe a debt to the fine people of St. Peter. Show your appreciation."

A chorus rose up from the ranks, "Huzzah! Huzzah! Huzzah!"

* * *

THE HORSE-DRAWN SLEIGHS slid out of town and up the Minnesota River to LaFayette, where they camped eighteen miles southeast of Fort Ridgely. The next day at noon the men and boys of Company B arrived at their post.

Fort Ridgely rested on a bluff high above the north side of the Minnesota River. Built ten years before under the direction of Captain Pemberton, currently a Confederate general, the fort was a collection of wood-framed buildings on three sides with a long, stone building on one end and another in the northwest corner. Other cabins and stables stood outside the perimeter.

"What kind of fort is this?" Will Sutherland complained as climbed from a sleigh. "There aren't any walls, just a bunch o' stone and wood buildings in a rectangle."

Gere overheard and answered. "The men who established this fort thought walls led to complacency. An open fort needs vigilance and a more active force."

Oscar Wall looked from side to side. "Well, they weren't too smart, were they? Ravines are all around us 'cept one corner. We wouldn't see attackers 'til they're right on top of us."

"Oh, Oscar," Marty Wilson admonished, "nobody's gonna attack us. We're just here ta be here. Don't worry so much."

"Like the sergeant said, I'm just being vigilant."

First Lieutenant Norm Culver, with his young son Charlie the drummer boy, and a burly man with a heavy dark beard, trudged across the snowy parade ground to greet them.

Gere quickly ordered the men into parade formation at attention.

"At ease men," Culver ordered. "Welcome to Fort Ridgely. You're now the guardians of the western frontier in Minnesota. The Upper Sioux, or Redwood Agency, we oversee is twelve miles up the river. Immigrant farmsteads dot the countryside. We are at peace and will remain at peace.

"You'll be bivouacked in the long barracks at the north end of the fort. You'll have plenty of room there," he gestured at the one-story stone building. "It was built to hold 400.

"This," he motioned to the man next to him, "is Sergeant John Jones, regular army, the only one left on the post. The red piping on his trousers tells you he is an artillery man. Sergeant Jones."

The big man spoke in a booming voice. "We have six cannon left here by the regular army. It's my intention to train you all in the methods of firing artillery. You'll drill until you can do it in your sleep."

"Fine," Jimmy muttered, "more drills, just cannons not muskets."

"Don't worry," Marty whispered back, "I'm sure we'll get our fill of all kinds of drills. What else is there to do?"

In fact, other duties did claim some attention. Care and feeding of the horses entailed stable detail and pitching manure. Since the fort had no well, water had to be obtained each day from a spring between the fort and the river.

March turned into April, and the vanishing snow left the fort's parade ground with a layer of mud. In light of those conditions, drills were held on the prairie beyond the compound.

Marching and drilling in the use of firearms remained the main task faced by Company B. Sergeant John Bishop stood before a squad of eight men and called out, "Load in nine times!"

"We learned all this at Fort Snelling," Willie Sturgis complained. "Why do we hafta keep on every day?"

"Because," Bishop replied, "you have to do it faster and better. Someday you'll be shooting with rebs coming at your face."

"I can git off two a minute now," Sturgis countered.

"You need to get three or four."

"Our guns are antiques." Jimmy held his up. "Smoothbore .69 caliber, we can't hit the broadside of a barn at 100 yards with these."

"I know it's difficult," Bishop answered, "but these are what the State of Minnesota could come up with for us. Demand can't keep up with all the new regiments being formed. We'll get new rifles when we go east. We don't need them here."

"What do your brother's men have?" Oscar Wall inquired.

Bishop sighed, "He's got .58-caliber rifled, percussion cap muskets."

"A fella kin put ten outta ten inside a two-foot square at 300 yards with them," Jimmy pointed out.

Marty Wilson agreed, "And right through a foot of pine boards at a hundred yards. What we got are like toys. We can't hit nothing 'less we git lucky."

Bishop offered, "Well, if it's any consolation some of the rebs are still using flintlocks. They could shoot at you all day, and you might never know it 'cept for the noise. Enough talk, load in nine times. Load!"

The men began to follow the nine procedures that entailed firing their weapons. The squad, in two files of four, moved their right feet back and formed a "T" between their right insteps and left heels. Holding their muskets at a forty-five degree angle into the air, the men reached into the little leather pouches near their belt buckles and produced percussion caps, which they slipped beneath the striking hammers of their weapons.

"Tear cartridge!" Bishop shouted.

Each man reached his right hand inside the powder satchel riding just above his right hip. Then each grabbed one little paper bag of gunpowder, ripped off the twisted top with his teeth, poured the gunpowder down a musket bore, pushed the paper bag into the barrel and then seated a sixty-nine-caliber lead ball. They then immediately slid ramrods from beneath the musket barrel and forced the bullet, paper, and powder to the base of the barrel by ramming them down the long cylinder. They followed the steps automatically without Bishop's prompts.

At the command, "Ready!" each of the soldiers brought his musket to full cock.

Then came, "Aim!" and the guns were pointed at a distant two-and-one-half-foot-square target. The men in the second row leveled their weapons over the right shoulders of the man in their front.

"Fire!" Bishop cried.

The eight muskets roared in a staccato volley. A soldier standing far off to the side of the target trotted over to the target to examine it.

He looked back at Bishop, shook his head and announced, "Nothin'. They all missed."

"Well," Bishop commented, "let's try again. Load in nine times."

Into Virginia

THE 1ST TENNESSEE REGIMENT rolled out of Nashville with steam and smoke chugging from an engine revved up to roar down the tracks at twenty to thirty miles an hour. The populace lining the tracks cheered, waved flags and handkerchiefs, and shouted hurrahs for Jeff Davis and the new Confederacy.

At stops throughout Tennessee—Chattanooga, Lynchburg, Knoxville and at hamlets in between, banquets and demonstrations greeted the regiment. It was one long, rolling celebration into Virginia. Word of an impending battle had them all bursting like overripe fruit with anticipation and excitement.

"Well, Sam," Charlie Miller spoke loudly, over the *clickity-clack* of the train wheels, "I sure hope we git ta Manassas on time. I wanna git in some action. Teach those Yanks a lesson. They should o' stayed north and not come down here. There don't need ta be no war if they jest leave us alone."

"But that's what it's all about, Charlie. They have to come down here to force us back into the Union. It's the only way to settle it."

"Well I'm ready ta show 'em they can't do it."

Nightfall on July 21st the train hauling the 1st Tennessee pulled into Manassas Junction, arriving amid a scene of jubilation. A band played "Dixie." Torches burned brightly, illuminating flags. The smudged and sweat-dried faces of gray-uniformed men sang along with the band.

As the wheels locked and the locomotive squealed to a halt, shouts of "Huzzah!" and "God Bless Jeff Davis!" greeted the Tennesseans.

"What happened?" Sam cried down from atop a box car.

"Ain't ya heard?" a torch-laden soldier called back. "We kicked 'em in the behind. The Yanks is runnin' back ta Washington with their tails between their legs." He laughed gleefully. "They couldn't git back fast enough. Threw off knapsacks, rifles, ammunition belts, anything that'd slow 'em down."

Another soldier shouted up, "And kin ya believe it? It was a teacher that saved the day, Jackson, he came from VMI, they're callin' him Stonewall, 'cause of what he did. He stood off the Yanks like a stone wall."

"Sam, I heard of a Jackson from Virginia Military Institute," said Charlie, "but they called him, 'Fool Tom.' They made fun o' him."

"Looks like he's no fool no more." Sam paused. "And we missed the battle."

Charlie mused, "Jest mebbe we missed the war."

From Manassas the train rolled into Staunton, Virginia. Another crowd of well-wishers greeted them like conquering heroes. They weren't. No one cared. There had been a great victory, and anyone in gray was part of it whether actually there or not. Three privates—Sam, John Smith and Bill Searcey—jumped from the boxcar, their faces glowing brighter with excitement than the afternoon sun.

"Sarge says ta go inta camp and git set up. Then we kin see the town," Smith marveled.

"Staunton is a big place," Searcey added. "A lot to do and a lot to see."

For young boys, many away from home for the first time, it all seemed like a moving fair or carnival. Joyous people everywhere, cheap whiskey, good tobacco, and games. Barkers called them out wherever they went.

Sam and the others walked past faro and roulette tables and gambling halls. "C'mon in, boys," a sweaty man in a cheap suit called as they walked by. "New game for you ta try, chuck-a-luck."

Searcey retorted, "Lots o' chuck and not much luck, I'll bet!"

"It's like they know we just got two months' pay," Sam pondered.

"My momma told me ta stay away from gamblers," Smith cautioned.

"Looky there." Searcey pointed to a sign reading "State Asylum for the Blind and Insane." He nudged Smith. "I wager she told ya to stay outta there, too. 'Less ya belong there."

"We can look it over tomorrow, boys," Sam commented. "There's lots to see in a place like this."

A woman, looking tired and wearing bright clothing, stood to the side. A red flower, which looked out of place, was fastened in her black hair. She crooked a finger at Sam and beckoned softly, "Come on over here, boy, I got somethin' to show you."

Sam reddened, put his head down and kept walking straight ahead as his friends giggled and hooted.

"Mebbe she's got some food for ya, Sam," Smith suggested.

"Or," Searcey chimed in, "a Bible. Bet she wants ta read the Bible with ya."

"All right, John," Sam countered, "maybe you should go see her. I'm sure your momma wouldn't care."

"No," Smith rejoined, "Momma *would* care. There's other stuff fer us to do."

The young solders continued on. They did visit the asylum and many other spots of interest in the town, including churches and schools. The next day they were all off again into the Virginia valley and Millboro.

It was there they bid adieu to the railroad, slung their knapsacks on their backs, shouldered their rifles and began to march, something most would continue doing for much of the next three years. Off they went, tramping and stomping along roads, trails, and through brush. At Valley Mountain, Virginia, the Rutherford Rifles, along with the 7th and 14th Tennessee Infantry, were formed into General Sam Anderson's brigade of General William W. Loring's Division, the Army of the Northwest.

As they trudged under the blistering July sun, they passed through Bath Alum toward the Alleghenies. Sam marched alongside Joe Cates. Strewn all along the trail were items discarded by overheated, exhausted soldiers: blankets, boots, hats, pants, sometimes good ones. Even pistols and Bowie knives.

"Wish I had time ta collect that stuff," Cates observed. "When I got home I could start a general store."

"You'd have a good start," Sam agreed.

"There's jest one good thing about marchin,' Sam."

"What's that?"

"You know. Everthin' grows up here. Berries, apples, peaches, even peas and potatoes not far off the trail. A fella kin sure could fill up his hat easy."

The next stop for the men was Warm Springs, which featured a refreshing but brief frolic in the tepid waters of the big, natural pool. As Joe, Sam, and John Smith lounged in the waters, they speculated over their mission.

"Anybody know where we might be goin'?" John wondered. "I heerd somethin' 'bout a place called Cheat Mountain."

"Ta find Yanks," Joe said. "Seems some of 'em don't know they's beat yet."

"There are lots of Unionists in western Virginia. I think we're trying to hold on to it," Sam reasoned.

Charlie raised his hand as if still in school. "So they got us joined up with some Virginians and put somebody called Bobby Lee in charge of us all. Anybody know anythin' about him?"

"He's West Point," Sam answered, "an engineer in the Mexican War. Folks say he's a smart one."

Cates snorted. "I heard folks call him 'Granny Lee.' He's too slow and never led men in battle."

"We'll see," Sam considered, "I just know we keep moving. I expect Robert E. Lee knows where we're going—Cheat Mountain or someplace."

"Now yer learnin', Sam," Charlie agreed. "It don't pay ta try to figure nothin' out. We're foot soldiers. We march. If they tell us to, we shoot. But we don't need ta think."

Two days later brought August. The regiment was camped at Big Springs preparing breakfast. A heavy white frost lay over the land like a white blanket.

"It's beautiful country," Bill Searcey observed as he tried to bite into a chunk of hardtack.

John Beesley slapped at a bug crawling over his corporal stripes. "Beautiful, sure. Two days ago it was hot 'nough ta fry eggs on a bald head. Today yer coffee'd freeze if ya don't drink it right away. It's way too early for this."

"We're in mountains, Johnny."

"And we're enjoyin' the bounties provided us by the Southern Confederacy. Good food for all and eleven dollars a month."

Charlie Miller shook a couple thin slabs of fatty bacon in the grease of a frying pan over an open fire. "Book says we're s'posed to git twelve ounces of bacon or twenty ounces of salt beef every day along with eighteen ounces of flour or twenty ounces of corn meal or hard bread. I ain't seen nothin' close to that yet. We're lucky the brush is full of berries and fruit."

Searcey held up another piece of hardtack. "We got plenty of this."

"And the meat's right in it," Sam agreed. "If you want to eat the meat separate, just boil it. The bugs'll come floating right out."

A lightning bolt split the morning sky, followed by another and yet another until the light show cast a continuous eerie glow all around. Rumbles of thunder followed, struggling to keep up with the lightning flashes.

"Ain't that a wonderment." Cates murmured.

Beesley stood. "You'll all be wondering why you didn't see to your shelters when the rain starts. See to your accoutrements and your tents."

"I've heard there be Yanks about," Cate advised.

Corporal Beesley peered into the distance and wiped raindrops from his eyes. "If there are, I hope we find them b'fore they find us."

On the 25th of August, the regiment marched to the summit of Valley Mountain. There they pitched tents and sent out scouts looking for Union patrols. On September 2nd, they marched farther north to Mingo Plat.

The entire regiment waited in camp with the anticipation something was going to happen. The arrival of General Robert E. Lee lent credence to their expectations. General Loring, Colonel Maney, Captain Ledbetter and other officers joined Lee in the open. They sat on camp stools around a smoldering campfire's yellow flickers of flame, like hands seeking help.

Joe Cates and Sam Davis watched from some distance away. Cates said, "Whole bunch o' bigwigs. Somethin's up, Sam."

"I think you're right. Let's walk over and find out."

"Yes, sir, General Davis. I see they got a place held for you."

"We'll just mosey over and stand by the trees that ring their site. Close enough to maybe hear things but not be in the way. In a few minutes it'll be dark and they won't notice us anyway."

Even after Ledbetter stirred up the fire and tossed on dry wood, the light didn't reach the trees Sam and Joe stood beside in the growing darkness.

Maney explained, "The Yankee's general, Reynolds, left Colonel Kimball in charge on Cheat Mountain. Our scouts tell us the Yanks have got one regiment there in a fort on the summit."

General Lee listened intently. "I've scouted the area myself. Reynolds has three regiments down in the river valley." He stood up, the flickering flames revealing a mustached face and blue cottonade uniform. His voice was calm, reasoned, as if nothing could excite him.

"General," he said gently to Loring, "those people have about 5,000 to put in play against us. So we are outnumbered by a couple thousand. But if we do this right, it won't make any difference."

"What about Rosecrans?" Ledbetter wondered.

"Too far away," Lee answered. "He won't be a factor."

"What's your plan, sir?"

Maney said something unintelligible.

"What?" Cates whispered to Sam in the nearby trees.

His buddy put his finger to his lips.

"That won't be a concern, Colonel Maney," Lee continued. "This is what we'll do. We'll launch a two-pronged attack: one on the summit against Kimball's fort, and the other into the valley on Reynolds.

"General Jackson, you'll take six brigades and create a diversion in front of the fort. Colonel Rust, your brigade will take the fort. General Loring, your brigades'll head into the valley and attack Reynolds. We'll engage three brigades independently. President Davis sent me here to retake Confederate land in western Virginia and to coordinate this army. If this works, both goals will have been met."

"How do I know when to attack the fort?" Maney inquired.

"Don't move until you hear a single gunshot," Lee answered. "That's the signal to begin it all."

"So tomorrow we move," Cates whispered.

"September 12th," Sam nodded. "Our holiday is over. Maybe it's time to do what we came here for."

A bolt of lightning slashed a jagged line across the sky, followed by a boom of thunder, which shook the earth. As the Maney and Cates reached their tents, torrents of rain poured from the sky. Sam looked at a lumpy form lying on a fallen tree trunk. In another flash of lightning he saw that it was a man, his head covered by a knapsack and a blanket over that.

"What are you doing?" Sam shouted at the form.

First one covering and then the other were peeled off until the form revealed itself as Charlie Miller. "Hi ya, Sam, the ground's gonna be soaked awful quick. I'm stayin' up here where it's dry. I'm off the ground and all covered up."

As Charlie slipped back under his shelter, Sam dropped down and crawled into his tent on the soaking ground.

The next morning dawned foggy with a mist of rain still in the air. The 1st Tennessee sloshed through mud and water into position on Cheat Mountain, then waited behind logs and stumps for the gunshot signal that would commence the charge. It never came.

One blue-coated soldier wandered out of some bushes, his canteen rattling. Bill Beesley shot and wounded him. That was the extent of action for the Rutherford Rifles. Late in the day Captain Ledbetter spoke to his company.

"The day was just messed up from the beginning. The rain, fog, the mountainous terrain, plus dense forest limited visibility. We couldn't see what we needed to. So, each of the three brigades wound up acting independently and never made contact with the other two.

"Then the federals acted from the fort on the summit and our Rust and Anderson pulled back. Down below, they couldn't move Reynolds from his entrenchments. After Colonel Washington was killed, General Lee called off the attack. It's over."

"Now what?" Joe Cates shouted.

"We march where they tell us to," Ledbetter replied. "We've got a new commander. Lee's been called back to Richmond. General Jackson'll take us through Virginia."

"Old Stonewall!" Charlie Miller shouted.

"More like Fool Tom!" another called.

"There'll be none of that!" Ledbetter responded. "General Jackson will be given all the respect due his rank and accomplishments." The captain paused and looked over his men. "Dismissed," he ordered. "Get a good night's rest. We march tomorrow."

The men gathered around cook fires before turning into their shelters. Some puffed on pipes filled with fine Virginia tobacco they'd managed to scrounge.

"Stonewall Jackson," Charlie mused, "he seems to be a fighter."

Joe Ewing poked a stick into the fire, causing a shower of red sparks to sprinkle onto the ground. "But he seems so odd. He rode by camp yesterday. His feet pulled way up in his stirrups on that old nag of a horse he rides. His wrinkled, dirty cap pulled down with the brim over his eyes."

"I've heard he likes to have lemons whenever he can git 'em," Cates said. "He likes to watch things, like battles, while sucking lemons."

"All the while holding out his left arm, to keep himself in balance," Sam interjected.

"I don't care how odd he is," Corporal Beesley replied, "just so's he wins battles."

"We'll follow him and find out," Cates concluded. He stood and stretched. "Now, let's hit the hay."

Tents were used for short tenures in camp. But the most popular shelter was a small hut made of logs, chinked and daubed like a pioneer cabin. These could be thrown up quickly, especially if an officer offered a reward for the first one completed. A jug of whiskey was a popular inducement. The walls were usually about eight feet high, topped by a tent-canvas roof, unless a very ambitious spirit inspired men to split logs into planks for the roof. Four to ten men, depending on the size of the mess group, would occupy the structure.

Cates led his compatriots into their log shelter, threw wood into the stone fireplace forming part of one wall, and settled down onto the floor to sleep.

On September 16th the regiment left Cheat Pass and marched back to the base of Valley Mountain. After settled into camp, word came to Jackson that General John Floyd was in retreat in western Virginia and needed his help.

Jackson ordered a forced march 100 miles to Sewell Mountain. The only consolation for the Rutherford Rifles was the scenery they marched through.

Tom Wade called back to Sam and Charlie Miller, "Ya ever seen anything this purty, even back home?"

The green valleys sloped down from low mountains whose peaks were sometimes enveloped in a misty gloaming. Lush, verdant fruit trees bore apples, peaches, and plums and seemed to reach toward the trail as if proffered by the hands of welcoming hosts.

"It's beautiful," Sam agreed. "Do you suppose we'll get some fighting in at Sewell Mountain?"

Charlie was hopeful. "Sounds like it. I heard we're after Old Rosey, himself, General Rosecrans. He's the one been chasing Floyd."

But it wasn't to be. Floyd had captured one line of the Union works in a charge two days earlier. Now he was entrenched and dug in. Near Sewell Mountain the Rutherford boys erected breastworks and stayed behind them until October, when Rosecrans retreated. A minor skirmish or two occurred, and shots were fired. But none involved the Rifles.

Along the foot of the mountains the regiment tramped to Harrisonburg, Lewisburg, and Kanawha Salt-Works before reaching Huntersville in early November. There the men had time to construct their log shelters again and vote in the national election. The Rifles voted for Jefferson Davis for president and split their votes between Ready and Gentry for Congress.

In late November they moved to Fort Maney, where they were ordered to build winter quarters. The men industriously chinked and daubed the walls. They even split logs into planks for stronger rooftops. Sam Davis and his messmates settled comfortably into their cozy, warm shelter. Outside a cold wind whipped across the camp as if angry the troops invaded its pristine landscape.

The soldiers were playing cards or writing letters home in the room's flickering candlelight when the door burst open. Corporal Beesley stepped in.

"Fer cripes sake!" Joe Cates shouted, "shut the door. This ain't no barn!"

"Sorry, men," Beesley apologized, "but I got news."

The men stopped whatever they were doing and looked expectantly at their corporal.

"Things've changed. We been ordered to join up with Stonewall again, this time on the Potomac. Seems the Yanks might start movin' on Richmond again, and we need to give 'em somethin' else to think about."

"It's pretty cold to do a march, John," Sam cautioned. "Most are still in summer uniforms, linsey-woolsey and cotton. Some have already worn through their gunboats, er, shoes."

"It's 200 miles to Winchester. I'm told we git winter clothing there."

"Will we actually have uniforms that match? Look at us. Some companies in gray, some butternut, some with blue pants, some even in blue altogether and looking like Yankees. Others have wool jacket blouses and some don't. Isn't uniform supposed to imply the same?"

"Jeepers creepers," Charlie Miller whistled, "sure kin tell somebody here went ta some college."

Beesley exhaled slowly. "All's I know is what I said, you'll get new winter uniforms and I expect they'll be alike. Fact is, Congress passed a new law. Some of you got fifty dollars a year for havin' yer own uniforms. No more of that. No more 'fancy Dan's' with bright colors and foo-fa-rah. Even if some rich fella wants to outfit a company or regiment, he'll hafta do it like Richmond says."

"What about hats?" Marion McFarlin asked. "I'm pretty partial to my wide brim. I don't want a little kepi with a tiny brim. I'll look like Stonewall."

Amid chuckles from the men, Beesley responded, "Head gear is still whatever you want to wear."

"What about rifles?' Sam inquired. "Some of the boys are still using flintlocks."

"Being replaced as quick as we kin get our hands on percussion rifles."

"Maybe we'll fight some Yanks and take theirs," Charlie grinned.

"Maybe," their corporal agreed. "We move out in two days, December 11. Christmas in Winchester."

A week later after tramp, tramp, tramping up the Shenandoah Valley past stately homes, bountiful fields and lovely farmsteads, the regiment reached Winchester. They had traveled through the breadbasket of the Confederacy.

"Sam," Charlie said as they neared the town, "I ain't never seen purtier land than what we just marched through."

"It's more than that, Charlie, I heard that one-fifth of the Confederacy's food comes from the Shenandoah."

"Wind's comin' up, Sam. I sure hope we git set up in camp soon. I want some of that one-fifth."

The first night in Winchester, a blustery wind bared its teeth, taking a bite out of everything in its way. It ripped the regiment's hastily set up tents from their stakes. Men huddled behind trees, in ditches—anywhere they could.

The next morning they were issued their new uniforms: long underwear, gray woolen pants and blouses, and overcoats—"great coats" as they were called. These were gray wool; some even came with short capes. Black shoes, called gunboats by the troops, without typical right or left configuration, also arrived.

"My, oh, my!" Charlie exclaimed. "I ain't never had clothes this fine!"

"And you might never again," suggested Marion McFarlin. "The Yanks'll tighten things up. This might be all ya get for the rest of the war."

"You mean a few months then. Hey, these pants are too long."

"Then cut 'em off," Corporal Beesley replied.

"What are these long, funny-lookin' pants fer?" a young man asked Sam.

"They're underwear. You wear them under your pants."

"Tarnation, what fer?"

Sam shook his head in bewilderment. "Just wear them."

The soldiers spent Christmas 1861 warm and toasty in their new clothes and rough cabins. Then the order came. The regiment was to head for Romney near the Maryland state line.

The 1st Tennessee was glad to have warm clothes because the march to Romney commencing January 1st would prove to be one of its most arduous. The men bundled up as best they could and hit the trail north. A storm hit them with all its fury, shrieking like a banshee and striking them hard and as sure as a gloved fist. Snow, wind, rain and sleet seemed to alternate their attack in waves of intensity. But one element was always present: the cold. As the troops marched, icicles formed on clothing, knapsacks, and rifles. Charlie Miller's uniform was literally encased in ice, his face turning blue.

Here and there along the way the bodies of dead men lay in the snow, frozen stiff as fresh-cut planks. The fresh snow grew packed by the tramping of plodding feet and turned dangerously slippery. Horses pulling the artillery caissons slid and slipped, injuring themselves and their riders or drivers. The pitiful cries of wounded animals mingled with the piercing howl of the wind.

Sam wrapped his arm around Charlie and urged him on. "Romney's not far off, Charlie, you can make it."

Charlie mumbled numbly, "I might be frostbit, but I ain't dead. Not yet."

"We'll get there. A farmer back a ways said this is the worst storm folks can remember hereabouts. I believe it."

"Let's just git ta Romney, Sam."

General Jackson passed them from the rear, his horse tentatively picking its way on the frozen path.

From the ranks a cry rang out, "Fool Tom, yer killin' us!"

Another shouted, "Yer crazy fer makin' us march in this!"

"Stop this confounded snow!" bellowed a man a few ranks behind Sam.

Jackson stoically continued on, seemingly oblivious to the cat calls.

When they finally reached Romney, the half-frozen, exhausted Confederate soldiers erected shelters as quickly as possible. They built bonfires outside and small fires inside their log structures. Some huddled in tents, quicker to set up, but much colder in the long run.

Gradually the men thawed. Snow melted in pots over fires and the hot liquid poured down the throats of distressed soldiers, including Charlie Miller. As Sam Davis slowly poured the warming fluid down his friend's throat, Charlie revived.

"The cabin's almost done, Charlie. We'll have you in front of a fire in no time."

"Thanks, Sam. It'll be good to feel my fingers and toes again."

After the bedraggled regiment had a day to recover, Captain Ledbetter had 'them assemble so he could address them. "Men, the Yankees have Banks and Meade in the valley. We're to march on them, hit 'em hard and drive them toward Washington. We've got to relieve the pressure McClellan's planning to put on Richmond. The Yankees need to start thinking about what we might do to their capital."

"Captain," a man cried from the back, "we ain't fit to march, let alone fight, and we sure ain't up to followin' Tom Fool."

A chorus of shouts rose in a wave of agreement.

Ledbetter held up his palms to quiet them. "I get that. Other company captains have relayed the same sentiment. But you can't go blaming General Jackson for the snow and how hard the wind blew. He had orders to get into the Shenandoah and fight Yankees. That's what he wants to do. Do you want to go back to Rutherford County and tell your folks you got here, but just didn't feel like fighting because you didn't like General Jackson?"

The company fell silent until Sam spoke up. "I don't know about the rest. But I'm sticking with the general."

Another called out, "I'm with him, too!" Choruses of assent followed.

But Thomas Jackson was not convinced. Other companies had refused to follow him. He marched back to Winchester to tender his resignation, but it was turned down. Jackson returned to Romney and the encamped army.

Sam's messmates huddled for warmth in their cabin, waiting for Jackson's next move.

"Well," Bill Searcey considered, "this sure ain't what I signed up for. I thought we'd fight Yankees and not sit around waitin' and freezin'."

"At least companies H and K got to see some Yanks up close when we were leaving Cheat Mountain," Joe Cates remarked.

"Only 'cause they led the regiment into an ambush and were in the front of it," a recovered Charlie Miller noted.

"Weren't much," Joe snorted, "once a few shots got fired and Captain Feild had the boys charge, the Yanks ran off."

Sam considered the conversation and noted, "I heard that officers ripped off their rank insignias and anything fancy on their uniforms."

"I heard that, too," Marion MacFarland agreed. "I talked to a fella named Sam with the Maury Grays, Company H. He said an officer told him he wasn't gonna advertise being an officer to make a better target for them to shoot at."

"Really," Sam chuckled, "do they think bullets have eyes and can decide who to hit?"

"Shoot at privates," Joe noted. "Officers are pretty worthless, it's the privates who'll be shooting at you."

John Beesley interjected, "Well, I kept my stripes on and, speaking of Company H, listen to this."

As the men all turned intently to Beesley, he spat a stream of yellow tobacco into the fire. It sizzled and bubbled. The corporal considered it briefly before he continued. "Sam told me this, too. Seems some boys went out on picket duty on one of them really cold nights to relieve some Georgia boys early in the mornin'. Sam says he came up to one o' the men standing against a tree. Told 'em he was reportin' for duty. The man just stood there in the dark like he didn't hear Sam. Sam reached out and touched 'im. The fella was dead, froze stiff standin' up. Another fella was standin' close by. Same thing. Eight others lay on the ground, some jest lyin' there or some curled up kinda like. All dead, all frozen. One fella had an icicle on the end of his nose. They was like statues, Sam said." Beesley grew silent.

"Makes me feel better," Charlie uttered laconically, "I jest froze my feet and hands."

"An' ya peeled the skin off like they was onions."

"How long we been here now?" Charlie wondered.

Sam thought for a moment. "Almost a month. It's February now."

"Well, we ain't done much more than sit here," Charlie complained. "Some boys got into little scrapes with Yanks, but not much. I'd just as soon go home as sit here."

"Don't let the general hear you say that," MacFarland cautioned, "he cracks a pretty mean whip around here. Talk like that could get you shot."

"Remember back in Winchester," Sam added, "first order read to us after being attached to his corps was to attend the shooting to death by firing squad of two men who had stopped on the battlefield to carry off a wounded friend."

"The general can be unreasonable," Cates agreed.

* * *

THE TIME WITH GENERAL JACKSON and the Army of the Northwest was over. Jackson would continue his Potomac Campaign in western Virginia and Maryland. But orders came from Richmond that the 1st Tennessee and the Rutherford Rifles were to return to Winchester, from which they were ordered west on February 17, 1862. Back in Tennessee, at Knoxville, the left wing of the 1st Tennessee, companies A, B, C, and D, was detached by Major General Kirby Smith and sent to the Cumberland Gap.

The right wing, companies F, G, H, I, and K, including the Rutherford Rifles, was sent to Chattanooga for garrison duty. Once rejoined by the left wing, the 1st Tennessee was ordered to board a train bound for Corinth, Mississippi. There they would be under the command of Albert Sidney Johnson to serve in the Army of Mississippi. But the train had room for only half the regiment. The right wing boarded. The left wing waited for another train.

Sam Davis and the Rutherford Rifles chugged into Corinth on March 15, 1862, and immediately were detailed building up the city's defenses.

To Shiloh

ON FEBRUARY 10TH the 2nd Minnesota left the area around Mill Springs and set off for Louisville. They were content in the belief they had played an important part in preserving Kentucky for the Union. They left behind twelve dead and had sustained thirty-three wounded, some of whom remained hospitalized as the others marched off. The regiment passed through Stanford, Danville, Perryville, Bardstown, and other hamlets before reaching Louisville on February 24th.

The arriving troops marched down the main street of Louisville, which was lined with loyal Union citizens who waved flags and banners from the sidewalk, windows, and porches. The marching men took heart from the joyous reception and proceeded with a smart and lively cadence.

Before the National Hotel in Louisville, the Minnesota troops assembled to receive a silk banner of appreciation from the "Loyal Ladies of Louisville."

Colonel Van Cleve then addressed the troops and townspeople.

"We thank you for your expressions of gratitude. Thanks to the heroism of these fine men, Kentucky will remain in the Union." Van Cleve paused while the citizens applauded boisterously.

"General Grant and his gallant men have captured forts Henry and Donelson on the Tennessee River and Cumberland River. The way to Nashville on the Ohio and Cumberland is now open. Grant's army is moving relentlessly down the Tennessee and will soon cut through the rebels' defenses. With good fortune, we will join him."

Loud cheers echoed down the street as the 2nd Minnesota resumed its march to the river and boarded a steamer, the *Jacob Strader,* at the levee. As the craft steamed down the Ohio River, Clinton Cilley and Judson Bishop stood near the bow. The paddlewheel churned through the dark waters of the wide river that February 24, 1862.

"The men sure like this better than marching, Captain."

"They should, Clint. In just a few days we'll enter the Cumberland near Fort Donelson and be in Nashville by the end of the week."

"Things sure didn't work out the way the rebs planned, did they?"

"No, Henry and Donelson were overrun. Instead of being shot at when we pass Donelson, we'll be cheered. General Buell is closing on Nashville and the town is being evacuated. Tennessee's governor, Isham Harris, is moving the capitol to Memphis."

"Not quite a year in and the first Confederate state capitol has fallen," Cilley acknowledged.

"For the last state to secede, this is a real blow to them. This city is an economic engine for their war effort. I've heard a plant there turns out 100,000 percussion caps a day. The Nashville Plow Works was making sabers." He paused. "I guess they were turning plow shares into sabers—not quite Biblical.

"Other plants turn out muskets, saddles, harness, and knapsacks. Looms there turn out thousands of gray uniforms. They got a railroad center, arsenal, and supply depot. We'll take 'em all. Captain, I sure hope we get there soon."

"We'll get there just as fast as this boat will take us."

On February 28 the steamer paddled past Smithfield, Tennessee, and cut off on the Cumberland River. On the first of March they heard cheers as they passed Fort Donelson. They arrived in Nashville on March 3. The next day the 2nd Minnesota set up camp three miles out of town on the Granny White Pike to be resupplied and await orders.

Rincie DeGrave and Charlie Orline quickly buttoned their tent together. Each man carried half of a two-man tent. It only took minutes to set up.

"Not as big as a Sibley, but I like it better," Rincie commented.

"Ya ever been in a Sibley?" Charlie wondered.

"Some last year," Rincie answered, "crammed in like a tin of sardines. Twelve men at least, and we had ta sleep with our feet to the center pole like a wagon wheel with twelve spokes. 'Nother thing, it was damn near impossible to breathe in a Sibley. If it was rainy or cold it got all closed up. I stepped in once on a damp, cool mornin', and the smell of twelve men after a night of burpin', fartin', and not washin' was about enough to make me puke."

"I never slept in one," Charlie said. "I was in a wedge, an 'A' because of the shape. 'Bout seven square feet, made for four men. But the army says six fit jest fine. We had ta sleep like spoons. When one turned over, we all had to."

"Wait 'til winter, Charlie."

"The winter quarters ain't much better," Charlie rejoined, "part wood, part canvas, and with a stove, but it sure gets smelly and stuffy there, too."

"Well, now it's spring, and we kin enjoy the comforts of our 'dog' tents."

"Dog tents are just fine, Charlie. When got time we can lift up the edges for air or put 'em on top of logs, kinda like a foundation."

"It's a regular palace," DeGrave laughed.

"What's so funny?" Dan Heaney wondered as he approached the two.

"Nothin', Sarge, just considerin' the good and bad of where we've slept."

"Well, I've got some more comforts to add to your list. Report to the commissary. You're being issued more clothing, rations, and ammunition."

"We get new blue suits!" Rincie DeGrave cried. "I bet they're wool."

"Finest wool a sheep can provide. Nice white cotton shirts, too. Just in time for summer."

Late that afternoon, after accumulating the bounties of the commissary, the men gathered for evening mess. John Fern and Aaron Doty joined Charlie Orline and Rincie around their cookstove, which rested over a hot fire.

Fern asked, "Lemme guess. Salt pork tonight with crackers and coffee?"

"Good guess," Rincie answered. "How'd you figure it out?"

"Because it's the same as every night," Doty replied.

"Well," Charlie announced, "we do have a little change tonight. Onions!" He held up several. "Got 'em off a peddler that came through camp."

"Good job, Charlie," Doty grinned, "variety is the spice of life, I've heard."

"But we hafta depend on peddlers to get it. I heard colored folks calling out they had pizen cakes. I wondered who'd buy a cake if it was pizened."

"Not poisoned," Doty corrected.

"Pissed on? Pissed on cakes?"

Doty laughed. "No. Pies. Pies and cakes."

"Oh, I shoulda got one."

Doty shook his head. "Charlie, you've gotta get off the farm more."

Over the next couple of weeks the men of the 2nd Minnesota enjoyed the relative comfort with a pleasant and healthy camp. The warming spring weather provided a welcome relief from the memories of Mill Springs.

A bugle sounded on March 15th calling the men of the 2nd Minnesota to assemble. As they stood in ranks, Colonel Van Cleve strode before them. Then he stopped to address the troops.

"Men, we're in for a march. General Grant's been ordered by General Hallack to proceed down the Tennessee River to the big bend near Savannah, Tennessee. "General Buell's army, of which we are part, will march there from Nashville. Tomorrow Alexander McCook's division will commence the march to the rendezvous point near Savannah. He'll be followed in order, one day apart, by the divisions of Nelson, Crittenden, Wood and Thomas.

"Our division, Thomas's, is last in recognition of our already having fought a battle. So we are in the rear and march on the 20th."

"I'd rather be in front," Clinton Cilley commented to Dan Heaney. "We should be rewarded for our experience."

"If the army moves fast enough, we'll all be there to fight," Heaney replied.

But nature had other ideas. Heavy rain drenched the army as they marched, turning the road into a quagmire in places. At times the road ahead was so crowded with the troops of other divisions that Thomas's Division stayed in camp and didn't march.

In good weather they could have pushed forward at a clip of twenty miles a day. But in the rain, they were lucky to slosh ahead for twelve.

Van Cleve announced to his officers, "Nelson, up front, heard from Grant. His division will be in Savannah on the fifth. He says Nelson doesn't need to hurry because the transports to carry him to Pittsburg Landing won't be ready to take him until April 8th."

"What's our objective, Colonel?" Judson Bishop asked.

"Corinth, Mississippi, just over the state line. We take it, we cut a main Confederate supply line to the east. Major rail lines stem out of Corinth."

"Where are the rebs?"

"In Corinth, waiting for us, I suppose."

Corinth, Mississippi
April 2nd

A LBERT SIDNEY JOHNSTON was a great man. At least, everyone seemed to think so. President Jefferson Davis considered Johnston the best general he had and placed him in command of all forces in the west.

Johnston wasn't physically imposing, being of medium height and weight. His hair, mostly dark despite his fifty-nine years, was streaked with white, was thin in front but lay heavily over his ears and collar. Johnston had served as a general in three armies, the Republic of Texas, United States, and Confederate. A West Point graduate, he'd attended at the same time as future Confederate president Jefferson Davis.

After resigning command of the United States Department of the Pacific in September of 1861, Johnston was placed in charge of the Western Department of the Confederacy. This vast area stretched from the Allegheny Mountains west. The critical line of defense ran raggedly from Arkansas north to Columbus, Kentucky, then through southern Kentucky into Virginia. Johnston established his headquarters at Bowling Green.

After the defeat at Mill Springs, followed by the losses of forts Henry and Donelson a month later, Johnston's army retreated to Nashville. But holding onto the city would place his army in imminent peril as larger Union armies closed in. On February 23 Johnston's forces left Nashville for Murfreesboro, just two days before General Don Carolos Buell's Union army marched into the city.

Johnston decided to concentrate forces with General Leonidas Polk and General Pierre T. Beauregard at the strategic railroad crossing site at Corinth, just over the Tennessee line in Mississippi. He led his personal command, the Army of Central Kentucky, south and ordered all units scattered throughout his territory south as well to avoid being cut off.

The Confederates planned to fortify Corinth and the surrounding territory heavily. They concentrated on the vital intersection of the north-south

Mobile and Ohio Railroad and the east-west Memphis and Charleston Railroad, considered a lifeline to the east.

By March 23, Johnston's forces had gathered around Corinth. On the night of April 2nd, their commander gathered his division generals at Rose Cottage to discuss a change in strategy. Around a table in the small building were generals Braxton Bragg, Leonidas Polk, William Hardee, and John Breckinridge. Albert Sidney Johnston, commander of the Army of the Mississippi, sat at the head and Pierre Beauregard at the other end.

In the flickering yellow candlelight, Johnston viewed the men he depended upon for victory. His dark eyes took them in one by one as he coursed the table. Bragg, hard and a strict disciplinarian—a competent leader who could command respect but not love from his men. Polk was a bishop in the Episcopal Church and a graduate of West Point, a big man who had had disagreements with Johnston in Kentucky but was loyal to his friend, "Sidney." John Breckinridge had been vice-president of the United States under James Buchanen. He had run for president himself in 1860 and had only joined the Confederate army in the fall of 1861. But once Bragg discovered that George Crittenden might have a drinking problem and accusations of his intoxication at Mill Springs followed, Johnston was forced to replace him with Breckinridge.

Hardee was perhaps Johnston's best commander. He had served as commandant at West Point and had literally written the book on army infantry drill and training, *Hardee's Tactics*, the military bible of Union and Confederate armies.

Opposite Johnston, at the other end of the table, sat Pierre Beauregard, hero of Fort Sumter. He had been rewarded for his early successes by being named second in command and chief advisor to Johnston, who had endured severe criticism for abandoning Nashville. Davis reasoned having a "hero" assist Johnston would mollify the press and quell public uproar over a retreat Davis agreed with.

Standing apart against a wall was another man, Isham Harris, the governor of Tennessee. Harris had left his new state capitol in exile in Memphis to travel with the army. Meanwhile Andrew Johnson, former U.S. senator from Tennessee, the only senator from a seceding state to remain loyal to the Union, had been named governor by Lincoln.

"I've received word from Colonel Forrest," Johnston began. "McCook's division is leading Buell's army down from Nashville. They're getting close but moving slow, bogged down by rain, mud, and baggage. But they have finally crossed over the Duck River."

"Where's Grant?" Polk wondered.

"Upriver at Savannah. Most of his men, about 40,000, are camped below Pittsburg Landing around a church. The closest are Cump Sherman's division about twenty miles away."

"Church got a name?" Polk inquired.

Johnston smiled. "Leave it to the bishop to ask that. Do you plan to hold services? Someone said the place is called Shiloh."

"Peaceful, pleasant name," Polk murmured thoughtfully.

"It won't be peaceful much longer," Bragg asserted.

Polk shook his head and announced, "I have important news. One of my division commanders, General Cheatham, reports that Lew Wallace's division is moving west in force."

Johnston mused, "Maybe to make another raid on the Mobile and Ohio Railroad. With Buell and Wallace on the move, now's the time to advance and strike the enemy at Pittsburg Landing before they get there."

Bragg pushed back his brown hair and looked around the table, his deep-set eyes glowing under heavy, bushy eyebrows. His full beard and mustache barely moved as he spoke in firm direct tones. "Grant will attack us as soon as Buell joins him. We have to be ready to send them all to Hell. Excuse me, Bishop," he looked at Polk. "Are we ready for them?"

Beauregard answered, "I've drawn up plans, maps, to see to the placement of our defenses. We have a strong position."

"Gentlemen," Johnston explained, "Right now we have 44,000 men ready for battle. Grant has a few thousand or so more. Buell's coming with about 18,000. I propose a new strategy. We won't wait. We won't allow Buell to reinforce Grant and hit us with a numbers advantage tipped greatly to their side."

"I agree, we must attack, destroy Grant before Buell can reach him."

"Sound tactics." Hardee agree.

"But risky," Bragg cautioned.

"We must not fail," Johnston continued. "The plan is for the corps of Hardee, Polk, and Bragg to concentrate within a few miles of the Union lines. General Breckinridge, your corps will be held in reserve. I want the other three to spread side by side in a huge arc. You'll burst from the tree line before the Union camp and drive them fast and hard. Overrun them and push them back to the river. Grant has erred in establishing his camp with their backs to the river. We'll push them right into it. You must proceed with vigor."

From the shadows, Governor Harris said, "I can tell you one thing, General, my boys will be ready. The 1st Tennessee is nearly here and ready to defend their state to the last man."

"Thank you, Isham. All must be ready. But if they don't get here tomorrow, they may be too late. Governor, I feel bad we're in this predicament. After forts Henry and Donelson fell, the door was open to Nashville. We couldn't hold it against the odds we faced, and so the most important city for both river and railroad transportation was lost. We'll get it back for you, Isham. I promise you that we'll get Nashville back."

"When will the attack commence on Grant?" Beauregard asked.

"As soon as we can, by the 4th I hope. I just laid out the parameters of the plan. The details will be drawn up. General Beauregard, that's your specialty. You'll plan where to march, what routes to take, the precise order of regiments, and the exact moment of attack. Grant will be caught off guard and we'll sweep his army from the field."

"It's better than waiting for them," Polk concurred.

"We need a rendezvous point for the army," Johnston noted, "somewhere north of here, not far from Sherman's camp."

Bragg considered, then suggested, "We passed a farm on the Bark Road, a place called Michie's. Lots of room to assemble, and the Ridge Road and Monterey nearly intersect it."

"How far?" Johnston asked.

"Around fourteen miles from here and about eight miles southwest of Pittsburg Landing."

"Good," Johnston agreed. "Our army's dispersed, and we must bring them together. General Polk, General Hardee, you'll move up from Corinth on the Ridge Road. General Bragg, advance through Monterey. General Polk, please call down General Cheatham's division from Purdy. General Breckinridge, move up from Burnsville and follow Bragg's route."

"This won't be easy," Polk cautioned. "We've got to bring thousands of men together in coordinated movement. They're scattered over thirty miles and must converge by various country roads to a selected point of concentration. Not easy for green troops. We're expecting some to cover twenty miles in a day."

"The boys can do it!" Bragg exclaimed. "They've been spoiling for a fight, most of them have never been in battle."

"Will you direct us from Corinth?" Governor Harris wondered.

Johnston looked at the man incredulously. "No, I'll lead my army from the front, not the rear. Once in position at Michie's, I'll call a council of war to finalize the plan of attack for you."

Johnston paused and looked at his bishop/general. "One thing, Leonidas, we could be fighting on Sunday."

"God understands that the righteous cannot always pick when it's best to fight. He will be with us."

Sherman's Camp

CUMP SHERMAN STEPPED out from a rough, unpainted plank building, a small, rectangular church. It more resembled a place to store grain than a house of worship. Folks called it Shiloh. Sherman considered the name, had heard it meant peace.

"Ironic," he mumbled to himself. "An army in a place called peace, all ready to fight, and I've made a church my headquarters."

The general surveyed the vista before him. What had been a wide, grassy plain was now a city of tents—"dog" tents, wall, and mostly Sibley. The pancake-flat ground spread out before him until it dropped steeply into a thick woods. Sherman's men were the forward division of the army. The slate-gray sky leaked a misty drizzle, adding more water to already sloppy ground.

Other divisions arrived at the landing about two miles behind him on the Tennessee River. Grant was nine miles away at the Cherry Mansion in Savannah, Tennessee. To the west spread high, open ground. The only water there was captured in ravines slicing unevenly into the earth. Even the drenching of the last few days hadn't filled them. The soil, left parched after a dry summer, had sucked up the water like a hungry piglet at its mother.

Sherman had an envelope in his hand. He called to a courier nearby, "Take this to Cherry Mansion. See it's delivered to General Grant."

"No rebs that way," the courier noted, "should be easy."

"The rebs are over that way." Sherman pointed toward the trees. "Patrols see them around the railroad."

"Pretty daring, aren't they, General? Ya think they might attack?"

"If I thought so, we'd dig in and build abatis and other barricades. But I'm confident we'll be moving on them before they're ready to move on us. They're holed up in Corinth for the most part. We'll pay them a visit once Buell gets here. My biggest problem is keeping the latrines dug and finding good water. The filthy stuff around here makes men sick.

"Now, sergeant, go to Grant."

As the courier bounded off on his horse, a lieutenant approached Sherman from the church.

"What did you tell General Grant, Sir?"

"That there's no reason to build defenses and I don't apprehend an attack upon our position."

Within an hour the courier trotted up to a stately brick house on the bank of the Tennessee. Two blue-clad guards blocked his way.

"What do you have?" asked one.

The mounted sergeant reached down and handed the envelope to him. "From General Sherman. See General Grant gets it."

As the guard took the paper, the courier wheeled his horse around and trotted away.

Minutes later, after reading the one-sentence message, Grant scrawled his reply. It read, "I have scarcely the faintest idea of an attack being made on us. I will be prepared should such a thing take place. Reports of rebs massing are rumors only."

He addressed an envelope to General Henry Halleck, Commander of the Western Department, Grant's direct superior. Then he handed it to his aide, Captain Rawlins. "Send it to Halleck," he ordered.

"Are we moving on Corinth?"

"Not yet, roads are too muddy and Buell's still a couple days away. When we do, the roads join about halfway to Corinth. The army will come together on the march."

"General Wallace is out of the way behind us."

"I'll keep his division there until we need him. I don't want a rebel cavalry running into us from back there. He can watch out for us from where he is for now."

"Captain, I think things are coming together nicely."

"I wish Buell would get here, General."

"He'll be here soon. The rebs are waiting for us. I don't care if they have to wait a little longer."

A flash of lightning zigzagged across the sky, followed by a rumble of thunder. In minutes, the skies opened up again with a drenching downpour. Grant and Rawlins walked onto the porch of Cherry Mansion.

"Nobody can fight in this," the captain observed.

"It's us that have to bring the fight to them," Grant replied, "and this army isn't moving until things dry out some."

Michie's Farm

ON APRIL 3RD Johnston's Army of the Mississippi began to maneuver into position at the rendezvous point at Michie's, eight miles from Sherman's camp at Shiloh Church. Sam Davis and the Rutherford Rifles were still traveling by rail a good day away from Corinth. Clint Cilley and the 2nd Minnesota were bringing up the rear of Buell's army as it marched to Pittsburg Landing, sludging along through mud like an army of pigs.

Johnston's Army of the Mississippi wasn't doing much better. Polk's apprehensions were well founded. Beauregard had set a timetable for each division to get into position for an attack on the fourth. It fell apart. The twenty-mile march became a quagmire of entangled men, wagons, and horses in the mud. Hardee's troops in the vanguard on Ridge Road held up the advance until 3:00 p.m. on April 3 as they struggled through mud that sucked them down with every step.

A courier from Johnston rode up to Hardee, who sat mud-splattered astride his horse yelling fruitless commands in an attempt to disengage his army from the sticky, red slush.

"General Johnston's compliments, sir. He wishes to know when you'll be in position."

The growing red in Hardee's face nearly glowed in the white of the general's goatee as he shouted in exasperation, "Tell General Johnston that if he could make it stop raining and dry this horrid road, we'd be ready within the hour. Tell him one of the guides he sent me led us off course until we corrected. Tell him having an army with any experience at all on getting ready for battle would be wonderful. Tell him . . ."

Hardee paused, then swallowed hard and resumed, more composed, "I think I've told him enough. We're trying to get through this mess and will get into position as soon as we can." He looked at his mud-caked army. "Just as soon as we can."

In his headquarters behind the advance, Johnston received the message from Hardee and turned to Beauregard in frustration. "We're getting more and more behind. I don't see how this can all come together by tomorrow morning. I fear your plan of march is too complicated for these conditions."

"It should work, General Johnston. But I can't control nature."

"All right. With better conditions tomorrow, we can still make this work."

It wasn't to be. The next day was even worse. On the 4th a torrential spring rain drenched the soldiers and ruined the roads even more. Seeking protection, some men wore great coats, others cut holes for their heads in blankets and draped them over their shoulders. Most just endured the rain and chill in their gray-woolen uniforms.

In a wooden shack along the roadway, Johnston conferred again with Beauregard. Rain plopped on the leaky roof of the small building. There were no chairs, so the two men stood in an open doorway that allowed in the gray, late-afternoon light.

"Twelve hours behind," Johnston muttered, "and Breckinridge didn't even start moving out of Burnsville until after noon."

He stared through the raindrops as his army plodded over the mud-soaked road. To the side, more troops waited to get in line.

Johnston shook his head, "General, look at the poor souls who have to stand and wait. They have no shelter, nowhere to go but alongside a tree if they can find one."

"Sidney," Beauregard agreed, "it's bad. Those men marching by are wading, stumbling and plunging through mud and water a foot deep."

"By God, this rain has to stop!"

"I believe Bishop Polk has entreated the Almighty about it."

"I pray the Lord is listening."

"Well, General Beauregard, we obviously won't be ready to attack any-time today. Tomorrow, the 5th, we'll try tomorrow."

It was still raining the next day when the Tennessee boys chugged into Corinth. The men climbed out of boxcars and assembled on the rail siding under gray skies and a light drizzle.

Colonel Maney stood on the station platform and shouted to his regiment. "We're not too late! General Johnston's moving into position, but there's been no fighting yet. If we march north directly, we can catch the Army of Mississippi and get in on the action. Are ya ready, men?"

"Yes!" arose a boisterous cry from hundreds of enthusiastic voices.

Maney grinned and turned to his captains. "Gentlemen, see to your companies and let's get moving."

Sam Davis smiled broadly at Joe Cates and Marion McFarlin. "Finally, we get to see some real action."

Cates laughed and asked, "Wasn't traipsin' all over the Shenandoah with Jackson enough action for ya?"

"That was just carrying a rifle around and not using it, Joe."

"At least we kept the Yanks busy and worried them we might attack Washington."

Captain Ledbetter appeared and shouted, "Fall into formation, we've done enough riding. It's time to march. We're heading north a piece!"

The lightness in their step soon diminished as the Rifles' feet were sucked into the muddy road. Yet, the Tennessee men pushed forward with a sense of purpose they hadn't felt for weeks.

Albert Sidney Johnston was beyond frustration. He consulted with Governor Harris and his planner, General Beauregard.

"It's still raining, and it'll be noon soon," he complained. "At least Hardee got into position by mid-morning, but Bragg still isn't in position."

"Sidney," Beauregard began tentatively, "I don't know how, but Bragg seems to have lost an entire division."

"I'll be damned!" Johnston exploded, "How in Heaven's name could he lose a division? That's about all I can take of this incompetence! Sergeant," he turned to an aide, "get my horse now!"

"What are you going to do?" Harris asked.

"Find the damn division, that's what."

In moments Johnston swung onto his saddled horse and splashed down the road.

"I've never seen him that upset," Harris observed.

"He's got a lot to worry about, Governor."

After several miles of hard riding, the general of the Army of Mississippi found the missing division of his army. They were on the road, miles in the rear, blocked by Polk's wagons and artillery at Mitchie's intersection. The sounds of shouts, cursing, whips cracking, and horses neighing filled the air. Men strained to extricate wagon wheels sunk in the morass that was the road.

Johnston stood tall in his stirrups as he observed the snarl of men, horses, and wagons. The general dismounted and strode angrily to the intersection. He roughly grabbed horses by the bridles and moved them along as he shouted instructions. "Get some order to this chaos!" he yelled. "I want this army moving!"

It took more time, but a semblance of a system replaced the chaotic scene. Still it was after 4:00 p.m. before the clogged intersection was clear and Bragg's missing division could tramp the four miles east to get into attack position.

A disillusioned Johnston rode back to where Beauregard and Harris waited in camp. He looked up at the heavens and thanked God that at least the rain had stopped. In fact, the sun was shining from a blue sky. He rode up to an expectant Harris and Beauregard.

"Is everything ready?" Harris inquired.

"Close, but there can be no attack today. Everything went wrong." He turned to an aide. "Tell my division commanders to meet me for a council of war at my headquarters set up behind Hardee's line."

Shiloh Church
April 4th and 5th

JUST AFTER 2:00 P.M. on April 4th, the rain slacked to a drizzle, General Sherman sat on a bench in the church examining a map. His head snapped up as a ragged volley of distant rifle shots reached his ears.

"What is that?" he demanded of an aide.

"Could only be pickets, sir. That's all we have out there."

"Get a patrol to find out. I want to know for sure."

A short time later Colonel Ralph Buckland, commander of the Fourth Brigade of Sherman's division, led his men to where the pickets were posted past the distant tree line.

Lieutenant Colonel Canfield reported to his colonel. "The pickets are all gone, sir, all seven of them."

"Gone?" Buckland wondered. "Where?"

"From the looks and sound of things, captured. I don't see any bodies. There are signs of rebel cavalry up ahead."

At that moment the skies opened and emptied a blinding rain on the men in blue.

"Will this never stop?" Buckland shouted at the sky. "Canfield, we still have to find those pickets. Take two companies of men and pursue."

The 72nd Ohio moved out and soon encountered the 1st Alabama Cavalry. The two forces reached out to fight in the driving rain like blind boxers seeking unseen opponents. When the Union soldiers tried to fire their rifles, the water-soaked powder refused to ignite.

The men formed a line and braced their rifles with the bayoneted barrels held at forty-five-degree angles in anticipation of an attack.

"Fix bayonets, prepare for cavalry charge!" Canfield commanded.

The Alabamans unsheathed their swords and were preparing to charge when the 5th Ohio Cavalry came to the rescue and joined the 72nd. The rebels scattered. The Ohio men chased after them for a quarter mile until they encountered a long line of Confederate infantry backed by artillery. As the big guns opened up on them, the federal troops fell back.

Buckland, soaking wet, reported back to Sherman. He stood at attention and saluted as a puddle of water grew around his feet.

"Whatcha got, Colonel?"

"We ran into reb cavalry and pushed them back deeper into the woods. Then we encountered rebel infantry and artillery. My cavalry managed to fire their carbines, but the Confederate force was superior and we fell back."

"Colonel," Sherman reprimanded, "do you have any idea what you almost did? You came upon a Confederate reconnaissance force, a scout detail, and you tried to start a general engagement. This isn't the time or place for a fight.

"General Grant will decide. I expect we aim to hit them at Corinth. There we can besiege them, cut their supply lines, starve 'em out. You could have caused a general engagement and put the whole army at peril. Buell isn't here yet."

"I'm sorry, sir, but it didn't seem like just a reconnaissance force."

"Our agents report only scouting details have come out of Corinth. Consider yourself lucky you didn't start anything big."

Little did Sherman realize that Buckland had run into the advance of Hardee's troops.

On the morning of the 5th more rifle shots echoed from the woods. Colonel Jesse Appier of the 53rd Ohio was alarmed and ordered the long roll sounded to assemble his troops. In Shiloh Church, Sherman heard the clatter of drums and rushed to where the men were gathering.

"Colonel, what are you doing?" he angrily shouted at Appier.

"We heard shots, sir!"

"Take your damned regiment back to Ohio. There is no enemy nearer than Corinth."

* * *

IN THE WOODS a Confederate captain called his sergeant. "What's the shooting for? We have orders not to shoot. Are you trying to tell the Yanks we're here?"

"Well, Captain, the men, they want to make sure that them rifles is still workin'. Everything's so wet. They wanna be sure they kin shoot all right."

"Tell them to stop. There's to be no shooting."

Orders or not, occasional gunshots still echoed from the woods to the Union camp.

A beautiful sunset lit the western sky as if a painter splashed pink and blue pastels on a canvas. It was a welcome sight for Johnston as he rode with Bragg and Polk toward his meeting site. All along the road they were greeted by soldiers in position waiting to move out. Frequent shouts greeted the generals. "When we movin'?" "We're ready!" Let's go git 'em!" Then cheers erupted.

Johnston reined in his horse and shouted, "Quiet! This is to be a surprise! Quiet!" He looked around to find an officer. "Captain," he called a man to him. "Pass the word ahead. No cheers, no shouts, no shooting."

Twilight faded to black as the command force gathered before a lively, crackling fire. Polk sat upon a log, while Beauregard, Breckinridge, Hardee, Johnston, and Bragg stood before the flames. A yellow glow played on the front of their cloaks and great coats. Johnston held out his palms for warmth.

"Gentlemen, we finally have all our men assembled and ready to be positioned. Tomorrow morning we'll attack."

"How will we deploy, sir?" Bragg asked.

"General Beauregard, lay out the plan."

Beauregard's eyes danced in the firelight as he explained. "We'll attack them in successive waves, each corps being in a parallel line behind the other. Hardee will lead the offensive, followed in order by Bragg and Polk. General Breckinridge, you'll be in reserve and move to the right."

"I had planned," Johnston added, "to maneuver our army so to turn Grant's left, cut off federal retreat to the river and their supply lines, and drive them back into the flooded Owl Creek bottoms. I telegraphed President Davis we would attack, Polk the left, Bragg the center, Hardee the right, and Breckinridge in reserve. General Beauregard has convinced me otherwise."

"To do as General Johnston suggests," Beauregard explained, "would have entailed more combat strength on our right. I plan for equal strength across the entire front. We'll sweep them from the field and into the river before they know what hit them. We begin early, get them at breakfast, about 6:30."

"Sidney," Polk wondered, "are you comfortable with this plan?"

"I've been persuaded. There's no time to modify it now. Move your divisions into position in the woods beyond Shiloh Church where Sherman's camped."

"I know my men are ready," Hardee interjected. "My advance units are already in position. Just waiting for the rest of us."

"Where will your headquarters be?" Harris asked.

"At the head of my army. You'll find me there if you need me. General Beauregard will be stationed behind the battle lines."

Bragg leaned over to Johnston's second in command. "You'll be callin' the shots, Frenchy."

Beauregard silently nodded assent.

"Where's Forrest?" Breckinridge wondered.

Johnston answered, "His cavalry is to the northwest at Lick Creek. They'll block the ford there. I'm moving the 1st Tennessee, just arrived, to help Forrest. Got a prayer for us, Bishop?"

All stood in a circle around the fire, removed their hats and bowed their heads as Polk began, "Precious Lord, we ask for your guidance and protection as we defend our beloved land from invaders who wish to end our way of life. May we fire straight and true. May we prevail with your blessing. Amen."

"Amen," the others solemnly finished.

* * *

AT NEARLY THE SAME TIME, just a few miles away, Sherman held a conference at Shiloh Church, his division headquarters. General Prentiss, 6th Division and General William Wallace, 2nd Division were joined by Sherman's 5th Division colonels: Buckland, Hildebrand, Stuart, Smith, and McDowell. The officers sat in pews as Sherman stood before them.

Sherman reported, "I've heard from General Grant that Buell is still at least a day away. We won't move on to Corinth for at least a few days."

"How is General Grant?" Prentiss inquired. "I heard his horse slipped and fell on him."

"The general's doing fine, but he's on crutches with a severely sprained ankle. It's ironic one of the finest horseman in the army is victimized by a riding accident. I'm in communication with him back at Cherry Mansion."

Colonel Stuart glanced at Buckland. "I heard Colonel Buckland had an altercation with a Confederate force near the tree line. Should we be concerned?"

Sherman glared at Buckland, who turned crimson.

"It was a reconnaissance force, nothing else. Johnston's army is holed up in Corinth."

Prentiss supported Sherman. "Colonel Peabody, my 1st Brigade commander, suspects the Confederates are nearby in force. He suggested we ready the troops to receive an attack. I asked what evidence he had. He had none and I won't operate on the basis of suspicion."

"That's wise," Sherman agreed. "We're under direct orders not to bring on an engagement. We've passed that directive down the line. Everyone should know. A battle, in the mud, in early April is not in our plans. We'll fight them on our terms, shoot them out or starve them out in Corinth."

"Wouldn't it be prudent to fortify?" McDowell suggested.

Now Sherman turned crimson as a red-hot stove. "This is preposterous! For weeks, old women have told us Beauregard is on his way, that Johnston has 100,000 men, no, maybe 300,000. I won't treat old wives' tales as gospel. Do you understand?"

No one with a contrary opinion dared express it under the glowering gaze of the red-haired general.

"General, thank you for transferring the 1st Minnesota Light Artillery to my division. We were light on big guns," Prentiss offered, changing topics.

"I agree. You seemed short in that regard. See to your men. Dry them out somehow. Maybe a break in this miserable weather will raise spirits."

"Hot food and dry clothing will do wonders for them," Smith asserted.

"Hot food we can do. Drying out wool uniforms may take a little more time. We should be all dried out before we march on Corinth."

* * *

THE RUTHERFORD RIFLES and the other five companies of the 1st Tennessee had marched toward Pittsburg Landing after disembarking their train in Corinth. They went into camp just off the Corinth Road several miles behind the main army and tried to rest on damp ground by laying blankets and tent halves on the ground. Some huddled under trees. No fires were permitted.

"Well, Sam," Andy Bates spoke in a low voice, "sounds like tomorrow's the day. For the first time we'll be in real action."

"Are you scared, Andy?"

"Scared? Maybe a little. It's funny thinkin' this might be the last time I ever see stars. Ain't they beautiful?"

Both men gazed through tree branches at a patch of twinkling, bright stars in the deep black sky.

"You'll be fine, Andy," Sam assured him. "Stay with me."

"Sure, but if the worst happens, y'all know my folks. Tell 'em I was thinkin' 'bout 'em."

"Of course, I will. But we'll get through it. The Yanks will run as soon as we hit them."

"Sam, do ya ever see General Bushrod, yer old teacher?

"Not much, just when he rides by sometimes. He waved at me once. He's head of the first brigade in Cheatham's Division. We're the second. I expect we'll talk someday."

Sam removed a worn, well-creased letter from a front pocket and carefully unfolded it.

"Watcha got?" Andy asked.

"A letter from a girl, Kate."

"Ya can't read it in the dark."

Sam chuckled. "I don't need light. I know the words from memory."

"What's she say?"

"That she misses me and wishes the war was over and that she's working with her father, a doctor and doing her part for the war."

"What's that?"

"That's not real clear. I suppose she'll tell me later."

"Good luck tomorrow, Sam, God be with you."

"He'll be with both of us, Andy."

The Battle of Shiloh
APRIL 6TH

IN THE DARKNESS a patrol of five companies under Major James Powell slid off into a night illuminated by the silver shaft of a quarter moon. Colonel Peabody trusted his own instincts more than the opinion of his division commander and had ordered his own reconnaissance. Powell marched down the Seay Field road looking for rebels. He found them.

Near dawn Powell encountered advance Confederate skirmishers less than a mile from the Union front. The rebels promptly attacked. The battle was on.

Powell shouted to an aide as his men retreated, "Get word to Prentiss. The whole reb army is on the way!"

Peabody himself rode back to Prentiss. The general was on his horse in front of his headquarters tent. Distant gunfire rang in his ears. "What have you done, Peabody?"

"We found them, General. Johnston's whole army is out there."

"Balderdash! They are in Corinth. I'll hold you personally responsible for bringing on this battle."

In an arrogant huff, the general rode off to see to his men.

In Johnston's camp behind Hardee's lines, the sound of rifle fire was met with alarm. Johnston turned to Governor Harris. "Someone started shooting too soon."

"Us or them?"

"It doesn't matter. The timing's wrong and we're farther from their camp than we planned. Sherman will be able to mobilize."

"Then there can be no delay."

Distant gunfire grew in volume and frequency, the sound swelling and filtering back like an ocean wave.

"Hardee has attacked. The battle has begun. Ready or not, we must prevail now."

77

Sherman's division was the forward salient of Grant's Army of the Tennessee. Their camp around Shiloh Church was like a picturesque painting on Sunday morning April 6th. Smoke tendrilled up from cook fires as men fried bacon and salt pork. The rising sun reflected a pinkish glow and glistened through haze on the dew-covered grass.

Sherman stood in front of the church and stretched his arms over his head. *Beautiful morning*, he thought.

Then he noticed a soldier running toward him yelling. Distant shots raised the hairs on the back of his neck. "What's happening?" he whispered.

"They're comin'," the man shouted as he ran. "The rebs are comin'!"

From the distant trees a long gray line burst into the open.

"My God, we are under attack!" Sherman exclaimed. "Sound the alarm!" he shouted at his bugler. As the bugle refrain began, men already scrambled for weapons, with officers frantically racing around to rally their companies.

To the southeast a suddenly convinced Prentiss had begun to mobilize, as bullets removed all doubt of the impending attack.

At Sherman's Shiloh Church encampment, Polk's and Hardee's brigades decimated the first line of Union defense in minutes. They smashed their way into the Union camps, where men deserted their still-cooking breakfasts and ran. Brigades under Hildebrand and Buckland reeled to the north.

Meanwhile Prentiss, with his units scattered in the face of Braxton Bragg's onslaught, tried to retreat northward. Sherman, pushed back nearly a mile, managed to rally his men and form a defensive line on the crest of a small hill.

The red-bearded general rode back and forth through his disorganized units, trying to bring order for a stand. To the Union's left, most of Prentiss's men gave ground grudgingly, stubbornly setting up a line two miles to the rear.

Polk's and Hardee's brigades burst through Sherman's camp. Many stopped to eat the food left cooking by the dispatched Union soldiers. Others began rummaging through the camp and tents. Some picked up new percussion firing Springfields, left behind in haste, and tossed aside their antiquated flintlocks.

Johnston was everywhere, galloping up and down the line rallying his troops, "We've got 'em on the run, boys!" he shouted. "Pour into them! Don't stop!"

He reined up before Isham Harris. "Governor, we've lost cohesion and unity of command. The waves Beauregard planned for the attack are non-existent. Polk's and Hardee's men are all mixed together. There are no divisions or brigades, just an undisciplined mob."

"Yes, Sidney, but aren't they a glorious mob! The Yankees are folding up before them like a cheap tent."

* * *

BACK AT THE CHERRY MANSION in Savannah, Ulysses Grant was eating a cold breakfast of bread and sausage, his injured leg stretched out on the floor as he read reports from his officers. His crutches were propped against the table. Grant's head snapped up as he heard a distant rumble. He hoped it was thunder, but he knew better. It was the faraway roar of cannon and musket shot. It could only mean one thing: Pittsburg Landing was under attack. He immediately began to scrawl on a piece of paper.

Grant called out to Rawlins, "Get this to Bull Nelson!" and handed the paper to his adjutant. "His division is the closest of Buell's army. He needs to get across from Pittsburg Landing so we can ferry them across."

"What about Lew Wallace?" Rawlins asked.

"I'll leave a message for him at Crump's Landing while I take a steamboat to Pittsburg. I want him to wait in reserve and stand ready. I'll let him know when to move. Now get me on the boat."

By 8:30 that morning Grant paddled into Pittsburg Landing and bedlam. A stream of panic-stricken Union soldiers flowed into the landing for protection. Grant's first command as he limped down the steamboat's gangplank was to demand order and a defense of the landing.

* * *

AS SHERMAN CONTINUED his retreat north toward Pittsburg Landing, he skirted the flood-swollen Owl Creek. Johnston could not bring enough pressure to bear from his right to cut Sherman off and push him toward the creek. Beauregard's plan of equal strength across the front was a detriment to that goal.

Generals McClernand and William Wallace had been camped farther to the north. They rushed to join Prentiss to slow the now disorganized but lethal Confederate advance.

Prentiss was frantic. He had started the day with 5,400, and only a fraction of them gathered for sanctuary in a sunken roadway. "Peabody, how many men do we have?"

"Near as I can figure, about 500."

"We can't hold on with 500."

"Look, General, here comes the 23rd Missouri."

A horseman jerked his animal to a halt in front of Prentiss. The general, still agitated, asked, "Colonel Tindahl, how many men have you?"

"About 500 hundred, sir, and Wallace is right behind me."

"How many men does he have?"

Tindahl briefly considered. "A thousand, maybe fifteen hundred."

Prentiss looked right and then left. "We'll hold 'em here, on this road, for as long as we can. Get 'em dug in. Maybe we can buy Sherman some time."

About 9:00 a.m. the fight at the sunken road began. Bragg's forces were launched in consecutive, disjointed attacks. The air filled with hissing, whizzing minie balls.

A Confederate soldier shouted over the din to his captain, "It's like we stuck a stick in a hornet's nest, the bees are flyin' and stingin' all over!"

In the slight depression called the "sunken road," Union soldiers, their faces blackened by gunpowder, desperately held on and turned back attack after attack.

An officer with a red stripe down his blue pant leg, indicating artillery, rode to Prentiss, frantically rallying his men. The officer shouted, "Lieutenant Pfaender, 1st Minnesota Artillery, reporting, sir. Captain Munch sends his compliments. Where do you want us?"

Prentiss quickly surveyed his line. "Thank God, artillery. There," he pointed, "on that elevated ground behind the road in the center. Blast the hell out of 'em."

At nearly 11:00 a.m. the 1st Minnesota Artillery rolled six cannons onto the rise, two twelve-pound howitzers and four brass James rifled guns. To their immediate left, Welker's Missouri Battery rolled into position. Almost immediately the Minnesotans encountered problems. The wooden carriage hauling a James Rifle snapped in two at the tail of the elevation screw, rendering it useless.

The Minnesotans faced an open field on the other side of the road. General William Wallace rode up. As he peered intently at the distant clearing, Wallace asked, "Captain, how many men do you have?"

"Full battery, sir, 125 men, 150 horses. One James is disabled. We'll try to fix it."

"Do us proud, men," he shouted, "we've got to hold this piece of land."

Pfaender, standing next to Munch, his battery commander, pointed and shouted, "Look, Captain, they're comin' again!"

Munch turned to his five remaining nine-man gun crews. Each soldier had specific duties in the firing of a cannon. "Load and fire at will!"

The shout of "prick and prime" rose from each of the gun crews. One soldier with each cannon placed a needle-like object in a hole at the near end of the cannon barrel. When pulled out by a long slender cord, the friction ignited a bag of gun powder and flung canister shot from the barrel.

"Fire!" shouted Munch, and four soldiers jerked the pins from the cannons. The fiery blast and roar of the cannons ripped across the field and decimated a line of charging rebel soldiers. Moments later the Missouri cannons erupted as well as the Confederates, shattered and bloodied, fell back.

Wallace shouted, "Hot work, men, hot work!" He trotted his horse to Munch. "Keep it up. My men are concentrated on the road. I've got to get back to them. Keep the rebs at bay. Across the field, they're in that log cabin with barricades in front. Blast 'em!"

Munch saluted, "Yes, sir!" Wallace rode off into the maelstrom of shot.

Minutes later a cannon shot slammed into a Missouri battery. Munch stared over at the mangled bodies and obliterated equipment. He watched with disgust as the survivors of the Missouri battery turned and ran to the north.

"Lieutenant," he shouted to Pfaender, "we have more gun crews. Take them from horse duty and send them to man the Missouri batteries."

"Yes, sir, but we have another problem. A James Rifle has a ball stuck half way down the barrel. We can't use the rammer for fear it'll explode, and we can't get it out."

Munch slammed a fist into the palm of his hand. "What more can go wrong!" he exclaimed. "All right, send another crew with both broken guns back to Pittsburg Landing. Maybe they can make one gun that works out of them. We still have four here."

Confederate soldiers stayed low. Marksman were sent out to pick off the gun crews. They crawled onto the field and into trees overlooking the battery position. Several artillerymen were hit by the snipers. Private Stinson grabbed his neck and fell, blood gurgling from his mouth as he lay on his back.

Munch, on horseback, cried at Pfaender, "We need infantry support fire!"

The lieutenant looked through the gun powder haze at the blaze of muskets blasting on either side. "I've asked. They've got their hands full."

A moment later Munch's horse screamed and fell dead with a ball in its head. The captain wrenched his leg from beneath the dead animal and struggled to his feet only to wince in pain as he grabbed his right thigh. Red blood seeped between his fingers.

"I've been hit, Lieutenant," the dazed captain cried. Then he tumbled to the ground.

Pfaender turned to a gun crew private. "Get the captain to the rear and ask for infantry support again."

The Union soldiers clung to the bottom of the sunken road as if they wanted to crawl beneath it. Braxton Bragg's troops poured relentless lead that cut through tree branches and skimmed the blades of grass. Bullets hissed through the air, occasionally thudding into flesh. The earth trembled beneath the prone soldiers as the concussion pounded from the cannons.

* * *

JUST AFTER THE BATTLE started, about 7:00 a.m., the 1st Tennessee Battalion was sent to support Colonel Nathan Bedford Forrest's cavalry at a ford on Lick Creek on the far right, east of the Confederate battle line.

"What're we doin' out here?" Joe Cates asked. "Listen. The fightin's to the west."

"Captain Ledbetter says we're to block the ford, to make sure no federals try to get away over it," Sam Davis replied. "And we're to scout to make sure no Yanks are around here."

"What time do ya s'pose it is, Sam?"

Sam regarded the sun above the eastern horizon. "I don't know, 9:30, maybe 10:00."

"Just listen, it's like sitting next to a train ferever. That roar out there, the guns, there's no stopping, ever."

"Well, it's quiet here."

"But it's not quiet over there," Cates persisted. "It sounds like all Hell is breakin' loose. No Yanks around here."

"If there was, Colonel Forrest would find 'em. He's the best."

Andy Bates rushed over. "Captain's comin'. I think he's got news."

Word spread. The company soon gathered around Ledbetter. He tried to calm his voice as he spoke, but the rising tone of his speech belied his excitement.

"Colonel Maney's satisfied that there are no federals in this area. We're to move north and join Bragg in the battle."

"What's going on, Captain?" Sam asked.

"Sherman's been pushed back between Owl Creek and the Tennessee. He's trying to rally his men back by Pittsburg Landing. Bragg's attack has stalled to the right of Polk. The Yanks are holding on in a depressed road, just a couple thousand of 'em. Bragg's tryin' hard to drive 'em out and we're needed to help him."

"Then let's get to it!" Charlie Miller cried.

In short order the 1st Tennessee marched north to the sound of the guns. Colonel Maney rode alongside his major, Hume Feild.

"Major, I just received a dispatch. I'm to report to General Cheatham, I'm to command Stephen's Brigade because Colonel Stephens has been injured. You'll command the regiment."

"How many regiments are in your brigade?"

"Ours and four more."

"You'll do us all proud, sir."

"I'm riding ahead to Cheatham. I'll see you at the front."

As Maney rode off, the handsome, dark-complexioned major called back to Ledbetter in line behind him. "Double quick, let's pick up the pace."

* * *

TO THE RIGHT of the Confederate forces, facing the sunken road, was a Peach Orchard and just north of that a small pond. Albert Sidney Johnston, accompanied by Isham Harris, had seemed to be everywhere in the battle. From the early overrunning of Sherman's camp to the stall at the road, Johnston could be seen rallying his men.

"Governor, tell my doctor to tend to the wounded Union soldiers we've captured. I'm going to lead a charge on the enemy position in that orchard. What time is it?

Harris reached into his pants and removed a pocket watch. "About 2:30."

"Bragg's been attacking the road almost five hours. We've got to break them."

As Harris dispatched the doctor, Johnston led a charge into the peach orchard. With a raised sword the general bounded his horse forward. He felt a sting behind his right knee but ignored it as his men braved the deadly missiles that shattered arms, legs, and bodies.

The charge was rebuffed. Johnston rode back to his staff. Harris was horrified to see his commander, whose face was deathly pale as he swayed in his saddle.

"General, are you wounded?"

Johnston looked down at his red pant leg and realized his right boot had filled with blood. He turned to Harris and mumbled in a voice just above a whisper, "Yes . . . and I fear seriously."

Harris and other officers rushed to the general and slid him off his horse.

"Where's the doctor?" a man demanded.

"Gone," Harris replied, "sent to tend to Union prisoners."

Seeking shelter, the officers lowered Johnston into a small ravine. Harris grabbed a piece of rope and desperately tried to apply a tourniquet. Johnston soon lost consciousness.

The governor looked up. "He's lost too much blood."

A few minutes later Johnston exhaled his last breath.

"Cover him," Harris commanded. "We can't let the men see him, not now. He was the best we had." He turned toward an orderly. "Get back to Beauregard and tell him what's happened. He's in charge now."

At that moment the 1st Tennessee marched by the scene. "What's goin' on over there?" Bill Searcy pointed.

John Beesley said, "Don't know. Looks like somebody important got kilt."

"Sam, I'm worried," Andy Bates whispered.

"God decides what'll happen, Andy. Watch your head and stay by me."

Up ahead Colonel Maney reached Major General Cheatham, commander of Polk's 2nd Division. To the whistle of bullets and the crash of cannon, Cheatham greeted Maney.

The general emitted a sigh of relief. "Thank God you're here. Stephen's left the battlefield, his fall shook him up pretty good. It's your brigade now."

"I came as soon as ordered. My regiment's still on the way."

"The federals are dug in on that road," Cheatham pointed. "Bragg's hit them with one attack after another and keeps being driven back."

"Why don't we just go around?" Maney wondered.

Cheatham considered his words before responding. "General Bragg is fixated on that spot. The men are calling it the Hornet's Nest because all the balls flying around sound like buzzing bees. Bragg's determined to take it, saying it'd be dangerous to go around and leave it in our rear."

Maney shook his head. "Seems like a waste of time and men. The federals are falling back towards Pittsburg Landing. We could attack the flanks and come back to the Hornet's Nest at our leisure."

"That is not what General Bragg wants."

"What do you want me to do?"

"They've held that spot five and a half hours. It's your turn to charge. There's a mass of federals near that cabin out there. Hit 'em. Drive 'em outta there. In addition to your regiment, you have the 7th Kentucky. But first we're going to soften them up some. General Ruggles's battery has been enhanced. He has over fifty cannon, and they're ready to blast into the Union line at close range. You'll follow his barrage."

Maney looked around and viewed his regiment approaching. "My men are here. I'll see they're deployed."

"When Ruggles's guns stop, smash 'em hard."

Maney greeted Hume Feild as the Tennesseans marched near. "Here's what you are to do. There's the nest of Yankees." He pointed across the field. "Set up a line, the 9th regiment on the left, the 1st in the middle and the 19th a little further down on the right. Put the 6th Tennessee and the 7th Kentucky in reserve. When the big guns stop, charge."

* * *

As THE BRIGADE FELL into line on the battle front, the small Union battery of cannons opened up on another force of charging Confederates. Pfaender and the 1st Minnesota Battery valiantly tried to hold the line, but the situation was turning hopeless.

Then it became worse. Hell seemed to open up on the beleaguered men fighting valiantly from the sunken road as the crashing thunder of Ruggles's guns spit flame and canister shot into them.

Wallace yelled at Prentiss, "We can't hold much longer!"

"See to the batteries. Can they hold?"

General Wallace raced through shot to the rise where the Minnesotans held. "Lieutenant, where's your captain?"

"Shot, sir. We sent him to the rear."

A bullet whizzed by Wallace and struck a corporal behind him.

The general's reaction was decisive. "That's it. Pull back. Bring your guns with you." Wallace turned and rode off.

A minute later a breathless orderly reached Pfaender amidst the cannons' roar. His mouth at the lieutenant's ear, he cried, "The general, Wallace, he jest rode off and he got hit. He's dead."

The lieutenant's face betrayed his shock. "His last order was to leave this position and fall back. That's what we're trying to do."

Amidst the calamitous roar of battle and screaming shells, the Minnesota pulled off the rise in order and fell back.

The roar from Ruggles's battery continued, then abruptly stopped. For a brief moment an eerie silence hung like a funeral shroud over the battlefield. Soldiers huddled down to avoid canister shot realized the barrage was over.

* * *

THEN FROM THE UNION FORCES, amidst trees, on the sunken road came a rifle volley. Bullets sizzled and whizzed all around. Sam and the others hugged the ground or clung behind trees as leaves sliced from branches floated down like big green snowflakes.

"Okay, boys," Maney shouted, "now! While they're reloading! Charge!"

The officers in Maney's brigade hurled the cry of "Charge!" The boys from Tennessee surged forward out of the woods across the open grass, slamming into the right and center of the Union line. A blood-curdling staccato yell emanated from their throats as the rebels desperately pitched into the federals.

Sam Davis raced in the front with Andy Bates just behind and a flag bearer waving the Stars and Bars alongside. They held their rifles diagonally with two hands, bayonets fixed on the end of the barrels.

The flag bearer took a shot to the head and slammed to the earth.

Andy hesitated, then grabbed the flag. "I've got it, Sam!" he yelled before racing to join his friend. But Andy dashed only about twenty-five yards before a federal bullet ripped into his chest, sending him tumbling to the ground.

Sam paused, looked back, then raced on, realizing he could do nothing for Andy, the growing red splotch on his chest signaling a fatal wound. Ahead, as the rebels charged into the blue line on the road, the Union left began to cave in and the whole line began to crumble.

As Sam reached the line, a Union solder stood up and leveled his rifle at him. Sam froze. His eyes focused on the marksman's eyes and the terror and hate burning in them. A thud from the side knocked Sam over just as the man fired.

John Beesley, who had knocked Sam down, rolled into a shooting position on the ground and snapped off a shot. The Union soldier tumbled onto the hard-packed roadway.

Beesley pulled Sam up. "Okay, ya seen the elephant. Now get yer head right and keep goin'!"

Sam shook his head as if to clear it, then picked up his rifle and resumed his charge into the blazing cloud of gun smoke.

* * *

THE UNION LINE continued to roll in on itself. Prentiss's beleaguered battalion found itself surrounded. Prentiss desperately tried to rally his men once again. For hours he had resisted what he now knew he must do.

"Colonel Tindahl!" he cried as the officer passed nearby. Tindahl crouched low next to Prentiss, who asked, "Where is General Wallace?"

"He's dead, sir, shot near the Minnesota battery."

Prentiss grimaced. "He was a fine man. Colonel, send up a white flag and pass the order. We have to surrender. We can hold on no longer."

"Did we do any good?"

"God only knows, I hope so."

As a white flag waved and word spread, the shooting gradually sputtered to an end. Sam and his brigade erupted into cheers as Colonel Maney rode onto the sunken road and encountered Prentiss.

"You put up a helluva fight, general, seven hours of it."

"Where's Sherman?" Prentiss asked.

"All your boys have been pushed back toward Pittsburg Landing. They're in a long line of defense from the landing west toward Owl Creek. Tomorrow we'll push 'em into the river if they don't give up. You're beat."

Tindahl leaned close to Prentiss and said lowly, "You saved the army, General, holdin' on here gave them time to organize a defense."

Prentiss turned and surveyed the chaotic scene all around. Men and horses were dead or dying. The cries of wounded men could now be heard in the absence of gunfire. Blood stained the earth of the road and the grass nearby.

"Maybe it was all worth it, Tindahl." He turned to Maney. "Colonel, I have men in need of medical assistance."

"Certainly, we'll do our best to care for them."

Two thousand and two hundred Union soldiers of the Hornet's Nest were taken prisoner at the sunken road. Their part of the battle was over.

* * *

AT PITTSBURG LANDING, Grant had organized a defensive line, stretching three miles to the west and north to River Road. Sherman's division held the right, McClernand the center. Remnants of Wallace's, Hurlbut's and Stuart's forces mixed with thousands of stragglers from other regiments on the left. Fifty cannon fortified the line.

Sherman had hurried back to the landing to meet with Grant.

"Where's Lew Wallace?" he inquired. "We could sure use him."

Grant answered, "I left him at Crump's this morning. He was to move out when I sent for him. I ordered him to move at eleven."

"He should have been here by now."

"He'll be here. We need him. Leave a way open for him. Nelson just arrived across the river. One brigade's been ferried across. We've got them on the left."

"Look," Sherman pointed, "here they come."

* * *

Two brigades led by General Withers charged across open ground, determined to smash a hole in the Union line. But concentrated fire drove them back. Beauregard, from his headquarters at Shiloh Church, considered another attack, then viewed the sun, an orange ball nearing the horizon.

He told Governor Harris, "Darkness will fall shortly. The men are exhausted. I don't want a night fight. It's six o'clock now. Frankly, we've won this battle. Call my officers together for a council."

Polk, Cheatham, Bragg, Hardee, and Breckinridge met with Beauregard, sitting on the church pew benches just as the Union officers had when Sherman addressed them.

"Gentlemen," Beauregard said, "General Johnston'd be proud of you. You've won this battle. I've sent a communication to President Davis to that effect."

Hardee wasn't so sure. "General, our strategy didn't work as planned. We had a chance to cave in their left and push them away from the landing. Instead, we only pushed them into a defensible position and not into the swamps."

Bragg bemoaned, "We lost a great opportunity. We still had an hour of daylight left. We should have attacked their line again and, by my count, we have just under 28,000 suitable for combat tomorrow."

"That's enough. The Yankees have about the same. We'll finish what we started and drive them the rest of the way into the river. I have Grant just where I want him. We'll whip him in the morning," Beauregard countered. "Besides, the men are exhausted. At least they can get a good night's sleep."

"Yes," Polk concurred, "enjoying the spoils of war, sleeping in Yankee tents, enjoying Yankee food, and acquiring what Yankee supplies appeal to them."

"What about Buell?" Cheatham asked. "I've heard from Forrest that he's close to the landing. Even General Prentiss is blabbing away that Buell will save the day for his army."

"I have a dispatch from General Hardin Helm in northern Alabama that Buell's heading for Decatur, not Pittsburg Landing," Beauregard rejoined.

"I sure as Hell hope you're right and Forrest's wrong," Breckinridge said.

"We lost a lot of good men today," Polk said softly. "Sidney was a great man. I heard that our Captain Thomas, the Union general's nephew, lost his arm. I hope he makes it."

Beauregard somberly replied, "I've sent a message across the lines to General Thomas. Sidney would be proud of what's been accomplished."

* * *

THE MOOD WAS DIFFERENT at Pittsburg Landing. Reinforcements brought hope. After the first troops of Buell's army crossed over around 5:00 p.m., others followed throughout the night. At 7:00 p.m. General Lew Wallace and his division marched into Pittsburg Landing. Wallace immediately reported to Grant, where he was reprimanded for his delay.

* * *

THE EXHAUSTED MEN of the 1st Tennessee collapsed after they retired to their former camp about four miles southwest of the landing. Some fastened shelter half-tents to use for the night. But most tried to find comfortable spots on the ground or under trees. They dug into their haversacks and eagerly ripped into salt pork and hardtack.

"After today, this is a meal fit for a king," Cates remarked between bites.

"It ain't much, and I can't enjoy it none," Charlie Miller said flatly. "We lost a whole buncha good boys today."

Sam's voice came from the darkness. "Andy Bates died. I was with him when he got hit. I couldn't do anything. I should have stopped anyway."

"No, you shouldn't have," John Beesley cautioned, "two men stopped charging to bring a wounded man to the rear. General Buell had 'em arrested for cowardice. He plans to have 'em shot. Like Jackson did, remember?"

"Bragg's a real hard ass," Cates said.

"But he's a fighter. With Johnston gone, we need every fighter we have."

"The Yanks are all holed up by the landing," Bill Searcey interjected. "I heard Ledbetter says we're to join up with Withers's brigade and wipe 'em clean tomorrow."

"Well, we better do it before Buell gets there," Sam advised.

"I heard Buell ain't comin' this way at all."

"I wouldn't bet the farm on that, Bill."

"Why'd Polk have us bivouac out in the open?" Miller wondered. "The rest of the army is under nice Yankee tents tonight."

Cates shook his head. "It was sure nice of Prentiss and Sherman's boys to leave 'em up for us. I just wish we was camped there. I wonder what they got for food and water."

A big plop of rain splatted onto Beesley's broad-brimmed hat. "Rain," he moaned, "not more rain!"

The skies opened up once again as the men tried to find whatever shelter they could. Most huddled in soggy blankets under trees and waited for dawn while they cussed the good fortune of those under Yankee tents.

* * *

ABOUT MIDNIGHT GENERALS Sherman and Grant stood beneath a tree near the landing. As the downpour emptied all around them, they stood in relative shelter and sucked cigars. The bright red glow of two cigar ends in the inky blackness was the only evidence of their presence.

In the distance the misty glow of yellow lanterns signaled the steady arrival of Buell's army. Grant laid out his battle plan.

"We've got about 45,000 with Buell's men. Tomorrow we attack the rebels. Buell and I will operate separately and coordinate on the division level. We'll counterattack at dawn."

"Who's going in first?"

Grant smiled grimly. "Lew Wallace, on our extreme right."

"Good, it's about time he sees action. Where was he all day?"

"Wandering around. He started moving for Pittsburg Landing at noon. He thought you were still at Shiloh. When he got there he found the whole Confederate army in his front. Now he could have fought through them to get to us, but instead he decided to march to the landing using crossroads on the river road. They countermarched onto the Shunpike Road instead of the River Road as I ordered. Wallace says he didn't get the order."

"We could have used him."

"He made a mess of things, but he can redeem himself tomorrow."

"Who will be on his left?"

"Your men, Cump, then a line of McClernand's; Tuttle, taking Bill Wallace's place; then comes Buell with Bull Nelson's, Crittenden's, and McCook's divisions." Sherman sucked on his cigar. "Well, Grant, we've had the devil's own day, haven't we?"

Grant looked up. "Yes." He puffed and blew a little cloud of cigar smoke. "Yes. Lick 'em tomorrow, though."

The Battle of Shiloh

April 7th

WHILE CONFEDERATE SOLDIERS struggled to endure another soggy night in camp, Buell's army continued streaming across the river by ferry to Pittsburg Landing. The 2nd Minnesota, in Thomas's division, was last in line, waiting to cross on the opposite side of the Tennessee River.

Beauregard, having sent his "complete victory" telegram to President Davis, went to sleep, not having ordered a resupply of ammunition nor building any defensive fortifications. "There's no need," he told Harris. "Grant will slip across the river in retreat tonight or we'll mop him up in the morning."

Colonel Nathan Bedford Forrest wasn't so sure. The Tennessee cavalry commander was on the move. Forrest was a self-made man. He was a plantation owner, real estate dealer and slave trader who had amassed a fortune. A man with no military training, he had a genius for war and, after enlisting as a private, Forrest had risen in rank at a seemingly impossible rate to become a colonel and the commander of a regiment of cavalry.

Forrest was forty years old, six-foot-two and 210 pounds. He had dark, wavy hair with a wide forehead. A bushy, dark beard adorned his chin. In the hard rain his cavalry, dressed in the blue uniforms of captured Union soldiers, rode near Pittsburg Landing.

Forrest and two officers stood on a rise of ground and watched the landing below. Captain William Forrest, the colonel's fifteen-year-old son and head of a company of scouts, peered at the yellow globes bobbing in the darkness, which guided ferries back and forth over the river.

William said to his father. "They're leavin', hightailin' it as fast as they can!"

Colonel Forrest watched intently and exclaimed to his son, "That's Buell's army comin' over, not Grant retreating! Beauregard thinks Grant will give up and cross the river. Just the opposite is happening. They'll be comin' across all night and about doubling what Grant's got. We should have broken them today when we could. I've gotta see Beauregard and tell him!"

Forrest looked at Captain Tom Kizer. "Get the men back to camp. I've got to personally deliver what I've seen."

Forrest swung onto his waiting horse and trotted down the muddy trail. The soft thud of hooves on the soggy earth hung in the air behind him. Then the sky lit up like a white chalk on a blackboard as a silver streak rose from the river toward the Confederate camps. A loud boom reverberated in the night air.

Gonna keep the boys awake, Forrest thought, *just noise with nothin' to aim at.*

From the river two gunboats continued to fling shot into the night. Noise and not destruction was the goal of the boat's batteries.

A mud-splattered Forrest burst into the camp of General Patrick Cleburne. He rode directly to the general's tent and demanded an aide awaken his officer. The Irish 2nd Brigade commander of Hardee's 3rd Corps appeared, bleary-eyed in the drizzling rain.

"General," Forrest reported, "Buell's crossin' the river to reinforce Grant."

"The devil, ya say! Are you sure?"

"I saw it with my own eyes. If the enemy comes on us in the mornin', we'll be whipped like Hell."

"You better find Beauregard."

"That's what I'm tryin' to do. Where is he?"

"Last I heard, around Shiloh Church. Check with General Chalmers or General Breckinridge. They should know."

When accosted by Forrest, neither of the two generals could pinpoint Beauregard's whereabouts, but both urged the cavalryman to find him.

Near the church, Forrest found General Hardee, who emerged into the rain from a dry tent. His right arm was bandaged in a sling.

"You're hurt, sir," Forrest noted with concern.

"Nothing, just a slight wound."

"General, where is General Beauregard camped?"

"Colonel Forrest, the general has moved his camp. He neglected to tell me or anyone else around here where he went."

"Sir, I've been to Pittsburg Landing. Grant's not retreating. Buell's crossing to reinforce him. We need to do something."

"Well then, colonel, you really do need to find General Beauregard."

"General Hardee," Forrest urged, "you have more experience than anyone here. I trust your judgment. Act on what I've told you. We can't just ignore Buell."

Hardee sighed. "I think it'll wait. In any event, you've got to find Beauregard."

The sky flashed brightly over their heads as another boom made the earth tremble.

"Shouldda sunk the gunboat," Hardee murmured as he saluted Forrest and retreated into his tent.

Forrest's search for Beauregard was fruitless. The colonel rode back to Kizer in his camp, unable to control his fury. "They don't care! Damn them! Four generals. No one knows where Beauregard is and no one cares! It was in our grasp to win the battle right here, maybe even the war. It's runnin' away like piss down yer leg because of fools who don't care!"

"What do we do, sir?" Kizer asked.

"Wait here 'til some idiot tells us to do some idiotic thing. Or maybe we'll just do what I decide we should do."

* * *

HARRIS AND BRAXTON BRAGG knew where Beauregard was. They were sleeping in his tent, although fitfully through a night of rain and the intermittent rumbles and blasts from the Union gunboat cannons. Bragg arose at dawn, stepped outside the tent and breathed deeply into the fresh morning air.

He looked at Harris, already standing beside a dead campfire. "Looks like a great day, Governor. Clouds cleared out." He pointed to the pink smudge on the eastern horizon that promised a blue sky above it.

Then, a deep rumble of artillery and a rapid clash and clatter of musketry rose up from their left. With alarm flashing across his face, Bragg shouted at the tent, "General Beauregard, the enemy is attacking!"

* * *

IN THEIR CAMP southeast of Shiloh Church, the Rutherford Rifles and the rest of the Tennessee Regiment had suffered through a wretched night. They were soggy through and through and bone weary. No fires were allowed, even if it were possible to get any started.

Sam Davis ripped off a chunk of hardtack and chewed it while gazing through dim daylight at fading stars up above. "At least it stopped raining. Looks like a clear day coming."

"Do ya suppose any Yanks are left at the landing?" Joe Cates wondered. "I heard they was runnin' off."

"We'll know soon, Joe."

The sound of distant rifle fire brought the answer.

"What's that, Sam? Can't be Yanks, can it?"

"Sounds like Grant didn't retreat. I expect we'll be busy soon."

* * *

AT 5:30 A.M. on the far right of the Union line, Lew Wallace's division charged forward in the vanguard of a massive Union counterattack. They met little resistance at first as Beauregard frantically tried to rally his forces to meet them. It wasn't easy.

"Where's Polk?" the general shouted at Harris.

"To the southwest somewhere. He moved his camp a few miles away. Cheatham took his division southeast to where they camped Saturday night."

"Get them here, send riders immediately." Beauregard looked to the sound of gunfire. "It's a mess up there. Our divisions are so mixed up, we have no unit cohesion above the brigade level. We need more men!"

"I'll see to it, general."

The mass of federal soldiers continued to rise like a great blue tide. Wallace's men crushed the brigade of Preston Pond. The Union front of Sherman's survivors, plus McClernand's men and Bill Wallace's force, now commanded by Tuttle, were joined by Buell's divisions on their left. Bull Nelson, Crittenden, and McCook rolled through the disorganized Confederates recapturing lost land from the previous day.

It took two hours to locate Polk and get his men into position. By 10:00 a.m., Beauregard had managed to stabilize his front line with the corps of Bragg, Polk, Breckinridge, and Hardee positioned from left to right. But they had already been pushed nearly into Sherman's old camp at Shiloh Church.

Cheatham's division, which included the Rutherford Rifles, rushed up the Corinth Road and were ordered to stop at the Hamburg-Purdy Road. Major Hume Feild's regiment halted directly across from the east end of the sunken road, just south of the George cabin. It was shortly after noon.

Charlie Miller knelt next to Sam. "Weren't we in this spot yesterday?"

"Pretty close. Look, see the Yank flags coming. They've about taken back the Hornet's Nest."

"Too bad, it took us seven hours to git it."

"Well, Charlie, they might want us to do it again."

Corporal Beesley circulated among the Rutherford boys. He came to Sam and Charlie, "The Yankee left has gotta be stopped. We need to regain control of the Corinth Road. Be ready to move."

"Not just the Rifles, I hope," Charlie urged.

"No, all of Maney's brigade. We're to reinforce General Withers."

In short order, rifle fire exploded from the thickets held by the Confederates south of the Hamburg-Purdy Road. The response by the Union troops created an unceasing roar of musketry. Sam fired, loaded and rammed as rapidly as he could, getting off three shots a minute. Each time after shooting, he rolled over on his back to reload.

Then the order came to charge. The brigade, led by the Rutherford Rifles let out a scream and sprinted over the road. As the Union forces fell back, Maney's brigade dug in and held their position.

Joe Cates fell in next to Sam. In alarm he noticed a red splotch growing on his friend's left arm. "You're hit!" he shouted over the rifle fire.

Sam looked down at his arm. "Can't be much. I don't feel anything." He removed a yellow scarf and twisted it around his arm, covering the wound.

Across from them, Sherman remarked, "I've never heard musket fire so severe."

As Maney held his position on the far right of the Confederate line, the rest were in peril. On the Union right, Wallace and Sherman's men relentlessly drove Bragg and Polk farther south. Beauregard ordered counterattacks from the Shiloh Church area. They were flung back.

To the left of the Rifles, Crittenden's Union division swarmed onto the sunken road. The Hornet's Nest was retaken. Still, Maney's brigade held their piece of ground. Then Tuttle reinforced Crittenden and poised to take the junction of the Hamburg-Purdy and East Corinth roads.

Cheatham shouted to Maney, "Get your men out of there! Fall back to Corinth! We can't hold 'em!"

Wherever Beauregard tried to hold a line firm, it was only a matter of time before it collapsed. His men battled against twice their number.

Breckinridge reported to his commanding general. "Sir, we can't hold the extreme right any longer. Cheatham has ordered Maney's brigade to fall back toward Corinth."

"We all need to get to Corinth. I need you to hold on here, at the church. I can spare only about 5,000 men. I'll leave you some batteries, mass them at the church and on the ridge south of Shiloh Branch. This army needs to retreat in an orderly fashion to Corinth. Hold on as long as you can and then follow us."

As the Confederate army began to withdraw en masse toward Corinth, Breckinridge's small force held the Union troops at bay on the Corinth Road until 5:00 p.m. Then they joined the rest of the army in a measured withdrawal.

Back at Pittsburg Landing, Grant received word of the retreat. Don Carlos Buell urged Grant to follow up. "Chase 'em all the way to Corinth if we need to. They're tired and hungry. We can take down the whole army now."

"General, we too are exhausted and hungry. My divisions have been barely holding on for two days. We have dead to bury, many dead to bury. There have never been this many men killed in battle on the whole North American continent. Beauregard and Corinth will wait."

"My men can keep going, general. It's a mistake not to seize the moment."

Grant sighed. "Not today. Frankly, we just don't have the gumption. Tomorrow I'll send Sherman out to make sure they're still heading for Corinth.

"I still say we should be on their tails now."

Grant's eyes shone brightly. "Yes, and I'm sure you'll convey your thoughts to General Halleck and both of you'll present a fine critique of my efforts here. I know these men. They had enough today."

* * *

ON APRIL 8TH CUMP Sherman marched down the Corinth Road with two infantry brigades and two cavalry battalions. They met General Wood's division of Buell's army and continued on.

"Well, Wood," Sherman greeted Buell's general, "we've found nothing but dead rebels so far. I wish we had more cavalry, though. They are more suited for reconnaissance and vigorous pursuit of a retreating foe."

"The rebs are probably back in Corinth by now," Wood responded.

Six miles southwest of Pittsburg Landing, skirmishers from the 77th Ohio Infantry marched in a heavy drizzle. They encountered trees toppled across the roadway for nearly two hundred yards. In the distance, beyond the fallen trees, the road led into an open clearing, where a rain-swollen creek gurgled through the grass.

In the clearing was the camp of Colonel Forrest and 300 of his cavalry. A field hospital tent stood in their midst. Forrest had urged his men to ready themselves the previous night, and their arsenal was prepared.

Forrest's cavalry regiment used shotguns, breech-loading Maynard carbines, and sabers. But the preferred weapon of the horseman was the Navy Colt revolver. It could get off six shots, and many men carried two on their belt.

The colonel, himself, liked pistols but favored his curved saber. He sharpened it from tip to hilt and slashed the enemy as he rode through them. Forrest was sitting on a camp stool polishing his sword when he heard the clump of horse hooves over the soggy meadow. Two horsemen, his scouts, raced their mounts up to Forrest.

One shouted breathlessly, "Yanks comin' through the trees on the road!" He pointed north. "They'll be here soon!"

"Cavalry?" Forrest asked.

"Infantry," the scout answered.

Forrest took a pair of binoculars from a pouch and stood in his stirrups. Viewing the road, he affirmed, "They're comin', all right, Ohio boys, maybe Sherman's. Infantry first, cavalry behind 'em. That's a mistake. Captain Kizer," he looked to his nearest officer, "General Breckinridge wants us to delay the Yankees at all cost. Here's where we do it. Assemble the regiment."

From the crest of a hill on the road leading to the clearing, Sherman watched his men advance. He turned to General Wood. "Well, Wood, looks like a camp of cavalry down there. I wish I was sure that's all. They could have a whole division back in those trees."

"And we have two brigades. What do you propose, general?"

"We've got infantry stumbling over fallen trees as if they've been pulling the cork all night. We should have cavalry ahead of them."

"Too late to switch 'em around."

"The infantry should lead the charge, Wood."

In the camp the distant roll of drums sounded from the Ohio infantry as they struggled over the logs and into the clearing.

"Mount up, boys!" Forrest called, and three hundred gathered in formation.

The Union troops were nearly halfway across the clearing to the rebel camp when they encountered the creek. They paused, searching for rocks to step on as they crossed or for shallow spots in the swift stream. The blue line broke up as men sought easy passage.

Forrest seized the moment. With his sword pointed toward the federals he screamed, "Charge!" Three hundred horses leaped forward to attack. The thundering regiment was upon the 77th Ohio in minutes. Shocked Union soldiers, some in water above their knees, unleashed a ragged volley and then scrambled to fix bayonets.

Once upon them, the cavalry smashed into the confused blue coats with shotgun blasts and the pop of carbines. Union soldiers ducked down and piled into each other as they tried to escape the onslaught. Forrest slashed through them, his blade soon red with blood.

The fleeing Union infantry spread their panic to the Yankee cavalry behind them, and horsemen fired quick shots in the general direction of the Tennessee cavalry before retreating. Forrest yelled, "Charge!" again as his men drew their pistols and spit lead in rapid fire at the Union horseman.

Through infantry and cavalry they rode, cutting a bloody swath as they went. Then Kizer pulled up. Before them, less than a hundred yards away, was a solid blue line of infantry, brigade strength at least.

"Lieutenant," he shouted to another officer, "we can't ride into that. There's too many. Call a halt and order them to fall back."

Both men hollered with all their might. "Fall back! Fall back!"

As the troops wrenched their horses' heads to pull them up to stop, Kizer peered into the distance before them. "Who's that?" he cried as a single horseman, oblivious to the fact that all others had retreated, charged singlehandedly.

"That's my dad!" Captain Forrest yelled as he put his stirrups to his horse.

Kizer reached out and grabbed the boy's bridle and held on to the horse. "Don't be a fool, they'll kill you!"

Colonel Forrest rushed pell mell into the swarm of Union soldiers. Clutching his horse's reins with his teeth, he drew two pistols and fired with deadly accuracy at close range until both Colts were empty. Then he drew his saber and cut and slashed in the melee.

A Union infantryman held his musket at close range and fired point blank into Forrest's side. The colonel rocked back in his saddle and grabbed his horse's mane to keep from falling off. Realizing his situation was desparate, Forrest reached down and pulled a startled Union soldier onto his saddle. Using the man as a shield, Forrest dug his spurs into his horse and bounded back toward his camp. Once he had broken clear and was out of range of Yankee gunfire, he dumped the soldier onto the ground.

"My compliments to General Sherman, boy," he called to the dazed soldier as he rode back to his troops.

Meanwhile the Rutherford Rifles with the rest of the army were pulling through knee-high mud that sucked them down with every step.

Joe Cates grumbled to Sam, "Mud's bad enough, but this stinks, too."

Sam kept his head down and didn't reply. The odor was putrid, and he didn't want to talk about the dead men and horses strewn along the road producing the stench. Corinth had to be better.

A young officer trotted his horse alongside Sam and Joe. "I thought we had 'em beat," he claimed. "Now look at us."

Sam glanced at the bedraggled, mud-splattered young captain. The horse, equally dirty, was bleeding from a long, shallow cut on his back haunch.

"We ain't a pretty sight," Joe agreed.

"Where y'all from?" the officer asked.

"Smyrna, Rutherford County," Sam said.

The officer brightened in spite of his surroundings. "I live not far from you, in Franklin, next county over." He reached down to shake hands. "I'm Tod Carter, guess I should say Captain Carter, 20th Tennessee."

"I'm Sam Davis, 1st Tennessee, private," he shook the proffered gloved hand. "And this is Private Cates."

"Davis," Carter mused as his horse sloshed along beside the marching men, "the name's familiar to me. Does your father have land dealings?"

"He does, he's done some buying and selling."

"I've dealt with him. Back home I was a lawyer."

"Ya don't look old enough." Cates studied the officer's slender, handsome face.

Carter straightened up in his saddle. "I'm twenty-two, and I was practicing law for a year before I signed up in May last year."

"Lots of people left a lot behind to join in this," Sam commented. "Some gave up more than others."

"Yes," Carter agreed, pausing to gaze at a body face down in the mud, "and some will never get it back. My brother has been a Yankee prisoner for five months. Good luck to you both. We'll meet again."

Carter set his spurs, and the horse splashed ahead down the trail.

* * *

THE 2ND MINNESOTA arrived on the battlefield the next day. They were given the task of digging trenches and helping to bury the dead, both blue and gray.

The March to Corinth

RINCIE DEGRAVE THRUST a shovel into the soggy earth and scooped up a heavy load of muddy dirt. He flopped it onto a pile and watched as his comrades lowered dead soldiers into a long, shallow trench.

"How many trenches ya figure we dug?" Aaron Doty wondered.

"Enough to plant 'bout 4,000 men, from what I hear, both blue 'n' gray."

"Funny, ain't it?" DeGrave observed, "some of 'em look like they's just sleepin', while others are all twisted up like they really suffered."

"Or was really scared," Doty considered.

"Well, anyway, once we cover these up, we're done."

"Rincie, do ya ever wish we'd got here in time to fight?"

DeGrave's eyes traveled along the long row of twisted bodies. "No, Aaron, I don't."

Doty pushed his shovel into the muck. "I dug graves back home, Rincie. There was some fine digging there. My favorite was the Catholic Cemetery. It was smooth, like slicing into a chocolate cake. What do ya think we'll be doin' next?"

"Movin' on to Corinth. I hear that General Halleck hisself has come from St. Louis to run the army."

"What about Grant, Rincie?"

"From what I hear, he's on the outs with Halleck."

"Din't Halleck write that book 'bout how to fight?"

"I heard he wrote one. Word has it he likes to move slow, build fortifications and out-maneuver."

"So, we won't be chargin' into Corinth?"

"Hard tellin', Aaron. But we just be privates. We'll do what they tell us."

On April 11th the commander of the Department of the Missouri, Henry Halleck, arrived at Pittsburg Landing. A shakeup in the 2nd Minnesota had taken place. Colonel Van Cleeve had been named a brigadier general in charge of volunteers. Lieutenant Colonel George moved up to colonel of the 2nd and Judson Bishop was promoted to major.

Clint Cilley, newly a lieutenant of Company C, was assigned the task of escorting Van Cleeve to his new assignment with Halleck. As they rode into the landing, they saw a mud-splattered General Grant standing in front of a large tent. A straight-backed, well-formed man dressed impeccably in civilian clothes strode briskly back and forth before the general.

As the two riders neared, they could plainly overhear the man's words. "Despicable! General Grant, despicable! You were unprepared and surprised at Shiloh. Your army was in terrible condition. Had Buell not arrived, your army would have been destroyed!"

Cilley murmured to Van Cleeve, "Who is that man?"

"General Henry Halleck."

Grant replied to Halleck in an even tone. "I beg to differ with you, sir."

Halleck's voice turned loud and haughty. "You beg to differ? Your army was without discipline or order. Immediate steps must be taken to put your force in condition to withstand another attack."

"What do you propose to do, general?"

"I shall reorganize this army. There will be three wings: the right under Thomas, he'll have three divisions of the Army of the Tennessee and one from the Army of the Ohio; Buell, with four divisions of the Army of the Ohio, will command the center; and Pope, fresh from his victory at Island Number 10, will lead the four divisions of the Army of the Mississippi on the left wing. We will move on Corinth with 100,000 men."

"What about me?" Grant inquired.

"You'll be my second in command. Your rank entitles you to it."

"What does second in command do?"

Halleck smirked. "Whatever I want you to do."

"Well, Colonel," Cilley said softly to his companion, "good luck to you."

Van Cleeve nodded. "Thank you, lieutenant. It looks like we'll all need luck."

* * *

THE 1ST TENNESSEE had also been reorganized. George Maney was promoted to brigadier general for his gallantry at Shiloh, and Hume Feild was elected colonel of the regiment.

Corinth's population of only 1,000 swelled nearly seventy times as Beauregard's various forces converged on the strategic railroad center. Two vital lines, the east-west Memphis and Charleston and the north-south Mobile and Ohio railroads, intersected at Corinth.

The terrain separating the little town from Pittsburg Landing twenty-two miles north was rolling and wooded, interspersed with swamps, roads, and streams. Even before the fighting at Shiloh, Bragg had begun the construction of entrenchments to protect the city. Ten miles of clay and timber mounds stretched around Corinth, reinforcing natural defenses of flooded streams and swamps.

All along the muddy roads leading into town, gray-clad soldiers staggered through discarded muskets, blankets, tent poles and wagon parts. Sometimes they rolled dead bodies to the side. Other times they simply stepped over them.

Sam Davis wearily remarked to Charlie Miller as they sighted Corinth, "Look at all those tents. It's good we still have railroads for supplies."

"Sure, but how many is hospital tents? I hear we got twenty thousand too sick to be worth anything. They can ship us food, all right, but men can't fight when they're crappin' their lives away."

"Dysentery," Sam agreed. "The water's bad and getting worse."

"Men gotta drink, Sam. Most don't know no better."

"The town's become a big hospital."

"Or a morgue. Some fellas got bad fevers."

"Typhoid, Charlie."

"It ain't right, Sam. We're losin' more men to sickness than we do fightin'."

"And we lost plenty fighting. Can we hold off the Yankees, Charlie?"

"We got entrenchments and swamps all over. It should hold 'em."

"Just for a while. There are three major roads leading from Pittsburg Landing. They might be muddy, but that'll just slow 'em down, not stop 'em."

Miller hefted his musket at Sam. "We got these to stop 'em."

"Yes, we do," Sam agreed.

* * *

HENRY HALLECK PAINSTAKINGLY planned every move. Every detail and maneuver of his army was accounted for. In a meeting with his wing commanders, Thomas, Pope and Buell, he explained his plan. The generals sat on camp stools as Halleck began. "I firmly believe that victory can best be obtained by massing troops, outmaneuvering and numerical superiority."

"I think I read that somewhere," Buell smiled, "like in your book."

"Those tactics served us well in the Mexican War," Halleck concurred.

"What about the weather factor?" Thomas asked. "We seem to get a downpour every day. It's hard to mass troops in the mud."

"It just takes a little longer," Halleck countered. "We'll engage the enemy at Corinth when we've massed our troops in his front. The wilderness nature of the terrain makes it almost impossible to march through, but we'll manage. I'm more concerned with reports of reinforcements arriving in Corinth giving rise to added confidence Beauregard will be able to repulse us."

"Add the heavy rains, washed-out bridges, and quagmires for roads, and the challenge is even greater," Pope added. "Besides, the rebs keep cutting down trees as obstacles to us."

"It's severely inhibiting our supply lines," Thomas relayed. "While you raise legitimate concerns, General Halleck, our men have more basic needs. They're hungry and we can't get enough food to them. So far they just curse our quartermasters, the cry of 'crackers, we want crackers' resounds from one end of my camp to the other."

"It's April," Halleck demurred, "the rains will stop and we'll be in position to put Beauregard in a vise. In the meantime, we'll move incrementally each day and fortify as we do."

"Tightening the noose around them," Pope agreed, "but I'm anxious to pitch into them now. Let me move out front and test them."

"No, my impetuous General Pope. You will not move out by yourself. We shall slowly tighten the noose."

* * *

IN CORINTH THE DEFENDERS sought to build up their fortifications. Joe Hall heaved a shovel full of clay onto a parapet. "It's the one thing we got lots of," he called to Bill Searcey. "No decent food, our clothes in tatters and the water is foul, but we got dirt."

"And we've got General Bragg," Searcey added.

"That ain't sayin' much," Hall complained, "he won't even let coffee or tobacco be issued to us and scant food when we get it. We need leaders."

Sam Davis considered a moment. "It seems like the farther up the chain of command we go, the worse it gets. Colonel Feild is a fine regimental commander. We all know the great job Maney did with us and now he's got our brigade. Cheatham didn't have much military training, but he's a fighter and his 2nd Division is our best. Even Leonidas Polk, our preacher/general, knows when to pray and how to fight."

"That brings us to Bragg," Searcy, "and that ain't much."

"It's why men are desertin'," Hall said.

"That and the fact many enlisted for a year and believe their time is up and they can go home."

"They should be able to go home if they wanna," Hall snorted. "They did what they signed up for. They got rights to go home."

Sam shook his head. "The Conscription Act pretty much says that once you're signed up, it's for the duration of the war."

"And Bragg shoots anyone who thinks different. We get to watch another one git shot tonight." Searcey frowned.

"Yes, it's sad," Sam concluded as he pitched another shovel of dirt.

Bragg would call his whole army together for executions of deserters. Early that evening they watched as a scrawny, trembling young man was tied to a post while a platoon of twelve lined up before him.

A hush like that before a prayer in church fell over the thousands of watching men while a captain cried, "Ready, aim, fire!"

The prisoner twitched from the impact of twelve rifle balls and then hung lifeless from the post.

"Let this be a lesson!" the captain shouted. "General Bragg won't abide desertion. The ultimate price will be paid by those who forsake their duty to their country."

"Damn Bragg to Hell," Searcey mumbled to Sam.

"Keep it to yourself, Bill. Bragg don't abide being cussed at, either."

"Sam, we're all gonna die for the glorious Confederacy. It just depends on how. Are we gonna get shot by Yankees, get shot by Bragg, starve to death, or get sick and die."

"Some will live, Bill. They can't kill us all."

"What 'bout the fella that was ten days late comin' back from leave. He woulda been better off dead. They whipped and branded him. They made us watch when they shaved his head smooth and then stripped him buck naked before some big fella peeled the skin off his back with a rawhide whip.

"The poor guy was screaming like a banshee, beggin' for mercy. What did that get 'im? Branded on both hips with a hot iron shaped like a D. He woulda been better off if they killed him."

"Bragg does fight, and we need to hold this ground."

"Sam, men fight better for a man they love than them's they hate."

"What about those they fear?"

* * *

HALLECK'S MASSIVE ARMY inched forward like a slow-moving turtle. Their three wings formed a twelve-mile front that edged forward ponderously, entrenched, and then crept forward again before entrenching again. John Pope slogged through mud nearly knee deep as he approached Halleck's tent. He stopped and pulled the top of his right boot to combat the sucking force of mud that grabbed at his boot like a hidden hand and tried to pull it off.

Pope futilely tried to brush splats of mud off his uniform before being escorted into Halleck's large circular tent. "Have you ever seen weather like this?" he asked his commander.

"Not under these circumstances. I want your report, General Pope. How are you proceeding?"

"Slow. The rebels fell trees to impede our progress, but sometimes it works to our advantage. We use the logs to build corduroy roads over the swamps. We're bearing down on the Tennessee/Mississippi border. I'd still like to move things along more quickly. My men are ready to attack."

Halleck sighed. "No, General Pope. I strongly believe in the French Doctrine of maneuver and fortification, particularly where amateur soldiers are involved, and that's what most of our army is, amateurs."

Pope countered, "I keep hearing rumors Beauregard is being reinforced and is going to hit us by surprise at Shiloh. Shouldn't we be proactive and hit him first?"

"That is why we entrench each day, so we're ready and won't be caught off guard as Grant was."

"How's Grant doing?"

Halleck stifled a smile. "Not well. I just received a note from him." The general held up a crumbled piece of paper. "He writes, 'I believe it is generally understood through this army that my position differs little from that of one under arrest.' He asks to be relieved or to have his position better defined. I expressed shock at his opinion and his questioning of my command structure. I told him that, as a friend, he should not require explanations from me."

"What do you expect General Grant to do?"

"Leave or stay, I don't care. I have found him useless." He chuckled. "'Useless' Grant, seems more accurate than 'Ulysses.'"

"He did capture Henry and Donelson."

"Luck and circumstance, certainly not generalship."

"Any other orders for me, General Halleck?"

"Just keep following the plan. We'll get to Corinth soon enough. Maybe things will even dry up."

Behind the lines at Grant's camp, the general's trunks were packed and waiting beside his tent for shipment. Inside his tent, Grant was busy packing his personal belongings when Sherman flipped the tent flaps aside and entered.

"Grant, what are you doing? Whether you plan a leave or are resigning altogether, neither is an option. You can't do it."

"Cump, I'm about as useless as teats on a boar. I can't just sit back and watch this happen. Maybe I was at fault at Shiloh. Maybe I could have been better prepared. I need to go back to St. Louis."

"Nonsense, if anyone was caught with their pants down it was me, not you, and Halleck has me commanding a division. He resents you, Grant, because you won battles and when he tried to deny you credit for your victories, Lincoln even came down on your side. Be patient. Things will come your way again. You're a fighter, and this army has far too few of them."

"My wife Julia, she—"

"For God's sake, Grant, we're trying to save our country. We need your help to do it. I don't want to hear about Julia or your children or your father or your store in Galena. I want you to stay and fight. You'll get your chance."

Grant rarely showed emotion, but swallowed a lump in his throat and grasped his friend's hand. "Thank you, Cump. I'll stay, bide my time. At least for a while."

* * *

FIRST LIEUTENANT CLINTON Cilley marched through the mud alongside his captain, Dan Heaney. Clint squinted his eyes and waved his hands in front of his face to ward off a swarm of gnats. "I don't know what's worse: the ticks, the mosquitoes, or the gnats."

"I'll take the gnats, lieutenant, I don't like anything that sucks my blood."

"I guess there are worse things."

"Take your pick. Rain, mud, not knowing if the food wagons from Pittsburg Landing will show up, getting shot at or sick. Yep, there are worse things than gnats."

"At least the lice provide diversion. The races are pretty popular," Clint added.

"It's amazing how fast some of 'em get off a tin plate."

"Especially when someone heats up the plate. It's cheating, and when one's betting on a race, horse or lice, one doesn't like to be cheated."

"Right, professor, no heated plates."

"I'm glad we're stuck with Thomas. You'd think the other Minnesota boys would have been with us."

"That's not how it works, Clint. The 5th is with Rosecrans and the 4th with Hamilton."

"Maybe it is better to spread the Minnesota boys around. Improve the other regiments a little."

"Too bad three companies of the 5th got left behind in Minnesota."

"Guarding frontier forts. Against what? Mosquitoes?"

"Certainly not Indians, Clint, there's never been a problem with them. But I guess it makes the new immigrants feel better to have soldiers around."

"Well, it's a shame they aren't here yet."

April at Fort Ridgely

A LONE WAGON ROLLED up the trail from the Minnesota River to Fort Ridgely. A teamster flicked his reins and clucked his team of two horses forward. Beside him sat a well-formed, athletic man with a bronzed face that seemed out of place in a Minnesota spring.

John Marsh, of Preston, returning from fighting in the East with the 2nd Wisconsin Infantry Regiment, had been frustrated with delays in forming a regiment in Minnesota. He'd crossed the river to LaCrosse and headed into Virginia with the Wisconsin boys. But a commission had been reserved for him in Company B of the 5th Minnesota. Marsh had come home to claim it.

By April 16th, the open prairie leading to the fort shimmered like a field of emeralds in the mid-morning sun. The fort compound was a duskier green blemished with smudges of brown dirt drying out after spring rains.

A tall flagpole stood in the center of the rectangular-shaped fort, which measured ninety yards across. An American flag fluttered in the light breeze as the eighty-six men of Company B waited in formation. The wagon stopped before them. Marsh dismounted. First Lieutenant Norm Culver strode to Marsh and clasped his hand in greeting. Culver's son, twelve-year-old Charlie, struck up a cadence on his drum while another man added the shrill whistle of a pipe.

A chorus erupted from the ranks with "Huzzah! Huzzah! Huzzah!"

Marsh held up his hands to silence the music, then saluted his new command. He turned to Culver. "I didn't expect such pomp and circumstance."

"We are very glad to see you! The boys think you'll get them one step closer to fighting rebs."

"That will come in time, Lieutenant."

Marsh faced Company B. "Thank you for your warm welcome. The *Chatfield News Democrat* calls you a gallant company, and indeed you are. I know you're anxious to go south to fight. That time will come. It's our task to make sure the frontier is secure in the meantime and be as ready as we possibly can to meet the challenges of war against the rebels."

"When do we get some real guns, Cap'n?" Jimmy Dunn questioned from the front rank.

Marsh stepped forward and took Jimmy's musket to examine it. "A .69-caliber flintlock retrofitted with a percussion cap." He hefted it. "All nine pounds of it." He looked to Culver. "All the men have these?"

"Yes, captain."

"No .58 caliber rifled muskets?"

"Not one."

Marsh shook his head. "You'll have to make the best of it here. I guarantee you, when we go south, when you really need good weaponry, you'll have it."

Three cheers of "Huzzah!" again rose from the men.

Marsh turned to Culver. "Dismiss the men and come to the headquarters building. Bring your second lieutenant and first sergeant with you."

Marsh and the teamster unloaded the captain's meager baggage at a white board-sided building with a wide front porch. The captain entered and found a sparsely furnished structure with a few rooms, one of which was his office, as evidenced by the bare desk in the middle.

Marsh sat easily behind the desk, warily testing out the wooden chair as it creaked beneath him. Culver stepped through the open door accompanied by Tom Gere and a stocky fellow with a full, bushy, dark beard.

They saluted. Marsh stood, returned the salutes and strode to the three to shake their hands. Culver introduced them. "This young man is Second Lieutenant Tom Gere."

"Beecher Gere's kid brother."

"Yes, sir." Tom answered.

"And this hairy fellow is John Jones, the other regular army man. Fought in the Mexican War. A native of England, but we don't hold that against him. His specialty is artillery."

"What artillery do we have?"

"Our arsenal is six guns, sir. Two twelve-pound mountain howitzers, two six pounders, a twelve-pound Napoleon cannon and my big baby, a twenty-four-pound howitzer with a 1,318-pound barrel."

Marsh chuckled. "That's a lot of firepower for a backwater fort. What do you do with them?"

"Captain, sir," Jones explained, "Things can be a bit boring here. I drill these boys, er, men. I teach them how to fire the cannons. It gives the lads something to do."

"And every night," Gere interjected, "he teaches some of the men sword exercise and bayonet drill. That's after drilling them in rifle manual-of-arms. All this will come in handy if we ever go south, and I expect to before long."

"Captain, is it true that a sixth Minnesota regiment is being formed?" Culver asked.

"Yes, that's true."

"Then we can go south, and they can take our place here."

"A likely scenario. How high are we above the river valley?"

"A hundred and fifty feet or so," Culver answered.

"I noticed some things riding in. You have ravines on three sides. I hope we're never attacked. An offensive force wouldn't be noticed until they're almost on top of us."

"Not likely, sir," Culver responded. "Relations with the Sioux have always been good."

"It's our job to help it stay that way."

"Captain," Jones suggested, "I'm breaking in a new gun crew. Would you like to watch?"

"I'd enjoy that."

"Then let's go to the firing range. The men are ready."

Jones led Marsh to a twelve-pound Napoleon cannon. Seven soldiers stood at attention, including Jimmy Dunn, Bill Perrington, and Oscar Wall. As Marsh observed, Jones began his instructions.

"Men, we established your positions on the gun crew earlier. So you do have some understanding this is complicated and dangerous work.

"The poundage on the cannon indicates the weight of the ball fired. A twelve-pounder fires a twelve-pound cannon ball. Some gun crews have up to nine cannoneers. Five or even three can do it, but not efficiently. Seven is a good number.

"Each man has his specific duty. As I call it out, step forward and perform the function. Numbers six and seven are in charge of the ammunition chests. They cut the fuses of the explosive shells to match the distance to the targets. They hand them to number five, who brings the cartridges forward to the gun."

Each man moved as Jones called out his number and did as instructed.

"Number two takes the round, puts it in the muzzle of the cannon. Number one pushes the cartridge down the barrel with his rammer. Number three pokes a wire pick down through the vent hole in the barrel. This opens the cartridge's bag of black powder. He wears a leather patch over his thumb and puts it over the vent hole to make sure there is no premature explosion.

"Number four will take a friction primer from the pouch on his belt and place it in the vent hole. The officer in charge of the crew, the gunner, stays behind the gun and sights the piece. When all's ready, a pull on a rope lanyard ignites the primer. The spark sets off the powder in the cartridge and fires the piece.

"Numbers one and two will watch the barrel to make sure it fires. In the smoke, noise and confusion of battle, it can be missed unless watched carefully. It'd be a disaster to reload a cannon that was already loaded.

"They are waiting for the two commands to set this in motion. Number four, prick and prime." He waited while the lanyard was set. "Gunner, fire!" The lanyard pin was jerked from the vent hole.

The Napoleon roared and lurched back several feet in recoil as a ball launched onto the distant prairie.

"Number one will now use the opposite end of his rammer to swab out any burning embers left in the barrel with a wet sponge. Then it starts over again. A good crew can get off two shots a minute. At least an additional four men are assigned duty with the horses."

Marsh smiled and clapped. "Excellent, men. You're learning fast."

"Not fast enough," Jones critiqued, "they've got a lot of work to do."

As the two officers departed, Perrington commented, "Well, I sure hope this helps us later on. Sergeant Jones sure knows what he's doing."

Wall squinted at the officers' backs. "Jones is too exacting. Nothing's good enough if it isn't perfectly right."

"I don't care," Jimmy said, "it gives us something to do. We'll never use what we've learned here, but in the South it might come in handy."

"We're an infantry regiment, not artillery," Wall corrected.

Jimmy laughed and signaled a mock salute. "Just like you, I'm here to preserve order and protect United States property. That's what they tell us. I just thought it'd be someplace other than Minnesota."

* * *

"Tell me about my command," Marsh asked Jones as they crossed the parade ground toward headquarters. "Most are from Preston or Chatfield, I see."

"All but eleven."

"Mostly farm boys?"

"Sixty of them, from the sixteen-year-olds who lied to enlist, to a couple in their forties. We have a few carpenters or clerks. A couple each of saddlers, machinists and printers. We've got a teacher, a baker, a gunsmith and a black-smith. Jimmy Dunn ran his father's hotel."

"Family men?"

"Only eighteen are married."

"I see you have John Bishop here. His brother Judson is a major now and moving up fast. What more can you tell me?"

"A third are foreign born, like me. Only one was born in Minnesota, Andrew Williamson, whose father is a missionary at the Redwood Agency. He's also our most educated, having earned a master's degree at Yale. They're a good bunch of lads, eager to learn. Five are over six feet tall, the rest a few inches under, not counting the drummer boy, Charlie."

"So what you're telling me is I command a company of good boys who know nothing of soldiering and have antiquated weapons. I know everyone is eager to head south to fight, but we need more time. This is a good, quiet place to get it."

The Siege at Corinth

THE MEN OF THE 2ND Minnesota and the rest of Halleck's army embarked on a tedious campaign of offensive entrenchment. Clint Cilley supervised the men of Company C and occasionally bent his back in shoveling with his men.

As Clint dumped a shovel load of heavy dirt on top of a four-foot-high mound, he encouraged the soldiers, "Keep it up, boys. Each day brings us closer to Corinth."

"Are ya sure?" Rincie DeGrave called. "It's the middle of May. At this rate we'll be in Corinth by Christmas."

"I don't know if we can move that fast. It's over five miles away," Charlie Orline countered.

"General Halleck knows what he's doing," Clint answered, "He'll get us there in one piece and take the town."

Rincie stood on a rise of ground and looked into the distance. Coal-black smoke from a locomotive signaled the arrival of another train. "Looks like they keep getting more supplies or more men or more of somethin'."

"That's why we have to do this right," Clint explained. "To make sure we're in position to stop those trains and starve out the town if we need to. Put your backs into it, men!"

* * *

IN CORINTH THE LABYRINTH of defenses surrounding the town was finished and its defenders awaited the eventual Union offensive. The 1st Tennessee's Rutherford Rifles grew impatient with the tedium.

Joe Ewing motioned to Sam Davis as stretcher bearers carried another lifeless body off to the burial trench. "Another one, Sam. We'll be diggin' another ditch soon."

Sam's eyes sadly followed the stretcher. "It's the water. Has to be. We're getting by with the food, but the water's foul. It stinks. You take your life in your hands when you drink."

113

Joe Hale commented, "I lick off dew in the mornin'. It gets me by."

"You better watch out," Ewing laughed. "Wearin' butternut, somebody might take ya for a deer in the meadow and shoot ya."

Hale ruefully shook his head. "That might be better than the fevers and gut aches that be killin' the boys now."

"Something good'll happen," Sam said hopefully. "Have faith."

Ewing held up his rifle. "I got faith in this, sure enuff, not no generals."

* * *

FORTIFYING AFTER EACH incremental advance, it took the Union army three weeks to move five miles. On May 26th they were finally in position.

John Pope had led Halleck's left wing. On May 3rd his aggressive nature overcame his commander's cautions. Pope moved forward and captured the town of Farmington only a few miles from Corinth. Instead of moving the center wing under Buell forward to join Pope, Halleck ordered Pope to withdraw and realign with the Union center. But the zealous federal general did not withdraw until attacked by Van Dorn a few days later.

Halleck ordered Pope to Pittsburg Landing, where they met in the commanding general's large circular tent. "General Pope," Halleck began, "I admonished you before to make no offensive moves without orders. Your impetuousness could jeopardize this whole operation."

"General," Pope countered, "we can crush them. This isn't a time to be timid. We have a glittering array of our best officers here—Grant, Sherman, Sheridan, McPherson, Logan, Buell, and Rosecrans are just a few. Let's use the superior manpower and talent we have and attack."

Halleck sighed. "Napoleon would mass his army here and lay siege. That's what I'm doing. They may very well have more men than we do. General Pope, you will adhere to our plan."

From mid-May on, the Union troops fought a series of minor engagements as they aligned themselves in front of Corinth. At Farmington, Russel's House, the Widow Surratt Farm, Double Log House, Surratt's Hill and Bridge Creek, the noose grew tighter and tighter around Corinth. By May 28th the federals were in full siege mode and within easy range of cannon fire into the city. Members of the 4th Minnesota and the seven companies of the 5th not still in Minnesota fought alongside Pope. The 2nd remained in the siege line.

* * *

BEAUREGARD MET with his generals in a house in the town on May 28th.

"We're in a sad state, general," Cheatham remarked. "Scouts report that we're outnumbered by better than two to one. The men know it, and they feel pretty low."

Isham Harris looked at Beauregard with remorse. "The hospital tents are full, and more men are lying out there with no shelter at all, dying of typhoid and dysentery. We've lost nearly as many men as we did at Shiloh."

"What do you suggest?" their general wondered.

Hardee, still recovering from his wound at Shiloh, grimaced. "We gotta leave, general, that's all there is to it."

Beauregard shook his head. "They'd be on us like flies on horse manure before we could get away."

"Not if we're creative," Forrest interjected. "It's been said I have a flair for the dramatic. Let's put some drama into this."

"What do you mean?"

"We move out on the Mobile and Ohio Railroad and take our sick, wounded, heavy artillery, and supplies with us. Every time a train whistles, we cheer like all get-out to make the Yanks think we're bein' reinforced."

"I like the idea," Beauregard considered. "Let's be even more theatrical. We'll set up dummy guns, Quakers, on the defensive line, leave some men behind to keep campfires burning and have regular drum rolls and bugle calls."

"I can do ya one better," Hardee continued. "Give some men three days' rations, send 'em out and tell 'em to prepare for an attack."

"We leave them high and dry? We don't tell them we're leaving? Is that right to do?" Harris questioned.

"The Yanks won't hurt 'em," Hardee answered, "they'll take 'em prisoner, but we'll exchange back for 'em later. The important thing is the army gets away."

Braxton Bragg offered another perspective. "I understand our predicament, but, General Beauregard, we're leaving a vital railroad junction without a fight. What will the reaction be in Richmond?"

"What choice do we have? Even if we tried to fight them off with our depleted force, it'd turn out the same. We have no drinkable water left."

Beauregard grimly nodded to his officers. "Gentlemen, see to your men. Tomorrow night we'll move out."

On May 29th the Union bombardment of Corinth began as Halleck's men maneuvered into position. The Confederate forces placed "dummy" cannons along their defenses and began to ship out their sick and injured men and supplies on the Mobile and Ohio Railroad.

Each time a train appeared, the remaining rebel soldiers emitted loud cheers and huzzahs. Sam Davis and others of the Rutherford Rifles set charges to blow up supplies that couldn't be transported. Throughout the day drums rolled and bugles blared. As twilight set in, campfires blazed all around Corinth, while Sam and his company marched unseen south to Tupelo, Mississippi.

* * *

CLINT CILLEY AND DAN Heaney watched and listened from the siege line. "Clint, it sure sounds like they got a passel o' reinforcements today."

"It looks like a lot more campfires than before. Do you think we should have attacked sooner, before they were reinforced?"

Heaney scratched the stubble on his chin. "Maybe, but Old Brains, General Halleck, seemed pretty sure of himself on this."

"We caught some rebs who say Beauregard's getting ready to attack. He must've been waiting for more men. It looks like he got them."

As the sky turned to ink, a huge explosion from Corinth sent red streaks streaming into the sky. "What in blazes!" Heaney cried.

"I don't get it," Clint said, "that couldn't have been from us."

By morning the fires in Corinth were only smoldering slivers of smoke smudging a blue sky. Sherman, Pope, Buell and Halleck, himself, surveyed the city with binoculars.

"It's so quiet," Sherman muttered, "and I don't see anyone. We've got a few prisoners, men out in advance. But I don't see anything now."

"Order a patrol in," Halleck commanded. "Let's find out what's going on."

A short time later a company of soldiers returned to Halleck after riding back from Corinth. "The place is empty, general," a captain reported, "no rebs there at all, just some civilians."

"What about all the cheering?" Halleck asked.

"An old fella told me it was all a show to make us think the trains were bringin' more men in when they was really taking their army away."

Pope slapped his dusty hat over his thigh and exclaimed, "They fooled us. Beauregard pulled the wool right over our eyes!"

Buell stuck out his hand to shake Halleck's. "We've won, general, the plan of Old Brains did it. We took Corinth and hardly lost a man. The victory is yours, general."

Under his breath Pope muttered, "We could have destroyed their army."

Mary Kate Patterson

MARY KATE PATTERSON returned home from the Elliot School in Nashville in June of 1861. Her family lived on Nolensville Road not far from the Rutherford County line in Rashboro. She found three brothers had left home to join the Confederate army. Only a sister, Margaret, two younger brothers, and her parents, Hugh and Ellen, remained.

Hugh, a well respected doctor in the community, kept certain activities secret, like his house being a way station for Confederate couriers needing safe haven. He also had access to medical supplies that were critical to the cause of the Confederacy. His home became even more important and his supplies more urgently needed when Nashville fell into Union hands in early 1862.

The turn in the war in Tennessee hit Kate hard. Determined to contribute to the "cause," she sat down for an earnest conversation with her father at a round wooden table in the kitchen after the rest of the family had gone to bed. An oil lamp's flickering yellow light reflected off the ceiling as Dr. Patterson beamed at his daughter. "You've been a great help, especially with all that's going on."

"My brothers are gone," Kate said. "Sam's in Mississippi. If I can't do something, why, I'll just burst! I wish I were a man so I could fight."

"Hold on, girl. You've got fire in you, but there are ways you can help here."

"I suppose you want me to be a nurse."

Patterson smiled. "I've got other plans, if you're interested."

"What do you have in mind for me?"

"Well, I wish I could fight too, but sometimes we do what we were cut out to do. I'm a doctor. People respect this place. I've agreed to shelter visitors, riders who need a place to stay."

"What kind of riders?"

"Some might call them spies. I prefer to consider them couriers."

"You want me to spy?"

"Not exactly. There's great need for medicinal drugs—quinine, morphine and such. You can be of service in that regard if you choose."

"How, Papa?"

"As a doctor, I have access to drugs. But I can't deliver them without attracting suspicion. We need to get them to our contacts in Nashville so they can get them to our troops. You can find ways to deliver drugs to people in Nashville. You can get by the Yankee security and through their lines."

Kate grew thoughtful. "How would I do that?"

"You've always been resourceful. Think about it. Decide what would work. I believe your cousin, Robbie Woodruff, might help. Kate, this is dangerous. Yankees would consider you a spy if they caught you. If you don't want to do this, I'd understand."

"Yankees invaded Tennessee, have our capitol, and are trying to change how we live. My brothers and Sam are risking their lives to save the South. I just heard from Sam about Shiloh. He's facing horrible, terrible things. I shall do my part. I can get through Union lines. It'd just take some planning."

"What have you heard from Sam?"

Kate clutched a folded letter in her lap but didn't open it. She knew what it said. "The army's on the march, Bragg's their commander now. Beauregard fell sick at Tupelo. The Rutherford Rifles have gone from Tupelo to Chattanooga."

"How's Sam doing?"

"He says fine. Why are they traipsing all over Tennessee, though?"

"Kate, you should know some things. If you hear the mournful song of a Bob White, it's likely not a bird, but a courier. During the day a raised shutter signals the coast is clear, a lowered shutter means stay away. A lit candle in a window at night is a sign to come on in."

"You've already set things up."

"I had to, it was time."

"I'll get together with Robbie tomorrow. I think this shall be fun. I've always wanted to fool Yankees."

"I don't think 'fun' is the word to describe this, Kate. I'm afraid we're talking about life and death here. I warn you, we can all be in danger."

"Our sacrifice is still small, Papa, compared to the privations our gallant army is going through. I do miss Sam . . . and my brothers, too, of course!" She blushed crimson in the yellow light.

Patterson laughed. "Your brother Charles's returning. He has been practicing medicine with the army but is coming back to help me, with more than just medicine. Ev's left the army as well. He seems to be assigned to some special duty in Nashville. I didn't ask what."

After Corinth

THE 2ND MINNESOTA marched into Corinth with the rest of George Thomas's corps. Colonel George rode at the head of the regiment, accompanied by Lieutenant Colonel Alexander Wilkin and Major Judson Bishop.

Captain Heaney and Lieutenant Cilley marched alongside their men down desolate, deserted streets.

Sergeant Sam Burnell spat a stream of yellow tobacco in disgust. "There ain't nobody here, Lieutenant. They jest made a buncha noise at the front door and slipped out the back while we was lookin' the other way."

"They played us for fools, Dan," Clint muttered.

"Now what do we do?"

"Chase after them, I guess. 'Old Brains' will have a plan, I'm sure of that."

Halleck did have plans. As his army marched into Corinth, he outlined them with his generals at his headquarters camp. "Gentlemen, there's been a reorganization of the army. President Lincoln ordered me to Washington to replace General McClellan as general-in-chief."

Buell exclaimed, "Congratulations, sir! The success of your operation here is a stark contrast to the failure of McClellan's peninsular campaign in Virginia."

Halleck beamed. "Thank you, General, but we have other changes. General Grant, you'll resume field command in what is now the District of West Tennessee. But your forces will be dispersed. General Buell, I want you to march towards Chattanooga, General Sherman to Memphis. One division will go to Arkansas, and General Rosecrans, you'll hold Corinth."

Grant muttered to Sherman, "I'm being treated like a neutered dog."

"It's better than second in command with nothing to do. Make the most of it."

"What's the objective, General Halleck?" Grant inquired.

"President Lincoln wants us to capture eastern Tennessee and protect the Unionists in that region. For now, we'll pursue Beauregard, hunt him down."

"An admirable goal," Pope commented. "But it's hard to catch a rooster once he's flown the coop."

The "rooster" was indeed hard to catch. Weeks stretched into a month of fruitless chase. Union troops gave up pursuit at Booneville, Mississippi. After returning to Corinth, the 2nd Minnesota marched off with Buell to a camp at Tuscumbia, Alabama. There, they rested.

* * *

THE CONFEDERATES marched directly south of Corinth to Tupelo, where a sickly Beauregard was replaced by Bragg in what would become the re-formed Army of Tennessee and 56,000 men.

In early July, Bragg held his own meeting to announce his next moves, just as Halleck had earlier. They met in the courtroom of the town's courthouse. Bragg stood before the seated officers like a lawyer about to address a jury.

"Men, we've had a temporary setback. It can and will be rectified. This is what we'll do. I'm shifting 35,000 men by rail to Mobile, Alabama, and then on to Chattanooga. It looks like Buell's on the way to Chattanooga as well. We'll link up with General Kirby Smith. Ol' Ted commands the Army of East Tennessee."

Leonidas Polk asked, "What do you intend to do once we join Smith?"

"Cut Buell's lines of communications, defeat him, then beat Grant."

"I you take 35,000 men," Forrest wondered, "what about the rest?"

"Generals Price and Van Dorn will stay back to distract Grant. I want Corinth retaken. Grant's army's been dispersed, so Corinth could be ripe for the taking."

"When do we leave Tupelo?"

"July 11th."

* * *

THE 2ND MINNESOTA had spent several weeks in camp before being ordered to march east. They progressed along the Memphis and Charleston Railroad, repairing it as they marched.

Rincie DeGrave took a mighty swing with a mallet and drove a metal spike through a tie. He paused, wiped sweat from his brow and proclaimed to Charlie Orline, "This here army's makin' us masters of all kinda things. Now we're railroad repairmen."

"I'd rather just be a soldier and fight rebs," Orline grumbled.

"It's all part o' soldierin', Charlie."

"At least we get paid for this work," Orline said, a little brighter.

"Twenty-six dollars for two months' work."

"Can't beat that with a stick, Rincie."

Clint Cilley walked by. DeGrave called out, "Lieutenant, when we gonna catch the other divisions?"

"McCook, Crittenden, and Nelson have a head start after Buell. Two brigades from our own division are a few days ahead of us, but we'll all get together soon."

Clint was accurate in his prediction. On June 27th, the march eastward resumed. Two days later, camp was made in an open field outside of Tuscumbia, Alabama.

After a morning drill, troops assembled around campfires to prepare their noon meal. Aaron Doty took a swig from his canteen and swiped water off his chin. "Ahhh," he proclaimed, "this is the best water I've had since Minnesota."

"And lots of it." Mike Rohan added. "Best stream since we got out here."

"Even got pork in the beans today. It's a real treat," Doty smiled.

As the men slurped beans from tin cups, they heard the drum roll to assemble.

"What's that for?" Rincies asked.

Sergeant Burnell called out as he hurried by. "The governor's here, Governor Ramsey, it's the Fourth of July and he's here to talk to us."

It was a day of patriotism. Generals Steedman and McCook both spoke. Then the Minnesota governor stood before his home state regiment. The portly politician beamed as he began to speak. "I'm proud of you boys, all of Minnesota is! You did great things at Mill Springs, Shiloh, and Corinth!"

Charlie mumbled out of the side of his mouth to Rincie, "Somebody oughta tell him all we did in Shiloh was bury people."

Ramsey continued, "I was proud to be the first in the country to offer troops when President Lincoln asked for them. You're not only the first, you're the best. I've seen many other regiments from other armies, and I want you to know I'm quite satisfied with how you represent our great state!"

Sam Burnell shouted, "Three cheers and a tiger for Governor Ramsey!"

From a thousand throats resounded, "Huzzah! Huzzah! Huzzah! Grrrrr!"

The camp time at Tuscumbia stretched into weeks. The band had been broken up and sent home, but the instruments remained behind and, with some creative bargaining with other regiments, enough men were assembled to become a quite proficient "bugle band."

Clint listened to them perform one night before reveille and remarked, "They've become the envy of the army."

Dan Heaney agreed. "Yes, they are, but it took a couple of weeks to put them together. Couldn't we have been marching after Bragg?"

"Well, Dan, apparently our commanders are on another time schedule than we are, and we don't control it."

On July 26th camp was finally broken and the army crossed the Tennessee River to Florence, Alabama. The next day, Sunday, a good number of the 2nd Minnesota decided to take advantage of civilization and attended a real church after morning inspection.

Many officers decided upon the First Presbyterian Church of Florence. The town itself was small, with just a few hundred inhabitants. Clint Cilley, Dan Heaney, and Judson Bishop walked down a broad street of tree-filled vacant lots interspersed with shops and houses. Enlisted men from various regiments followed the officers down the street.

Near the center of town was a plain red-brick church. A wooden, white-painted steeple rose from the middle of the church front. Dozens of blue-clad soldiers followed the officers as horse-drawn carriages, skillfully driven by black slaves, trotted up to the church gate.

Women in voluminous hoop skirts emerged from the carriages wearing bonnets adorned with wildflowers. Young boys and girls tumbled out of many conveyances and hurried up the stairs to the house of worship.

Well-dressed men, preferring horseback to the overcrowded carriages, dismounted and tied their mounts to hitching posts.

As Clint walked into the sanctuary, he encountered three rows of pews with high backs and high seats upholstered with long, mattress-like cushions. There were long footrests and pew doors that closed once the family was seated.

A gallery ran around three sides of the church. In the gallery facing the pulpit was the organ loft. Black slaves sat in the east side gallery. Young men were on the west side. The galleries were supported by pillars on each side that obstructed entrance to the pews beneath them so that women, in their wide skirts, found it difficult to enter the pews. Therefore, these pews were reserved for bachelors.

As the regular parishioners took their seats, Buell's men interspersed among them where there was room. Most of the local people were women and children, their men off in the Confederate army. About one-third of the nearly full church were regular members. The rest wore blue.

The soldiers heartily joined in on the opening hymn. The Right Reverend Dr. William Mitchell read from scripture to an attentive congregation. The minister was broad shouldered and stocky. His dark hair was combed back and fell to mid-ear. He wore a heavy, dark mustache and chin beard and was dressed in a white collar and black clerical robes.

Dr. Mitchell announced, "Let us pray."

Clint reverently bowed his head with all the others.

Dr. Mitchell said, "Lord, may You grant Your divine blessing upon the president of the Confederate States and upon all the authority under him."

Clint opened his eyes a slit and watched for reactions. Many soldiers' heads had snapped up, staring harshly directed at Mitchell.

"Lord, we ask that You bless our Confederate army and the members of First Presbyterian fighting for our freedom. May those trying to bind us to that government attempting to destroy our way of life be defeated. May confusion and defeat overwhelm our enemies who have invaded our soil and threaten our institutions and liberties. Amen."

"Treason!" The shout echoed from the back, followed by exclamations of "traitor!" and "rebel!" Some indignantly got up and walked out of the church. But most stayed, including Clint, Heaney, and Bishop.

Mitchell climbed a few steps into his raised pulpit and began his sermon. It was presented in a dignified and graceful manner. Clint was impressed with the simple, earnest, on-point words. He was almost willing to forgive the prayer that preceded it.

Then, with a crash, the church doors were flung open and the tramp of marching feet down the center aisle echoed through the sanctuary. Colonel John Harlen of the 10th Kentucky advanced to the pulpit.

"Sir," he said, "you will cease this service at once. Consider yourself under arrest for treasonous remarks and for urging others to commit treason."

Pastor Mitchell closed his sermon book and gracefully stepped down from the pulpit. He bowed his head and replied, "At your service, sir."

As soldiers seized the minister and marched him down the aisle under arrest, shouts and taunts rose from the congregants. "No!" shouted a stout woman who thrust a flowered umbrella at a soldier. Others sobbed and pleaded. "For God's sake, don't shoot him!" a woman cried out.

Some rushed over to Major Bishop. "Please, sir," a woman appealed, "help our pastor, don't let them harm him."

Bishop held down his hands to quiet the crowd. "I'm sure he won't be harmed. Don't worry. I'll try to intercede, but I don't know what will happen."

True to his word, Bishop did intercede on Dr. Mitchell's behalf, but his words of intercession fell on deaf ears. Dr. Mitchell was sent north under arrest.

Fort Ridgely
July 1862

THE PRAIRIES AROUND Fort Ridgely came alive in an explosion of color as wildflowers bloomed. Big blue-stem grasses grew ten feet and resembled a vast ocean as they swayed in the breeze.

But at Fort Ridgely, the same routine continued. The men drilled with cannon and rifle, did stable and latrine duty and occasionally marched out on patrol into the countryside. All seemed peaceful and sanguine on July 4th when a delegation from the Redwood Agency, twelve miles upstream, came to visit.

Among them was Colonel John Galbraith, the federal Indian agent for Redwood and Yellow Medicine agencies. The title, "colonel," was honorary, not military. Captain Marsh greeted the dozen from Redwood and, while the others were shuttled off to watch drills and demonstrations commemorating the holiday, the long, lanky agent met with Marsh in his office. He took a chair across from his desk with an expression of concern.

"Captain," Galbraith began, his Adam's apple bobbing as he spoke, "if the treaty money doesn't get here soon, we'll have problems. There's a shortage of food on the reservation. The Sioux are getting hungry."

"When was it due?"

"When the prairie grass is fit to graze. That means early summer, and we're past that now."

"Mr. Galbraith, as I understand it, once a year this payment is to be made to the Dakota in money, food, and goods. Can't you give the food and goods now and the money later?"

Galbraith sighed and shook his head. "That's just not how things are done. All three must be given together. We have over 7,000 Indians to round up when we do this. I'm not going to do it two or three times.

"Also, the traders are involved. Each of the two agencies has a half dozen or so traders working there. They extend credit to the Indians knowing the government will pay them what's owed.

"If we give them food, the Sioux won't come back when the money's here because they know most, or all, will go to the traders anyway. It just throws off the whole system if we do this piecemeal."

"Where is the food?"

"Our warehouses at Redwood and Yellow Medicine are full of grain. As soon as the annuity payment comes, they'll get it all."

"What do you want from me?"

"Keep order. A show of force should keep 'em quiet."

"I don't like this. Colonel Galbraith, you have the means to keep peace by simply releasing food, but you want me to show a threat of force. You have two reservations along 150 miles of the Minnesota River with Indian villages and two mission enclaves in between. I have about eighty men. We can't cover all of that, and I don't want a war here against Indians."

"Getting the money here would defuse any unrest."

Marsh shook his head. "I don't control that, but I'll ask for men from Fort Ripley."

"I expect you to keep the reds under control."

"There's never been a problem before, Mr. Galbraith. Do your part as well."

On the fort parade ground, Jimmy Dunn and seven others went through their cannon firing drill steps as John Jones called out the commands. The agency visitors and other soldiers shouted huzzahs as a launched cannon ball splintered a distant target.

"Take that, Jeff Davis!" Jimmy yelled.

"Hot shooting for farm boys!" Jones beamed.

As the gun crew shook hands all around, the assemblage broke up to gather for an outdoor feast. Jimmy walked toward the long table holding the bounty of roast pork, fruit, and berries. He encountered Margaret Hern, one of the post laundresses whose husband was off fighting rebels.

She lugged a large basket of freshly washed clothes as she trudged across the fort compound. Jimmy left his friends and approached Margaret.

"Miz Hern, what are you working for today? It's the Fourth of July."

"Laundry don't take days off. If I don't do it today, I got more tomorrow."

"Let me help," Jimmy offered as he hefted the basket and followed her toward a long string of wet clothes hanging from a line in the sun.

"Thank ya, Jimmy. Yer a good boy."

The boy grinned. "I'll bring ya a slice of pork. Take some time off."

The woman smiled. "You know where to find me. Over there by the wash kettles." She pointed to the large black pots of bubbling water.

Jimmy joined his comrades as they filed on both sides of the food table. He looked over at another wood plank table where officers and agency personnel were sitting. "Oscar," he asked Private Wall, "who are they, the one-armed man and the pretty girl?"

"I heard people talking, the man is called Nathan Cates. He's a trader at Redwood. The girl is a teacher at the agency."

Jimmy took two plates and filled them with food. "You must really be hungry," Oscar noted.

"One's for Miz Hern."

The next day the visitors from Redwood boarded a steamboat and journeyed the twelve miles back up the river to the agency. Marsh, true to his word, sent a request for troops to Captain Hall 125 miles to the north, at Fort Ripley. He also sent out a squad of twelve to march on the river flats to provide a "show" for the immigrant settlers.

They marched in squads of two with little Charlie Culver beating out the time on his drum. Jimmy marched alongside Will Sutherland. Sergeant John Bishop kept them on a brisk trek through the green river bottom.

Will remarked to Jimmy, "Sure is purty, ain't it?"

"Sure is. The German folks down here know how to farm and keep up their homesteads. Nice solid log houses, good outbuildings and most of them have only been here a year or two."

As they passed by a farmstead, a pretty young girl waved at them from the yard in front of her house. "*Guten tag!*" she shouted.

"*Guten tag*," Jimmy cried back, "*Auf weidersehn!*"

"I didn't know you knew German," Will commented.

"Just a little, *nicht so gut*. But I worked in a hotel. Germans came through."

"Do you speak Injun, too, just in case we run into any?"

"Nope, I don't speak Sioux. Wish I did, though. They seem pretty friendly."

"They don't seem to cause no trouble. They stop by the cabins ever now 'n' then. But I heard somethin' from the Redwood folks yesterday. The reds are gettin' a little worked up 'cause the treaty payment ain't been made. Part of the pay is food and they're gittin' hungry."

"I thought a lot of them worked as farmers. We got government agents that have been teaching them how, don't we?"

"I heard that one-armed fella talkin'. He said they had a bad crop last year and that some is farmin' but lots of 'em are still tryin' to live like they used to. He says it's the farmer Injuns against the blanket Injuns. Some of the blankets have got somethin' goin' called a Soldier's Lodge. They want the old ways back again. He thinks things might get a bit dicey."

"I wonder if us marching around out here has something to do with that."

"Ya never can tell, Jimmy, ya never can tell."

"I hear the Indians called Sioux and Dakota. What's the difference?"

"None. They're the same thing. I heard that Chippewas called 'em Sioux. It means something like snake. They used to fight each other. They call themselves Dakota. I guess we use both."

Bragg on the Move

AFTER REORGANIZATION, Bragg's army stayed in Tupelo over a month. General Bragg was a stickler for drills and made sure his men stayed occupied, but time still weighed down on the private soldiers.

Sam Davis and his comrades sat around a campfire eating sloosh on a hot July late afternoon. "I thought we'd be outta here by now," Joe Cates proclaimed between munches.

"Soon," Corporal Beesley said, "sometime in the next coupla days I think."

A rattling of distant gunfire drew their attention. "Another poor soul meets up with Gen'rl Bragg," Bill Searcey observed, "that's the third one today."

"No slackers, no deserters," Cates added, "Bragg's justice is swift."

"Didja see that boy yesterday?" Cates recalled, "not mor'n sixteen. Face still smooth as a baby's butt. Slackin' off on his detail, they said. Bragg had 'im hung up between two trees and whipped thirty-nine times."

Sam bit off a piece of sloosh. "I think some of the boys fight more out of fear of General Bragg than love of country."

"Some?" Cates rejoined, "how 'bout most? At least Yankees don't make us all watch every time somebody gets shot or whipped."

"It's pretty much all we'd do," Searcy said, "with little time left over to fight."

"Well, I'm sure ready to move," Sam said. "I'd like to get back to middle Tennessee."

Cates snorted. "Ya got any partic'lar reason for that, like maybe some girl in middle Tennessee?"

Sam blushed as the others snickered and laughed.

The next day, July 11th Bragg ordered his Army of Mississippi to move out. They herded into railroad cars and rode the rails to Mobile, Alabama, then to Montgomery, to Atlanta, and finally to Chattanooga.

* * *

THE 2ND MINNESOTA and the Army of Ohio continued a slow, somewhat leisurely progression through Alabama and Georgia, hindered by rear-action attacks by Forrest's cavalry. But Buell seemed to be in no great hurry to reach Chattanooga.

On August 3rd they reached Athens, Tennessee. Dan Heaney had been promoted to a staff officer, and on July 10th Clint Cilley had been named captain of Company C, in Bishop's 2nd Regiment of the 2nd Minnesota in Robert McCook's 3rd Brigade.

Athens was a desolate, ruined little town, the last city in Tennessee to lower its Union flag. But in May Turchin's brigade of federal soldiers had mercilessly plundered the place. Its citizens met the approaching Union army with sullen silence behind closed doors.

Dan Bailey, Captain Cilley's new lieutenant, spoke under his breath to Clint. "It's too quiet, I don't like this."

Clint warily eyed faces peering from behind shutters and curtains. "They can't be blamed, Lieutenant. Turchin's men pulled this place apart."

"Buell is so strict. How'd he let it happen?"

"It wasn't Buell. He tried to have Turchin disciplined. Our general was infuriated. But all they did was court martial Turchin. Buell wanted him kicked out of the army. He got promoted in the end."

"Captain, have you heard how General McCook is doing?"

"He's been sick since Tuscumbia. He rides in an ambulance carriage up front, about a half mile ahead of us and the dust. I hear he hasn't been able to dress or sit up."

"With Forrest's raiders out there, I hope he's got a good escort."

Two days later Bob McCook continued his ambulance ride a good half mile ahead of the army. The dust created by thousands of marching feet made an already sick man feel worse, so getting ahead of it was a blessing.

Attending McCook were two staff officers and a driver. Captains Miller and Brooke rode on their horses in front. McCook lay on a makeshift bed inside the carriage.

The road became more and more narrow and twisting as they traveled. Smith noted to Brooke, "The brush and trees are getting thicker on both sides. It'll be tough to turn around if we have to."

"It can be still be done," Brooke answered, "but not so quickly. Let's hope we don't have to."

"Forrest is out here somewhere. Fresh from Murfreesboro."

"He captured a whole brigade. I heard he got half of 'em and then said he didn't come to do half a job and took the whole bunch."

Smith added, "The Minnesota boys talked about a regiment, their 3rd. Seems their officers surrendered them to Forrest at Murfreesboro without a fight."

"So," Brooked concluded, "they're out of the war until an exchange is made."

"They'll likely send 'em back to Minnesota for a while. I hear they're mad as hornets. Say, what's that up ahead?"

Brooke peered intently, then his face registered alarm. "Rebs!"

Smith shouted at the driver, "Turn around, now! Reb cavalry coming!"

McCook's pale face appeared from the carriage. "How many?"

"Too many for us, general. We've gotta run!"

The driver strained at the reins, jerking the team of horses around. The two Union officers fired shots to hold the ambushers at bay. But that bought only about thirty seconds. The ambulance finally made a cumbersome about-face and, with the driver frantically whipping his horses, they began a mad run back to the federal forces down the road.

The Confederate cavalry thundered alongside the carriage, yelling and firing revolvers, splintering the wooden side walls of the ambulance.

McCook shouted from a carriage window, "Driver, stop and pull over! We can't outrun them!"

The driver futilely strained to pull the reins back with all his strength. Still the horses forced their way ahead. More shots were fired into the ambulance. The terrified horses lurched off the road into an overgrown thicket, where the thick brush caught the carriage and pulled it to a stop.

A Confederate lieutenant pulled his horse up before the driver and looked into the ambulance. "Don't bother none with that one," he told a sergeant, "ya got the other two."

"Yes, sir, we caught 'em both a ways back. Union patrol is up ahead."

"Then let's go." The officer touched the brim of his hat, nodded at the driver and rode off with his men.

Minutes later the head of the Union column arrived. General McCook had been grievously wounded and was taken to the nearest house alongside the road. The brigade camped around the house, but pursuit of the Confederates was hopeless without a Union cavalry nearby.

The next day the general died in the farmhouse. Enraged members of the Ninth Ohio, McCook's regiment, burned every nearby building in revenge. Colonel Van Derveer replaced General McCook as brigade commander.

On August 7th the Army of the Ohio reached Winchester, Tennessee. They encamped for twelve days, while, Bragg's forces arrived in Chattanooga.

Fort Ridgely
August 18, 1862

THE EARLY MORNING SUN splashed over the green parade ground of Fort Ridgely, greeting everyone with a sparkling freshness. A Monday, Company B had enjoyed the previous day of rest.

They stretched and yawned as Charlie Culver blew reveille, then rose to meet the dawn, refreshed. After assembly and early drill, they welcomed breakfast—hot coffee, bacon, and bread freshly baked by the fort cooks.

Will Sturgis, Jimmy Dunn, and Andy Williamson sat in the stone commissary building, savoring their meal. "A fine way to start the day," Will grinned.

"Sure is," Jimmy grinned. "I think we're gettin' closer to goin' east. They let Norm Culver go with the Renville Rangers, fifty lucky boys gettin' to go south."

"And Sheehan went back to Ripley with his men," Andy asserted. He continued hopefully, "Sure looked like trouble at Yellow Medicine, but Sheehan got it sorted and calmed down. Now it's more peaceful than ever here. We'll get sent to fight rebels soon, I'm sure of it."

"That coulda been bad at Yellow Medicine," Jimmy said, "with 5,000 Indians demandin' food. When he said no, they attacked the warehouses. Sheehan pointed cannons at 'em, told 'em to hold on and got Galbraith."

"We was standin' in a line, a hundred holdin' back thousands. If Sheehan hadn't got Galbraith to give 'em food, I don't know what woulda happened."

"Galbraith told 'em he'd release food at Redwood. They came but he'd changed his mind," Andy added. "The traders got scared they wouldn't get paid."

Will shook his head. "Things got ugly. A trader yelled, 'If yer so hungry, go eat grass or yer own dung.'"

"At least the agent allowed them to leave the reservation to hunt," Andy said. "When the government money gets here things'll calm down and we can leave."

"Marsh must think things are settled down," Jimmy noted, "or he woulda kept the Rangers and not sent Sheehan back to Ripley. A hunnerd men here yesterday and are now gone, 'cause we don't need 'em."

"Ya know what?" Bill Perrington observed with a mouthful of crisp bacon. "When stuff was goin' on with the Sioux at Yellow Medicine, it was kinda excitin'. I hate to say it, but sometimes I think havin' a little action around here with Indians'd be better than sittin' around doin' nothin'."

"You want an Indian war!" Jesse retorted. "Yer crazy!"

"Oh, not a *big* one," Bill chuckled. "Jus' somethin' little ta pass the time."

Will Sutherland burst into the commissary. "The money's here! A wagon just rolled in with the Indian annuity payment. Seventy thousand in gold!"

"Don't that beat all?" Will Sturgis clapped his hands. "Now everybody'll be happy and we'll be outta here. There goes your Indian war, Bill."

"It's a great day, boys!" Jimmy agreed.

Company B went about morning drills with new vigor. Even latrine detail seemed less laborious. A change was coming, they could sense it. Soon they'd be joining the rest of their regiment in the south.

Lieutenant Tom Gere joined John Marsh in headquarters where a trunk rested in the corner. "It's really here!" Gere exclaimed. "I just hafta see it!"

Marsh walked to the trunk and flung it open. Glistening gold coins flashed in the sunlight beaming through a window.

"Captain, will we be leaving here soon, to fight rebs?"

"I haven't received any such orders, lieutenant, but I'd guess this improves our chances." He paused and sat at his desk. "You know, Tom, war isn't the glorious thing it's made up to be. I was at Bull Run with the Wisconsin boys. It was ugly and dirty. Men died, and they didn't just lie down pretty, like for an undertaker. Bodies were ripped apart, brains splashed into us. Glory don't last long. Sometimes what you wish for isn't what you get."

Tom straightened. "I want to fight to save the Union, sir."

"I know you do. It's a noble ambition. But nobility is fleeting."

The loud clatter of a wagon pulled by the thundering of a team of horses galloping into the fort alerted Marsh. He sprang to his doorway. An open wagon, filled with women and children and driven by a sinewy, middle-aged man, jerked to a halt in front of Marsh, standing with Gere on the porch.

The man leaped from the wagon box and scrambled onto the porch. "There's been murder at Redwood. The Sioux . . . they's killin' everybody!"

Marsh paled. "How can you be sure? Who are you?"

"I'm Dickenson, I'm sure. I was there, at the agency. They started the killin' 'bout seven this mornin'. Men, women, children, they didn't care. They jest killed 'em. Folks ran. The reds ran 'em down on the prairie and killed 'em , too. Then they started on the homesteads. I saw them dead on the way here."

Jimmy Dunn listened nearby, his face revealing dread and excitement.

Marsh turned to him. "Private, tend to these folks. Give them sanctuary. Lieutenant Gere, join me in my office."

Marsh returned to his desk and pulled a pocket watch from his pants. "Ten o'clock," he noted. Then he scribbled a message and handed it to Gere.

"This is an order bringing Sheehan back here. Send someone on a good horse to get this to him. He can't be too far yet. I've gotta go down to Redwood to find out how bad this is. I'm hopeful Dickenson exaggerated, but we have to be sure. If he's right, we have to settle this down."

"How many will we be taking with us?" Gere asked.

"Not 'we.' I'll take a couple platoons, about forty-five men. You stay here."

"Sir, I want to go with you."

"You're the only officer here besides me. Sheehan and Culver are gone. I'm experienced in combat. I must go. You have to stay. Assemble the garrison, I want to speak to them." Marsh hesitated. "Tom, how old are you?"

"Nineteen, my birthday's next month."

"I want to see you make twenty. Now get to work."

"Yes, sir!" Gere saluted and walked into the bright sunshine. Men were already gathering around headquarters, curious about the news that flashed like lightning across the post. Others, on foot, horseback and in wagons, were streaming into the fort. Gere glanced at the note as he stood on the porch.

Marsh had written, 'Lieutenant Sheehan, It is absolutely necessary you return with your command immediately. The Indians are raising hell at the Lower Agency. Return as soon as possible."

Gere called to Jim Meade, "Corporal, find the best horse you can and find Lieutenant Sheehan and Company C. Give 'em this. Get th'em back here."

Then Gere turned to Charlie Culver. "Sound the long roll for assembly."

Within minutes all eighty-six soldiers of Company B were assembled on the parade ground near the flagpole in the center of the compound. Marsh, a grim expression chiseled into his face, stood before his command. "Men, there's been an uprising at the Lower Sioux Agency. Reports say there have been murders and other outrages. We must go there. Many times in the past the Dakota have been cowed by a show of force. They backed off a couple weeks ago at Yellow Medicine when cannons were trained on the warehouse. I fully expect they'll back down and stop their depredations if we stand firm.

"I ask for volunteers. Could be perilous duty. Who among will come with me to Redwood?" The entire company stepped forward. "Thank you," Marsh acknowledged. "I wish all of you could go. But some must stay. Lieutenant Gere, count me off forty-six, including Peter Quinn. We'll need an interpreter.

"In one-half hour we'll be on the march!" he shouted to his men. Turning to Gere: "See they're issued a day's rations and forty rounds of ammunition."

Peter Quinn sadly prepared to leave for the Redwood Agency. A premonition of disaster hung over him like a black cloud. He trudged to the sutler's cabin. Ben Randal had just returned from a buggy ride with his family, a ride cut short by the urgent flight of refugees to the fort.

Randal was concerned about his friend's sadness. "Peter, I'm sure all will be good. The captain fixed things out at Yellow Medicine. He'll do it again."

Quinn brushed back his white hair and forced a smile. "Maybe you're right. But, Ben, I just don't feel right about this. I came to say goodbye."

Randal stuck out his hand, "Then, goodbye to you, Peter, but you'll be back by nightfall, I wager."

The interpreter looked with remorse at a passing wagon of bedraggled and frightened passengers, one with blood stains soaking through his shoulder. He looked back at Ben. "Goodbye, tell my friends—"

"Tell 'em what you want when you get back."

The twenty-nine remaining men of Company B stood at attention and saluted as Captain Marsh mounted his mule. He looked down at Gere. "I'm confident we'll calm things down. Once the teams are ready and the wagons loaded, send them after us. We'll begin the march now."

"Good luck, Captain."

Marsh nodded, snapped a salute. "Forward!" With Quinn astride a mule beside him, Marsh led the forty-six onto the road to the agency. Charley Culver and Oscar Wall stood in the ranks of those left behind. The drummer boy beat out a cadence that hung in the air behind the departing soldiers.

The company trod in a column of twos with Jimmy Dunn marching next to Will Sutherland. Once away from the fort, they encountered more groups of refugees hurrying past them in search of sanctuary at Ridgely.

"They're like scared rabbits. See their faces, I never seen folks so afraid."

Sutherland agreed. "I wonder what we're gettin' ourselves into."

"The captain, he's fought before, he knows what to do."

"Go back!" a man shouted from a passing wagon. "Yer fools if ya think ya can do anything with that puny bunch!"

"Eyes front!" Marsh commanded.

The column continued on high ground above the river valley flats. After about three miles, two wagons overtook the marchers, and they all crowded aboard. The four-mule teams pulling each wagon quickened their pace.

Will squirmed in the tight, crowded wagon. "Well, Jimmy, we can't hardly move, but at least we'll get there quicker."

Jimmy looked at the August sun burning down like a hot coal. He wiped sweat from his forehead. "I'd rather walk and not bake with a bunch of sweaty men. I feel like a lump of beef in a bubbling pot of stew."

Ole Svendson, newly arrived from Norway, looked down at the river. "Vhy don't ve cross da river now? Vhy do we hafta vait to cross?"

"River's too high here," Sergeant John Bishop responded, "and too swift. The only safe place to cross is at Redwood."

The two wagons rolled along, Marsh and Quinn riding alongside. Refugees bound for Fort Ridgely increased. Panic and hysteria were painted across the faces of nearly everyone. Many called on Marsh to turn back. He nodded politely, thanked them for their concern and continued on.

John Whipple of Faribault, at the Redwood Agency on business, had fled early in the attack. He galloped up to Marsh and reined in his lathered horse. "Captain, turn back, get some artillery. There's too many of them!"

"Thank you, Mr. Whipple, but we'll proceed."

"Captain, don't be a fool. The Sioux know you're coming. They'll be ready. Their blood's hot."

"How did this all start, what do you know?"

"What I've heard, a small party of Sioux were coming back from a hunt northwest, up at Acton. I don't know particulars, but some bad blood got stirred up, and the Indians killed five white people, two of them women. Looks like the Sioux saw no turning back and attacked the agency this morning. Killed the traders first. If the annuity'd come, maybe this wouldn't have happened."

"It came this morning," Marsh replied.

Whipple blanched. "Too late. Go back, captain, I'm warning you. Go back!"

"Look at those people." Marsh gestured to those hurrying by. "See the panic in their eyes? They depend on us to protect them. If we turn yellow and run back to the fort, we'll be the same as them. They'd be protected by cowards. No soldier worth his salt would turn back and leave defenseless women and children between the Indians and ourselves. If I order a retreat without even fighting, I'd be dishonored and deserve to be shot. We'll continue on and end this madness."

Jimmy had listened intently to the conversation. He leaned to Will and whispered, "The captain's a brave man. I'd follow him to Hell."

"Let's hope you don't get the chance."

Nearby, Whipple shook his head sadly at the troops' plight, applied a whip to his horse and galloped off.

About six miles out, halfway to Redwood, the column began to spot mutilated bodies along the way. They found a family of four dead, their hacked-up bodies smoldering in the ruins of a burned-out cabin.

Marsh turned to his men. "Out of the wagons, form into columns of two again. We'll march in from here."

The men marched on in silence, sickened by what they had seen. "Two was just kids," Sutherland bemoaned.

"Look! Over there!" Jimmy pointed across the river. In the distance, several Indian horsemen ran down two fleeing men who couldn't outrace horses.

Several stopped in rank and leveled their rifles to shoot.

Marsh commanded them, "Shoulder arms! There'll be no shooting. You can't hit them at that distance, anyway. March on."

Three more miles brought the troopers to the top of a long slope that descended into the valley. The sun blazed above them as Marsh, on mule back, surveyed the scene below Faribault Hill. The floor of the river valley was covered by tall prairie grass. Up the Minnesota River on the far side of the river, pillars of heavy smoke rose like fingers reaching into the sky.

"It's the agency, they've burned it," Marsh announced. "Three miles to the ferry. We cross there."

"Captain," Peter Quinn sidled his mule next to Marsh, "we've reached the point of no return. I urge you to turn around, don't go down there."

"Mr. Quinn, we saw all those lying dead on the prairie. Those running for their lives to the fort, those still in their cabins with no idea what's happening, deserve a chance. We are their chance."

With that, Marsh drew his sword from its scabbard and shouted, "All but cowards will follow me!"

Redwood Ferry

ORTY-SIX MEN DESCENDED the slope toward the valley with their captain. At the bottom of the hill was a farmstead owned by a trader and farmer, David Faribault. Twenty-five people, mostly women and children, burst from the cabin where they had sought refuge.

David's wife, Nancy Faribault, mixed-blood daughter of a Fort Snelling officer, reached Marsh first. Breathlessly, she said, "I heard gunfire this morning. A man on horseback shouted, 'Run away. Indians are killing everybody at the agency!' We headed for the fort. Dakota overtaken us. They left us alone because I'm mixed blood. But they slaughtered two wagonloads of others with us."

Marsh saw the horror-stricken group behind Nancy. "What about them?"

"They fled the agency. We gave them refuge, but the Dakota will find them."

"Ma'am," Marsh advised, "soon the Sioux will be occupied with my men. Get going for the fort." He looked back at his hot, sweaty men. "With your permission, we'd like to draw water from your well before we move on."

Nancy said, "Sure, but you're crazy to go to the agency! They'll kill you all."

"Thank you, ma'am. We appreciate the concern. But we have a job to do."

As Company B's men filed by the well, bayonets glistening in the sun, the Fairbaults and refugees began to scurry down the road to the fort.

Marsh addressed his men. "The ferry's close. From here on, tall grass borders the trail. Be vigilant."

"Captain Marsh," John Bishop cautioned, "shouldn't we deploy flankers?"

Marsh considered sending men to the sides. "No, we'll stay together."

The company had filed about halfway down the river bottom when Marsh halted them. "Proceed single file. Spread out." He turned to Bishop. "It'll be harder to hit us if we're not in ranks."

Jimmy moved on, then stumbled and fell. He scrambled to his feet and looked back. "My God!" he cried in horror, "I tripped on a man! He's slit from his belly to his chest, dressed-out like a deer!"

Sam Stewart called, "There's two more bodies in the grass over here."

In all they found ten dead in the grass either side of the road. Just after noon the soldiers halted at Redwood Ferry. The body of ferryman Charlie Martel, lay disemboweled near his ferry boat.

Marsh took a measure of his surroundings. Tall grass mixed with hazel and willow tree thickets on shore, with sandbars left after the river's flood. Down-river, thickets were larger along the river. The pulley system that transported the boat to the agency side looked intact except where loosened from a post.

Across the river, the agency stood on a high bluff. A trail twisted through thick underbrush and young trees up the face of the bluff to the agency.

Marsh asked Quinn, "How far down do you suppose that thicket goes?"

"About two miles, captain."

"It looks to vary in width. Twenty feet here, a couple hundred feet there."

"Look, captain!" Bishop pointed across the river. An Indian wearing a feathered headdress and dressed in buckskin stood on a half-submerged tree trunk.

"It's White Dog," Quinn identified, "a cut-hair agency employee, Galbraith fired him when he took over."

Marsh and Quinn dismounted. Quinn called out to White Dog in Dakota. The Indian replied. Quinn translated the message for Marsh, "He says to come across. Everything's just fine. It was bad Indians, maybe Chippewa, who did this. He says they don't want to fight and there'll be no trouble. He wants us to come over to the agency for a council."

"Do you believe him?" Marsh wondered.

"Something ain't right. He's Upper Sioux from Yellow Medicine. I don't really know him. He don't belong here."

Bishop said, "I saw 'im last summer at Upper Sioux with Standing Buffalo."

The captain told Quinn, "Ask him why he's at Redwood."

Quinn asked. White Dog answered, "He says he's visiting. Again he urges we go over. He says Dakota are up at the agency and want to council."

"Quinn, ask what happened."

The interpreter asked, then listened to the reply. "He says they had some trouble with the traders but you can fix it with the Indians and that everything will be all right."

Marsh turned his back to White Dog and ordered his men, "Prepare to cross on the ferry. Sergeant Findley, secure the ferry, make sure the pulley works and move the men to the riverbank in ranks."

Bishop had gone to the riverbank to fill his canteen. Shortly after Marsh issued his order, the sergeant rushed up to him. "As I bent down to get water, I noticed the water was dirty, roiled up. Twigs and leaves floated down in it. Something stirred up the water upriver. I think they're crossing over, they wanna surround us. I'm sure I saw Indians in the brush on the other side."

Bishop climbed atop a sandpile for a better view. He shouted to Marsh, "There's a ravine over there, ponies in the brush. Must be Indians in there, too."

"Quinn," Marsh snapped, "ask why ponies are over there."

White Dog suddenly leveled his rifle. Quinn yelled, "Look out!" The Indian's shot was followed by a volley. The underbrush came alive as rifles blasted and Indians screamed. Quinn tumbled to the ground riddled by bullets.

Will Sutherland fell face down into the river. A bullet passed through Will Blodgett's lung and out his shoulder. But most of the volley had gone high, and Marsh ordered his command back to the ferry house.

Suddenly, from the tall grass behind them, another volley erupted. Dakota screamed war cries. Soldiers fell in their ranks. Dakota warriors poured from the grass and closed off the road leading back to the fort.

Marsh coolly called out, "Steady, men, get to the top of the riverbank."

Bullets whistled through the air all around the soldiers. As the Dakota rushed the riverbank, Marsh ordered a volley. Jimmy Dunn stood shoulder to shoulder with his friends. Their muskets mowed down onrushing Indians.

The Dakota kept coming, not giving the soldiers the needed twenty seconds to reload. The painted warriors, naked except for breechcloths, charged headlong into them, and a desperate hand-to-hand struggle ensued.

Jimmy swung his rifle butt and lunged ahead with bayonet slashing. The soldiers' fight was desperate, their lives held in the balance. It became a frantic struggle with every man for himself. Four men, led by John Bishop, made a break for the ferry house, cutting their way through anyone in their way.

Only Bishop reached the house. He found it and the barn across the road filled with Dakota warriors firing at him. He sprinted down the road between the two buildings as bullets whizzed around him. A ball smashed into the butt of his musket; another sliced across his leg. Bishop kept running.

Meanwhile, Marsh and most of the company made their stand on high ground by the riverbank. They fought desperately, trying to hold on as dead Dakota piled up around them. One by one, the little band of soldiers was being cut off from the command and killed.

Marsh recognized that a fight in the open would result in the total annihilation of his command. He ordered his remaining men to move southeast.

"There!" he shouted, pointing, "that little woods along the river, no Indians are there yet. Follow me!"

Marsh and his men battled inch by inch to the trees and thicket. The captain and thirteen of his men found refuge in a cover of willow and hazel. The Dakota riddled the thicket like a hailstorm with buckshot and ball.

But at least with some cover, the bluecoats could load and return fire.

John Bishop had made it to the road just beyond the ferry house. He stopped abruptly as he encountered a Dakota brave in the road just ahead. The Indian raised a shotgun and quickly blasted both barrels.

Sand kicked up at Bishop's feet. "Missed!" he exclaimed. He snapped his musket up and pulled the trigger. An empty click greeted him.

In the frenetic race to reload, Bishop lost. The Dakota had slipped a shot into his breech loader and was aiming while Bishop was still ramming shot down his barrel. John felt something under his left armpit raise his arm. He looked down to see a rifle barrel protruding from under his arm. The rifle spit lead. Flame and smoke burst from the barrel. The Indian warrior screamed, flung up his arms and tumbled back, dead. Bishop turned to see Jimmy Dunn.

"Is your gun loaded?" Jimmy asked.

"It will be soon as I cap it. Why aren't you with Marsh?"

"Got cut off. The road's clear, let's move. You lead. My gun's empty."

The two sprinted down the road only a few hundred feet before a band of Dakota rose up and blocked the road again. Five Indians emerged from the grass and headed toward the soldiers. Bishop gestured at the high grass to the south, and the he and Jimmy ducked into it.

The warriors, eager for the chase, pressed Bishop and Dunn from the south and west as they crawled and ran over the grassy river bottom. Then the two circled back to the thicket just south and east of the ferry.

They moved toward the heavy gunfire and found Marsh clinging to his position with his shrinking band of survivors. As the Dakota closed in, Bishop and Dunn joined the fight. No other soldier would make it to the thicket.

The handful of soldiers, cut off from all others, fought on. Blodgett and Sutherland, thought to be dead, were still alive but grievously wounded. They managed to crawl off into the brush. Others made their own stands. Some escaped. Most were cut down.

Marsh turned to Bishop. "We're holding them off, but it's only a matter of time. We're running low on shot. We've got to go to the fort under cover."

"Captain," Bishop said, "we'll have cover for only two miles. What then?"

"We'll figure that out later. Move the men back. Keep 'em firing."

In the trees beside the river, Marsh and his men were in a running battle with the Dakota. The maelstrom of lead fired by the Indians clipped leaves and sent them drifting to the ground as if it were a fall day.

Soldiers fired back, moved south with grass and trees for cover, then shot again. Ole Svendson took a ball in the shoulder and thudded to the earth.

Jimmy shouted, "Ole's down. He needs help!" Three others joined Jimmy and helped carry Ole.

Marsh's voice rose above the staccato gunfire. "We're keepin' 'em back! Every step we're closer to the fort. Make every shot count. We're getting low!"

By four o' clock the fraught band of soldiers had struggled down the riverbank to the end of the protective thicket. From the trees on the edge of the thicket, Marsh and his men stared out on open ground.

"Decision time," Marsh announced. "How many are left?"

Bishop answered, "Fifteen, some wounded, though."

"Findley? Trescott?"

"Dead. I'm your only sergeant. Corporal Besse's dead, too."

"We have ten miles of open prairie to Ridgely. See the Dakota moving down the fort road? They'll cut us off if we keep going. Can we make a stand here?"

"Captain, I checked. We got about four cartridges per man. We won't last long."

"Dark is still five hours away. We can't use the night to escape, either."

"We're in kind of a jam, aren't we, sir?"

"Well, it'd be suicidal to fight them out in the open. Here, with no food, little ammunition, our backs to the river and the Dakota closing in on three sides . . . well, that's not much of an option, either."

"What should we do, captain?"

Marsh's weathered face creased as he pondered his options. He watched intently as the Indians rode on the trail north of the Minnesota River. "We cross the river. There aren't any Indians over there. At least none I can see."

"What does that gain us?" Bishop countered, "They'll just cross and cut us down over there."

"It's a desperate gamble. But just maybe, if we get across first we can pick them off like sitting ducks when they try to come over. I don't think we have any other choice."

"I can't swim!" Levi Carr announced. "This is crazy!"

"I'll stay with ya, Levi," Jimmy assured his friend.

"Look," Marsh continued, "I'll go first and find the best way to cross. It might not even be over your head, Private Carr."

"It's fifty yards across. There's a current," Bishop advised. "Be careful, sir."

Marsh waded into the river. His sword and pistol above his head, he crossed. The river slowly rose up his body. Finally, too deep to wade, he discarded his weapons and swam. Whether he cramped up or the weight of his soaked uniform and boots dragged him down is unknown. But Marsh began to struggle in the swift current. "Boys, I need help!" he shouted.

Jimmy, Brennan, and Van Buren swam out toward Marsh, who slipped beneath the surface. Brennan dove, resurfacing holding Marsh by the wrist. But the strong, swift current pried Marsh out of Brennan's grasp and swept him downriver. The current tugged him under again. He never came up.

The three would-be rescuers were stunned as they returned to the others.

"I had him," Private Brennan sobbed, "I'll never forget the look on his face. I just couldn't hold on. Hard as I tried, I just couldn't."

The grief-stricken soldiers returned to the north side of the river under a bank back in the thicket. John Bishop was the highest-ranking man left.

Jimmy Dunn, rivulets of water still running off his drenched uniform, put his hand on Brennan's shoulder. "You did your best you. Don't be hard on yerself. You tried. We all did."

Will Hutchinson looked to Bishop, who hobbled toward them on his wounded leg. "Sergeant, what now?" he asked.

"Don't know. I guess we have the same options Captain Marsh outlined."

"Except the option of crossing the river is gone," Jimmy proclaimed.

"Then what do we do?" Levi Carr cried.

Bishop shrugged and scrutinized the land before them.

"Why has it got so quiet all of a sudden?" Jimmy wondered.

Van Buren peered cautiously out of the thicket. "Where are the Indians? I don't see them anywhere this side of the river."

"My God!" Bishop cried. "Our prayers are answered! Look, the Indians found a ford. They must've thought we crossed and decided to follow us."

"But we're still here," Brennan marveled.

Bishop's eyes regained a gleam. "This is our chance. While they try to ambush us on the south side, we'll move out on the north. The sun is starting to set. There's a high bank just to our left on the prairie. We need to move out and get behind that bank. It'll screen us from the Indians and, God save us, we'll make it to the fort. Some of you carry Ole. Let's go."

Jimmy turned to Will Hutchinson as they crept through the prairie grass toward the base of the hill. "Out of the jaws of death we go, Will."

Fifteen hopeful men trudged along the bank, then proceeded along the river until dark. Then they climbed the bluff to the north and reached the fort road. Progress was slow, made slower by needing to carry Svendson.

Jimmy was helping with the wounded man, and Ole's blood had soaked the boy's shirt. Bishop called a halt, asking for Jimmy and Will Hutchinson. "We're about five miles out. I want you to go on ahead and make sure the fort's still in our hands. I didn't hear cannon fire today, so I believe we hold it, but I can't be sure. Tell Lieutenant Gere what happened and that we'll be coming in."

Jimmy stood ramrod stiff and snapped his best salute. "Yes, sir!"

Dunn and Hutchinson disappeared like mist into the darkness.

* * *

Tom Gere had spent a day filled with apprehension but had not let that deter him from his duty. He had to strengthen the defenses of the fort.

He knew that Sheehan must be at least thirty miles away and would not arrive until the next day at best. Until then, under his command, he had twenty-two men fit for duty. Without help, the Dakota would overwhelm them.

Scores of civilians still streamed into the fort. They'd have to be used in the defense. Ben Randal, post sutler, was a veteran of Ridgely. He'd come in 1853 and helped build the fort. Gere put him in charge of organizing the civilians.

Randal reported to Gere, "We've got hundreds of folks camped in here. I've put the women and children in the long barracks. There are dozens of men. Problem is, they're farmers. They don't have guns. We have only ten more rifles. We did an inventory of the arsenal and found twenty old dragoon carbines. Whipple calls them condemned muskets. They're hardly worth wasting powder on. But a man named Heffron used to be here in the regular army. He's fixed 'em up so they're useable. The blacksmith's cutting iron rods into slugs. We'll get them into the hands of folks who can shoot but we're still short of guns.

"Being as we have no well, I've had up every tank, tub, and pail brought down to the spring and filled. If they attack us we'll be cut off from the water.

"Whipple was an artillery man in the Mexican War. He's volunteered his services to Sergeant Jones."

"Thank you, Mr. Randal. I've had barricades made between buildings and posted sentinels around the fort. I pray Marsh gets back soon and Sheehan and Galbraith reinforce us. One thing, why did they build a fort on a plateau with ravines on three sides? Do you realize how difficult it'll be to see the Indians if they attack? They'll be on top of us before we know it."

"Captain Pemberton wanted a garrison always alert, on the offensive."

"Pemberton, isn't he a Confederate general at Vicksburg?

"The same. Yep, he's a northern man fighting for the Confederacy."

"I wish he were here trying to defend the fort. I'd wish him luck."

"Lieutenant, I wish to God Marsh would get back."

"Mr. Randal, I do, too."

Later, two forms emerged from the darkness of the agency road. At a picket's challenge, a voice said, "Dunn and Hutchinson from Marsh's command."

Gere met them at the headquarters building. The young lieutenant was shocked. Both men were disheveled, their uniforms ripped and bloody. Jimmy's blue blouse was caked with blood.

"What in all creation has happened?" Gere demanded.

Jimmy spoke, his voice choked with emotion. "The reds. They hit us at the ferry. Fifteen is all of us that's left. The captain's dead, lieutenant."

"No! Are you sure?"

Jimmy nodded. "Pulled under. He drowned leading us across the river."

"Where are the other thirteen?"

"Down the road a little, not far. Sergeant Bishop has them. Finley and Trescott are dead, too."

Gere turned to a picket. "Send some men out. Bring in Bishop. Send me Corporal Sturgis." He looked back at Dunn and Hutchinson. "Dr. Mueller's moved into the building behind us. Go see him now."

In the headquarters building, Gere scrawled a message at Marsh's desk. A rap sounded at the door and Willie Sturgis entered.

"You wanted to see me."

He handed the corporal the note. "Marsh and half his command have been killed. Get the best horse in the fort and take this message to Governor Ramsey in St. Paul. We need help. Stop in St. Peter. Galbraith and the Renville Rangers are likely there. Tell them what has happened and that we need them back here immediately."

"I'll ride like Hell, sir!"

"May God be with you."

Bragg in Chattanooga
AUGUST 1862

BRAXTON BRAGG'S ARMY of Mississippi encamped just outside Chattanooga, but the commander proceeded immediately to a hotel in the city. It was July 31st and a courier had brought a message from General Edmund Kirby Smith asking for an immediate conference. Smith was commander of the Army of East Tennessee.

Bragg, with three staff officers, entered the hotel and found Smith sitting alone at a table in the dining room. General Smith stood up and saluted. He was of medium height and build, had a receding hairline, a dark chin beard that stretched in a line over his cheeks on both sides, and a bushy mustache. He was thirty-eight years old.

"General Bragg, welcome to Chattanooga," Smith proclaimed.

All four took seats around the table as Bragg responded, "Well, at least I beat Buell here. This was his goal as well. When he comes, we'll have the good ground here."

Smith got right to the point. "General, I don't think you should fight him here. I just received a report from John Hunt Morgan, who returned from spending most of July riding through Kentucky. His cavalry was raising hell in Buell's rear as well. They captured 1,200 federal soldiers. He paroled 'em all, but kept hundreds of their horses and destroyed massive quantities of their supplies."

Smith paused. "General Bragg, that's not what I want to talk to you about."

A bit taken aback, Bragg said, "Then what do you want to talk about?"

"The opportunity that awaits you in Kentucky. I believe tens of thousands would rally to our cause if given the opportunity. If you arrive with a show of force, they'd flock to us and bring Kentucky into the Confederacy."

"What about Buell?"

"Apparently he's been delayed by supply difficulties helped along by Forrest's harassment. His army is moving slowly. It's like Lincoln said about McClellan,

146

'He's got the slows.'" Smith chuckled, then continued. "Lincoln won't let Buell sit in Chattanooga with you having free rein in Kentucky. You'd be a threat to Ohio and points east. Buell will have to come after you and, with your present army and the new recruits you'll surely garner, we'll whip those Yankees."

"What do you propose?"

"My Army of East Tennessee will march into Kentucky to dispose of the Union defenders of Cumberland Gap. Then we'll join you. Together we can maneuver into Buell's rear. He'll be forced to give us battle to protect his supply lines. Once Buell's beaten, we move farther up north, where the local populace will be overjoyed."

"You're right to go first. My army's exhausted and must rest."

"We'll fight a grand battle in Kentucky. We can establish a Confederate frontier at the Ohio River."

"General Smith," Bragg said, looking directly across the table at him, "you've been given an independent command by President Davis. But I command the west. How do you see this?"

"Sir, once our armies are combined, your seniority applies. I'll be under your direct command."

Bragg contemplated a few moments, then replied. "This is an intriguing plan. If going north gains me a new army and a new state for the Confederacy, I think it's worth the trip. If President Davis agrees, we head to Kentucky. There's one holdup. You can feel free to maneuver into Kentucky. But my artillery is still on the move here from Corinth. I won't leave without it."

Bragg left Smith and returned to his army's encampment. There he met Generals Cheatham and Hardee waiting by his headquarters tent. "Gentlemen, I trust you haven't had to wait too long for me. I need to talk to you about a couple of things."

The three men entered the tent and sat on camp stools. Cheatham and Hardee listened intently as Bragg outlined the plan urged by Smith.

"So," Cheatham encouraged, "it makes sense to me. Are you up to it?"

"If Davis is, yes. Kirby Smith will head to Knoxville. We'll work in conjunction with his army and move into Kentucky. It'll relieve pressure on Chattanooga because Buell will have to head north after us and also distract Grant from Vicksburg. We only have a single rail line going east from Vicksburg, and we have to keep Grant occupied. Price and Van Dorn are still watching Grant. They'll engage him soon.

"But I have another concern for you. It takes more than soldiers and guns to win wars. We're in Tennessee, where Union forces occupy our capitol and much territory.

"I need to know what's happening with Yankee troop movements, what's being said in newspapers and anything important about enemy resources. My commanders must be informed of all enemy operations that can be ascertained."

Hardee hesitated, clearing his throat. "You want spies."

"Spies. I suppose they can be called that, or couriers. We need both. We need men to find out military secrets, and we need men to carry the messages between commanders. It could be the same people doing both, but not necessarily."

Cheatham was pensive. "It's risky business, general."

"But vital."

"Then I'll find someone interested. Are we going near Nashville soon?"

"As soon as I get approval from the president, I expect we'll pass by there."

"The men I have in mind live near Nashville. I'll set up a meeting for when we get there."

"I'll leave the recruitment up to you."

Attack on Fort Ridgely
AUGUST 20

UGUST 19TH FOUND the beleaguered force at Fort Ridgely in desperate straits. Some 350 refugees joined Gere's command of twenty-two, fortified by Bishop's fifteen survivors. The pleas sent for reinforcements from Sheehan and Galbraith had gone unanswered. If and when Sturgis got to St. Paul, relief would still be days away.

Fear reflected in the faces of women, children, and many of the civilian men. The soldiers fit for duty manned posts on the fort's perimeter. Others were under the care of Dr. Mueller and his wife, Eliza. Tension felt like a smothering blanket as they waited—for help, for an attack, for something to happen.

About mid-morning, Jimmy Dunn leaned against a barricade between the commissary and long barracks at the northwest corner of the fort, the only area that didn't face a ravine. He laid his rifle on top of the makeshift wall and asked Levi Carr, "Didja ever think we'd get back here?"

"No. I thought for sure we'd all die in the thicket. Thing is, did we just escape death there to get killed here?"

Jimmy's brow furrowed. "We live and we die the way we was meant to."

"Well, Jimmy, I sure hope we're meant to live here."

"Look!" Jimmy pointed out onto the prairie. Then his voice turned into a shout. "Here they come! Lieutenant Gere! Come quick!"

A large mass of Dakota Indians had assembled on the open prairie to the northwest. Gere rushed over and sighted them through a telescope. He climbed upon a wagon near the barricade to get a better look. Watching intently, he relayed, "They're all listening to a man talking. It looks like he's giving a speech. I think it's Chief Little Crow. He's really getting into it, shouting, waving his arms, pointing at us.

"I wish I could be sure that's him." He looked away from the telescope and hollered, "Does anyone here know Little Crow?"

Margaret Hern was near the position delivering hot coffee to the soldiers. She called back, "I know him. Once he offered three ponies to my husband for me. He liked how I sang."

Gere handed her the telescope. After a moment Margaret gave him her answer, "It's Little Crow, all right. There's no doubt about it."

Other Indians spoke. Then the lieutenant noted with surprise, "They're leaving. Small groups, bigger groups . . . they're leaving."

"Why?" Jimmy asked. "Why aren't they attacking?"

"I think Little Crow wants them to, but they have other ideas."

"Good for us," Jimmy observed.

Little Crow's band of 400 Dakota decided not to follow their leader's demands that they attack Fort Ridgely. Instead, they moved eighteen miles south to attack the village of New Ulm.

The delay was a godsend for the fort. Shortly after the Indians rode off, Sheehan and his fifty men of Company C trotted into the fort. The scene resembled a community celebration as the soldiers and refugees cheered and Charlie Culver's drum beats resounded. Women wiped tears from eyes now filled with hope.

That evening, about six o'clock, Galbraith and the fifty men of the Renville Rangers also arrived. Norm Culver and a half dozen Company B men who had been with the Rangers were with them.

Gere greeted Galbraith, then asked. "When did Sturgis reach St. Peter?"

"About three in the morning. We left a few hours later and force marched the forty miles to get here."

"How long did Sturgis stay at St. Peter?"

"Just long enough to get another horse. Then he was off to St. Paul."

"I hope he's got the word to Governor Ramsey by now."

"It's a long way, but he was riding hard."

During the night, four who had been wounded or separated from Marsh at Redwood straggled into Ridgely. Four others including Blodgett, badly wounded, made it back at two in the morning, Will Sutherland at 9:00 a.m. on the 20th, and Charlie Beecher just before noon. An eighth man, Ezkiel Rose, would turn up in the river town of Henderson.

Fort Ridgely now had 160 soldiers and about twenty-five civilian men ready to defend the fort. Gere turned command over to Sheehan, explained what had been done to ready the fort for attack, then winced and rubbed his jaw.

"What's wrong, Tom?" Sheehan asked.

"Doc says I've got the mumps."

Sheehan laughed in spite of the situation. "Well, I hope you can pull a trigger if you need to."

"I'll be there, Tim."

"Your preparations have been excellent. I want vigilance maintained on the barricades, but I've talked to Sergeant Jones, and we have an important fallback. I want cannons manned at each corner of the fort. Whipple, Mc-Grew, Jones, and Bishop with their crews will blast them out of the ravines."

"If they had attacked last night or even this morning, we couldn't have stopped them."

"We're still in a tight spot, Tom. We'll be outnumbered when they come, probably four to one or more. They likely even have better guns than we do. We'll need the cannons."

"So Jones's spending all that time drilling the men wasn't a waste."

"On the contrary, it just might be our salvation."

Tim Sheehan was adamant discipline be maintained. He said to Ben Randal, "It's absolutely necessary to keep order among citizens as well as soldiers. Therefore, I'm going to swear them all in. Gather your contingent at the flagpole."

* * *

As Randal assembled his men, fort women were in the ammunition magazine cabins located two hundred yards northwest of the fort. Margaret Hern was among the women making cartridges in the magazine in their stocking feet. They feared shoes could somehow set off the volatile gun powder.

Margaret gave instructions to a young girl. "Take a piece of paper, give it a twist, drop in some powder and an iron slug or a ball, and give it another twist."

"Why isn't the magazine in the fort?" the girl wondered.

"So the fort doesn't blow up. Just do as I said and quick."

* * *

Randal's twenty-five men raised their right hands and swore to Sheehan to "defend the United States against all her enemies."

"All right, men, to your posts." Randal ordered.

A low hill rose on the northwest prairie. Sheehan posted a sentinel there to watch for Dakota. Shortly after noon on August 20th a single shot rang out and the sentinel, with other pickets, raced back to Ridgely crying the alert. "Indians! Indians! The Sioux are coming!"

Charlie Culver beat the long roll while Sheehan, on a mule, shouted, "To your posts!" He led forty-eight men, two squads, onto the west prairie.

They waited in ranks while Sheehan watched Dakota warriors halt just out of musket range. Another squad raced double quick to the southwest corner. One Indian trotted back and forth on a black stallion. Three others joined him.

Sheehan turned to his sergeant, John Bishop, "That's Little Crow on the black. I think he wants to parlay. I'll go out there."

"Lieutenant, you're needed here," Bishop cautioned, "I'll go out."

Bishop walked a short distance from the fort and called out to Little Crow, "Come closer. Our lieutenant wants to talk to you."

"You want me to ride to where you can shoot me. I don't think I will do that. Give up the fort and leave. We will let you go down the river in peace."

Bishop turned crimson and shouted, "I was at Redwood Ferry. We were offered peace there, too. Then we were ambushed!"

Suddenly a rattling of gunfire erupted from behind Bishop.

Sheehan cried, "It's a ruse. The attack's on the northeast! Hold your ground here! I expect another attack!" Then he spurred his mount back to the fort to supervise the assault.

The gun crews raced to their posts in the fort, McGrew to the northwest, Whipple the northeast, Bishop the southeast, and Jones the southwest.

Dakota warriors, unseen until they charged, burst from the ravine and seized several of a row of six log cabins forty yards from the wall of the long barracks. The Indians blasted three separate volleys into the northeast opening. Gere and thirty-five soldiers raced double quick to the northeast and poured fire into the Dakota as they emerged from the ravine.

Two of the log buildings were occupied. John Jones's pregnant wife, Maria, found herself trapped when gunfire erupted. She slid behind an iron stove, which saved her from a ball fired by an Indian from a window. Men of Company C burst into the cabin to rescue her.

In a building used as Dr. Mueller's hospital, the suddenness of the attack surprised everyone. Mueller and his steward hurried to help patients out of the building save one. Will Blodgett was sound asleep. Awakened by gunfire, Will stared around the empty room and knew he'd have to save himself once again.

The wounded soldier had forty yards to traverse between the hospital cabin and the long barracks. Just seventeen, Will could barely move due to the severity of his wounds. With painstaking slowness he edged his way across the open space. Bullets whizzed past him like a swarm of bees. He felt the rush of air as lead balls shot by his cheek. Finally he reached the west end of the barracks safety without sustaining any new wounds.

A soldier grabbed him and helped him up the steps into the barracks. "My boy," he said, "I never thought you'd get across."

At the southwest corner, the hammer fell on the second prong of Little Crow's attack. With attention to the northeast, Dakota warriors streamed from the ravine and threatened to flank Sheehan's men, who were still on the prairie. In an exposed position and under fire, the men made a "rapid retreat."

Sheehan met his men as they raced, ordering them back into ranks. This exposed them to gunfire from the northwest. Some men tried to break ranks.

"Let us fight from cover!" one yelled.

Their lieutenant pulled out his pistol and commanded, "Stay in ranks. I'll cut down the first man who tries to leave."

The soldiers obeyed and fell back into line. Then three fell to enemy fire. Sheehan saw the desperation in his men's faces and realized his folly. His plan to mass their rifles in volley fire was foolish. He let them run for cover.

Whipple rolled his mountain howitzer into position and dropped shells into the ravine. Firing on both sides on the north end of the fort became intense. In the stone barracks, the women and children were sent to the upper floor, while soldiers fired from the long row of windows on the north side.

From the northwest corner Jim McGrew's gun crew had a hot fight. Jimmy Dunn slid a canister ball into the cannon barrel and rammed it in. The gun had been rolled out to fire on the Indians attacking from the northern ravine. A blast from the howitzer raked into the Dakota.

Under fire from Whipple's and McGrew's guns and a counterattack by men of companies B and C, the warriors who had taken the northern out buildings were driven out and into the ravine. A barn, held by Dakota, nearby burst into flames when hit by a shell.

Then, at the southwest corner, a second attack burst from the ravine. Jones, Culver, and the Renville Rangers desperately fought back. Jones's six-pounder cannon blasted shot and shell into the ravine, driving Indians back and holding them at bay.

Cannon roar shook the earth during then ceaseless firing. Jimmy was sent to Sheehan with a message from McGrew. He darted across the parade ground zigzagging and covering his face like he was running through a hornet's nest.

"Lieutenant, Sergeant McGrew says we're startin' to run low on ammo."

"I've ordered the men to conserve. But powder for the cannon is critical. It's what's holding them back." He looked to the northwest at the two little buildings on the prairie.

"We have plenty of powder out there. We'll have to get some. Tell Mc-Grew I'll send men out there to bring back powder. Give them cover."

Private Andy Williamson, youngest son of missionary Dr. Thomas Williamson, volunteered to lead a detail to the munition buildings. The sun beat down mercilessly in the heat of battle as the squad of men strained to haul heavy crates of ammunition back to the stone buildings of Fort Ridgely.

It was two hundred yards to the buildings. McGrew sighted his weapon for his gun crew. "This is the only place where they can't attack under cover. We've got to keep 'em back, m'boys!"

Jimmy called back, "We'll make 'em pay if they don't!" and rammed another shell home. The crew lobbed shot after shot to keep the Dakota back, while Williamson and his detail toiled an hour to bring in gunpowder and shells.

After the attacks stalled in the northeast and southwest, the attack became general around the fort. For five hours gunfire was incessant.

Bill Perrington shouted to Jimmy, "Bullets are coming down like rain!" He aimed his musket only to have a ball smash into the firing mechanism, tearing off the hammer. Astonished, he turned his gunpowder-streaked face to Jimmy.

In spite of it all, Jimmy replied laconically, "Well, I sure hope yer not bored. Enough action for ya? I could find you an umbrella for the raining bullets."

Bill shook his head. "It's more than I bargained for. Keep your umbrella."

Sheehan was everywhere, moving amongst his men, giving orders and offering encouragement. Women and children huddled closer together and trembled on the floor of the second story of the long barracks as bullets sliced off chunks of stone outside. Some shots smashed through windows and ricocheted off an opposite wall. Margaret Hern efficiently collected a basin full of lead balls to be recast and fired back at the Dakota.

Many of the outbuildings were engulfed in flames. Fire arrows arched in the smoky blue sky and embedded in the wooden shingles of the officers' quarters. A mixed blood, Joe Coursolle, grabbed a ladder and an axe and climbed to the roof. Arrows and bullets all around him, Joe whacked out the fire.

The air over the fort hung thick with heavy, black smoke from muskets, cannons, burning buildings and burning hay in the barn. And then it just stopped. The Dakota left the battlefield and retreated back to their villages.

At Fort Ridgely a strange silence hung over the bloody, powder-stained, exhausted defenders. Then they erupted in cheers when they realized the day's fighting was over.

* * *

OVER EIGHTEEN HOURS of hard riding through perilous terrain saw Willie Sturgis reach Fort Snelling 110 miles away. He was fortunate to find Governor Ramsey meeting with Adjutant General Oscar Malmos at the fort. The governor read Gere's note and dispatches from St. Peter, then ordered Malmos to ready four companies of the new 6th Infantry Regiment.

"See they get to Fort Ridgely with the utmost promptitude," Governor Ramsey commanded.

A former fur trader and Minnesota's first governor, Henry Hastings Sibley, was placed in charge of the relief force. With haste they could have been outfitted and made the journey west to Ridgely within forty-eight hours.

But Sibley's expedition didn't get moving until the next day. They traveled by steamboat to Shakopee, where Sibley complained about a lack of supplies and munitions, refusing to go farther until the necessary supplies reached him.

Sibley had no scouts, so he relied upon information from travelers coming from the west. He was told by a man from St. Peter that "the whole Indian force is in arms, and they are waging a war of extermination."

The former governor wrote Governor Ramsey. "It will require a far larger force than I have, and it would be as well for you to send up, without delay, at least 500 men, with arms and equipments. I shall take position to protect the settlements until reinforced. A hell-for-leather dash down the valley and across the prairie to Fort Ridgley seems reckless. I need more guns, more ammunition, and more provisions."

His expedition had traveled twenty-five miles in twenty-four hours and was now camped for the night. Sixty-five miles from where Sibley wrote his letter to Ramsey, John Jones sent rockets streaming into the sky, etching silver and red streaks onto a background of black.

Jones shouted, "We're still here! See! We're still alive!"

Jimmy Dunn looked up as a flash illuminated the American flag whipping from the flag pole in the night breeze. "By God, I hope Sibley sees that, Will."

Hutchinson nodded. "Or at least the folks in New Ulm."

Then another jagged flash cut across the sky. Lightning, followed by a low rumble like a hundred of Charlie Culver's drums. Then the skies opened up and rain plopped in big drops

"This is all we need," Will muttered disgustedly.

"Don't complain," Andy Williamson rejoined. "I was raised with the Indians at my father's mission. They don't like to do much in rain, especially fight."

Jimmy asked, "Andy, I heard folks from Upper Sioux came by. What happened to 'em?"

"My brother-in-law was sent ahead to see what was happening here, Sheehan told them to keep going. He wouldn't let them in."

"What! Why not?"

"He said they were safer on the prairie, that he couldn't guarantee we could protect them and if we were attacked again they all might be killed."

"He might be right," Jimmy concurred, "but how did they get away from Yellow Medicine?"

"A friendly Indian, John Other Day, warned them about what had happened at Redwood. They evacuated before an attack came there. Some have been killed on the prairie, but most escaped alive."

"I hope they make it to Fort Snelling."

"One funny thing, Jimmy. I was told a Confederate officer's been seen in Little Crow's camp recently."

"Why would they make up a fool thing like that?"

"Maybe it isn't so farfetched. Think about it. An Indian war on the frontier would keep Minnesota troops here instead of fighting rebels and would likely cause Lincoln to divert troops here who've been fighting in the South."

Jimmy whistled. "Ain't that somethin' if it's true."

"We'll likely never know, Jimmy."

Another flash of lightning seared the sky, and a crack of thunder rattled glass in a nearby window. Will called, "You guys can keep gabbin' if ya want, but I think we should get outta this rain."

The two nodded and followed Will into the crowded long barracks. They watched through bullet-shattered windows as lightning cut through the darkness.

Then a shot rang out and a picket yelled, "Man comin'!" followed by a distant voice crying, "Don't shoot! I'm white!" Moments later a man stumbled over a barricade into the fort compound. Sheehan and Gere raced across the grounds to him.

The man gasped, "I'm from New Ulm. They shot my horse. Hit the town yesterday. A few got killed, but we drove 'em off. We need help, soldiers."

Sheehan sadly shook his head. "I'm sorry, sir, we have no men we can send you. Look around. We're just holding on here."

It rained in the Minnesota River Valley into the morning of August 21st. The soldiers of Fort Ridgely spent the day bolstering their defenses with more lumber, cordwood, and sacks of oats. They dumped shovelfuls of dirt on rooftops in an attempt to fireproof them. Women continued work on cartridges and melted spent bullets, molding them to fit the muskets.

Sheehan met on the parade ground with his officers and civilian leaders. "Men, we're running low on food. I want you to cut rations in half."

Dr. Mueller informed them, "And I'm running low on medical supplies. I've got about a dozen under my care. I'm about out of any painkillers."

"Do your best. Have you lost anyone?"

"No one brought to me has died. Blodgett's just holding on, and three were killed outright."

"Another problem sir," Sergeant Jones added, "you can smell. The sanitary conditions of over four hundred people in a two-acre area are atrocious."

"Keep digging latrines."

"Sir, we're digging defenses."

"Then we'll live with the smell and everything else." Sheehan looked to the east. "Sibley has got to get here soon. He just has to."

* * *

SIBLEY WAS AT BELLE PLAINE, fifty-five miles away. He had sent Captain Hiram Grant and 150 men toward Fort Ridgely but then received a report that that the fort had fallen and been burned. He recalled Grant, advising that they meet in St. Peter, which would become his base of operations.

Sibley next sent a dispatch to New Ulm, "I will not go out on a fool's errand to find out about Fort Ridgely, not with the entire Dakota nation waiting out there on the prairie to wipe out my command. We will leave for St. Peter Friday evening."

Little Crow and his warriors remained in their lodges, waiting for a break in the weather. The chief's sullen spirits were buoyed by the appearance of 400 warriors from Yellow Medicine. While their leaders and most Upper Agency Dakota had chosen to not fight, they had not held back those who wished to do so. On the morrow, Little Crow's force would be doubled.

Friday dawned bright. Amidst the soggy conditions, Fort Ridgely was nearly out of water. A detail, with a detachment of armed guards, ventured down the bluff to the spring. To their dismay they discovered that the Dakota had smashed the clay reservoir holding the water supply. It took precious time but the soldiers hurriedly rebuilt it, then loaded barrels with water and hauled them by wagon back to the fort. Then all defenders hustled vigilantly to resume their posts.

That same morning Little Crow and 800 warriors rode across the heavy dew and rain-damp prairie to the fort. They came down both sides of the river and then divided to approach the fort from different sides.

Jimmy, in the northwest corner with McGrew's gun crew, gazed out over the prairie. "I wonder where they'll be comin' from this time?"

"Out of the ground, like the devils they are," McGrew answered.

They did come out of the ground. As the sun was just past its mid-point above them, pandemonium broke out everywhere. Dakota braves sprang out of the ravines all around the fort in a simultaneous attack. Screams, war cries, and the roar of musket fire resounded as if the gates of Hell had been thrown open as Dakota rushed the fort through smoke and fire.

The defenders blasted back from the barricades and barracks. Cannon fire erupted from all four corners of the fort. Jimmy strained with Bill Perrington and others of the gun crew to roll their 12-pounder out onto the prairie, where they fired canister shot down the ravine.

The furious fighting raged all afternoon. The Dakota fired unceasing volleys into the fort. Flaming arrows launched into the air, but thudded into wet dirt and damp shingles on the rooftops, where they extinguished.

Another crisis point came when the supply of ammunition once again ran dangerously low. In the stone commissary, men cut three-quarter-inch slugs from rods. Jimmy Dunn brought explosive artillery shells that contained lead balls and powder. He pried the shells open so Eliza Mueller, Margaret Hern, and other women could fashion cartridges from them.

Late that afternoon the Renville Rangers, many of whom were of Dakota and French blood, heard taunts and voices coming from the southwest ravine.

Lieutenant Gorman hurried to Sergeant Jones to alert him. "Sergeant, I think they plan to concentrate their attack where we seem to be most vulnerable, the southwest corner. My men are hearing things."

Jones surveyed his position. Two wood-framed buildings, a two-story officers' quarters on the west, and the headquarters building on the south— none had the security of the stone buildings anchoring the other end of the fort.

To make matters worse, beyond the perimeter of the fort, the Dakota were using two outbuildings as a staging area for an attack and shelter to pour fire into the fort. Jimmy sprinted up to Jones, who stood on the porch of the headquarters, and shouted above the din, "Indians are movin' across the prairie, looks like they want to join up with reds in the ravine right in front of you."

"Blast the hell out of 'em," Jones ordered.

"We can't. They're movin' outta range."

Jones hesitated, then looked to the center of the fort, where the massive twenty-four-pound cannon rested. "Tell Lieutenant McGrew to wheel over the big howitzer. You can hit 'em with that, m'boy. Lob some more into the ravine while you're at it. If they all hit us at this spot, we can't stop 'em."

A few minutes later a tremendous boom like an enormous crack of thunder rattled the earth and reverberated down the valley. It blasted near the Dakota as they traversed open ground toward the ravines. After a series of shots, the warriors held back at the risk of being blown to smithereens while trying to converge in the southwest.

Shot rained like deadly hail from the outbuildings—Ben Randal's sutler store, and a mule barn stable, 300 feet directly behind headquarters. On the second attempt McGrew's cannon shot burst the store into flames.

It was a different matter with the stable. "I can't get a clear shot at it without exposing my men to murderous fire," Jones explained to Sheehan.

"Do something," Sheehan pleaded. "We must stop them before we're attacked again."

Once again Jones coolly contemplated, then looked at the headquarters, now doubling as a hospital with wounded soldiers on the porch being tended to by Eliza Mueller. Jones called to his gun crew, "Move the six pounder to the front of the headquarters."

"What are you going to do?" Sheehan demanded.

"Just watch, sir," Jones calmly replied.

Once the cannon was positioned and loaded, Jones called, "Mrs. Mueller, would you be so kind as to open the front door of the building and then go down the hallway and open the back door."

Shocked, Eliza stammered, "You . . . you don't mean to . . . No, you can't!"

"Mrs. Mueller, I beg your pardon, but I can do this. Now, please . . ."

Eliza did as instructed. From the parade ground, the view through the house to the gunsmoke-wreathed stable was clear. Jones knelt behind his cannon and sighted it. Then he rose up and announced, "There'll be a demonstration here shortly. I'd advise those of you on the porch remove yourselves."

Some scampered, other assisted. from the front of the building.

Then Jones called, "Prick and prime!" and then "Fire!" With a roar followed by flames, the cannon spat a six-pound explosive shot down the building's hallway and into the stable beyond. In an instant an explosion shattered it and engulfed the building in flames.

"Now, wheel back to the corner!" Jones yelled. "They'll be coming soon!"

After the six-pounder was positioned again in the southwest, the Dakota warriors once again erupted like specters from the ravine 175 yards away. Jones watched and waited. Soldiers returned a blistering fire from the barricades.

Then Jones cried to his crew, "Fire!" A withering blast of canister shot sent hundreds of shards of metal streaming into the onrushing Indians. A ranger yelled in Dakota, "Come back. We are ready for you!"

It was too much for the attackers. They stopped short of the barricade and retreated, dragging their dead and wounded with them. After six hours of desperate fighting, it was over. The Dakota had come within twenty feet of the defense line. But the cannons had been too much for them.

Cries of "Huzzah! Huzzah!" rose from the fort, followed by a general cheer. Jimmy Dunn waved his hat in the air. Margaret Hern came out of the nearby commissary and joined in the celebration. Jimmy raced over and hugged her. She beamed at the powder-blackened, sweat-streaked face of her young friend and exclaimed, "You did it!"

"We all did it, Mrs. Hern!"

Then she sobered. "But it was a shame, wasn't it. That this had to happen. If the money had only come sooner. If the treaty had been followed."

Jimmy was not in the mood to consider the whys and why nots of what had happened. He just grinned, "But we won!"

* * *

As the Dakota slipped away into the looming darkness, Colonel Sibley and three companies of his command marched into St. Peter twenty-five miles away. There Sibley penned a message to Governor Ramsey claiming the journey had been "very fatiguing, due to execrable roads."

Sibley met with a friend, an old scout named Jack Frazer, who claimed Little Crow had attacked Fort Ridgely with 1,500 men and that all warriors from Ridgely to the Missouri River, some 5,000, would be joining in.

The exaggeration was more than enough to keep Sibley in place. He advised that he would not leave St. Peter without reinforcements.

* * *

At the fort a hopeful stillness hung over them all. Sheehan ordered his defenses to be buoyed up on Saturday morning in expectation of another attack, while praying it wouldn't come.

Gere reported to Sheehan, "The women have done great work, and the final cartridges have been distributed."

"How many per man?"

"Six."

"Six shots each. That won't hold them."

"The cannons are running low, too."

"Well, Little Crow doesn't know that. I sent a message to him, had it posted onto a split stick on the prairie."

"What did you tell him?"

"I advised him to stop the slaughter of women and children or the 'Great Father in Washington' would send enough troops to kill them all or drive them to the Rocky Mountains."

Ben Randal, out of breath, rushed up to the officers. "I just got word the Sioux were seen moving in large numbers down the south side of the Minnesota. But they didn't come this way. Looks like they're going toward New Ulm again."

"God help them," Sheehan murmured.

The defenders of Fort Ridgely endured four more days of intense trepidation until 175 cavalryman led by Colonel Sam McPhail rode into a cheering throng in the fort. The siege was finally over. Willie Sturgis rode at the front. He looked at his friends and proclaimed, "You're alive!"

Middle Tennessee
LATE AUGUST 1862

O N AUGUST 28 BRAGG'S ARMY finally received its artillery and left Chattanooga on a race into Kentucky, where he would join forces with Kirby Smith. Once it became plain Bragg was heading north, Buell was diverted from his approach on Chattanooga and sent north. He was ordered to place his army between Louisville, Cincinnati, and Bragg.

Sam Davis took the occasion of his army's movement north to make a request. "Captain, sir," Sam began, "we'll be passing real close to my home at Smyrna. Could I have a few hours' leave and stop off there?"

Captain Ledbetter hesitated briefly. "We're going to move fast around Nashville. You can have tonight, but you must catch up with us tomorrow. Don't be late, you know General Bragg won't put up with being late. He might charge you with desertion, and we wouldn't want that."

"No, sir, we wouldn't. I'll be on time, thank you."

It was late afternoon when Sam trotted down the path to the house where he grew up. Slaves shouted greetings, but this time they seemed a little more subdued. As before, his mother and father hurried down the porch to greet their son. Jane, still pregnant, wrapped her right around Sam and kissed his cheek.

Sam peered over to a pasture next to their barn. He put two fingers into his mouth and whistled. Instantly, a beautiful dapple-gray stallion trotted from around a corner of the barn. Sam grabbed an apple from a low hanging branch and said, "I'll be right back. It's been awhile since I've seen Brandy, too."

John and Jane watched as Sam hurried to the pasture. "He's always loved that horse," John observed.

"The best thing you ever gave him. Too bad he can't take him along."

"Brandy's too good a horse to go off to war. Besides, Sam's infantry. He doesn't need a full-time horse."

Sam rubbed his horse's nose as the animal nickered and then crunched into the fresh apple. "Next time home I'll ride you, boy. We'll take three rail fences again. Be good to Oscar, don't let him bother you with any of his jokes. Remember when he took you to the general store and asked for a pound of nails. Then when asked what kind he said, 'Toe nails,' and rode off laughing."

The young man sobered. "There's not much to laugh about now." Then he smiled and patted his horse's neck. "But wars don't last forever. I'll be back."

Sam delighted in entertaining his younger brothers and sisters with stories of his experiences. Slave children gathered near as well as he regaled them all with his exploits. His brother Oscar asked, "Didja ever see Bobby Lee?"

"Sure did, when we were marching by Cheat Mountain. He's a fine-looking man. I hear his army would march through a brick wall for him."

"What 'bout General Bragg?" sister Margaret wondered.

Sam paused. "He can be hard. Lots of boys don't like him much. But he fights, and we'll follow his lead. Where's John?" he asked about his half-brother.

His father answered, "Down in Shelbyville, kind of mysterious business. A rider came by, gave John a message, and an hour later the boy said he was off to Shelbyville."

"That's kind of funny. Well, greet him for me."

After Jane fed her family a fine meal in Sam's honor, her son excused himself. "I've got to be back tomorrow. I'm sorry I didn't have much time here. But I have to go."

"You gotta go pay a visit on the county line, don't cha?" Oscar asked.

The children giggled and Sam reddened slightly.

"Yes, I'm going to stop and visit the Pattersons."

"You mean Kate," Oscar teased.

"I guess so," Sam grinned.

After his mother handed him a bag full of slices of smoked ham and other victuals, Sam was eager to get onto his horse. A young black boy led it to him. Sam placed his arm over the younger boy's shoulder.

"Thanks, Coleman. Where have you been?"

"Pickin' cotton on da back forty."

"You were a great friend growing up. I miss you."

"We done everthin' together, Mastah Sam. Take me with you."

"No, Coleman. Maybe some other time. Not now."

A look of disappointment swept the younger boy's face.

Sam tried to encourage him. "Don't be sad. Next time I come back we'll go hunting, just like we used to do."

Coleman grinned. "Those was good times!"

"There'll be more."

Sam easily swung onto his horse with the grace of an expert horseman. He paused, waved at his family assembled in front of the house and trotted away down the roadway.

LaVergne was only nine miles north of Smyrna on the way to Nashville. Sam knew his army was skirting the city to the west, so he was on target to meet up with his regiment as planned. His time with Kate would be brief, but it was all he could hope for.

* * *

As Sam trotted up the trail to LaVergne a meeting was taking place some thirty miles to the south at Shelbyville. In a small inn room, five men gathered around a table. A single oil lamp illuminated the room.

Three wore Confederate uniforms. They were generals Cheatham and Hardee, along with Captain Henry Shaw. The latter was of medium height and nondescript in many ways. Clean shaven, he wore his dark hair short.

The other two other were civilians, solidly built, robust young men. The more handsome one brushed his dark hair from his eyes and spoke. "This is a real honor for us Rutherford County farm boys to be asked to meet up with two generals and a captain. Me and Al didn't think twice about coming here when we got the word, but why?"

General Cheatham removed his hat, revealing a full head of gray, curly hair that flopped over his ears. "Because whenever my staff asked about who in the area around Nashville would be most qualified for the venture before us, the names of John Davis and Alfred Douglas kept coming up."

"All right," John wondered, "so just what is this venture?"

Cheatham spread his hands and leaned back on his creaking chair. "Men," he confided, "tactics and strategy in war depend on more than just soldiers and guns. We need to know things about the enemy. We need to know what they're thinking, where they're going, how many are there. You can help us with that."

"You want us ta spy?" Al said incredulously.

"Not exactly. Oh, some of what you do might be a little borderline spying, but mostly we need men to deliver information that others, spies if you will, have obtained."

"Both of us were wounded," John countered, "we're healed now and hoped to rejoin our regiments."

General Hardee interrupted, "Your regiment commanders recommended you. You know this area. This is how you can best serve the Confederacy."

"All right, what do you want us to do?" asked John.

"First," Cheatham said, "we need you to recruit another ten or so. Two isn't enough. We want daring unmarried young men, who are excellent horsemen. John, you know all the woods, ravines and rivers between Nashville and Chattanooga. Find others who know the terrain well, too."

"Tell us more, General," John asked, "just how will this work?"

"This is," he gestured to the captain, "Captain Henry Shaw, your contact."

Shaw looked earnestly at the two young men. "You'll be the eyes and ears of the Confederate forces in Tennessee. You'll pick up newspapers and other bits of information about the federals you think helpful. Other agents will do more in-depth investigations into Yankee activities."

"Spying," Al interjected.

"Call them what you will. I like to think of this in terms of a postal service. You'll be mail deliverers, couriers. You'll go to the post office, actually our agents, and pick up packets you'll then deliver to me. I'll rewrite in code as needed, and other couriers will take messages to Bragg in Alabama or Chattanooga or wherever he is, maybe even Kentucky."

John frowned in concentration, then turned to Al. "I'm game if you are."

"If this is the way to git the Yankees outta Tennessee, I'm all in, too."

"Excellent!" Hardee exclaimed as Cheatham glowed in approval.

"Start recruiting right away," Shaw suggested. "We need to get this in operation soon. Oh, one other thing. Forget the name Shaw, my alias will be E. Coleman. That's how I'l sign my dispatches. You're now members of Coleman's Scouts. I'll pass among you and the Yankees as an old itinerant herb doctor. I might even look a little shabby. But it'll be me, and you'll see me from time to time. Don't let on you know me or who I am. Understand?"

Both John and Al nodded.

"Well, boys," Cheatham shook their hands, "let's get to work."

* * *

SAM REACHED the Patterson house after dark. A lit lamp glowed from the front window. Sam rapped softly on the door. A woman inquired, "Who's there?"

"Sam Davis."

The door flung open, and Kate Patterson wrapped her arms around Sam and kissed him. Then she stepped back, tightened her night robe around her neck and snapped, "Can't you write more?"

"It's hard—"

"Who's there, Kate?" Dr. Patterson spoke from the shadows.

"It's Sam, Daddy."

"Sam Davis, let me look at you, boy! He's a little skinny, don't you think, Kate?"

"Maybe, but he still looks good to me!"

"Come in, Sam. Sit down. Ellen!" he called to his wife, "get us some coffee and that good bread you made. Maybe we can fatten Sam up a little."

"Where are you going, Sam?" Kate asked.

"Up toward Nashville. Our army's going by on the way to Kentucky."

"How long do you have?"

"Not long, Kate. I have to be back with my regiment in the morning. Why a light in the window this time of night? You didn't know I was coming."

"Travelers come by, Sam," Dr. Patterson answered.

Sam thought that odd. "What kind of travelers?"

"The kind Yankees would like to find. Sometimes soldiers, sometimes men with dispatches. We put them up if they need a place."

"Are they spies?"

"I don't ask 'em what they are, Sam, long's they believe in our cause."

"Where's Ev?"

"Everand's in Nashville, I don't know what my boy's doing in the middle of the federals, but I'm sure he has a purpose."

Sam took a sip of coffee and munched on a thick slice of bread. "Real good, ma'am," he smiled at Ellen. Then he tried to stifle a big yawn. "I'm sorry, I guess I'm pretty tired."

"You can sleep in Ev's room. When do you have to leave?"

"Before dawn."

"I'll make sure you're up in time," Kate offered. She looked at her parents. "I'll see he gets settled in tonight."

"We'll wait here while you show him the room," her mother said.

Kate led the way upstairs, down a short hallway and to a sparsely furnished bedroom. She lit a lantern, and they embraced.

"Couldn't you have come any earlier? We have no time. My parents won't let me spend time with you this late in a bedroom. It's not seemly."

"There'll be plenty of time later, Kate. What've you been doing?"

"I help out my father with some nursing. I also assist our travelers and other visitors when I can. I'm involved with some other things to help Ev."

"Doing what?"

"It's better you don't know. Don't worry."

Sam swept Kate's curls off her face and admonished, "Please be careful. You live in Yankee-held land. Someday our army will come to take it back."

"There's someone I wonder about. Says he's a cattle buyer. He comes by often inquiring about the availability of cattle. Funny thing is, we usually only see him just before or just after federal troop movements."

"Watch out for him, Kate He's fishing around here and not for fish."

"It's funny," Kate added, "I've never seen him with a cow."

"Kate! Come on down!"

"Oh, Mother, wait a moment."

They kissed again and held each other close. "I can't wait for this war to be over," she murmured into his ear.

"That day will come, Kate, I just hope it's soon, too."

Tears flooding her eyes, Kate turned and hurried down the stairs.

* * *

IT SEEMED AS IF Sam had just fallen asleep when he felt his shoulder being lightly shaken. "Wake up, Sam. It's near daylight."

Through bleary eyes in the darkened room, he recognized Kate. "Already?"

"Yes. Father has coffee on and breakfast for you."

Sam sniffed. "I smell bacon frying."

"It's ready for you."

Kate returned downstairs. Sam dressed and descended to the kitchen, where hot coffee, bacon, eggs, and more freshly baked bread awaited him. He devoured the delicious, hearty breakfast, then rose to peer out the window. A sliver of pink on the eastern horizon signaled the start of the day and the need to rejoin the 1st Tennessee.

Kate handed Sam a small bundle wrapped in brown paper. He removed the paper to reveal a fine pair of boots.

"I know how scarce and important good footwear is to a soldier. You'll make good use of them."

"Good boots are a godsend, Kate. Thank you very much."

"You're welcome," she smiled at his obvious appreciation. "I had Robert saddle your horse. It should be ready."

"Thank you, Dr. Patterson. You've been most hospitable. I hope to get back this way again soon."

"Do us proud, boy."

Sam nodded and stepped through an open door into the fresh, early morning air. Kate followed him and clung to him while Robert, a young slave boy, held the bridle of his horse.

Kate gazed up into Sam's face and pleaded, "Be careful. Don't try to be a hero. Just come back." Then they kissed.

"Kate, with you waiting for me, I have to take care. You're who I have to come home to." With those words hanging in the air, Sam swung onto his mount and trotted north.

The Fifth at Corinth and Minnesota

WHILE COMPANY B at Fort Ridgely recovered from the Indian attack, Kirby Smith's army had bypassed the Cumberland Gap, leaving a small holding force to neutralize the Union garrison. Instead of rejoining Bragg, he'd move north into Kentucky. Bragg was on the march north. Buell, after facing supply delays and harassment from Forrest, turned away from Chattanooga to head north, first to Nashville, then in pursuit of Bragg.

Meanwhile, Bragg ordered Van Dorn and Price to harass Rosecrans in the west around Corinth, and Robert E. Lee began his intrusion into Maryland.

Companies A and E through K of the 5th Minnesota were led by Colonel Lucius Hubbard, serving in the 2nd Brigade of Rosecrans's Army of the Mississippi. The 4th Minnesota Regiment was also with Rosecrans in Mississippi.

General Sterling Price and General Earl Van Dorn had moved into northern Mississippi. Price occupied the town of Iuka, thirty miles east of Corinth. Grant sent two armies on a double envelopment of Price. Rosecrans would move in from the southwest with three divisions of Grant's own Army of the Tennessee, under General Ord, advancing from the northwest.

The attack was to be simultaneous, but Rosecrans and the Minnesotans opened up on Price first. Ord was to move in when he heard Rosecrans open up. A phenomenon in battle called the "acoustic shadow" resulted in Ord's inability to hear the battle sounds just miles away. He did not attack, and Rosecrans's men battled alone throughout the bloody afternoon of September 19th.

Price's beaten forces escaped Iuka on a road left unguarded by Union forces. They joined up with Van Dorn and on October 3rd and made a vigorous attack on Rosecrans's defense line around Corinth. The 5th Minnesota was bivouacked on the northwest edge of the town to the rear of the defense trench lines.

Company A was on sharp-shooting duty and positioned in advance of the line. The rest of the regiment stood in line awaiting orders. At about 11:00 a.m.

on October 4th, Confederate batteries opened up with a thunderous volley. Both sides poured everything they could into each other with muskets and cannon.

The 5th stood impatiently in reserve. Over most of the line, Van Dorn's assault had been firmly withstood, but just to the right of the Minnesota boys, a breach opened in the Union line. Confederate soldiers, after capturing Union batteries, surged toward the streets of Corinth.

Unless the gap in the line was closed, Rosecrans's army's rear would be in peril as rebel columns drove into the streets of the town.

The 5th Minnesota companies closed the gap, pouring relentless volleys against the flank of the Confederates and driving them back. They could justly claim they had saved the day in the second Battle of Corinth.

* * *

BUT BACK IN MINNESOTA. the rest of the 5th continued to man forts. Company B stayed at Fort Ridgley, with C at Ripley and D at Abercrombie while the 6th, 7th, 9th, and 10th regiments served under Sibley.

They were joined by the 3rd Regiment after their surrender and parol at Murfreesboro. After several battles, Sibley finally moved down the Minnesota River Valley in force after Little Crow. The six-week war culminated at the Battle of Wood Lake on September 24, 1862, where Sibley's forces defeated Little Crow.

Most of Little Crow's followers retreated into the Dakota Territory. Others were captured or surrendered in Minnesota. In retribution, over 400 Indians were put on trial. Thirty-eight were hanged from one gallows in Mankato on December 26th. The 8th and 9th Minnesota regiments served as guards at the execution.

The war had claimed over 700 lives of white settlers and soldiers. New Ulm lost 190 buildings and thirty-four of its citizens before driving off the Dakota in their second attack on the town, which came the day after the second attack on Fort Ridgely. The number of Indian dead is unknown.

Throughout the rest of 1862, the 8th and 9th Minnesota regiments patrolled the western frontier. By the spring of 1863, Jimmy Dunn's prayers were finally answered. Companies B, C, and D of the 5th Minnesota were sent south to join the rest of the regiment.

The Minnesota regiments left behind had another mission ahead of them: pursue Little Crow to the west and guard the Minnesota frontier.

Into Kentucky

ON AUGUST 26TH Judson Bishop was named lieutenant colonel of the 2nd Minnesota and John Davis, major.

Lieutenant Clint Cilley joined his men encamped around a fire. Rincie DeGrave called to him, "Didja hear anything about the Indian war?"

"Just that 250 died the first day in the river valley, mostly Germans. Fort Ridgley held, but we lost nineteen Fillmore County boys at Redwood Ferry."

"It's terrible," Charlie Orline spat a stream of tobacco. "Only worse thing woulda been if the fightin' was by our homes, not in the Minnesota Valley."

"I'd desert, go home," Rinice said, "if the fightin' was in my backyard."

"Well, you're lucky it's not."

"When we gonna do somethin' 'sides just marching?" Aaron Doty asked.

Clint scratched chin stubble. "That's why I came by. Colonel Bishop just met with higher ups. Seems Bragg's left Chattanooga, going north into Kentucky. That likely means he's on his way to the Union supply depot in Louisville. So gentlemen, we're turning north too. We go to Nashville and then after Bragg."

"We get to fight!' Doty asked eagerly.

"Well, for sure we get to march. I think we'll catch up to him eventually."

When the 2nd Minnesota reached Nashville on September 7th most of the Union army had crossed the Cumberland. The Minnesota regiments were ordered to encamp at Nashville while other divisions watched Bragg's movements.

The Confederates were farther up the river, north of Nashville. By the 14th the entire army was north of the Cumberland and moving into Kentucky. The race for Louisville was on.

* * *

THE RUTHERFORD RIFLES had remained at Chattanooga until Polk's and Hardee's divisions arrived. Then they crossed the Tennessee River on flatboats and marched to Sale Creek, Tennessee.

At their camp Joe Cates, Will Searcey, and Sam Davis were joined by Corporal John Beesley, "Got any news for us?" Cates wondered.

"Jest that Bragg is mad as hell. General Smith was s'posed ta join up with us. But he's off on his own. What's good is that Smith's got Lexington."

"So," Sam said, "we're going into Kentucky as two armies, not one force."

"It might work as long as Buell doesn't manage to beat us both separately." Beesley paused. "We'll have to see which of us gets to Louisville first."

"What's our company strength, Corporal?"

"Still right around 150. We've had very few losses so far."

"God's with us," Searcey claimed.

Sam retorted, "The Yankees say the same thing."

"Well, we'll have to see at the end I guess," Cates concluded.

Through early September, the Army of Mississippi crossed the Cumberland Mountains to Sparta, Tennessee, then moved forward to ford the Cumberland River near Gainesboro, Tennessee. They reached Glasgow, Kentucky, and rested a few days. On September 15th they flanked Bowling Green.

Meanwhile, General Simon Bolivar Buckner, of Hardee's division, had surrounded the small Union force at Munfordville. Federal Colonel John Wilder turned down requests for surrender on September 12th and 14th.

On the 16th Bragg's full army, including the 1st Tennessee, moved into position near town. Another demand of surrender was sent to the Union commander. Wilder, under a white flag, journeyed across Confederate lines to meet Buckner. Confederate pickets blindfolded him and took him to Buckner.

Wilder shook hands with the general and confessed, "I'm not a military man, but I know I'm in a tough spot. What would you do?"

Buckner, flattered, but taken aback asserted, "Sir, this is not how things are done. It's not my place to give you advice."

"I need proof you have the superiority you claim for my surrender."

Buckner smiled grimly. "Follow me."

Wilder trailed the general up a small rise where Wilder gestured down the slope. Before them stretched a massed force of nearly 30,000 Confederate troops. "Colonel," Buckner said softly," you are outnumbered at least five to one."

The federal colonel paled and turned to Buckner, "You have my surrender, sir, anything else would be willful murder."

"Thank you, your surrender is accepted. I was born here, I didn't want to attack my home town."

After the surrender at Munfordville the rebel army continued on to Bardstown as conquering heroes. Bands played "Dixie" and "The Bonnie Blue Flag" as they marched through towns. Pretty girls waved and tossed flower bouquets. Tables filled with food greeted the soldiers as they marched.

"Well, Sam, ya sure kain't beat this," Joe Cates grinned.

A young girl shouted, "Hurrah, for our southern boys!"

Sam laughed, "No, you can't, and boys are joining up. Kentucky will be ours. Smith has taken control of the center part of the state, capturing Lexington and Richmond. He's got folks scared in Cincinnati even."

"Are we gonna jine up with Smith soon."

"I don't know, Joe, I'm not a general."

"I heard we got Camp Dick Robinson and it's full of all kinda good things."

"I hope so Joe. Clean clothes, food, and shoes would be good."

Sam's wishes all came true at the camp. In addition they were able to wash and bathe. Southern girls delivered cockades for all the soldiers who fastened them to their hats. There were even dances and parties.

Buell's Army of the Ohio pressed on with urgency toward Louisville. Bragg left his army and journeyed to Frankfort, Kentucky, to meet Kirby Smith. On October 4th, Simon Buckner met with the two other generals.

"Sir, I must protest," Buckner complained, "your visit to Frankfort distracts from our mission."

"I have come here to discuss plans with General Smith," Bragg asserted, "and to honor the inauguration of our Confederate Governor Richard Hawes. It's important we show our support for the morale of the people of Kentucky. They must know we remain committed to them."

"Are the Yankees doing the same thing with their governor?" Buckner wondered. "General, I've received word from a spy in Buell's army. The Yankees are at least ten miles from Louisville. Attack Buell before he reaches the city."

"I don't think so. It's time to join up with Smith. We haven't yet combined."

Bragg spoke at the inauguration as well as Buckner, who gave a stirring speech as a son of Kentucky. Afterwards Buckner asked Leonidas Polk to convince Bragg to attack Buell. Once again Bragg declined the request to concentrate his forces and attack at Perryville.

Governor Hawes glanced at a hazy sky at a distant rumble. "Rain?"

"No, cannon." Buckner corrected.

The inaugural ball was canceled due to the Union armies approach.

Perryville

BRAGG'S DELAYS at Munfordville and Frankfort allowed Buell to reach Louisville first. When questioned by Cheatham, he replied, "After we took Munfordville, I could have continued on and fought with Buell over Louisville, or joined up with Smith and together fought Buell. We don't have to beat him in Louisville to take the city. We'll beat Buell at a place of our choosing, drive him out of Kentucky and establish a Confederate frontier at the Ohio River."

In Louisville, Don Carlos Buell met with his second in command, George Thomas, who reported, "Bragg and Smith are in Frankfort giving speeches."

"We beat them here and have had time to reorganize. I've heard that new recruits have joined the Confederate army in Kentucky. Well, Pap, thousands have joined us as well."

"How do you plan to keep Bragg and Smith from joining forces?"

"I'll dispatch General Sill toward Frankfort with 20,000 men. Bragg went to Frankfort without his army. Sill will act as a diversion to keep Smith in place. I'll move on Bragg's army with three corps, 55,000 men."

"Are we ready, General? I find our army undisciplined, without suitable artillery, in every way unfit for active operations against a disciplined foe."

"They are the army we have, Pap. They'll do the job."

"We need fresh water."

"Yes, we'll have to find some."

The approach of Sill's army broke up the celebration festivities in Frankfort. Polk was left in command when Bragg went to Frankfort. On October 3rd the approach of the large Union force caused the Confederates to withdraw eastward and occupy Bardstown.

Along three separate roads Buell's three corps converged on Bardstown. In the 5th Brigade of General Van Cleve marched the 2nd Minnesota. The Confederates deployed two wings of 16,800: the right wing, commanded by General Polk, with one division under Ben Cheatham, including the 1st Tennessee; the left wing was led by General Hardee.

Bragg, in Frankfort preparing to fight Sill, ordered his main army to concentrate at Versailles. Hardee dispatched a message to his commander that the rapidly approaching Federal III Corps made concentration at Perryville a necessity.

Bragg wrote, "The village of 300 has an excellent road network with connections to nearby towns in six directions. That gives us strategic flexibility and will prevent the federals from reaching our supply depot in Bryantsville. It also has a very good source of water and we need some."

The area hadn't had significant rain in months. The early October heat was oppressive for both men and horses. West of Perryville, rivers and creeks provided a few sources of drinking water. Most were reduced to puddles. Still, even stagnant patches of water were desperately sought after.

On October 7th Buell reached the Perryville area as Union cavalry skirmished with Confederate rear guard for much of the day. The commanding general rode into camp with the III Corps led by General Charles Gilbert. Buell was greeted by General Thomas and his other two corps commanders, Alexander McCook of the I Corps and Thomas Crittenden of the II Corps.

The five men gathered in a Sibley tent to discuss strategy. "Bragg is in Perryville," McCook announced. "They're building defenses and deploying infantry."

"So this is where they want to fight." Buell cast a steely gaze at his generals. "Well, let's not disappoint them. We shall attack. I want all three corps to move into position at three in the morning and attack at ten tomorrow."

"What about water?" Gilbert asked.

"Take it as you find it. There are ponds west of town."

Hardee established a defense across the three roads leading into Perryville from the north and west with three of Buckner's four brigades. On the evening of October 7th, the final Confederate forces began to arrive. Cheatham's brigades marched through the night for Perryville. In Polk's division were Maney's brigade, Feild's regiment and Ledbetter's company, the Rutherford Rifles.

The company trudged as quietly as they could through the musky heat of the Kentucky night. Sam Davis marched alongside Joe Cates, whose lips were cracked and his tongue swollen. He continued to dehydrate as sweat rolled down his forehead.

"Joe," Sam rasped through parched lips, "we'll find water at Perryville. I know we will."

Joe continued to march with no response to Sam's comment.

Sam called out, "Joe, Joe!"

"Leave 'im be, Sam," Will Searcy urged, "he's sleepin'."

"But he's marching, Will."

"That may be, but he's sleepin' just the same. I'll answer ya. Yep, I sure hope we get somethin' to drink soon."

Around midnight the hot, thirsty, weary force reached Perryville.

* * *

THE 2ND MINNESOTA, in Gilbert's Third Corps, endured hardships as well. On the night of the 7th, they halted in Doctor's Creek valley about three miles west of Perryville. Clint Cilley approached his men in Company C, gesturing in the moonlight toward the dry creek. "There are small pools. Guards have been posted to keep horses and mules away, except for those reserved for them."

"Lieutenant," Rincie DeGrave called, "I ain't had a good drink of water for a week. Now we drink mud?"

"It's wet. You may break ranks."

With that command, the men of Company C scoured the creek bed for puddles of water. Some scrambled on hands and knees and slurped the precious dirty liquid out of holes like thirsty dogs.

They rested in the creek basin, sleeping on the ground without tents. Early the next morning they continued in search of water toward Perryville.

* * *

AT 1:00 A.M. BUELL sat on a chair in the Dorsey house a few miles due west of town, his right leg stretched out onto another chair. A fall from his horse had left him unable to ride and having to oversee the battle from the house.

His staff officers and General Thomas were busy with reports and dispatches. Buell called to Thomas, "Pap, the shooting should start soon. All divisions must be on the move in a couple of hours."

Thomas said, "There's been a delay. The I and II corps aren't in position."

"Delayed? How?"

"Apparently they deviated several miles from their line in search of water."

Buell shook his head in disgust. "When will they be in position?"

"I don't know. It's unclear."

Buell turned to an aide. "Prepare a dispatch for each of my division commanders: 'The attack will be delayed until October 9th. You will complete your division's deployment and avoid a general engagement today.' See that Crittenden, Gilbert, and McCook get copies of this."

Fate intervened in the presence of algae-covered pools of water in Doctor's Creek. Troops from the 10th Indiana and 7th Arkansas collided as they frantically sought the foul fluid. Shots were fired. The battle began at 2:00 a.m.

Buell and Gilbert, realizing that the cork was out of the bottle, decided to go ahead and fight. General Philip Sheridan was ordered to seize Peter's Hill. The Battle of Perryville was on. Bragg was still in Frankfort, believing Sill's attack there was the major thrust by Buell's army.

He ordered Polk in Perryville to attack and defeat the "minor" force there, then bring the army to Frankfort to unite with Smith's men. Early that morning, Polk dispatched Bragg that he would attack vigorously. But the former bishop changed his mind and went into a defensive position. Concerned he could hear no gunfire, Bragg rode to Perryville to take charge, arriving at 10:00 a.m.

After a quick survey of the battle line, Bragg met with Polk. "General," Bragg exclaimed, "I'm appalled at your line. There are gaps, and you're not properly anchored on the flanks. McCook's Yankees are north of town. We've got a big battle coming, and you're not ready."

"Sir," Polk protested, "you said the attack would be on Frankfort."

"Well, it's coming here. The federals have two corps out there, McCook to our right and Gilbert in our front. We'll realign into a north-south line and attack the Union left *en echelon*, one division after another."

"Which divisions?"

"The federals are on Mackville Road. Cheatham will begin a left wheel movement there. Then Patton Anderson's division will strike the Union center, followed by Buckner's division on the left. I want Powell to take a brigade to hit 'em farther south on the Lebanon Pike. See to it, General Polk. Get them ready to move."

* * *

FROM THEIR POSITION on the right, the Tennessee boys waited as the opposing lines drew up on either side north of Perryville. Sam watched the blue coats take position on a hillside. Each side eyed the other's movements. When the Union troops moved left, the Confederates matched with a parallel march to their right.

In the eerie calm before the storm, silence fell over the field. "What's goin' on Sam?" Joe Cates whispered, afraid to break the tense quiet.

"Waiting, sizing each other up, I guess. Something'll break soon."

At 12:30 the calm burst with an explosive flurry as Cheatham's artillery erupted. Bragg held back the infantry while Union troops filed in, extending McCook's line to the north, where an artillery battery was placed on Open Knob, a high hill on the northern end of the field.

Cheatham adjusted his position, then began the assault by crying, "Now! Give 'em hell, boys!"

Polk, the Episcopal bishop turned general, responded, "Give it to 'em, boys. Give 'em what General Cheatham says!"

Expecting to hit an open flank in the Union line, General Donelson's brigade found it massing into the Union center. The 16th Tennessee Infantry charged into a battery of cannon and halted in a depression, coming under heavy fire from the Ohio infantry and the eight cannon on Open Knob, 200 yards to the north.

Cheatham then ordered Maney's brigade to take Open Knob and relieve the pressure on Donelson's men. As the Union troops concentrated on Donelson, the Rutherford Rifles and the rest of Maney's troops approached the Knob undetected through some woods. They moved to the right, pausing at a spring to savor some gulps of the life-sustaining water and fill their canteens.

Sam and his friends waited in tense anticipation for the order to attack. Then it came. The Rifles burst from the cover of trees and over rock fences. Sam ran alongside Joe Cates as they scrambled up the base of the hill.

On Open Knob, brigade Union commander General Jackson fell mortally wounded. General William Terrill took over and redirected his fire to force the Tennesseans back. Through the blizzard of bullets, they hunched their shoulders, as if in a snowstorm, and kept advancing.

Shot after shot roared from the Union cannon, shaking the ground. The storm of metal shattered into the charging Confederates, ripping and shredding them apart. Smoke wreathed the hillside, and gunfire flamed through it.

In a brief pause, Will Searcy shouted to Sam, "Looks like we gone to Hell!"

"I see the devil!" Sam shouted back. "He's up on the hill!"

Then the rebels surged forward again through the smoke, fire, and lead.

* * *

TERRILL SHOUTED to his major, "I'm not gonna let 'em take the cannons. Hit 'em with a bayonet charge!"

Seven hundred seventy Illinois soldiers raced down the hill, fixed bayonets gleaming in the sun. Sam deflected a thrust and fired-point blank into his Union attacker. In front, Joe Cates turned his rifle into a club and smashed it into a bluecoat's face.

Then Joe turned to Sam with an odd smile on his face. Confused, Sam saw his friend grab his chest, then watched as blood oozed between his fingers before he crumbled to the ground. The momentary interlude was broken by another bayonet thrust at Sam. It sliced alongside his arm as he dodged. Sam slashed out with his own bayonet, finding its mark in the man's chest.

More Illinois reinforcements streamed into the fight. Briefly both armies held their own. Then Maney's artillery opened up and pounded the knob defenders. The boys from Tennessee swarmed up the hill, sweeping the Union soldiers from the crest.

The rebels continued west, down the reverse slope of Open Knob, through a cornfield and across Benton Road. There they encountered another steep ridge fortified by twelve Union cannon under General Alexander Starkweather.

The struggle continued in a field filled with ten- to twelve-foot-high cornstalks. As Union soldiers advanced into the cornfield, they couldn't see over the corn and were shocked to find Terrill's brigade retreating through the same field. Terrill himself shouted, "The rebels are advancing in terrible force!"

The Union general turned to make a stand and sent 200 men on another bayonet charge. They were smashed by oncoming Confederates. As Union soldiers had to hold their fire to avoid hitting retreating comrades, cannon fire from the ridge blasted among them, causing numerous friendly-fire deaths. Then the Rutherford Rifles and 1,300 more Confederates lined up and fired a withering volley that decimated the Union regiment.

The 2nd Minnesota had fallen in line to the rear and right of McCook's position. About noon they heard musket and cannon fire, but no order was given to advance. They waited in ranks until late afternoon, when their water supply again gave out. A company was detailed from the regiments in the division to find water.

It fell to Clint Cilley, under Colonel Bishop's direction, to make the search down the valley to the left. Carrying all the canteens of their regiments, the company pursued its quest. The roar of artillery and rattle of rifles grew louder as they moved along. Finally they found a pool and begin filling canteens.

Clint stood in silent amazement as he looked into the distance. "Private DeGrave," he called, "there's a really big battle going on out there."

Rincie followed his gaze. "We're in full view of the reb cannons."

"Lucky they don't care about us. They're too busy fighting McCook."

"Why aren't we fightin'? It looks like they could use us."

"I don't know, private. I really don't know."

The company returned to their previous position and, canteens were distributed. An order came to relieve McCook. They moved out a half mile into a strip of woods. There they waited, far back in trees and blind to what was happening on the battlefield. An occasional misaimed shell fell among them, but no one was hurt.

A mile to the west Buell waited. Sounds of battle were muffled or didn't reach him at all. The shadow echo phenomenon once again swallowed the sounds of battle. Therefore, Buell kept a large portion of his army in reserve, including the 2nd Minnesota, who waited for an order to join the battle.

As Buell ate dinner with General Gilbert in his headquarters house, he could hear cannon fire from his own ranks. Near the center, to McCook's right, Phil Sheridan had opened up his cannons to support McCook's besieged division.

Angered and misunderstanding the situation, Buell snapped at an aide, "Send a dispatch to Sheridan to cease the insane target practice. Doesn't he know a battle is about to take place?"

In the confusion, Sheridan ceased fire, but he hadn't been practicing. Through the cornfield the Rifles and other Confederates faced Starkweather's hill. The 1st Tennessee stormed the northern end of the hill, while the remainder of Maney's brigade attacked straight up the slope.

Strong rifle and artillery fire drove the Confederates back. But a second charge by the attackers resulted in a vicious hand-to-hand onslaught that brought Sam Davis and his comrades to the crest of the hill in the middle of the batteries. Pushed down the back slope, the Union forces regrouped. Led by General Terrill, they charged back up the hill. Exploding shot crashed above the Union soldiers. A piece sliced into Terrill, killing him.

Starkweather had managed to salvage six of his twelve cannon and moved them one hundred yards to the west atop another ridge. This time the Union soldiers had artillery, a stone wall and a steep slope running down from their position. Maney and Stewart's men tried three times to scale the hill. After the final failure they fell back to Open Knob.

The Confederate *en echelon* attack had continued with Anderson's division, to the left of Cheatham, hitting the Union center. A stalemate followed until attacks from the Confederate left by Buckner put pressure on the Union position.

As Anderson and Buckner battered the Union forces back, Bragg ordered Colonel Sam Powel to silence a battery in front to their left. Powel advanced, expecting to encounter an isolated battery and not the entire III Corps, which had not been engaged. Once they hit Sheridan's division, the Union soldiers lit into Powel and chased them back.

They ran as if in a steeplechase, jumping fences, crawling through ditches and ducking through cornfields with Union soldiers in hot pursuit. The rebels ran all the way into Perryville, where they took shelter. Strangely, Sheridan's men were recalled.

Bragg's pincher attack had stalled. They had forced McCook to mass his men at Dixie Crossroads, but the northern jaw of the pincher had been stopped at Starkweather's Hill, and the southern jaw ground to a halt when Cleburne could not dislodge Harris and Lytle's brigades.

On the far right of the Union line, General George Thomas wondered about the distant gunfire and sent a message inquiring into it. The reply told him not to be concerned, that McCook was doing a reconnaissance.

McCook had repeatedly asked for reinforcements. About 3:00 p.m. he sent a staff officer to ask for assistance from the nearest III Corps unit. The aide encountered 1st Division commander General Albin Schoepf, who sent him on to General Gilbert, who in turn ushered the man in to see Buell.

"What do you need men for?" Buell asked incredulously.

"General, sir, don't you know? All Hell broke loose north of town. McCook is just barely holding on."

"Nonsense, I've heard a few scattered shots, and what little artillery I heard was practice rounds."

"I'm sorry, sir, but you don't understand. There's a very big fight going on just a few miles from here. General McCook must have help."

Buell looked in bewilderment at Gilbert. "Can this be?"

The general looked at the bedraggled, sweat-stained, exasperated officer before him. "I think we should believe him, General Buell."

"All right, send two brigades of Schoepf's division to McCook. And, by God, find out what's going on!"

The reinforcements buoyed McCook as General John Liddell's forces attacked him less than 100 yards east of the Dixie Crossroads. Liddell's men, wearing captured Union trousers, fired at their distant targets. Cries of, "You are firing upon friends; for God's sake, stop!" echoed back to them.

Polk decided personally to find out who had been victimized by friendly fire. To his shock, he discovered they were not victims of friendly fire but of the 22nd Indiana, who had been confused by the blue pants of their attackers. Polk had ridden into the Union army.

His aide riding next to him whispered, "How the hell do we get out of this sir?"

"We bluff. Follow my lead. As of now, I'm a Union officer."

Polk rode down the Union line shouting orders, including "Cease fire! No shooting until further orders!" Then he galloped back to Confederate lines and shouted to Liddell, "Open fire!"

Hundreds of muskets opened up in a single volley, ripping into the Union troops. Liddell shouted to Polk, "Let's go get 'em, General."

Polk, unnerved by his escape, glanced at the setting sun and cried, "No, darkness is falling. We've done enough!"

McCook's men consolidated 200 yards to the west. Battered and beaten but not destroyed, they had made it through the day. The shooting of October 8th stopped.

In the gloom of the trees the 2nd Minnesota had missed another big battle. As their officers and men stood in the dimming light, Judson Bishop approached Clint. "Can you hear them? Listen." The rustle of grass and the firm tread of footsteps indicated an approaching army behind them.

"I hear them, sir. They're Union, aren't they?"

"Yes, I caught a glimpse of the Stars and Stripes."

A moment later the sound of a thousand snaps reverberated. "Wha . . . ? Bishop questioned. Then realization hit him. "They cocked their rifles! Down! Everyone hit the dirt! Get down!" Bishop yelled. Then, at the top of his lungs, "Don't shoot, we're the 2nd Minnesota! We're Union troops!"

"Just in time, we're Union too!" came the response from the rear.

Clint turned to 2nd Lieutenant Jude Capon. "That was close. Another few minutes and this would have been more than just another battle where all we do is dig graves."

"I heard men talking," Capon replied. "Why didn't we fight? About 30,000 of us stood by while McCook and his boys nearly got slaughtered. We could see it, Clint. We weren't even that far away."

Somberly Clint continued, "He went largely unaided, neglected and abandoned. Mostly, no one fired a shot or moved a step in his relief."

"It's a sad day, Lieutenant."

Both commanders were surprised at the battle's conclusion. Buell finally came to the realization a major battle had occurred and he had held much of his army in reserve. At 9:00 p.m. he met with his subordinates at the Crawford House near the battlefield.

* * *

"WE HOLD THE FIELD," Bragg asserted, "we've driven them back over a mile. They never attacked Frankfort. I thought they would. Tomorrow can be our day."

"Sir," Buckner countered, "I've just received word. Crittenden never fought today. His division never fired a shot. General, we were outnumbered the way it was, but Buell held a whole division out of the battle. They held us off with one hand tied behind their back."

Cheatham said, "We have over 3,000 casualties. Some regiments had heavy losses. The 1st Tennessee lost over half its men dead, wounded or missing."

"Not near enough Kentuckians joined us," Buckner continued. "Maybe some for cavalry, but not infantry, and not enough of the former, either."

Kirby Smith, who had come from Frankfort, leaving his army there, insisted, "For God's sake, general, let us fight Buell here! We can still beat him."

"We have to withdraw," Bragg concluded. "Look at what's happened. Van Dorn and Price were beaten at Corinth. Lee failed in his Maryland campaign. We have a victory, however isolated. Defeat here will cost not only my army but the bountiful food and supplies we've taken from the Yankees."

* * *

CHEATHAM SAID, "THAT REMINDS ME, I heard one of my Tennesseans say this was one hard-fought, close battle. If it was two men wrestling, it would've been a 'dog fall.' Both sides think they won; both got whipped."

"One more thing," Bragg added. "With the whole southwest in the enemy's possession, my crime would be unpardonable if I kept my noble little army ice bound here, without tents or shoes and obliged to forage daily for bread."

In firelight the battered survivors of Company I, the Rutherford Rifles, sat near a fire, their hollow, still-thirsty faces reflected in the glimmering flames.

Sam poked a stick into the burning wood. Red sparks shot into the black sky. "We lost Joe Cates today. I saw it. He was right in front of me."

John Beesley looked around. "Anybody see Will Searcy?"

"Dead," Charlie Miller said softly, "I saw him fall."

Sam remorsefully poked at the fire again. "I heard we won today. Captain Ledbetter said so."

Joe Hall shook his head. "If this is winning, I sure don't ever wanna see what losin's like."

The Army of Mississippi withdrew from Perryville to join up with Kirby Smith. They made their way southeast toward the Cumberland Gap and Knoxville.

Buell sent Crittenden's division on a halfhearted pursuit and then pulled back. But the Army of the Ohio claimed victory. It had driven Bragg from Kentucky and saved the state for the Union.

Kate Patterson

KATE PATTERSON AND COUSIN, fifteen-year-old Robbie Woodruff, rolled along in a buggy on the trail from LaVergne to Nashville, about nine miles away. Kate snapped the reins and clucked to her two-horse team.
"Heads up, stay on the road, be good to the Yankees."

Up ahead was a checkpoint near the Nashville city limits. A half dozen young Union soldiers blocked the road. Kate pulled to a halt in front of them.

"Johnny," she exclaimed, flashing a charming smile at a young blue-clad soldier, "they had you working here two days ago, don't you ever get a rest?"

"I asked for the duty," the young man smiled back, "just on the chance you might be comin' by."

"You know I have a maiden aunt in Nashville, Johnny. I'm bringing her some necessities. Billy, Charlie, good to see you again. You've got new friends. Introduce Robbie and me, you know we both like to meet handsome men."

Sheepishly the other three approached, "This here's Alex," Johnny pointed at the nearest, "and these are Frank and Donald. Here's your pass to Nashville, Miss Kate," he handed a piece of paper to her.

"So pleased to meet you. I'm kind of regular here, boys. I'll see you again soon." With a little wink in the men's direction, she flicked the reins to roll ahead.

Frank grabbed the bridle of one horse and looked at the other soldiers. "Ain't we supposed to check things out and make sure she's not got nothin' with her?"

Johnny, Billy and Charlie were amused by his suggestion. "This here is Miss Kate and Miss Robbie, look at 'em. Have you ever seen such pretty, innocent lookin' ladies? They come by here all the time. We used to check things over some, but they never had nothin' bad. Now we just let 'em go through after I give 'em a pass."

184

Frank released the reins. Kate snapped them over the horses' rumps. She smiled demurely, waved and blew a kiss as she rolled by.

"My, oh, my!" Robbie uttered softly, "that was kind of close."

"They would have found nothing. Those farm boys aren't smart enough to check for a false bottom in this buggy. Always keep on the good side of Union officers. Be sweet. Flirt even. It's how I get my passes."

"What are we bringing today, Kate?"

"Blankets, boots, spurs, the bulky things I can't fit around my waist where I carry the morphine and quinine."

"Do you think they'll ever get on to us?"

"Just keep being nice and smile pretty, Robbie. It's worked so far."

"Have you heard from Sam? Does he know what you're doing?"

"Sam's back in Tennessee. I think the army's going to Murfreesboro. He doesn't know what I'm up to."

"He'll be close. I bet he comes by."

Kate's eyes showed her longing. "He better."

The buggy with two pretty ladies rolled uninterrupted through Union lines and into Nashville. Soldiers and citizens mingled along the streets and in the shops as the girls passed. They stopped at the corner of Union and Cherry in the heart of the city.

"Just wait in the buggy," Kate told Robbie, "I'll be right back."

In a general store, Kate approached a sleepy-eyed old clerk, who gazed at her over wire-rimmed glasses. "Miz Patterson," he said, "what can I do you for?"

"Just the usual, Mr. Parsons."

The old man reached under his counter and produced a wrinkled slip of paper. He handed it to her. "Remember, you don't know where you got this."

Kate laughed. "I'll just say it came from a post office."

"There's lots of post offices around here."

"Some in hollow tree trunks, under rocks—you never know where the mail might be delivered."

Kate walked back into the afternoon sunlight and boarded the buggy. Robbie looked at her. "Where?"

Her older cousin unfolded the slip of paper and read, "Same as last time. The building in the alley off Jackson Street."

Minutes later the buggy clattered down a side street, where Kate reined the horses up in front of a wood building with a wide front door. A face appeared at a window. In moments, the door swung open and Kate drove the carriage into the darkened building. One large room, likely used for storage, dominated the space with a small room in the back.

When the door shut, sunlight from three high windows illuminated the room. Kate rushed into the arms of the man who had opened the door. Another man stood in the background.

"Ev," Kate cried, "every time I see you, I'm relieved you're still here."

"They're not on to me yet, baby sister. John Davis is here. You know 'im."

"Of course," she smiled at the tall man, Sam's brother, as he came out of the shadows. "Have you heard from Sam?"

"Nothing recent, ma'am. What do you have for us?"

"Open the bottom and find out."

As John and Ev Patterson began unloading blankets, boots, saddles, and other accoutrements, Kate retired to the back room for privacy. She emerged with a basket of packets she had been secreted under her garments.

"Morphine and quinine," she explained, "Father says about $500.00 worth."

John Davis whistled. "This'll really help out. The army's always short of drugs. People have a funny habit of getting shot or sick pretty often."

"How will you get this out of here?" Robbie wondered.

Ev explained, "Riders come by and take it. No one suspects a new saddle is going out to Forrest or wherever, when some fella is just riding out of town. The Yankees are a lot less suspicious of people leaving Nashville than of those coming in. They seldom search anyone going out."

"What do you have for us?" Kate inquired.

Ev handed her a packet. "Newspapers, troop movements, personal items. Put them at the 'post office' on Nolensville Road."

"The hollow tree?"

"That's the one. Is all well at home, Kate?"

"It's all quiet, save for the fellow who claims to be a cattle buyer. He still comes by, usually when Yankee troops are around, and he never has any cattle."

"Watch out for him."

"We will. Now we better go. I want to get us home before nightfall."

As the buggy rolled out onto the street the two men watched. "You've got a brave sister, Ev," John observed.

"Or a very foolish one."

"Either way, she's one good-looking woman."

"And that'll either get her in trouble or keep her out of it. It depends on how she uses that attribute."

About halfway home, Kate drew her buggy to a halt. Robbie jumped out and hurried to the side of the road. There she stuffed a packet through a hole in a tree trunk. "It'll be there to get picked up tomorrow if the squirrels don't get it," the girl smiled.

"Or the Yankees," her cousin replied.

As they reached the Patterson house, the girls were alarmed to see a dozen solders astride horses in the yard.

"Yankee patrol," Kate murmured. "I'll do the talking."

The buggy came to rest before the house, and a Union captain stepped off the porch and approached Kate and Robbie.

"Miss Patterson," he greeted, "your father doesn't seem to have seen anything out of the ordinary. How about you?"

Kate smiled sweetly and lowered her eyes, "I'm honored you paid us a visit and think we can help you. Robbie and I are just returned from Nashville. A band of cavalry passed to the north of us. I think it was General Forrest."

"Thank you, ma'am," the captain tipped his hat. "We'll look into it."

After the soldiers rode off down the dusty road, Robbie shook her head. "We didn't see any Confederate soldiers."

Kate laughed. "No, but there's no harm sending Yankees off on a wild goose chase."

Dr. Patterson came off the porch. "They're coming by more often. I wonder if they're getting suspicious."

"That this is a headquarters for spies, couriers, and Coleman's Scouts," Kate fanned her face in mock fear, "I hope not."

"Our cattle-buying friend came by again this morning,"

"Any cows this time?"

"Not a one, Kate. He says he wants to buy your mother's fat one, though."

"Funny, isn't it. He's here in the morning and a Union patrol comes in the afternoon. Have you let our boys know he was here?"

"Your brother Charlie brought word when he went to our clinic in town. So far no one's been able to find evidence he's a Yankee spy. The fellow covers his tracks real well."

A few days later was Christmas Eve. Ellen Patterson, daughter Margaret, and the two young boys, along with Kate and Robbie, prepared the house for Christmas. The aroma of bread wafted from the kitchen adjoining the dining room as the women prepared decorations for a pine tree braced in the middle of the living room. Doctors Hugh and Charlie Patterson were at their office in LaVergne and would be returning before nightfall.

Ellen happily hummed as she strung ornaments on the green branches. Suddenly Kate uttered a loud, "Shsssss! Listen!"

From outside came an unmistakable "*Bob-White, Bob-White*," call.

"Raise the shutter, Robbie," Kate urged. "We have company."

A minute later came a soft rap at the back door. "Who's there?" Ellen Patterson asked.

"Private Richard Adams, Alabama Cavalry."

Ellen cautiously opened the door to reveal a uniformed, slender young man with a scraggly beard that looked like it had given up trying to grow full.

Adams stepped into the house. "Jake will stand guard at the door," he motioned to second private outside, "and Johnny's back in the woods with the horses. Do you have any word for us?"

"The cattle buyer," Kate answered, "was by last evening *and* this morning. He asks all kinds of questions. Most have nothing to do with cattle."

"Like what?"

"Like where are my brothers? Do we see anything 'suspicious' going on?"

Jake stuck his head through the doorway. "There's a man comin'. He's crossin' the field to the right, a little behind the house."

Robbie rushed to a window. "It's him!" she exclaimed, "the cattle buyer!"

"Come in," Ellen urged Jake. Then, turning to Adams, she informed him, "There's a loft above the kitchen, get up there."

Just after the two scrambled up into the loft, a sharp rap sounded on the front door. Ellen opened it to find a lumpy, middle-aged man in a cheap, wrinkled suit standing before her.

"Miz Patterson," he began, "I've been walking around all day checking on cattle, I'm sure nuff real hungry. Can you spare a bite?"

"Certainly. We don't turn away travelers, especially on Christmas Eve, and you aren't even a stranger. We've seen you enough around here some think you're part of the family."

Ellen Patterson bustled into the kitchen to prepare food while the girls took the man into the dining room. Kate demurely asked, "Such a fine man like you, well spoken, handsome, you've got bigger things going on than buying cows, don't you Mr. . . . ?"

"Jones," he smiled slyly. "You could say I have other enterprises. Lots of things are happening 'round here. People like to know about such things."

"Who likes to know what?" Kate smiled, leaning toward him.

"Well, for one thing, Tennessee's becoming a Union state again. Nashville has a Union-sympathizing governor, Andrew Johnson, but rebels are still about, and we . . . er . . . they need to keep track of them."

"I thought Ishman Harris was our governor," Margaret asserted.

"Not anymore, Missy, no more rebel governors in Tennessee."

Ellen placed a plate of sweet potatoes and sliced ham before Mr. Jones. He beamed, "I'm much obliged, Miz Patterson.

"So what do you do?" Robbie inquired, "To help out, that is?"

"I watch for Confederate activities. Then I report to federal agents what I see. Have you seen any suspicious characters about?"

Ellen feigned thoughtfulness, "Why, just this morning, remember Kate, a Confederate soldier came through here. I think his name was Private Adams, three others were with him. They seemed very well informed."

"Where did they go?"

"I'm sure they went to Nashville by way of LaVergne."

The women continued to talk, mixing gossip with real news while Jones happily devoured his plate of food. Adams and Jake, listening from the loft, decided to make a move. Stealthily Adams climbed down the ladder from the upper room. Jake clumsily slipped, and his foot made a *thump*. Jones momentarily looked up.

Kate, dropped a large plate, that shattered on the floor.

Ellen began to loudly berate her daughter. "How can you be so clumsy? That was my last good, big plate!"

The woman stomped toward her daughter and overturned a chair that crashed to the floor. Kate cried out her remorse. Through the bedlam the ravenous man kept eating while Adams and Jake crept up behind him.

Jones felt the cold steel of two pistol muzzles on the back of his head. A voice behind him said, "Unbuckle yer belt and let yer arms fall to yer sides."

"I'm just a farmer, stopping by," Jones asserted. "Let me finish eating."

"You take another bite, and it'll be yer last," Adams sinisterly proclaimed. "Now do what I said."

Jones dropped two pistols to the floor.

"Whew weee!" Jake exclaimed, "Them's two real purty Colt army pistols."

A further search of Jones revealed a packet of papers. "Just livestock notes," the man protested.

Adams closely examined the papers, then declared, "This, in a very clever code, reveals the movements and position of the Confederate army."

Ellen interrupted. "Who are you two? Mr. Jones is a guest in this house. You just get out of here and leave him alone!"

"Sorry, ma'am," Adams replied. "He's going with us. Small mercy is shown those who would reveal our army's secrets."

As the three men left through the back door, the girls laughed. "Well," Ellen claimed, "that was very well done, if I do say so myself."

"Mr. Jones is a guest in this house. You just get out of here and leave him alone!" Kate mimicked as she laughed more.

"I think we've seen the last of Mr. Jones," Robbie concluded. And they had.

Aftermath

PRESIDENT JEFFERSON DAVIS called his Mexican War compadre to Richmond. He asked Bragg to explain the charges brought by his officers about how he had conducted the Heartland Campaign into Kentucky. The long, slender Confederate president stroked his white goatee as he viewed the general sitting across the desk from him. *Bragg looks a little puffed up,* he thought, *like a rooster trying to impress a hen.*

"Mr. President," Bragg began, "we won at Perryville. I know that some cast aspersions on my conduct of the battle. The fact remains, we captured food, supplies, and cannons, and Buell pulled back."

"General Bragg, you left Kentucky. It's completely in Union hands now."

"Sir, I had no choice. I had to—"

Davis stifled the comment with a wave of his hand. "I've seen the report. I know your reasons. I'm concerned about these comments from your subordinates." He placed his hand atop a stack of papers. "You have senior generals asking me to put Joe Johnston in charge. One says he'll never serve under you again. Another wants to challenge you to a duel. I've even heard from privates complaining of your heavy-handed treatment of them."

Bragg squirmed. "They're not in my place. They don't know all the factors I must consider. Discipline must be maintained or I'll have no army."

"General, I'm not going to remove you from command today. But you are nearing the end of your rope. I served with you in Mexico. You're a fine officer, and I trust you. Try to work more closely with your generals and do the job I have confidence you can do."

"Thank you, sir, I plan to head to Murfreesboro. We will regroup there."

Bragg's army had been reorganized into the Army of Tennessee.

* * *

DON CARLOS BUELL was not as fortunate as Bragg. His failure to follow up Perryville with an aggressive pursuit of Bragg cost him his job. That army was now the Union Army of the Cumberland, and Lincoln had named Major General William Rosecrans commander, telling him to be aggressive or be replaced.

* * *

IN MINNESOTA companies B, C, and D of the 5th Minnesota remained on garrison duty until replaced by the 8th and 9th Minnesota regiments. December found Jimmy Dunn at Fort Snelling, glad that his long wait was nearly over. The company was going south.

Cheers and excitement greeted the news, but something seemed lacking.

Jimmy sat in a warm barracks with Oscar Wall and Andy Williamson. "Sure, the boys seemed happy, but something don't seem right," he said.

"I thought they cheered pretty good," Andy noted.

"It should have been louder. I think the boys have seen what war is and ain't so thrilled to fight rebs anymore."

"Maybe they're thinking about those who aren't here. Trescott and Findley and Captain Marsh."

Andy looked around the room and muttered, "Lots of the boys took it pretty hard."

"Well, I know one thing," Jimmy asserted. "Whether they cheered as loud as they could or not, these boys want to fight rebs, and they will."

"And soon," Oscar agreed.

* * *

SAM DAVIS and the Rutherford Rifles marched back through the Cumberland Gap from Kentucky. They followed the trail to Knoxville, reaching it in a snowstorm. After spending the night outside in bitter cold, they boarded a train for Tullahoma, Tennessee. They remained there until November 22nd before heading home to Murfreesboro and Rutherford County. To be near home at Christmas seemed a real blessing for the men of Rutherford County.

Other regiments of Bragg's army went on to Chattanooga, then back up north to Murfreesboro, Tennessee. There Bragg planned to spend the winter.

On the tenth of October, the 2nd Minnesota began its march south from Kentucky. Along the way they frequently interrupted their procession with encampments and duties. At one point they spent ten days clearing out and guarding a railroad tunnel. At Gallatin, Tennessee, they guarded a ford. On a couple occasions they endured raids by the cavalry of John Hunt Morgan.

They spent Christmas in Nashville and were ordered back to Gallatin on the 26th, where they drilled, foraged and pleasantly encamped.

Murfreesboro

STONES RIVER

WITH WARTIME, Christmas Day brought a stark foreboding that overshadowed the joy of the season. Union troops under Rosecrans left Nashville and marched toward Murfreesboro. LaVergne lay in between, and the Rutherford Rifles had been sent to the small town on picket duty.

In the Patterson home, Kate gathered in the warmth of their dining room with her parents, brothers Robert, James, Ev, and Charlie, and sister Margaret.

"A beautiful day," Kate observed, "and not a Yankee in sight."

"I wonder if they got anything from your captive, Mr. Jones," Dr. Patterson said.

"All I know is they took him away. I don't think we'll see him again."

A soft *clink* came to a front window.

"Who could that be?" Charlie asked. Ellen moved a lantern onto a table in front of the window.

Moments later they heard a rap at the door. Dr. Patterson opened it. Sam stepped in. Kate raced to him and wrapped her arms around him in joy. The men slapped him on the back in greeting. "I had to stop by," Sam explained, "we were so close, in LaVergne, and it's Christmas."

Kate forced a pouty expression. "I'd've never forgiven you if you hadn't."

"But I can't stay long. We're moving out, back to Murfreesboro. Rosecrans will be here tomorrow."

Hugh Patterson looked concerned. "Why don't you stand and fight?"

"I think we will, sir, but not here. The ground's better for us around Murfreesboro."

"Well, sit down," Ellen urged. "We were just about to eat."

As all sat to their Christmas repast, the conversation bounced from family to local events and back to the war.

"Your brother John is with us, you know," Ev explained.

193

"I've heard some things, but they're pretty vague. What are you doing?"

"We're scouts for a man called E. Coleman—not his real name. We deliver messages and goods when we can."

"I help them, too," Kate said proudly.

"You!" Sam said with concern. "It's too dangerous!"

Kate replied soothingly, "Not if it's done right. The Yankees don't suspect me at all."

"She's very good," Ev explained.

"Please be careful." Sam looked at Kate, then around the table. "All of you, be careful."

A short time later Sam announced he had to return to the Rifles. Kate followed him outside. "I heard you were hurt at Perryville. Are you all right?"

"Just a little slice on my arm from a bayonet. I'm fine."

"No ill effects?"

Sam wrapped his arms around her. "Do I feel strong enough to hold you?"

Kate answered him with a kiss and whispered, "You be careful, too. Don't worry about me. You're the one with bullets whistling around you and bayonets coming your way."

Sam kissed her again and disappeared into the night.

That night only half a mile separated the Union and Confederate pickets near LaVergne. On the 26th the Union soldiers advanced. The Rutherford Rifles fired and fell back, shot again and retreated. They continued to fall back until the night of December 27th, when they camped on the Thomas Hord farm near Stones River by Murfreesboro. There Bragg determined to make his stand.

Cavalry regiments under Forrest, Morgan, and Wheeler harassed Rosecrans's march from Nashville. On December 29th Wheeler's 2,500 rode entirely around the Union army, destroying supplies and capturing ammunition.

Earlier, on December 13th, the 2nd Minnesota and their brigade were ordered to join their division at Murfreesboro. They set out from Gallatin, then were turned around and marched back. Fears of an attack by John Hunt Morgan kept the Minnesotans in place for two weeks.

Bragg's forces had been camped near Murfreesboro for over a month. The Army of Tennessee was divided into two corps, led by Hardee and Polk. Hardee met with Bragg and questioned his battle plan.

Hardee asserted, "General Bragg, this isn't the place to fight them. The ground's too flat. Father south the Duck River Valley would be much more defensible. Even the Stewart River area just north of here would be better."

Bragg was perturbed. "No, general, this is the place. In this rich agricultural area I can provision my army, and holding this town blocks the path to Chattanooga. I can't surrender another inch of Tennessee to the Yankees. We have to hold here. They have a slight numerical superiority, but we have a much stronger cavalry. Wharton will make them pay. He'll savage their rear and supply lines.

"The Yankees are stretched out on a four-mile front northwest of town. We'll make a line parallel to them. You, General Hardee, on the west of Stones River and Polk on the east. You'll hit their right flank at dawn on the 31st, turn them in on their rear and cut them off at their base, the Nashville Pike."

"I don't like the ground, General Bragg."

"You don't need to like. Just fight."

Ironically, Rosecrans had proposed nearly the same battle plan. The main difference was timing. He ordered Tom Crittenden to attack the Confederates right after breakfast on December 31st. Bragg instructed Hardee to launch his attack on the Union right earlier, at dawn.

The two lines were about seven hundred yards apart through the night of the 30th. In the cool stillness, a strange battle broke out. Not of bullets, but music. From the Union lines a band played "Yankee Doodle" and "Hail Columbia." From across the line floated the strains of "Dixie" and "The Bonnie Blue Flag." Then one band began to play "Home Sweet Home" and thousands of soldiers from both sides joined in song.

At first light the next morning they began killing each other again as Hardee's men smashed into the Union right. McCook's division was pushed back three miles by a frenzied Confederate attack.

By noon the Union line had been forced back in right angles to the original line of battle. Rosecrans recalled Crittenden's attack on the Confederate right flank and rushed his forces to McCook to stem the rebel advance.

Rosecrans raced across the battlefield with his aide, Julius Garesche, overseeing his men and troop movements. By the time he got to McCook, his uniform was covered with blood.

"Are you hit?" McCook inquired anxiously.

Rosecrans's face was ashen. "No. Garesche was right next to me when a cannonball took his head off."

A second Confederate wave under Polk swept into Sheridan of McCook's division. Cheatham, Cleburne, and General Jones Withers hit Sheridan. But the Union general was the only one who had anticipated a rebel attack, and he had alerted his men at 4:00 a.m. They were ready to fight and held their ground for four hours until they ran out of ammunition. They then regrouped and fell back in a defensive position on the Nashville Pike.

The Rutherford Rifles were ordered to move forward and support Withers, whose troops were facing stiff resistance near the Wilkinson Pike. Bragg called General Breckinridge for support but received a reply that Breckinridge was threatened by an attack and could not move this troops. He made a piecemeal attack near twilight to little effect. Yet when darkness fell, Bragg held the field.

He held a conference that night with his commanders. In a house near Murfreesboro the Confederate officers analyzed their day. Bragg was of mixed sentiment. He sent a message to Davis reading, "The enemy has yielded his strong position and is falling back. We occupy the whole field and shall follow him. God has granted us a happy New Year."

But Bragg was not satisfied. He believed that, without blunders by some of his generals, the victory would have been complete. He turned on Breckinridge. "General, you were instructed to attack the Union left and claimed you couldn't because Crittenden had too strong a force before you. He wasn't there. There was little resistance facing you. Crittenden had been moved to reinforce McCook on their right. Obey my orders, general," he concluded angrily.

Polk interceded, "We lost 9,000 men. It was a bloodbath."

Bragg launched into a defense. "By ten in the morning we had captured twenty-eight cannon and 3,000 Yankees. I'm sure the enemy suffered greater losses than we did. If orders had been adequately followed, and if I hadn't been given false reports, we would have crushed them. Tomorrow we shall."

Hardee inserted, "I pray that's true. But, General Bragg, we were to cut off Rosecrans on the Nashville Pike, his base of communications. To do that we had to overrun them from the start. Failing to, the result was we pushed the Yankees back into a defensive position by the pike. That made them stronger where we were trying to cut them. They grew stronger as they concentrated, and we grew weaker as we spread out."

Bragg concluded, "We're still on the verge of complete victory. Do your jobs, gentleman."

* * *

ROSECRANS HELD A COUNCIL of war in the wavering light of a campfire before his tent. Sheridan, Crittenden, Thomas, and McCook joined their commander, along with other brigade commanders. The general had a strong face. He wore a brown mustache and a closely trimmed beard that extended onto his cheeks. His dark hair was cropped mid-ear and neatly combed.

He opened with a sad, solemn commentary. "I suppose you've heard my chief of staff, Colonel Garesche, was killed today. You may not realize he has been my friend and confident since we went to West Point together. Julius was a good man, but there was a strangeness about him. You see, he had a dream in which he was killed. His premonition was he wouldn't survive his first battle. His priest brother confirmed his dream as an omen of disaster."

The general's face sagged with emotion. "We were riding together to address an emergency in our line. Confederate artillery saw me and fired. Julius took the shot. He was almost Christ-like in his sacrifice. I just wanted you to know."

Thomas Crittenden softly replied, "War is hard, General. It hits even commanders in a personal way. We are all sorry."

General Rosecrans shook his head as if to wipe clean the sad thoughts from his mind, then offered, "All right. Enough maudlin thoughts. We have a battle yet to win. Tell me what you think."

Rosecrans listened as his generals debated strategy. Several voiced the opinion they must retreat or would certainly be cut off and defeated by Bragg.

Crittenden countered them. "Yes, we were pushed back and our battle line is shorter and concentrated, but we're unbroken. General Sheridan, my hat's off to you. You lost three of your brigade commanders, yet you held on for four hours in a slaughter pen, losing a third of your men.

"Colonel Hazen, they kept hitting you on the left flank in the Round Forest. Your line held."

Hazen said, "It couldn't have be held without McCaskill bringing the 3rd Kentucky in to reinforce us."

McCaskill added, "We would've fought to the last man to hold it."

George Thomas paced in front of them. "I will not fall back and shame the brave men who so valiantly fought here today." His eyes glared as he snapped, "This army does not retreat. This is a good place to die."

Rosecrans offered the final exclamation point. "We will stand and fight from this spot of ground!"

* * *

Little fighting happened on January 1st. Van Cleve's division moved across the Stones River to some high ground, and the Union line strengthened. But each side spent most of the day caring for their wounded and burying their dead. Wheeler's cavalry continued to harass the Union line of communication on the Nashville Pike.

On the afternoon of January 2nd, Breckinridge's troops were ordered to assault Van Cleve's division on their new position, a hill east of Stones River. After being driven back, the Union troops unleashed a relentless volley into the attacking Confederates.

Then from Crittenden's troops came devastating fire, from forty-five hub-to-hub cannons, from a ridge overlooking McFadden's Ford. Twelve more cannon from the southwest smashed into the Confederates from the side.

In an hour Breckinridge lost 1,800 men, and his attack stalled. Thomas ripped into the gray line with a shattering counterattack. Hanson's brigade of Kentuckians lost a third of its men in the Yankee onslaught. The Confederates retreated as night fell.

Breckinridge, a Kentucky native, rode among the destroyed Kentucky brigade. "My orphans, my poor orphans!" he shouted. "You can't go home. The Yankees have Kentucky!"

During the night Rosecrans received more supplies and men. Wheeler failed in his attempt to capture ammunition-filled wagons. Bragg could do nothing but retreat. He wrote to Davis, "The federals have 70,000 men. I have 20,000 fit to fight them."

The Army of Tennessee withdrew from Murfreesboro to Tullahoma thirty-six miles south, while Rosecrans moved in to fortify it as a Union stronghold. When urged to pursue the Confederates, Rosecrans replied, "Bragg's a good dog. But Hold Fast's a better." Each army had lost nearly 12,000 in casualties.

The Rutherford Rifles went into winter quarters at Shelbyville, Tennessee. The 2nd Minnesota had not been sent to Murfreesboro and remained at Nashville.

Abraham Lincoln wrote Rosecrans, "You gave us a hard earned victory, which, had there been a defeat instead, the nation could hardly have lived over."

The Vicksburg Campaign

O N DECEMBER 12, 1862, companies B and C of the 5th Minnesota joined Grant's army and the rest of the 5th Regiment at Grand Junction, Tennessee, in preparation for a campaign through central Mississippi.

Jimmy Dunn was overjoyed to be reunited with his regiment. His enthusiasm was obvious at his camp with Andy Williamson and Levi Carr.

"Just talked with Lieutenant Gere. He says his brother, the lieutenant colonel, told him we're goin' to Vicksburg with Grant. Isn't it grand? We're finally gettin' to do what we signed up for."

"I sure didn't sign up to fight Indians," Andy agreed.

"Poor boys from Company D got left behind," Levi reminded them.

"Lieutenant Gere says they'll be comin' next month. Then the whole regiment will be together."

"Not all together," Andy corrected, "we lost nearly thirty fighting the Dakota, and Oscar Wall was mustered out when he got hurt."

Levi nodded. "It was all horrible, but it made us better soldiers. We've been shot at. We've been tested. We'll be ready for the rebs."

"How'd ya like to be one of the regiments left behind?" Jimmy asked.

"Not exactly left behind," Andy corrected. "From what I've heard, the 6th, 7th, and 10th are goin' into the Dakota Territory with Sibley to hunt down Little Crow."

"Don't forget the 8th," Jimmy said. "They're staying in Minnesota on patrol."

"What about the 9th?" Levi wondered.

Andy replied, "Rumor has it a couple companies are going west with Sibley. The rest will eventually join us."

"Well," Jimmy said, "I'm not sure where we're goin', but I know it ain't west to fight Indians."

* * *

THE ARMY REACHED Oxford, Tennessee, before rebel cavalry cut communication and supply lines. Late in December Grant established winter quarters along the Memphis & Charleston Railroad near LaGrange, Tennessee. There the army underwent complete reorganization. The 5th of Minnesota became part of the 2nd Brigade, 3rd Division 15th Corps commanded by General Sherman.

The 5th, with other troops, left at year's end in search of Nathan Bedford Forrest, a tough mission. They endured severe weather, inadequate shelter, and sometimes scanty rations. All the while they chased the elusive Forrest through west Tennessee with only an occasional skirmish to tease them along.

After two weeks they rested at Jackson, Tennessee, before being ordered to join Grant at Memphis. While Confederate armies continued to hold Union forces in check in the East, generals Grant, Curtis, and Butler had driven deep into the western half of the Confederacy.

George Curtis soundly defeated Confederates in Arkansas at Pea Ridge, relieving rebel pressure on Missouri and allowing Grant to move south unhindered to the Mississippi. Ben Butler and naval officer David Farragut captured New Orleans, cutting the western Confederacy off from the sea.

When the 5th moved south with Grant in March, they knew if they could capture Vicksburg, nearby Port Hudson would fall and the Mississippi River would be totally controlled by Union forces.

Only Vicksburg stood in the way. The city rested on a high bluff on the east side of the river, overlooking a hairpin bend. Any boats heading down the Mississippi had to face a gauntlet of artillery. To the north, the city was protected by impenetrable swamps and Chickasaw Bluffs. To the south, more swamps and another fortress city, Port Hudson, guarded that approach.

Grant had several different plans to take Vicksburg, while Confederate commander Pemberton had one big decision to make: stay or leave. Orders from President Davis were explicit: Vicksburg and Port Hudson must be held.

But this differed from the belief of General Joe Johnston, commander of the Department of the West. Johnston believed the two cities were both useless militarily and should be left for the Yankees. Indecisive and unsure whom to please, Pemberton dug in at Vicksburg to make a stand.

Attempts had been made to take Vicksburg since the spring of 1862. In May, Farragut ineffectively shelled the town. On December 20th, Sherman left Memphis with 32,000 men. Meanwhile, Van Dorn's rebel cavalry destroyed Grant's main depot at Holly Springs, Mississippi, while Forrest raided the Tennessee railroads. This caused Grant to halt his advance on Vicksburg and retire northward. His first attempt to take Vicksburg ended in failure.

On December 29th Sherman attacked the Chickasaw Bluffs north of Vicksburg and was repulsed with heavy losses as Pemberton rushed in reinforcements. Sherman retreated north to Helena, Arkansas. The second offensive had failed.

General John McClernand tried next. He came down the Yazoo River and was driven back by Confederates at Fort Pemberton. Admiral David Porter, commanding a squadron of gun boats, tried to traverse narrow bayous but was forced to abandon his expedition due to intense gun fire from Confederate marksmen.

After weighing his list of options, Grant decided on a new approach, which would shield his boats and troops from the artillery. They would dig a canal. Sherman was placed in charge.

Where the Mississippi formed the hairpin bend around a neck of land across the river from Vicksburg, Grant reasoned, by coming down the river on the west side of the neck, they'd be shielded from the guns. They'd then dig a canal across the neck, move their boats over and cross the river below the artillery.

Minnesota boys were handed shovels and told to dig a ditch a mile long and wide and deep enough for deep draft vessels. Jimmy and Willie Blodgett stood knee deep in muck, spading shovels full of slop from the ditch.

"Is this what ya signed up for, Jimmy?"

"Naw, I wanted to be a gambler. Now I'm the ace of spades."

The men chuckled. Levi Carr asserted, "They coulda brought in contrabands to do this and left us to do soldierin'."

"I'd feel better about it," Jimmy said, "if I thought it'd work. This is just a big mess. But, remember, Grant thinks we can crush the rebellion."

Andy Williamson paused and leaned on his shovel. "I wonder if Pemberton's watching us and laughing. He was a northerner until he got married to a southern belle. He even spent two years in charge of Fort Ridgely. I met him there."

"Let's dig faster, boys!" Jimmy called. "Andy has a friend up there. He wants a reunion!"

Dig they did. But when they were almost across and ready for the canal to be filled with water, the river level fell, leaving the canal bed higher than the river.

"Well, this is a switch," Will Blodgett observed. "We're the second try at a canal. The last time, it flooded and filled up with silt and mud."

"Two useless ditches," Jimmy agreed, "one with too much water and one too little."

Next, Grant decided on another approach for getting around the Vicksburg guns. Again Sherman got the job. Twenty miles above Vicksburg, where the Yazoo River joined the Mississippi, it intersected with a body of water called Steele Bayou. But first it ran through a series of rivers, bayous, and streams.

By loading troops into ironclad gunboats, Sherman planned to take his men on a two-hundred-mile roundabout journey through a labyrinth of brush, forest, and water infested by snakes. Eventually they would emerge on dry land below Vicksburg and sweep over the city's defenses from the rear.

Company B and the 5th Minnesota joined Sherman on what became an ill-fated venture. The first day they made sixty miles by slashing through over-hanging trees with saws and axes. The next day, Confederate sharp-shooters raised havoc with the gunboat crews. Sherman's infantry drove them off and they continued, only to find a bend in the river had become a morass of cut timber assembled there by the rebel army.

Sherman proclaimed it "the most infernal expedition I was ever on" and ordered a retreat.

Grant met with McClernand and Sherman in his camp north of Vicksburg. "Cump, I've been asking you to do the impossible. I'll try again."

"Well, Grant, what do you have in mind?"

"First off, I'm done trying to take Vicksburg from the north."

"How do you propose to get by the artillery and swamps?"

"I'll divert their attention. I want Colonel Grierson to take his 1,700 cavalry and head to Mississippi. Colonel Streight will head to Alabama with another 1,700. That should keep Forrest busy. General Steele will move his men north, and you, Cump, will demonstrate around Vicksburg."

"What will be happening while I'm demonstrating?"

"General McClernand will be taking his corps down the west side of the river, to New Carthage. After your exhibition, you'll join him over the river and march south with him."

"General," McClernand questioned, "Vicksburg's on the east side of the Mississippi. If I march my men on the west side, how will we get across?"

Grant chuckled. "I'm going to have Porter's fleet run the batteries under the cover of darkness. They'll bring you over."

"That's pretty risky," McClernand commented.

"I've tried everything else. We've tried frontal assaults, going through a tangled jungle of a bayou, we've even tried to dig canals twice. This is it. This is what will work."

On March 29th McClernand's XIII Corps begin to march down the west side of the Mississippi, hoping to rendezvous with Porter's boats at Hard Times, Louisiana, Grant's staging area below Vicksburg.

On the night of April 16th, as the diversionary forces of Grierson, Streight, Steele, and Sherman began to move, Porter's fleet tried to pass beneath the Vicksburg bluffs and its massed artillery.

Pemberton's cannons blasted into the gunboats. Cotton bales on the riverside were set aflame to illuminate the watercraft as they passed. Porter's fleet was damaged. Some gunboats were sunk. But most of the fleet got through and continued safely down the river.

Now Grant was in position to engage his plan. He intended to cross the river at Caffe Point, opposite the Confederate fortress at Grand Gulf. But Porter's attack from the river failed with the loss of a gunboat.

Meanwhile, Sherman's attack against the Yazoo Bluffs north of Vicksburg deceived Pemberton and caused the Confederate commander to concentrate north while Grant was moving south.

Failing to take Grand Gulf caused a minor change in Grant's plan. They would now cross at Bruinsburg, Mississippi, farther south and beyond Confederate guns. On April 30th McClernand's and McPherson's forces began to cross. The 4th Minnesota was in McPherson's XVll Corps.

The only Confederate cavalry in the area had been ordered away to pursue Grierson's raiders. Confederate General John Bowen had no "eyes" to tell him where Grant had landed.

Grant's forces were traveling light. The only food they carried was what fit in their haversacks. Grant announced, "All I'm bringing with me is my toothbrush." Unintentionally, McClernand had provided an impetus for his men to move quickly, but he had forgotten to issue his men rations.

The Union army pushed rapidly toward Port Gibson. On May 1st, after a stalemate between Bowen's forces and Union troops on the Rodney Road leading to Port Gibson, McPherson devised a turning movement that would render untenable the entire Confederate right flank.

Bowen was maneuvered out of position and left Port Gibson after ordering the defenses at Grand Gulf be abandoned with the powder magazine exploded and the artillery destroyed.

Grant headed to Grand Gulf, where he took his first bath in weeks and conferred with McPherson and McClernand. "I've heard that the Confederates expect us to move on Vicksburg now. They've crossed over the Big Black River Bridge and have fortified the roads going north. But we're not going north."

"Where are we going?" McPherson inquired.

"East to Jackson. We'll take their capitol in the home state of their president. The roads are open. The Black River's between Jackson and Vicksburg. They're on one side. We're on the other. They can't risk leaving Vicksburg and couldn't catch us anyway."

"They have no army to oppose us?" McClernand surmised.

Grant shook his head. "I wish it were that easy. I'm told Joe Johnston's come up to defend Jackson. General Gregg has a force there, too. Sherman left Chickasaw on the 2nd. He should be here soon, then we move out."

On May 8th Sherman caught up with Grant and McClernand. McPherson's corps was ahead, where he defeated a Confederate force at Raymond on the 12th. The 5th Regiment had drawn duty on the skirmish line and marched out in front and on the flanks of Sherman's and McClernand's corps as they continued on toward Jackson. McPherson joined them on the road.

The Minnesotans relentlessly marched on the 13th, almost constantly exchanging rifle fire with retreating Confederates. "Why are we the ones that hafta do this?" Willie Blodgett cried.

"'Cause we're so good at it, I guess," Jimmy answered.

"I've had enough being out front exposed to gunfire. I had enough of it at Redwood Ferry to last a lifetime."

"Where do ya wanna be?" Jimmy teased. "Back home, all safe with yer mommy?"

A shot whistled by. Jimmy snapped off a bullet in return.

"Tomorrow you'll be back in the ranks, Willie boy, don't worry."

The sun was an orange ball balancing upon the horizon when the Confederates decided to make a stand at Mississippi Springs. After a sharp exchange of gunfire, the rebels were dislodged when an order came to halt and bivouac for the night. As the Minnesotans sat around campfires, some playing cards in the flickering light, others singing or munching hardtack, division commander General Tuttle rode up. "Exemplary work, men. First rate. I need you to do it again tomorrow. Keep up the advance and move forward at four o' clock in the morning, maintaining your position as skirmishers."

Groans and mumbling, even a curse from the darkness, greeted the general's words. Tuttle turned to Colonel Hubbard. "Tell your men they're the best I have at this assignment. We need them to continue their fine work."

As the general rode off, Hubbard repeated his words of encouragement. Jimmy poked Willie in the ribs. "See? What'd I tell ya."

"It ain't fair!" Willie shouted.

Hubbard answered, "Just do your duty. We all have our tasks."

The next day the 5th skirmished all the way to Jackson. Tom Gere rode to Hubbard as the men paused on the edge of a clearing. Before them, about a mile distant, was a stand of timber.

Gere cautioned, "Colonel, we've got a smooth, open field here with nothing for cover. There's a ditch about halfway to the trees. It looks full of brush, but I'd be surprised if there wasn't something else in there, like a rebel army."

"Tell the men to advance with caution. Be ready to shoot."

They'd moved thirty yards from the ditch when Confederate skirmishers and infantry opened up on them with a heavy volley. The Union soldiers fell prone on the grass and fired back.

"Stay low!" Andy Williamson shouted.

"I sure will," Jimmy responded as he fired, then rolled over to reload on his back. "Weeds and grass might hide me a bit, but it sure don't give much cover."

"Here they come!" Gere yelled as gray- and butternut-clad soldiers rose up from the ditch and rushed toward them.

"It looks like Fort Ridgely, boys! Let 'em have a volley!"

A blast of fire and smoke roared from the grass. The attacking Confederates fell back, likely because the main column of the Union army had reached the area and advanced to support their beleaguered regiment of skirmishers.

The rebels scampered to the rear where the main body of their army waited. Hubbard ordered his men to advance. The Confederates had taken a position on the opposite bank of a bayou separating the Union soldiers from the town.

As the 5th advanced, a tumult of grapeshot and canister from a cannon battery on the bayou ripped through them. Two batteries of Union artillery were brought up and, after nearly an hour of sharp fighting, forced back the rebels.

* * *

THE PREVIOUS DAY, Joe Johnston had arrived in Jackson to discover General John Gregg only had 6,000 men to defend the town. Johnston was ordered by Secretary of War James Seddon to proceed at once to Jackson to take command.

Faced with two divisions of federal troops, Johnston told Gregg, "We don't have enough troops here to make a defense. More are coming, but they aren't here yet. I want you to fight a holding action. Buy us time to evacuate so we can get out of this town. Then fall back and let the Yanks have Jackson."

"Just let 'em have it?" Gregg questioned.

"We can't hold it, General. We'll take it back later. If you try to stay, you'll be slaughtered."

At about five o'clock Hubbard shouted, "Charge!" and the 5th, followed by the main Union column, raced double-quick into the Confederate entrenchments. They braced with bayonets fixed into the defenses and found them mostly empty. The army of Joe Johnston had evacuated Jackson, but not before sending an order to Pemberton to attack Grant at Clinton, about ten miles to the west.

As most of Sherman's and McClernand's divisions turned to advance on Vicksburg, the 5th Regiment stayed behind on provost duty in Jackson. They destroyed the railroad and anything thought to be of value to the Confederacy before leaving the town on the 16th.

Grant's Army of the Tennessee marched nearly directly west of Jackson toward Vicksburg. The 4th Minnesota in McPherson's division was among them. Pemberton, with three divisions and 23,000 men, had moved out per Johnston's order and had left Edwards Station east of Vicksburg. His troops were now in the open between the Union army and the city. On May 15th after the Battle of Jackson, he had to make a decision.

Pemberton fathomed the ground before him. The Pennsylvania native with the Virginian wife turned to John Bowen, a division commander next to him.

"Johnston wants us to hit Grant at Clinton."

Bowen shook his head. "It's still too dangerous. Grant has supply trains moving from Grand Gulf to Raymond. They're a much more inviting target."

"I wish Johnston were here."

"He was late getting here in the first place," Pemberton complained. "Now he's retreating with his army up the Canton Road." He paused and considered. "Let's hit Grant's supply train."

The next day while the Confederate army was marching on the Raymond-Edwards Road after Grant's supplies, another order came from Johnston. It repeated his demand that an attack be made at Clinton.

Pemberton ordered a countermarch. But they didn't reach Clinton before encountering Grant at Champion Hill. The Confederates drew up into a three-mile defensive line along the crest of a ridge.

After early skirmishing, Grant arrived on the scene at 10:00 a.m. He sent McClernand's corps to assault on the Union left and McPherson's corps on the right. Sherman, with the 5th Minnesota, was well behind, having left Jackson later.

It became a battle of attack and counterattack with McPherson more heavily engaged. Bowen's and Stevenson's divisions pushed the federals beyond the crest of the hill on the Union right but couldn't hold it for long without help. The 4th Minnesota was ordered to the right flank.

Pemberton ordered William Loring to transfer his men from the southern line, where the fighting was light, to the crest to help Bowen. He refused, citing a strong Union presence before him.

Grant's men then smashed into Bowen with Stevenson driving them back. Pemberton had only one escape route left, back to Vicksburg. He ordered his men to fall back onto it. Loring found himself cut off and with only one alternative: try to find Johnston and join him.

On the night of May 16th, Pemberton fell back to a defensive position at the Big Black River in front of Vicksburg, while Union troops followed him, taking Baker's Creek Bridge and Edwards in the process.

The Confederates, commanded by John Bowen, fortified the east bank of the river to hold back the Union pursuit. Behind cotton bales and abatis the rebels waited. Union artillery burst upon them. Then a Union charge surged from a rocky prominence, across the front of the rebel forces, through waist-deep water and into their breastworks.

The defenders, in a mass panic, broke and ran across a railroad bridge over the Big Black River and then set fire to the bridge. Nearly 1,700 were captured and many others drowned. Pemberton's forces limped back into Vicksburg with less than half the numbers they'd had at Champion Hill.

Vicksburg was a veritable fortress, strongly fortified, inaccessible in many approaches. Earthen forts connecting elaborate earthworks crowned the heights around the city. Abatis of fallen timber blocked all avenues into it. Pemberton had only 18,500 men left for defense, but they were resolute behind six and a-half miles of hills, knobs, steep angles, redoubts, lunettes, and gun pits. The line, anchored on the Mississippi River on each end, curved around Vicksburg.

On May 19th Grant drew his forces around the defenses and attacked, assuming the Confederates would have low morale after their defeats and would be vulnerable. Sherman's force attacked but ran against a six-foot deep, eight-foot wide ditch, beyond which was a seventeen-foot wall with abatis before it and withering musket fire. After heavy resistance, the Union army withdrew as Grant waited for the rest of his army to arrive. He would have 35,000 with more on the way. He determined to prepare better and try again.

Johnston had found safe haven away from Jackson and was reorganizing his command. He sadly relayed to his staff officers, "General Pemberton should have headed north when he had the chance. Now he's backed into a corner with no way out. I warned him he was fighting for something with no military value. We could have used his army out here. Now he has no chance. By staying in Vicksburg, he sealed his fate and the fate of the city."

"Can't we give him aid?" a captain asked.

"I'm getting reports of steamers unloading troops north of Vicksburg. Grant will have twice the army he has now very soon. They'll either attack Pemberton and defeat him or will besiege him and starve him out."

Fatigued, bloodied, hungry and yet exulted, the Minnesota regiments before Vicksburg, the 3rd, 4th, and 5th, settled in to camp.

Levi Carr watched as members of the 4th marched by. "Huzzah for Minnesota boys!" he shouted as they stepped proudly.

One shouted back, "We're sure more than home guards!"

Levi turned to Jimmy. "What's that mean?"

"That's what they call some western troops when they first got here, meanin' they wasn't fit to do anything but guard their homes. I guess they showed 'em at Champion Hill."

"I wish we coulda fought there too, Jimmy."

"Lots of battles and none of us fought in all of them. The 3rd didn't really get into any. But they're here now."

"What do we do, Jimmy?"

"First off, get some food in our bellies. Then we do what General Grant tells us to do. We're just privates, Levi."

Ample supplies came down the Mississippi north of Vicksburg, and the Union soldiers' empty haversacks were soon filled with a bounty of food.

The Confederates were now bottled up in Vicksburg with four divisions and the town populace trapped inside their lines of defense. Despite being repulsed by a bloody barrage on the 19th Grant's army was in high spirits. As the general rode by, Jimmy Dunn shouted "Hardtack!" Soon soldiers up and down the line were yelling, "Hardtack, Hardtack!"

On the night of May 21st the army was fed beans, hardtack, and coffee. They were ready to fight the next day and sure of victory. The city and its defenses were under barrage all night. Two hundred-twenty cannon blasted from the east while Porter's gunboats bombarded from the river side.

At 10:00 a.m. the Union assault was launched. Their line curved parallel to rebel defenses, with Sherman's corps to the north of Vicksburg, McPherson in the center, and McClernand to his left. Sherman tried to mass his men and force through a narrow corridor. Murderous fire drove them back. McPherson's men closed within a hundred yards and then were stymied.

All along the front, Confederates poured lead mercilessly at the blue-clad combatants.

The boys of the 5th Minnesota were on Sherman's left, advancing down a wagon road.

The order to charge came as Tom Gere shouted the command, "We can't move in line of battle. Charge by the flank!"

That circumstance saved many of the Minnesotans from certain death. The 11th Missouri was the leading regiment, thus was first to emerge, running by flank from protective timber. Its men melted down like candlewax from rebel gunfire, which came from the right and left of the road they were concentrated upon.

By the time the 5th reached the battle line, heaps of dead and wounded were piled on the site as if Confederate soldiers were using them as an obstructive abatis. The Minnesotans knelt behind the bodies and used them as barricades as they fired back at the Confederates.

Gere looked to the right and shouted, "Get over there to the fallen timber and ravine! It's the best cover around!"

The regiment scrambled over dead and wounded bodies and dived into the protective ditch and timber. There they waited until nightfall, when they crept back to safety in the rear.

Grant held a council of war. He was distraught at McClernand for giving, in his opinion, confusing reports. Sherman held up a hand and offered, "Yes, mistakes were made, but this was just plain murder. We can't take this place by assault."

Grant sighed. "Then we'll put them under siege. I had hoped to avoid a protracted engagement here. But we have no choice. We'll take Vicksburg. It's just a matter of time."

The Tullahoma Campaign

ON THE FIRST OF FEBRUARY, the 2nd Minnesota Regiment trod over rough, narrow, dirt roads toward Franklin in search of Wheeler's cavalry. It was a futile search. Colonel George, in ill health, was given leave to return to Minnesota. Lieutenant Colonel Bishop took command.

Much of February was spent foraging for food and making sorties after rebel cavalry. On March 2nd camp was established at Triune, about halfway between Murfreesboro and Franklin. After being ordered to guard a ford on the Harpeth River, the 2nd encountered a Confederate patrol and took sixty prisoners.

General John Schofield became division commander, and the bugle band had more time to practice and perform. Each night a concert of fine music echoed over the Tennessee woodlands.

For most of March and all the way into June, the 2nd was based at Triune. They had occasional excursions after rebel patrols, but much time was spent in drill and formations. One highlight came on the first of May when the regiment received new shelter tents called "pup" tents.

"What a wonder!" Rincie DeGrave exclaimed as he held up his half of a light canvas tent. "All ya need to do is find a friend to hook up the other half with, and ya got yerself a home."

"Right," Charlie Orline agreed, "now all ya need to do is find a friend."

As the men around laughed, Clint Cilley addressed them. "I'm glad to see you men enjoying yourselves. You'll find these new shelters will be quite handy. Each of you will carry half a tent. This will allow us to reduce the number of wagons needed for each regiment from thirteen to three, and only one mule for officer's baggage."

Rincie smiled broadly. "Tell us, Captain Cilley, last month we got new Enfield rifles, this month new shelters—yer spoilin' us. What's next?"

Cilley sniffed and laughed. "Maybe a bath. You fellas could use one."

"No," Rincie countered, "I've decided no baths 'til I get back to Minnesota."

"And that, my friend," Charlie rejoined, "is why you'll sleep alone."

With Rosecrans anchored at Murfreesboro and Bragg at Tullahoma, thirty miles south on the Duck River, both spent much of that winter and the spring of 1863 sending out fruitless cavalry raids and bickering with superiors over their intentions for their armies. The Confederate defensive position ran along the Duck River from Shelbyville to Wartrace.

Bragg was concerned Rosecrans would try to seize the strategic city of Chattanooga, vital for its railroad connections and the gateway to northern Georgia. His cavalry protected each flank and a front of seventy miles. Fearing an attack would be made on his left, Bragg placed Leonidas Polk with his largest corps entrenched at Shelbyville.

Eight miles to the right, William Hardee was positioned in Wartrace, from which he could reinforce three passes through the Highland Rim, namely Bell Buckle Gap, Liberty Gap, and Hoover's Gap.

Rosecrans kept his army in Murfreesboro for six months. He built a fortress and resupplied. Heavy rains struck middle Tennessee in the spring of 1863, and Rosecrans was reluctant to traverse the muddy roads.

Lincoln, Halleck, and Secretary of War Edwin Stanton all urged the Union commander to resume his campaign against Bragg. The president wrote, "I would not push you to any rashness, but I am very anxious that you do your utmost, short of rashness, to keep Bragg from getting lost to help Johnston against Grant."

Rosecrans replied, "If I were to start to move against Bragg, he would likely relocate his entire army to Mississippi and threaten Grant's Vicksburg Campaign even more. By not attacking Bragg, I am helping Grant."

Such logic befuddled Lincoln and Halleck, who again urged attacking Bragg.

The Tennessee boys encamped at Shelbyville became bored and restless during their lengthy stay there. Time was passed playing poker and chuck-a-luck. Money for gambling was long gone, so corn kernels substituted for cash.

Assemblies to witness punishment for various transgressions were still common under Bragg's discipline. All of Cheatham's division was called out to witness the execution of a young boy, seventeen or eighteen years old.

Sam Davis watched as the boy rode before them in the back of a wagon, sitting upon a coffin. Joe Ewing grumbled, "They gonna make us stand here and watch whilst they set the post to shoot 'em at and dig his grave? Couldn't they at least already have that done?"

A young officer answered, "General Bragg wants it to make a big impression. Making a show of it will dissuade others from desertion, slacking, cowardice, or whatever. At least, that's the hope."

Sam studied the officer. He was a young man, blonde, close shaven, slight of build, with a good face. Then he remembered. "Sir, I knew I saw you somewhere! After Shiloh, when we were marching back to Corinth, you rode by and spoke to us. You're Tod Carter. I'm Sam Davis. You had dealings with my father."

Carter beamed in recognition and shook Sam's hand. "We don't seem to be meeting up in the happiest of circumstances."

"I don't see you much. You're with the 20th Tennessee?"

"Yes, but I'm in the Quartermaster Department."

"We're not far away. Do you get home to Franklin?"

"It hasn't worked out for me yet. I hope to soon. But the Union army has a garrison in Franklin."

Joe Ewing asked, "Since you're with Cheatham, maybe you can tell us. When we gonna get outta here and do something?"

"They don't tell me, private. Our main task is to defend Chattanooga. We are in position to do that. Rosecrans has been in no hurry to do anything, either. It looks like as long as he sits, we sit."

They fell silent as the digging finished and the regiment chaplain walked up to the condemned man. The chaplain read from the Bible. The whole regiment knelt for a prayer. A general came up and shook the boy's hand just before he was tied to a post.

An officer then shouted to a rifle detail, "Ready, aim, fire!"

The stillness of the morning was shattered by the roar of musket and screams from the boy. "Oh, oh God!"

Then all watched with a sickening silence as the boy's head dropped onto his chest while his body remained tied by a rope to the wooden post.

Joe whispered to Tod Carter, "I never wanna see one of these again."

* * *

THE 2ND MINNESOTA stayed based at Triune. Occasionally they marched maneuvers in the hot sun. After hearing the sound of artillery firing near Franklin, the regiment was moved in that direction. After a day-long march in hot, sultry weather, the night became pitch black with flashes of lightning creasing the inky sky. A downpour turned the road soft and slippery, and men often slipped and tumbled into the mud.

After a ten-hour march, Captain Cilley guided his men into Franklin. All was peaceful and calm, the Union garrison apparently asleep, with no Confederates to be seen. They spent the night on village lawns waiting for the dawn.

Throughout the day they made a futile search for evidence of rebel soldiers. Then on June 6th the regiment returned to Triune, where the regular routine of battalion and brigade maneuvers and guard duty resumed.

After previous unheeded messages, General Halleck sent a blunt note to Rosecrans. "Is it your intention to make an immediate movement forward. A definite answer is required, yes or no."

Rosecrans responded, "If immediate means tonight or tomorrow, no. If it means as soon as all things are ready, say five days, yes."

In a week the general of the Union Army of the Cumberland finally decided the time was right. On June 23rd Rosecrans's army was on the move in a campaign to drive the Confederates out of middle Tennessee and take Chattanooga. The 2nd Minnesota fell into formation, ready to go where Rosecrans chose to send them. It was raining when they left Triune, and it would rain for fourteen of the next seventeen days.

The Minnesota regiment was part of an elaborate feint by Rosecrans. Bragg felt the main attack would be on Shelbyville on his left flank. At the same time, the XXI Corps division of John Palmer moved to Bradyville, well beyond the Confederate right flank. There he could push back Confederate cavalry and get into the rear of the rebel forces.

Rosecrans called his corps commanders together to explain the elaborate plan he'd spent six months concocting. He announced, "We'll slide Granger's corps to the left, covering the Shelbyville approaches, and perform a giant right wheel of the army. Bragg will be focused on Shelbyville, where he has a strong force. He thinks we'll be on his left, but we'll hit his right.

"I want General Thomas to march southeast on the Manchester Pike and head for Hoover's Gap on Hardee's right. The gap is lightly manned, so speed is of the essence. This is where we'll smash them hard. Our secret weapon has arrived, the seven-shot repeating Spencer rifle. I'm anxious to see them work."

On June 24th Rosecrans's army moved out on the three gaps. Wilder's brigade of mounted infantry reached Hoover's Gap nine miles ahead of Thomas's main body. Six miles to the west, McCook's forces attacked Liberty Gap.

Wilder's "Lightning Brigade" raced into Hoover's Gap and drove off the 1st Kentucky Cavalry. Then they dug in with their Spencer repeaters at the ready and prepared to hold their position in the face of a Confederate assault.

* * *

IN HEAVY RAIN two Confederate brigades moved into position, one led by Bushrod Johnson, Sam Davis's teacher in Nashville, included the 20th Tennessee. They charged the gap, screeching the "rebel yell," facing a withering volley from the federals. Expecting the usual respite while the defenders reloaded, the Confederates charged on, only to be cut down almost instantly by another volley and another and another as the Spencer carbines cut them to pieces.

Johnson pulled back after losing a quarter of his men, nearly 150. The gap was secure when Thomas arrived. He grabbed Wilder's hand. "You've saved the lives of a thousand men today. I didn't expect to get to the gap for three days."

"Well, sir," Wilder responded laconically, "I think we kind of surprised them with the Spencers. They didn't know what hit 'em."

* * *

AFTER ONE DAY of fighting through heavy rain, the Union army held two of the gaps and was in position to turn Bragg's right flank. As the 2nd Minnesota sloshed through the mud on a skirmish line, Aaron Doty called out to Clint Cilley, "What's this battle called, Captain? Where are we?"

"I guess historians will find names for the battles, private. But I've heard officers call this the Tullahoma Campaign."

"What's a Tullahoma?" Rincie DeGrave wondered.

Doty thought. "Near as I can figure, 'Tulla' is Latin for 'mud' and 'homa' means 'more mud.'"

Clint looked at Doty and burst into laughter. "I think you're right, and I went to Harvard and took Latin."

* * *

ON JUNE 25TH the Rutherford Rifles marched into Tullahoma to bolster Bragg's defenses there. Bushrod Johnson, with Bates's division, renewed his attempt to drive the Union troops out of Hoover's Gap. Cleburne resolved to do the same at Liberty Gap. Both were unsuccessful. Rosecrans moved his army forward until they stalled in the quagmire of a road as rain continued to fall.

Bragg met Polk and Hardee, his commanders in Tullahoma, on June 26th. In the drab living room of a procured house, Bragg was livid. "It was a feint at Shelbyville. I should have known! Rosecrans intended to hit us hard on the right all along. That's what I have cavalry to tell me. Where were Forrest and Wheeler?"

Bragg's face flushed, his brown-and-white beard quivering. "Tom Crittenden was moving through Bradyville and behind us, and no one reported it to me. Incompetence!"

"What do you suggest now that we know?" Hardee asked.

"General Polk, march your corps tonight toward Murfreesboro, through Guy's Gap, and attack the Yankees from behind at Liberty Gap. General Hardee, you hit them from the front."

Polk blanched. "This is impossible, General Bragg. We've already been driven out of the gaps and repulsed when we tried to retake them. With their repeating rifles, it'd be a suicide."

"The real threat," Hardee added, "will come from Thomas. He'll break out of the gap like a wild horse."

"We need better understanding," Polk complained. "Communication with your commanders is poor."

"Our position here at Tullahoma is unsuitable," Hardee added.

Bragg straightened his back and glared at his generals. "General Johnston and I are in agreement. Move your force in the direction of Manchester and delay Rosecrans. That'll give me time for a counterattack. Those are your orders."

Polk and Hardee walked from the house together. Hardee spat a brown stream of tobacco and muttered, "Bragg's an idiot. I'll do my best to save an army whose commander's an idiot."

Bragg called off Polk's attack when he realized the impending threat posed by Thomas. Hardee ordered his men at Hoover's Gap to fall back towards Wartrace and not Manchester. Rosecrans was able to complete his plan to outmaneuver and outgun Bragg at every turn.

After Tullahoma was flanked, Bragg withdrew on July 3rd as Rosecrans was preparing for a frontal assault. The Rutherford Rifles and the Army of Tennessee began a march to Chattanooga. Once in the vital railroad hub, Bragg knew he needed help and luck to hold it. But Rosecrans was in no hurry.

Stanton urged Rosecrans to follow up and obliterate the retreating Confederates. Instead, the general regrouped away from Chattanooga and once again took his time in developing a plan. Newspapers would call Rosecrans's Tullahoma Campaign one of the most brilliant military maneuvers in the entire war. But Lincoln and Stanton were not satisfied, believing their general had passed on the opportunity for a more complete victory.

Vicksburg Falls

AFTER HIS ASSAULTS on Vicksburg failed, Grant settled in for a siege. A twelve-mile semicircle front anchored by the river on both ends was matched by Grant's network of trenches and ditches, some so close to the Confederate fortifications fuse grenades could be thrown by hand into their midst.

The hot sun of late May scorched both sides and created another problem. Dead bodies of men and horses in the trenches and terrain between the armies began to decompose and wreak. Wounded men cried out in pain and desperately begged for water.

Jimmy Dunn covered his ears and urged his sergeant, John Bishop, "I can't bear to listen to this. Can't we so somethin'?"

"I heard General Grant thinks a ceasefire'll make the rebs think us weak."

"Weak? Doin' nothin' while men are dying in front of us is what's weak."

Grant relented. A truce was called, allowing both armies to tend to their dead and wounded. Side by side, men wearing blue and gray carried comrades, dead and alive, off the battlefield.

Once the truce was over, Confederate marksmen peered over parapets at their own peril as Union snipers took deadly aim. Yet Grant was not content. With his friend "Cump" Sherman, he looked over the mass of entrenchments.

"We need reinforcements. I can't cover twelve miles with fifty thousand men. Plus cover the enemy's other movements."

Sherman observed the distant fortifications and agreed. "Too bad we couldn't take them when we attacked."

"I only have one regret about our two assaults. We failed. Halleck's sending more men. We need them. Kirby Smith's rebels are raising hell across the river in Louisiana, and Johnston's still behind us in Jackson. He could move on us any time."

"At his own peril," Sherman surmised.

"I do not like sieges!" Grant proclaimed. "I hate just sitting and waiting for something to happen. We must take advantage of the inequalities of the

216

ground to start mines, trenches or advance batteries. But if a regular siege is what's in the cards, I'll just out-camp them and incur no more loss of life."

"We could dig under them and blow them up," Sherman suggested.

"Cump, I like the idea of explosives. Kill 'em from far off, less loss for us. I feel good here, if we need to venture out twenty to thirty miles after reb patrols, we can."

"How will Ord be?"

"Fine. You know him. Certainly better than McClernand, that self-serving politician general."

"It was a bit grand of him to take credit publicly for our successes around Vicksburg."

"His self-promotion gave me the opportunity to replace him with Ord. I have little regard for political soldiers; he did nothing to raise my esteem."

On June 7th Confederate raiders sought to cut off Grant's supply line at Milliken Bend up the river. Black Union soldiers, aided by fire from gunboats, suffered heavy losses but drove off the rebels.

An almost continuous barrage poured into Vicksburg from gunboats in the river and artillery on the land. As the days grew into weeks, the conditions in the city turned perilous. Grant tried to seal off prospective aid to Pemberton by sending a force to the Louisiana side of the river to keep troops of Kirby Smith and Dick Taylor at bay, then sent a division to the Black River Bridge to watch for Johnson's movements. His troops totaled 77,000, affording Grant the luxury to move them around. The three Minnesota regiments waited in the ever-tightening circle around Vicksburg.

The threat posed by Dick Taylor caused Grant to send Sherman's 2nd Brigade under Joe Mower, including the 5th Minnesota, up the Yazoo River. At Satartia on June 4th and at Mechanicsville on June 6th rebel forces were badly beaten. But another menace was surfacing.

Tom Gere addressed the men of Company B. "Taylor is back over the river. He's regrouping and approaching Vicksburg from the west. He's got an army of Texas and Arkansas boys—tough as nails. Colonel Hubbard says that the 2nd Brigade's crossing into Louisiana to stop them."

Sergeant John Bishop regarded his men. "I think we're ready to do it, sir!"

Shouts of "Huzzah!" burst from a hundred throats.

Gere smiled. "Dick Taylor doesn't have a chance!"

On June 14th the 2nd Brigade found Taylor's army at Richmond, Louisiana, just off the Mississippi River. The 5th once again drew skirmish duty as the whole regiment was deployed in the vanguard of the brigade's advance.

Bishop, marching with Company B, called out, "Easy, men, watch your step. Nice flat ground ahead, nothing like what we faced at Vicksburg."

"Skirmish line again," Charlie Beecher complained.

Jimmy Dunn looked at Ole Svendson. "We keep doing what we're good at."

About a mile from Richmond they encountered the Confederate skirmish line, strongly fortified. Gere rode in front of his men. "Just got word, men," he called. "Fix bayonets. We're going to charge."

"After Vicksburg, a piece of cake," Jimmy yelled. "Lotsa room, flat, let's go!"

Colonel Hubbard rode up, lifted his saber, pointed ahead and cried, "Charge!"

With a loud "Huzzah!" from the ranks, the regiment, followed by the entire brigade, raced forward. They overwhelmed the skirmish line and burst into the town facing only light resistance. Dick Taylor and his troops were already in retreat making for the cypress swamps of the interior.

Grant kept the 2nd Brigade on the west bank of the Mississippi for the duration of the siege in case Taylor or other Confederate forces reappeared. Behind the levees, on the Louisiana shore, batteries were erected. Each night hot shot and shells were thrown into Vicksburg.

Pemberton stood on a parapet with his staff officers and viewed his predicament. He turned to a major and asserted, "We can't hold much longer. Grant's tightening his line around us. Vicksburg's getting blasted to bits. I'm amazed only a few have died."

"It's the caves, sir. We counted about five hundred of 'em. The whole population is dug in. They've even moved furniture, fixtures, and paintings into them. It's food we need, for our army and the town."

"Funny, we have all the ammunition and guns we need. Even the constant shelling doesn't bother me as much as the food shortage."

"Horses, mules, dogs have become scarce. I've even heard that rats are becoming a delicacy. Half of our soldiers have been hospitalized."

"I know that many are sick, major."

"Malaria, scurvy, dysentery and diarrhea, all related to bad or no food. Sir, they're eating their shoes. The amazing thing is that the people don't want us to give up. They're still with us. Where's General Johnston?"

"It's too late for Johnston. We're outnumbered more than two to one. I can't be responsible for what'll happen if we don't surrender. The innocent, women, children, the men in town, to say nothing of our army, have no way out of this. We can't fight our way out, we can't wait them out, and we're getting no help. We have to surrender."

"When?" a colonel asked.

"A few days. I know these people. If we surrender on July 4th, their holiday, we'll get better terms."

On July 1st the earth under the Confederate defenders was rocked for the second time in a week. Just six days earlier, a mine dug under rebel fortifications was loaded with 2,200 pounds of gunpowder and set off. The resulting crater was forty feet wide and twelve feet deep. But when Union soldiers charged into it, they literally became sitting ducks for rebel marksmen. Artillery shells with short fuses were rolled into the crater by defenders. Only after ladders were lowered in were the Union soldier's extricated.

The July 1st crater wasn't as deep, and no attack followed. Engineers were ordered to plan another, more effective underground attack. The order became moot when Pemberton sent Grant a note on July 3rd asking for surrender terms.

Grant met with Sherman and Ord. "It's over, gentlemen," he announced.

"What terms?" Ord asked.

"I've responded as I did at Donelson, 'unconditional surrender.'"

Sherman hesitantly looked at Grant. "Are you sure that's such a good idea?"

"What do you mean?"

"There are 30,000 sick, starving men in that town. We'll have to feed them, care for them, then watch over them and bring them to a prison camp."

Ord added, "It'll tie up our army for months."

Grant considered, then nodded his head. "I'll relent on my terms and parole them to their homes. I think many of these men want nothing to do with war anymore."

On July 4th the surrender became official. With the fall of Vicksburg and Port Hudson, the Confederacy was now cut in half. Abraham Lincoln proudly announced, "The 'Father of Waters' again flows unvexed to the sea."

After Vicksburg, the 5th Minnesota rejoined Sherman's XV Corps and pursued Joe Johnston's retreating army, fleeing eastward. After the pursuit was called off, the 5th went into camp at the Big Black River.

The 2nd Minnesota, after the Tullahoma campaign, retired to camp at Winchester, where they remained a month.

The Rutherford Rifles went into camp south of Chattanooga and were largely inactive until September. For Sam Davis, however, a change was in the offing.

Sam Joins the Coleman Scouts

ARLY JULY FOUND SAM and the Rutherford Rifles camped just south of Chattanooga. The 1st Tennessee had been combined with the 27th Tennessee to form a Consolidated Regiment.

They were under the command of Colonel Feild and placed in Maney's Brigade, Cheatham's Division, Hardee's Corps, in Bragg's Army of Tennessee. The soldiers were listless and bored on a late afternoon in camp.

Sam, with Bill North, Charlie Miller, Marion McFarland, and Bob Jones ate sloosh around a campfire. Others played cards. In the distance the soft, haunting strains of a song reached them.

"'Lorena,'" Charlie muttered, "I thought it was banned."

"It's a pretty song," Sam commented, "The men love it."

Bill poked a stick in the fire, stirring up red sparks and embers, "So pretty that men desert when they hear it so they can get back to their own Lorena's."

"Make ya miss Kate?" Charlie teased.

"I don't need a song for that," Sam responded.

Bill idly blew smoke off the end of the stick, "Things ain't goin' too good fer our side."

"We ain't beat yet." Jones decreed.

"We've been driven out of Middle Tennessee," Sam observed.

Charlie spat into the fire and watched it sizzle, "Put on top of that we lost Vicksburg and Lee lost at Gettysburg. Things sure ain't tippin' our way."

"We got a long ways ta go before we're beat." Marion remarked, sounding more hopeful than positive, "we still got Chattanooga and jest maybe the Yanks'll git tired of fightin'."

"Attention!" someone called and the men scrambled to their feet and saluted. A general stood before them accompanied by a tall, slender man.

"John!" Sam exclaimed, "It's my brother, John, and General Johnson, my teacher in Nashville!"

A look of concern passed over Sam's face like a dark cloud, "John, everything's all right at home, isn't it?"

John smiled, "All is fine at home. But we need to talk to you about something. That's why we're here."

The general greeted all and then walked apart from them with John and Sam. They stood under a tree while Bushrod Johnson conferred with his former student, "Sam," he said, "it seems like a hundred years ago, but it's only been a couple. Remember I said I might be coming to you if we had special needs."

"I remember."

"General Cheatham was asked by General Bragg to put together a group of couriers, young men, unmarried, good horseman who know the territory."

"I'm one of them," John said, "With Alf Douglas I've been putting a band together. We want you."

"What do couriers do?"

"Scouts are sent into enemy territory to gather news concerning troop movements, to secure newspapers and obtain any vital information about enemy resources."

"You want me to be a spy?"

"Not necessarily a spy," Johnson corrected, "a courier delivers messages, some from spies, but he doesn't exactly do the spying."

John cleared his throat, "I won't steer you wrong. The Yankees might not see the difference between a spy and a courier. This is dangerous but very important work."

Sam questioned, "And you're in charge, John?"

"Alf and I are the first recruits, we've added more, but the man in charge is Henry Shaw. He goes by a fake name, E. Coleman. You'd be a member of Coleman's Scouts."

"I wonder what Kate would think?"

John looked at General Johnson, then responded, "Her brother Ev is one of us. And, Sam, Kate helps us too."

"What! It's too dangerous. She's a woman."

"Sam," Johnson replied in an even low voice, "it's not uncommon for women to be agents. There are many on both sides. We find they come under less scrutiny and less suspicion."

"Both sides?"

John resumed, "Of course the Union has spies as well. In that light Bragg and Rosecrans have an agreement by which each one can send scouts into the other's lines, dressed in their own uniforms and armed."

"If they're captured," Johnson continued, "they're to be treated as regular prisoners of war."

"We found out Rosecrans was moving on Stones River because of the scouts," John added.

"It didn't do us much good." Sam rejoined. "We still lost."

"Yes," Johnson replied, "but it could have been much worse had we not been alerted. The scouts are the army's big eyes. The result of a battle, the fate of the nation can hang upon the report of a scout. They're chosen for known bravery, intelligence, coolness and ability for this kind of activity. Henry Shaw was a born scout. You could be one as well."

"You just want me to leave the Rifles, what about my friends?"

"Yes," John agreed "and this comes with General Cheatham's endorsement. You're to become one of Coleman's Scouts on detached duty from the 1st Tennessee. When we're done recruiting, there'll be about a hundred scouts. Some of your friends will likely be added. Any ideas?"

Sam looked around, "I can think of a couple, Josh Brown and Billy Moore."

"We'll talk to them later, as we need more. Brother, will you be one of us?"

Sam clasped his brother's hand in a firm shake, "I'll be a Coleman Scout."

Sam and John rode out away from Chattanooga to the north. John explained, "Nashville is still important to us. Even with the Yankees running the town. A lot of what we do is in and around Nashville and almost all in middle Tennessee."

Chattanooga

HATTANOOGA WAS CRUCIAL to the Confederacy. After Tullahoma, Lincoln and Halleck insisted Rosecrans move quickly to take the city assertng that seizing Chattanooga would open the door for a Union advance to Atlanta and the heart of the South.

The rail hub had a line going north to Nashville and Knoxville and south to Atlanta. It produced iron and coke and was located on an important navigable river, the Tennessee. Peaks and ridges around the city made it very defensible.

Rosecrans demurred. He would move on Chattanooga when he felt he was ready and the time was right.

Bragg was well aware of the menace he faced from Rosecrans and the delay suited him. By the end of July he had 52,000 men in Chattanooga with another 17,800 on the way with General Buckner. Their arrival brought more good news. More troops would be heading Bragg's way under General James Longstreet. The down side was that Buckner was not a friend of Braggs and would join Polk and Hardee, whose lack of respect for their commander had continued to grow. Buckner blamed Bragg for the loss of Kentucky, and a merger of his troops into Bragg's left him without a command.

It was all too much for the general who had called Bragg an "idiot." Hardee requested a transfer into Mississippi, which was granted. Hardee was replaced by General D.H. Hill, a malcontent who ran afoul of Robert E. Lee.

And so in early August Bragg gathered Polk, Buckner, and Hill to review his plans. In an empty dining room, around a table in a Chattanooga hotel they gathered. Bragg spread out a paper on the table and smoothed it with his right hand, "The gentlemen in Richmond want me to renew our offensive against Rosecrans. They promise more reinforcements from Mississippi."

"What's your response General," Polk asked.

"There are many geographical and logistical challenges to be met. I would prefer Rosecrans battle these obstacles while we remain in this very defensible position. I'm also concerned about Burnside's force threatening Knoxville.

"So I'll let Rosecrans run around north of the Tennessee River and concentrate my two corps here in Chattanooga, covering our flanks with cavalry."

"When will Longstreet arrive? Buckner asked.

"No firm date has been given me. Just that he will be coming."

"So," Polk intoned in his best ministerial tone, "here we wait."

* * *

HALLECK DELIVERED another order insisting Rosecrans advance his army and report daily the movement of each corps until they crossed the Tennessee River.

Rosecrans responded that the "tone of your letter is one of reckless deceit and malice. I would be courting disaster if I did not delay my advance until at least August 17," insisting he needed time to accumulate enough supplies and transport wagons to travel long distances without a reliable communications.

He concluded, "The Cumberland Plateau that separates our armies is a rugged, barren country over thirty miles long with poor roads and little opportunity for foraging. If I'm attacked by Bragg while advancing I'll be forced to fight with my back to the mountains and poor supply lines. I must be better prepared."

On August 16th the Army of the Cumberland moved out. The 2nd Minnesota broke up their camp at Winchester. In blazing sun they marched. After a couple hours, a they hit a downpour of rain. The army marched on until the roads were so crowded with troops and wagon trains they camped for the night.

It took nearly a week of pushing heavy wagons up steep, narrow, torturous roads, then toiling down steep descents to reach the Tennessee River Valley. The 2nd camped on the river at a spot where it was broad and deep.

Clint Cilley reported to his men in Company C, "We'll spend a few days here recovering. Take care. On the south side of the river are rebel pickets. We'll picket this side. Don't make yourselves too good a target for Johnny Reb."

For a couple of days rebels across the river took potshots at Union soldiers close to the river. Then Union marksman were posted to answer. Both sides decided to give up shooting and hurl words at each other instead.

Eventually an unofficial truce resulted in both sides bathing on opposite river banks. Aaron Doty, waist deep in the water, called across. "I got a couple nice chunks of salt pork here. Anybuddy got some tobacco. I'd swap ya."

A rebel on shore shouted back, "Done deal, meet ya in the middle."

The men swam to the mid-point of the Tennessee and exchanged pouches.

"Take care Billy Yank, Ah ain't had a good bit a meat in ages."

"Likewise with tobacco, Johnny. I miss my chaw."

Soberly the rebel said, "Keep yer head down, boy. Don't git it blowed off."

"Watch yers too, Johnny," and the two swam to their respective shores.

Meanwhile the lumberman of the 2nd Minnesota's Company F were hard at work near the mouth of Battle Creek where it flowed into the Tennessee constructing scows and rafts for a crossing.

Colonel George returned from sick leave to reunite with the regiment. He saw the raft building and asked Bishop, "When will the crossing take place?"

"End of the month. Doesn't look like the rebs expect us to cross here. They've got men watching, but not enough to stop us or put up much opposition."

"I have to leave again on the twenty-seventh. But a battle is coming and I'll be back in time for it."

"We'll be over there to the east," Bishop pointed, "on our way to Chattanooga."

On the evening of August 29th four companies of the 2nd Minnesota crossed the river. By noon the next day the entire brigade was over, while all other divisions of the Army of the Cumberland were crossing above and below. A bridge was constructed at Bridgeport, Alabama, to allow free supply of goods by wagon. By September 4th the crossing of the whole army was complete.

The 2nd marched overland on September 1st to the foot of Raccoon Mountain west of Chattanooga. Private Dan Black called from the ranks as Clint Cilley passed by, "I seen a sign that says, 'Nick a Jack.' What's that?"

Clint paused and then kept pace with Black, "See that waterfall," he pointed ahead at a rushing, rumbling flow of water. "Behind it is a cave. They call it 'Nick a Jack.' In it is a large deposit of salt petre."

"What's that fer?"

"It's used by the rebs to make gun powder. You're in the bowels of the Confederacy when you're in there."

The soldiers marched up the western slope of Raccoon Mountain, an arduous journey up the Nick a Jack Trace. September 6th they reach the summit and began the descent on the 7th. Lookout Valley and Chattanooga drew near.

John Wilder, with his Lightning Brigade of mounted infantry, moved north of Chattanooga and another Rosecrans's plan of deception was carried out. His men pounded on tubs and sawed off planks of wood and tossed them into the river from where they'd float to Chattanooga.

In the city a crisis was brewing. Bragg once again conferred with his officers from the hotel dining room. "Rosecrans is moving on us. General Johnston's sending two divisions and Lee has dispatched a corps under Longstreet, but they won't get here for another week. The Yankees are much closer."

"General," Hill said, "I've had reports of sawn-off planks being fished from the river. The Yanks must be making rafts to cross over north of us."

"I know. I heard those reports days ago. We've been preparing for an attack on our right, to the north."

General Cheatham stated, "There are three passable roads to Chattanooga with Union corps on every one: McCook, Thomas, and Crittenden. By September 9th, Rosecrans's army will be in our rear. Activity north must be a feint. He's coming at us from our south and west, the left, not the right!"

"Then we're being out-flanked," Bragg realized. "We needed help sooner. We looked north and were blind to the west. We have to evacuate. Otherwise, we'll be trapped here just as Pemberton was at Vicksburg."

"Where do we go?" Polk asked.

"Into Georgia. We'll fight Rosecrans there, then take Chattanooga back."

The next day the Army of Tennessee left Chattanooga and marched toward LaFayette, Georgia. The following day Rosecrans occupied the city. He telegraphed Halleck, "Chattanooga is ours without a struggle. East Tennessee is free."

This time an exultant Rosecrans was determined to follow up his victory and pursue Bragg, who he supposed was retreating to Atlanta not just twenty miles away at LaFayette.

His supposition was fueled by the comments of Confederates posing as deserters. But Thomas met with his general and cautioned, "A pursuit of Bragg at this time is unwise. Our army is too widely dispersed and our supply lines are tenuous."

"General Thomas," Rosecrans countered, "I'll not let Halleck chastise me again for being hesitant. I believe Bragg is ripe to be had, just like a bright red apple. This is what we will do. McCook will swing across Lookout Mountain at Winston's Gap and use his cavalry to break Bragg's railroad supply line at Resaca, Georgia.

"Crittenden will move into Chattanooga, then turn south in pursuit of Bragg. You will continue your advance toward LaFayette."

With the Coleman Scouts

SAM DAVIS WORE civilian clothing as he rode into Chattanooga, going toward the train depot on Market Street. He stopped and listened as a seedy man in a cheap suit harangued before a group of onlookers.

A battered suitcase lay open on the side of the street with rows of bottles strapped into it. The man held one high and proclaimed, "Are ya having trouble sleeping at night, feelin' anxious, can't relax, worried about what the Yankee's are doin' in yer town. Take this here," he held up a dark-brown pint bottle, "Valerian root will settle you down just fine. It worked for kings and queens of Egypt. What do ya think Alexander took to settle his nerves when he invaded Persia? What let him stay cool, calm and collected in battle? This here, Valerian Root. "One thin dime, that's all it takes to kiss your worry's good bye."

"Ah kin go to the saloon and Mary's Garden of Eden, fer that!" a man yelled.

"That so?" the salesman said. "What about yer wife. Does she tag along?"

He paused as everyone laughed. Then he reached into the suitcase and took out another bottle. Holding it up, he cried, "What about this! Do you have bronchitis, fevers? Ever git bit by a snake? Black cohosh'll do wonders fer you.

"And for the little woman in yer life," he said, looking directly at the heckler, "it kin take care of hot flashes, night sweats, and mood swings. One thin dime and you won't have to take her with ya to the saloon no more."

"Now you convinced me," the heckler said and put a dime in the salesman's hand for the bottle. He waved at the laughing crowd and walked away.

Sam dismounted and walked alongside the street as the salesman continued. A man sat on a goods box at the train station. Sam peered closely, then called out, "Mr. Sharp, it's good to see you. What brings you to Chattanooga?"

The man looked up at the bronzed, mustached young man before him. He looked like he could be a soldier. His bearing suggested it but the wide brimmed hat and overcoat he wore were not uniform issues.

He shook his head, "Sorry, but I don't believe I know you."

Sam thrust out his hand and clasped the man's, "It's me, Sam Davis, your student in Smyrna."

"Sam!" Alfred Sharp rose from the box. "It's great to see you." He lowered his voice. "Last I heard you were off fighting with Bragg, where's your army?"

"I've been detailed as a scout."

"Where are you operating?"

"Middle Tennessee. We have orders to go in again next week."

"Will you get back to Smyrna?"

"If I get within fifty miles of home, I'll make a dash to get there."

"To see Kate?"

Sam laughed, "Her and my family too."

Sharp reached into his pocket, "Will you deliver a letter to my wife?"

"Certainly," Sam took the letter and put it in his pocket.

"There's a big battle coming isn't there Sam?"

"The Army of Tennessee left Chattanooga without a fight. We'll be taking it back come Hell or high water."

"Good luck to you, boy."

"Good bye, sir." Sam turned to walk away.

"Sam," Sharp called, "you were the best student I ever had."

Sam smiled and crossed the street, passing the salesman still talking. Sam went into a general store and addressed the clerk, "Are you Mr. Halquist?"

The gray haired, bespectacled man answered, "I am. What can I do ya for?"

"I'm told this is a post office and you might have a letter for a Mr. Coleman."

The man sobered and furtively looked from side to side. Assured they were alone in the store, he reached under the counter and took out a packet.

"Here ya be. Now git out, it's safer that way."

Sam nodded and walked into the street. He noticed the salesman was gone. After watering his horse and feeding it some oats in a stable, Sam trotted out of town. A couple miles south was a stump where he was to leave the packet.

When he approached the designated spot, he was surprised to find someone sitting on the stump—the salesman from Chattanooga.

"Good afternoon, boy," the man said.

"Good afternoon." Sam paused not knowing what to do. He couldn't leave the packet in the stump with the man was sitting on it.

The man continued to sit, smug and content. After a moment he asked, "Can I help you? I'm tired. I think I'll just set up camp right here on this stump."

"Is this a good spot?" Sam said. "It might rain. This is out in the open."

The man looked up into a clear blue sky and laughed, "Don't look much like rain. I think this is a good place to camp."

"Really, sir, I could carry your case for you, to a better spot."

The man laughed again, "I've played you enough, young Mr. Davis." He stood and reached to shake Sam's hand.

"How do you know me? Who are you?" Sam spoke in alarm.

"Why I'm just an itinerant herb doctor. Dr. Henry Shaw at your service. Or you can call me by my other name," his face lost all mirth, "E. Coleman."

Sam jumped from his horse, "You're Coleman?"

"Yes, I'm your captain, the man your brother recruited you to join."

"But I've never seen you."

"There was never a need. You've been doing a fine job getting information and leaving it at our drop offs.

"What about now?"

"You've been reassigned. You're to report directly to your regiment?"

"Why?"

"I don't know. I assume it's just temporary. You have something for me?"

Sam handed over the packet. Shaw took it and hefted it in his hands, "Some personal things for General Bragg. I'll tell him you got it for him."

"How's my brother, John."

"One of our best scouts. Kate Patterson's doing fine work as well."

"I wish I could see her."

"I'm sure you'll be near Smyrna. Good luck to you and get back to me soon. We need more like you and your brother."

* * *

JIMMY DUNN and the men of the 5th Regiment remained at Big Black River for a month after Vicksburg. They were sent on campaigns into central Mississippi to break up Confederate communication lines. A series of small sorties and engagements followed. They were assured by Captain Gere that something big would come their way. So they waited.

Chickamauga

THOMAS'S LEAD DIVISION under James Negley intended to cross McLemore's Cove and use Dug Gap in Pigeon Mountain to reach LaFayette and cut off Bragg. But once Negley entered the cove Bragg's forces under Hill and Hindman were poised to spring a trap. But miscommunication and failure to follow through on Bragg's orders allowed Negley to elude the trap. Rosecrans, realizing that his force had narrowly escaped, abandoned his plan for pursuit.

"This is a matter of life and death," he told Thomas, "I'll concentrate my forces and withdraw as a single body to Chattanooga. I've ordered McCook and the cavalry to meet up with you."

On September 13th Polk was ordered to attack Crittenden as he moved from Ringgold to Lee and Gordon's Mill on Chickamauga Creek. Polk hesitated and missed his opportunity, much to Bragg's consternation. For the next four days both armies were on the move. Rosecrans continued his attempts to bring his army together as Bragg tried to counter his moves as in a game of chess.

The Confederate commander called for a council of war of his officers. Before Bragg's tent they listened as Bragg outlined the situation to them, "McCook's at Alpine. I fear the federals might be planning a double envelopment that could crush our army. We have limited options. I believe our best chance of success is to forge an offensive in the direction of Chattanooga."

His officers assented. Polk spoke up, "I believe we all agree with you sir."

"Fine," Bragg snapped, "see your belief translates to following orders."

By September 17th, three Union corps reached Stevens Gap and were in a better position for attack. Still, Bragg believed he had a new opportunity. Longstreet with two divisions had arrived from Virginia and Bushrod Johnson had moved in from Mississippi with another division.

The next day Bragg ordered Johnson, "Move north and advance toward Chattanooga. You'll either draw Rosecrans out to fight or withdraw. We'll approach West Chickamauga Creek and cross with our corps in four places. I've been countering Rosecrans moves for six months. He expects me to do it again. I'm going to stand and fight."

Through the 18th, the 2nd Minnesota waited in their camp with the army's procession passing them. Colonel George had rejoined them and assumed his position of commander. A feeling of foreboding enveloped them like a thick fog. Troops and wagon trains continued to move to the north until 5:00 p.m., when the 2nd was ordered to fall in line.

They began a long, cold, march through the night, tromping about a quarter mile per hour, stopping at intervals long enough to get cold and stiff but never long enough to build a fire. Men were forbidden to leave the ranks and some fell asleep, sinking onto the road while others slept standing up.

As dawn broke it became apparent a big battle was imminent. Clint Cilley turned to his sergeant, Will Mills. "Watch the brigades and batteries leaving the road going east. We've been forming a line of battle all night, in the dark."

A rider galloped up to where Company C was formed, he saluted and asked, "Are you Captain Cilley?" When Clint said he was, the rider said, "You've been assigned detached service with brigade headquarters. You're to report immediately to Colonel Van Derveer."

"What about my company?"

"Your lieutenant will take command."

Bewildered, Clint turned to Harrison Couse, "Well, this is a surprise. Take over, Harry. They're good boys. You'll know what to do."

Clint promptly departed to headquarters.

At 8:00 a.m., as they stood in ranks on the LaFayette-Chattanooga Road, word passed down the line that the 2nd Minnesota had twenty minutes to eat breakfast. In five minutes hundreds of little fires heated hundreds of coffees pots and fried bacon. Hardtack was moistened and toasted. Just as some began to eat, a horseman galloped up, "Take arms and march immediately!" he yelled, followed by a bugle call to assemble.

With a barrage of profanity, the 2nd Minnesota fell into ranks, their breakfasts largely uneaten.

On September 19th, Thomas moved into position on the left flank of the Army of the Cumberland. Bragg mistakenly thought Tom Crittenden's troops at Lee and Gordon's Mill was the end of the Union line, but Thomas was arrayed behind him.

A Confederate charge was ordered on the advanced divisions of the Union left. The battle was on. The area between Chickamauga Creek and LaFayette Road, where much of the battle would be fought, was a broken, rolling landscape filled with a dense growth of trees.

Rosecrans, with his staff officers, became agitated after receiving a dispatch. They met in a small house, Widow Glen's, along a road. "Bragg's actually going to fight! Longstreet's near with reinforcements. I think it's prudent for us to withdraw to Chattanooga."

"In the middle of an attack?" an officer questioned.

"We'll march north, each unit taking turns protecting the others as they pass by. Like a game of leap frog. We fight as we withdraw."

"We leap frog to Chattanooga?"

"Yes, pass the order on."

Word came to Bragg Rosecrans was moving north. Bragg turned to Isham Harris. "If we can inflict a massive defeat on them, we can change the course of this war. We have reinforcements coming from east and west. The opportunity is near to cut Rosecrans's army in half and destroy it. We can and must do it."

Forrest's dismounted cavalry opened up on the Union left. By noon Cheatham's division of Tennessee regiments had crossed the creek and were moving into action at double quick. Cheatham sent in Maney's brigade to replace Jackson, who had run low on ammunition. Lead rained from the sky and thudded around them as the Confederates ran, reloaded and fired in an effort to help Forrest.

Through the thick woods, firing as they marched, the 1st Tennessee relentlessly moved like a slow wave on the federals two hundred yards distant. For two hours both lines held, a contest as to which side could load and fire fastest.

Shot poured in on the Confederates from the sides. They were in danger of being surrounded. Bedford Forrest galloped up and shouted to Colonel Feild, "Your flanks are collapsed. You're almost surrounded!" Retreat rang out.

The woods filled with smoke and fire as Feild's boys fell back. An officer raced up and asked, "Is this Maney's brigade?" When affirmed it was, he ordered, "Attention! Forward!"

The frenzy of lead centered like a vortex of death over the patch of vine and woodland. Shells whistled and thudded all around; the very earth trembled.

Bragg continued his onslaught, though Longstreet's entire corps had not arrived on the scene. He launched attacks across Chickamauga Creek. Union Colonel Minty's cavalry, protecting Reed's Bridge, was flanked and forced back, in such haste that they neglected to destroy the bridge behind them.

Minty's withdrawal left Wilder's federal regiments guarding Alexander's Bridge in a position they couldn't hold. They also withdrew.

The 2nd Minnesota marched near the left flank. In brigade order, they proceeded to the east on Reed's Bridge Road. They expected to find a destroyed bridge and were ordered to find and attack the one rebel brigade thought to have crossed, then hold the ford to prevent more Confederate troop crossings.

But the bridge still stood. Instead of one isolated rebel brigade, they encountered several. Van Derveer spat in disgust, "Everything they told us is wrong. They only easy part is we won't have to 'find' the rebels. They're all right in front of us. Their whole army looks like it's between our line and the creek."

Clint Cilley, now on brigade staff, commented, "I hope we can see them through the trees and brush."

With Indiana and Ohio regiments with them, the Minnesotans marched along a ridge. The sound of musketry to the south caused them to turn and advance down an easy slope toward the sound of guns.

They encountered a mass of Confederate soldiers, and furious gunfire began.

Rincie DeGrave sighted and fired as lead balls dropped like hail. "Sarge!" Rincie called, "I can't see them! But shot is all around like gnats in a swamp!"

Artillery shells ripped into the trees, sending splinters everywhere. An eruption of cheers followed by the screech of a rebel yell sent shivers through the Union ranks. The big guns ceased, the rattle of rifles nearer, and the rain of lead thicker.

"Lie down, men!" Lieutenant Cosgrove shouted, "Hug the ground!"

DeGrave, stretched out between Black and Doty as missiles whizzed above, "Don't wish you was gophers and could dig holes?" he cried at them.

"What's that?" Doty pointed.

In the distance a ragged blue line rushed toward them—at first a few, then more and more. Cosgrove yelled, "Hold your fire! Those are Union men!"

In panic they ran straight at the brigade, faster and faster as they frantically tried to outrun the yelling, shooting rebels behind them. Like a stampede of cattle, Union troops—officers and men—passed over the 2nd Minnesota to the rear.

Once their own men were clear, Van Derveer's brigade could see the charging gray forms coming at them. Cosgrove urged, "Steady boys!" Then, "Fire!"

A volley ripped from the Enfield rifles of the 2nd Minnesota and smothered the yelling rush of the Confederates. The rebels stopped in their tracks, then returned fire. They stood for a few minutes, taking and giving fire. Then they fell back.

During the fighting, the 2nd Minnesota operated as stretcher bearers and carried wounded to a makeshift hospital in the rear of the fighting.

Reports came to Van Derveer the Confederates were flanking on the left. He ordered Cilley, "Tell the regiment to face to their left. By filing left they'll be facing east. That's where Johnny Reb will come from."

Clint gave the order. The 2nd was in position to successfully repulse the attack. Cilley, still on the scene, shouted at Bishop, "The rebs are continuing to pass a large force to our left. We need to turn north and gain the road!"

The regiment was on the road, parallel to where they had been but facing the opposite direction. The wounded carried to the rear, were now in front.

An eerie silence swept over the battlefield as from out of the under growth and trees came an advance of Confederates. Their cadence was steady and deliberate—no rebel yells. Only silence.

Bishop stood and cried out, "Shoot to kill! Make every shot count!" The Minnesotans opened up on them. The order of rebel march was decimated. They regrouped and came on again, preparing to charge.

Then the artillery behind the Union troops opened up with canister and shot. Great holes shredded their lines, and shards of metal cut them down like a farmer's scythe. About sixty yards out from the Union line, they began to waver. At forty they broke and ran.

Quiet reigned on their part of the battlefield. To the southwest the rattle of muskets and boom of cannon continued, as the battle drifted south. Van Derveer reported to his brigade and regiment commanders, "We're to move south and camp for the night. It looks like our part of the fight is over for today. Have them eat what food they have, no fires until tomorrow morning. This battle isn't over."

At 6:00 p.m. Bragg had not given up on his idea of pushing Rosecrans south and cutting him off from Chattanooga. He ordered Patrick Cleburne to attack the Union left, which had been quiet for hours.

Thomas had been consolidating forces, and Baird and Johnson's Union divisions were in the rear of Thomas's withdrawal to the west. At sunset Cleburne launched an attack with three brigades. In the limited visibility of smoke, haze and dimming light, the assault quickly became chaotic. By nine o'clock Baird and Johnson had been driven back inside Thomas's new defensive line.

Bragg had set up headquarters at Thedford Ford, south of the battlefield. His staff and corps commanders met to plan the second day of the battle. The general in command of the Army of Tennessee summarized the day,

"Night finds us the masters of the ground, after a series of very obstinate contests with largely superior numbers."

Polk reminded Bragg, "Unfortunately our attacks were launched in a disjointed fashion. We didn't achieve a concentration of mass to defeat Rosecrans or cut him off from Chattanooga."

Breckinridge continued, "We were wrong about the location of Rosecrans's left wing. It cost us two splendid opportunities. The sporadic attacks sapped our strength."

Bragg pounded his fist in his hand and snapped, "We still hold the field. For tomorrow I'm reorganizing the Army of Tennessee into two wings. General Polk, you'll command the right wing with Hill's Corps, Walker's, and Cheatham's Division. You'll initiate an attack on the Union left at daybreak, beginning with Breckinridge's Division. "I've been informed General Longstreet arrived by train from Virginia. He'll command the left wing with Hood's Corps, Buckner's, and Hindman's Division of Polk's Corps.

"Where is Hill?" Polk asked.

"With his corps," Bragg answered.

"You've demoted him? Does he know?"

"He will do what we ask," Bragg concluded.

* * *

ROSECRANS HELD HIS own council of war with most of his corps and division commanders. Assistant Secretary of War Charles Dana attended the meeting, representing Lincoln and Stanton.

George Thomas said, "Our army got pretty beat up today. We only have five fresh brigades available. The enemy's been receiving reinforcements and now outnumbers our forces."

"You're right, Pap. That rules out an offensive for us," Rosecrans agreed.

"Well, you better not be planning a retreat," Dana asserted.

Rosecrans fidgeted. "We'll remain in place, on the defensive. Remember Bragg retreated after Perryville and Stones River. He could do it again."

"Don't count on it," Thomas concluded.

* * *

James Longstreet arrived at Bragg's headquarters at 11:00 p.m. and found the general asleep. He awakened him and Bragg explained his battle plan. "Pete, thank God you've come. I'm glad Lee could spare his "Old War Horse."

"This seems to be a place of reckoning. I'll do what I can."

Chickamauga, Day Two

BRAGG'S ARMY did not attack at daybreak on September 20th. There was confusion among his commanders. Hill didn't know his role in the coming battle. The courier responsible for delivering written orders to Hill couldn't find him and returned to headquarters without telling anyone.

Breckinridge was at Polk's headquarters, but no one told him he was to initiate the attack. The assault had to be delayed.

The battle continued at 9:30 a.m. Coordinated *en echelon* attacks were to proceed leftward along Confederate lines to drive the Union south away from escape routes to Chattanooga.

Had the attack happened four hours earlier, Thomas wouldn't have been ready. The delay allowed his men to dig in. Union forces built up defenses as well.

Breckinridge hit the Union left. Three brigades smashed into Thomas's breastworks. When Breckinridge found the end of the Union left, he realigned two brigades to straddle LaFayette Road and move south behind a Union brigade.

Thomas called to Cilley, "Captain, we need to get more men in there to stop them. What do we have?"

"Brannan is in reserve and we have Colonel Van Derveer's brigade."

"Send them in."

The 2nd Minnesota deployed to the left of the Union line. They passed through a pine thicket, while Indiana troops lined up on their left and Ohio behind them. A large open field lay before them, a strip of woods to the north.

Suddenly the air was alive with bullets, and a thin line of gun smoke formed at the edge of the woods to the left. Bishop ordered a left wheel, and the Minnesotans rolled left to face the fire. They opened up a volley, then charged to the edge of the woods, driving the rebels back. They opened up on the Confederates again. Van Derveer ordered the second line of Ohio troops to charge in as well. The result was a breakup of the enemy's front. Cilley rode back to Van Derveer at a gallop, when his horse pitched forward sending Clint flying over its head. Dazed, Clint looked back at his dead horse and stumbled on to Van Derveer, who inquired, "Are you all right, Captain?"

"Fine, but I need another horse. You've saved the rear of this army. Your men did some hot work here."

"We've got a ways to go."

"There's a little lull here. See to your wounded."

A rebel force attacked again, taking the field Van Derveer's brigade had won, then left. Clint came from Thomas and spoke with Van Derveer. "The battle's shifting toward Horseshoe Ridge, by the Snodgrass house. Follow me. I'll lead you to General Thomas."

Maney's Brigade with Polk's Corps was held in reserve. They listened and watched as the mayhem washed by them. Leonidas Polk himself rode up to General Cheatham, "Longstreet's moving the Yanks this way. We need to drive them that way and crush them between us. Move your division. Attack at once."

Cheatham turned to his men and shouted, "Forward boys. Give 'em Hell!"

After marching forward in various turns and formations, the order came, "Fire at will! Charge and take their breastworks!"

Tennesseans screeched a rebel yell, racing at the Union breastworks. From under head logs, Union soldiers poured a wave of lead. Undaunted, the rebels stormed onto the breastworks and planted their flag. The Yankees broke and ran.

On the Union right a critical moment came. A Thomas staff officer asked Rosecrans for assistance. He responded, "If I move out a division it'll expose the flanks of neighboring ones. I need to consult, make sure the line isn't disrupted."

Rosecrans did consult and sent an order to General Thomas Wood. Wood opened the order, questioned it with his staff officer, "I'm ordered to move my division to the left to support another division. That makes no sense. I'm already supporting the right flank of that division. If I move, it'll leave a hole in the line."

"Another division must be coming to fill it."

"Twice I've been upbraided by Rosecrans for not immediately obeying orders. I'll move three brigades as ordered, but they better fill the hole we'll leave."

As Wood moved his men out and created a gap, Longstreet launched his attack. His wing under General John Bell Hood hit the huge hole in the line and streamed through it. Then he wheeled his force north to destroy the Union army.

Thomas rode down to meet the Minnesotans as they ascended the slope at Horseshoe Ridge. "They're coming, Colonel," he called to Bishop, "I'm glad to see you in such good order."

Rosecrans and most of the rest of his generals and army bolted to the north. Thomas, joined by General Granger's men, made a stand on the ridge at a high point called Snodgrass Hill. On the southern slope, in front of the 2nd Minnesota, Confederates advanced up the slope, rank following rank in close order.

Colonel George shouted down the line, "Aim carefully. Make every shot count!" As a volley ripped from Union guns, Confederate lines melted away. They hunched their shoulders, bowed their heads and kept coming as their comrades fell beside them.

The rebels fell back, regrouped and came on again to be riddled again by volley after volley from the hill. The slope was littered with bodies of men in gray. Thomas sent Cilley to Van Derveer. Once again as he approached the colonel, Clint's horse was shot out from under him. As he gained his feet, he encountered a retreating regiment of Union soldiers.

Clint drew his pistol and aimed it at the retreating soldiers, then grabbed the American flag from their color bearer and shouted, "This is a time for heroes not cowards. Follow me! Follow the colors."

Carrying the flag high, Clint Cilley dashed back into the breach of the battle. The withdrawing soldiers turned and followed him, pushing rebels back. Miraculously General Steedman's brigade filled in on an open right flank.

A strange quiet enveloped the battlefield around 5:00 to 6:00. Then just before dark another attack in the 2nd's front was driven back. An hour later Clint reported that General Thomas ordered a quiet withdrawal to Rossville. Under Cilley's direction the army disengaged.

The 2nd Minnesota was among the last Union troops to leave the bloody field. They would join the rest of the Union army at the sanctuary of Chattanooga. First, at Rossville Gap, they did an accounting. All 384 men of the regiment were accounted for. Thirty-five were dead, 113 wounded, fourteen captured, and 222 present for duty. Not one man was among the missing.

They had been vital in saving of Rosecrans's army by keeping Bragg occupied while the Union army escaped to Chattanooga. His determined stand on Snodgrass Hill earned George Thomas the title, "Rock of Chickamauga." But the battle was a resounding Confederate victory. Bragg's men moved on to Chattanooga to occupy the heights around it.

Forrest was critical that Rosecrans's escape route was not cut off and urged an immediate assault on the city, but Bragg preferred to recover and wait.

Meanwhile the Union forces dug in with defenses in Chattanooga.

Sam Davis as a Scout

SAM'S ASSIGNMENT back to infantry duty lasted only a few days. He didn't take part in the Battle of Chickamauga but scouted for the infantry. A few days after the battle he was given a pass from General Bragg which read:

> *Headquarters, Gen. Bragg's Scouts, Middle Tennessee, September 25, 1863—Samuel Davis has permission to pass on scouting duty anywhere in Middle Tennessee or south of the Tennessee River he may see proper.*   *By order of Gen. Bragg.*
> *E. Colman, Captain Commanding Scouts.*

Richard Anderson, a Coleman scout, awaited delivery of "mail" at Coleman headquarters in the hills of Campbellsville, Tennessee, about fifteen miles from Pulaski, roughly seventy-five from Nashville. A courier line ran from there to Chattanooga and Nashville. Sam rode in with scout Will Hughes carrying dispatches. Sam Roberts and Anderson greeted their riders.

Anderson grinned. "Sure was good news from Chickamauga. Bragg must be happy."

Sam demurred, "I'm not sure I've ever seen the general really look happy. Guess he must be pleased. But the Yankees got back to Chattanooga."

"Trapped like rats in a cage," Roberts observed. "How's Nashville?"

"Full of Yankees," Hughes offered. "That blasted Andrew Johnson walks around like a peacock. I'd sure like to trim his feathers."

Anderson added, "The only senator from a seceding state who remained loyal to the Union. Now Lincoln makes him governor of Tennessee. I don't call him governor, I call him traitor."

"He'll git his comeuppance once we git Nashville back," Roberts said.

"Here are your dispatches." Sam handed over the packets to Anderson.

"Good. We'll get them to Chattanooga. Where are you off to?"

"Back to Nashville."

On the way north Sam stopped in LaVergne at the Patterson house. Kate and Robbie were harnessing a team of horses when Sam rode up. Kate brightened and flashed a smile at him. She ran into his arms and held tight.

"I was worried about you, Sam. There was word you were back in the infantry. You could have been killed at Chickamauga. Many of your friends were."

"I was only transferred temporarily and not to fight, to scout for it."

"Where are you going?" When Sam told her he was bound for Nashville, she said, "Blast, I've got to go south to pick up some 'mail' and make a delivery. I can't wait. Another courier will be by to pick it up."

Sam's face showed his disappointment. "I hoped we'd have a little more time."

Kate said, "It'll be over soon. Then we can have all the time in the world."

"Be careful, Kate. Take care of yourself."

"You're in more danger than I am, Sam. I worry about you."

The moment was too brief, both bound by duty in opposite directions.

Eleven miles southeast of Nashville, Sam rested under a cedar tree about an hour before the sunset. The moon was already rising, casting a bright silver glow. As Sam moved onto the pike, two men emerged from a woods.

When a voice called, "Who are you?" Sam retreated into the grove and drew his pistol. He shouted, "Who are you?"

A voice returned, "A Confederate scout."

Sam responded, "Phil Matlock, is that you?"

"Yeah, it's me. Sam, is that you?"

The two men happily greeted each other in the fading sunlight. "Jim," Matlock spoke to his companion, "this is Sam Davis. He's a Coleman scout. Sam, this is Jim Castleman, he scouts for Carter, with me."

The two shook hands. "Where are you going?" Sam inquired of Matlock.

"I just visited my parents' home. I don't have an assignment."

"Then come to Nashville with me."

Dressed as civilians, the three caught a ride with a black man driving a two-horse wagon just south of Nashville. That night they paid $15.00 at the St. Cloud Hotel for one room for two nights. They went to the dining room for dinner.

The three sat together at one very long table. At the other end was a collection of Union officers. Three looked to have been wounded. One wore a general's stars and was imposing with his trimmed black hair and neat dark beard.

Matlock gestured and whispered, "Look there. It's Rosecrans himself."

Sam watched intently, then commented, "The former commander of the Army of the Cumberland, himself, right in front of us."

"Former's right. That's what happens when you lose battles," Castleman said.

In their room the three men took count of what they had between them and came up with $350.00 in greenbacks and one pistol each.

"So, Sam," Matlock asked, "what are you here for?"

"Buy cheap whatever I can get that our men need. I'm to meet a contact tonight. Are you willing to contribute?"

Castleman chuckled, "There's more greenbacks to be had than just these. Just leave a little left over for clothes."

The next day in the town a man named Nute Watson, a former schoolmate of Sam's at the military school in Nashville, approached Sam. They greeted each other, then Nute proclaimed, "I can buy anything the Yankees have. They'll sell their guns, hell they'd sell their mothers if there was a market."

Sam handed Nute $150.00. "We need six shooters, Colts, navy or army. Place them in the usual place . . . you know, the coal house."

A short, stocky man walked by them, accompanied by a young, handsome man with dark curly hair and a short black mustache. They were laughing boisterously and the shorter man playfully slapped the younger man on the back.

Nute wrinkled his nose like he'd smelled something bad. "There goes Andrew Johnson, our governor."

"Who's the young man with him?" Sam wondered.

"An actor, fella named John Wilkes Booth, those two get together whenever Booth's in town. They chase women and whiskey together."

"Seem like an odd pair," Sam noted.

The three then went back to the hotel for supper. Later Watson returned, met with the three and informed them, "I bought thirty-eight pistols with scabbard and belts. All are Colts. I put 'em in two sacks in my coal house."

"Thank you," Sam nodded, "we'll pick them up.

The men then went to a clothing store and purchased hats, boots, pants woolen shirts and drawers. At 7:30 p.m. they mounted newly bought horses and rode to Nute's house where they picked up the pistols, then rode out of Nashville.

About midnight they reached Phil Matlock's father's house. Sam, elated, slapped his friends on the back. "We did the job and got out safe. At least thirty-eight men are going to be really happy with new pistols."

They all laughed heartily and then Matlock sobered and asked, "Can we take Chattanooga back?"

"We know Rosecrans won't be stopping us. He's gone. Old George Thomas's commander now. I'll bet on Bragg. He's an ornery cuss, but he'll fight."

The Fight for Chattanooga

ROSECRANS HAD BEEN stunned by his defeat. He ordered former Confederate fortifications bolstered in a tight three-mile semi-circle around Chattanooga, thus giving up a strong defensive position on Lookout Mountain. Thomas strenuously objected. Rosecrans ignored him but became indecisive and psychologically unable to take action to lift the siege of the city.

President Lincoln noted, "Rosecrans seems confused, stunned like a duck hit on the head."

The most immediate problem—all supply lines but one leading into Chattanooga were controlled by Bragg's army. The one open line was a torturous path nearly sixty miles over Walden's Ridge from Bridgeport, Alabama. To make matters worse, late September heavy rain washed out the mountain roads.

A wagon trail near the Tennessee River was closed by Confederate sharpshooters who riddled to pieces a sixty-wagon supply train. No pasture was available, and the horses were put on quarter rations. As a result, soldiers in the city were put on short rations, and horses and mules died. Relief for Chattanooga was sent in the form of 800 wagons of supplies.

Forrest was livid when he met Bragg. "For thirty-six hours after Chickamauga, you did nothing but allow Rosecrans to dig in. The Yankees are ready to move out. Give me infantry and I'll force them out!"

Bragg relieved Forrest and put Wheeler in command of cavalry. On October 1, Wheeler's cavalry attacked the 800 supply wagons, cut Rosecrans's supply lines, attacked and burned hundreds of the wagons and shot or sabered hundreds of mules. Rations grew slimmer in the city.

Bragg had three courses to take. As he mulled them over with his generals they were outlined. "We can outflank Rosecrans by crossing the Tennessee either below or above the city, assault the Union force directly in their fortifications, or starve the federals out by establishing a siege line."

Breckinridge was emphatic, saying, "Flanking is impractical. Our army is low on ammunition, and we have no pontoons for river crossing."

But Longstreet, Lee's most trusted general, suggested the flanking option. "Let's move to the west, flank Rosecrans and cut him off from middle Tennessee and his path of retreat."

"What about a direct assault?" Simon Buckner asked.

"Too costly. They're well fortified. We will lose many men."

General Hill said, "My intelligence says Rosecrans has only six days' rations."

Bragg pondered, then replied, "I think our option's clear. We'll lay siege to Chattanooga, cut off their supply lines and try to find the means to cross the Tennessee. We're in a strong position outside the city. We have the high ground."

The Confederate army fortified Lookout Mountain and Missionary Ridge. Off one bend of the Tennessee River to the east was Raccoon Mountain. South of the city, the river, and the Union supply lines were the high grounds of Lookout Mountain to the south and Missionary Ridge, a long prominence running east of Chattanooga in a line from the northeast to southwest.

As Bragg's men settled in to starve the Union soldiers into submission, Bragg had his own problems. His quarrels with his generals had reached a boiling point. On September 29, he relieved General Hindman, who had failed in his attack at McLemore's Cove, and General Polk, who delayed his attack on September 20 at Chickamauga.

The result was insurrection. On October 4 twelve officers sent a petition to Jefferson Davis demanding Bragg be removed of command. Davis came to Chattanooga to review the complaints personally. In the company of the twelve petitioners and Bragg, Davis listened. Longstreet had a private heated discussion with Davis in which he bitterly criticized Bragg's lack of direction.

Regardless, Davis decided to leave Bragg in command but alter the command structure. After Davis returned to Richmond, Bragg promptly dismissed D.H. Hill and Simon Buckner.

* * *

The Union had its own contentious command situation. On September 29 Secretary of War Stanton ordered Grant to go to Chattanooga himself as commander of the newly formed Military Division of the Mississippi, which included the territory between the Appalachians and the Mississippi River.

He was also instructed to send Sherman with 20,000 men to Chattanooga from Vicksburg. General Joe Hooker, with 15,000 more, was transferred from the Army of the Potomac in Virginia to Tennessee as well.

Before leaving Vicksburg, Grant was given the option of replacing Rosecrans with Thomas. He discussed the alternatives with Sherman. "Frankly, Cump, I don't think much of either of them. Rosecrans is in a daze from what I'm told. Also, I've been given reports he plans to abandon Chattanooga. That can't happen. One other, and this is the killer. It's one thing to lose a battle and have the spirit crushed of your men and officers," he held up a letter, "but as an Ohio captain points out, it's a horse of a different color when you lose confidence in your commander as they have in Rosecrans."

Sherman sighed, "But Thomas is so slow. He's not stupid, but he'd take an hour to analyze if two and two really equals four. Don't we have anyone else?"

"Stanton sent Hooker. He's no answer. He had his chance at Chancellorsville."

Sherman grimaced like he'd just bit into a sour lemon. "Old Fighting Joe told Lincoln his headquarters was his saddle. After he lost the battle, Lincoln told him he's got his headquarters where his hindquarters ought to be."

Grant chuckled. "So what do we do? He might be slow, but I'm inclined to name the 'Rock of Chickamauga' as the press is calling Thomas."

"More like the rock head of Chickamauga."

"Cump, don't worry. If a promotion's in order I'll move you over Thomas, I don't care if he's senior or outranks you. You've been with me since the start, through good and bad. He does his best, is loyal and wins, just takes his time."

"Well, I'll go with you on that. He's from Virginia and stayed with us."

"Even after his family disowned him. I'll telegraph him immediately."

"Things have changed haven't they? Remember after Shiloh when Halleck turned your Army of the Tennessee over to Thomas and kicked you upstairs to do nothing. Well, who's running the show now?"

"I guess the bottom rung is on top now," Grant said simply.

Grant telegraphed Thomas, "Hold Chattanooga at all hazards. I'll be there as soon as possible." Thomas replied, "We will hold the town until we starve."

Rosecrans went to Nashville where Sam Davis ate at the same table with him in the St. Cloud Hotel.

Maney's brigade watched over Chattanooga from Missionary Ridge and Lookout Mountain. Tod Carter, still on the quartermaster's staff, looked down at the activity below and commented to William Ledbetter, "They've got a very strong position, good fortifications, and nearly impregnable breastworks."

"They should. We built them."

"They have one route for food, and we're harassing that line," Carter added and then continued, "At least we have a rail line open to Atlanta."

"It's not working very well. Talk to the brass about it. Our rations are cooked up for us ten miles in the rear. Then we get three days' rations at a time. My starving men eat it all in half a day, then starve for two and a half more days."

"We're still better off than they are. They have a strong defensive position, but we don't have to attack them. We can just sit here and starve 'em out."

"Tod, look at our men. Hollow eyed, ragged clothes, full of lice. Some pickin' kernels of corn out of the mud to eat. I don't think they feel better off."

"General Bragg will see to it. I'll tell him."

"Bragg's a buffoon. President Davis came to see him. I wouldn't be surprised if Bragg's removed."

"I guess we'll know soon."

Davis decided to stick with Bragg. At their low point, the soldiers stood in ranks while President Davis and his staff thundered by on horseback. Instead of cheers, cries for food were shouted at the leader of the Confederacy.

* * *

IT WAS NO BETTER in the Union camp. When Grant reported to Chattanooga on October 23rd the soldiers also suffered privations. Thomas informed his commander, "We're down to four hard cakes and a half pound of pork per man over three days. We can't get food through. Wheeler keeps cutting the only line we have and it isn't reliable anyway."

"Pap," Grant replied, "we'll just have to open another way."

The next day the chief engineer of the Army of the Cumberland, General William F. (Baldy) Smith, reported to 110 East First Street. Grant had claimed the house after learning its owner had joined the Confederate army.

Grant greeted Smith in the living room, converted into an office.

"Good to see you, Baldy. I hear you have a plan for me."

"I do. You seem to have procured a very serviceable headquarters."

"It's near the river, has a high position on a hill, a wide two-story porch with a good view, and, best of all, it was empty. What's your plan?"

"I gave this to General Rosecrans, but he didn't implement it. I believe I can help you open a more reliable supply line to the troops in Chattanooga."

"That'd be wonderful. Explain it."

"We need to seize Brown's Ferry and link up with Hooker's men arriving from Bridgeport, Alabama, through the Lookout Valley. If we can do that we can open a reliable, efficient supply line."

"I've looked at maps," Grant pointed to one laid out on a desk. "Let me trace this. Brown's Ferry crosses the Tennessee River from Moccasin Point where the road follows a gap through the foothills, then turns south through Lookout Valley to Wauhatchie Station, then west to Kelley's Ferry, a place on the Tennessee that can be reached by Union supply boats."

"Yes," Smith added, "and a force at Brown's Ferry would give real problems on the right to any Confederate position moving into the valley. The key is to take control of Brown's Ferry."

"Baldy," Grant slapped his palm on the desk, "I like it! We have to open up the line. We're going to follow your plan to do it."

Grant planned to have his men join up with Hooker's, but that army was delayed. Grant sent General Hazen out on his own. In the early morning of October 27th, Hazen's men boarded boats in fog and no moonlight. They were undetected as they floated past the Confederate position on Lookout Mountain.

* * *

THEY OVERWHELMED a small Confederate force above Brown's Ferry and were in control by 4:40 a.m. A rebel counterattack was repulsed, and General Law sent a request for help to Longstreet. The general exclaimed to an aide, "This is nothing but a feint. They have to have bigger intentions."

"Should we tell General Bragg?" a staff officer asked.

"No, he's got more important worries."

A short time later Bragg found out about the seizure of Brown's Ferry and ordered Longstreet to retake it. Once again Lee's "warhorse" decided not to act. As a result, Baldy Smith's men had no opposition as they worked to strengthen their hold on the bridgehead.

Midafternoon the following day, Hooker's army marched through Lookout Valley and were united with Hazen at Brown's Ferry. A joyous George Thomas telegraphed to General-in-Chief Halleck, "We've opened a Cracker Line. In a few days I expect to be pretty well supplied."

Bragg's siege remained in force. But a sizable gap in it now allowed the Union forces in Chattanooga a steady supply of food and supplies. As each army eyed the other, it was imminent that one must eventually attack the other. It was just a matter of time.

Sam Davis

WHILE THE 2ND MINNESOTA and 1st Tennessee watched over each other around Chattanooga, the 5th Minnesota was largely in camp or moving to another camp somewhere else, or engaged in minor skirmishes. For weeks they were at Black River. During the late summer and early fall they saw two expeditions to Canton, Mississippi. On November 5th, orders came to go to Memphis by steamboat and from there to La Grange, Tennessee.

General Hubbard noted, "Indecision and confusion of purpose seemed to be the controlling influence in these back-and-forth movements. At least it gave the men exercise and kept them in condition for more serious work."

* * *

SAM DAVIS HAD a more active fall. In November of 1863 a small band of seven cavalry from the 4th Alabama approached a cabin north of Athens, Alabama, after dark. A lantern flickered through the cabin windows.

When Lieutenant Cal Hyatt approached and rapped sharply on the door, someone inside called out, "Who's there?"

"A friend," Hyatt answered.

The door opened and a middle-aged man let Hyatt in. A lantern burned in the corner of the cabin. A form lay in a bed and several people sat on chairs around it.

The man said to Hyatt, "I can't guide you tonight. Someone in my family's real sick."

"We have a mission we have to see through," Hyatt responded.

"I know. I got you a substitute." He motioned to a corner. A man stepped out of the shadows. "This here's Sam Davis. He's a scout. He'll guide you."

"I'm going that way anyway," Sam advised.

"We're to go to Fayettville and Winchester to watch for Union troop movements," Hyatt explained. "Are you ready to go? I want to make Fayettville by morning. It's near ten o'clock now."

"Let's mount up," Sam replied.

The night was pitch black until bolts of lightning cast a shimmering silver glow through the darkness. But Sam successfully guided the little group through the rain and night to their destination.

Early the next morning, soaked and tired, they had breakfast in a hotel in Fayettville. Then they divided their squad in two: three men riding toward Winchester with Lieutenant Hyatt and three others going northeast with Sam.

A rendezvous point was agreed to for that evening at the home of a relative of Sam's six miles from Fayettville. They ate and spent the night there, then hit the trail again early the next morning.

About a mile from Fayetteville they crossed a road near a river. The road hugged the bank for a while, then extended along the base of high hills to the east. Just before the road turned abruptly to the west the eight men rode across a small creek and went up the slope of a hill toward the courthouse.

High rail fences ran along either side of the road as Newman Cayce and Sam rode about fifty yards in advance of their comrades.

"Well, Sam, no one can see us through this fence."

"Unfortunately, we can't see what's going on on the other side either."

As they rode around the turn to the west they stumbled onto a column of Union cavalry. Sam held up his hand. "They don't see us. They're watering their horses at the creek."

Cayce said, "The rest of their column extends back toward town."

Sam smiled, "Let's have some fun."

He drew his revolver. Cayce followed suit. Both men opened fire on the head of the Union cavalry in the water. Confusion reigned as the two Confederates emptied their six-shot pistols and galloped back toward Hyatt and the others as the Union troops rallied and charged after them.

Sam laughed as they met Hyatt, "Come on, Lieutenant, we just stuck a stick in a hornet's nest and stirred up some bees. They're coming right along."

The band of eight galloped down the Huntsville Road. They swerved out of the lane and fled eastward in woods between two hills. The federal cavalry thundered by, clueless as to where their prey had fled. Hyatt's band circled back and watched their pursuers until they went west. That night Sam rode on ahead to report to a Confederate column near Huntsville.

After two days, Sam bid his new comrades farewell. Cayce clasped his hand and asked, "Can't you go on out with us?"

Sam answered, "No, I can't leave here yet. I'm one of some special scouts for General Bragg. We've been sent to find out the location of the federal troops in Middle Tennessee, the strength of the garrisons, and the works.

"Those I report to are now around Columbia and Pulaski. I have some information, but I must see them and get what information they have and see it gets delivered. Then I'll go back to the army."

Hyatt's band rode south, Sam north. On Friday, November 13, Sam crossed Stewart's Creek by Smyrna. Under the cover of night he rode to his homestead. As he entered, his mother burst into tears and held him tight. His father offered a firm handshake. They sat at the kitchen table eating cold meat and bread.

"We don't hear much about what you're doing, boy," his father said. "That's probably for the best."

Sam nodded. "The less who know about the Coleman scouts, the better it is for all involved. It's why I came here so late."

"Wasn't it enough for Cheatham to make your brother, John, a spy? Did they have to recruit you, too?" His mother shook her head sadly.

"I can accomplish much more for our cause doing what I'm doing than being in the infantry, and I'm not a spy, I'm a courier."

"Sam," Charles continued, "your mother and I are proud of you no matter what you do. But we do have a parent's right to worry. You're in a dangerous spot."

"All war is dangerous."

Jane opened a closet door. She came back with a coat and held it out to Sam. He smiled. "Union overcoat, nice and warm. How'd you dye it dark brown?"

"Walnuts. We can't have you wearing blue. That *would* make you a spy."

"Thank you, mother. I can't stay long. But I'd like to see my little brothers. I'm especially anxious to see the baby."

Jane ushered Sam into a bedroom where his little brothers, Charley, four, and Hickman, two, slept. Sam bent over each and kissed them on the forehead.

Sam studied them. "Hickman's growing fast, not really a baby anymore, and he wasn't even born when I left." He reached down and gently touched the little boy's hand, "Pleased to meet you, Mr. Davis," he whispered.

Jane said, "Folks say he looks like Daddy and acts like Mommy, just like you."

Sam said, "If that means I'm handsome like my father but have the fine, even disposition of my mother, then I'm blessed. But I don't think I'm equal to either of you in those regards. Maybe Hickman is.

"I hope I get a chance to watch him grow up."

"Just take care of yourself. Where are you off to?" Charles wondered.

"Better you don't know, but I expect I'll pass by the Patterson's."

Goodbyes said, Sam disappeared into the night. He traveled and tended to business the next day, arriving at the Patterson house shortly before daybreak on Sunday. Kate met him on the front porch. "They're watching the house," she said in a low voice. "We have to be careful."

"I'll go to Rain's Thicket," Sam said. "Meet me there. Could you bring me breakfast and spend the day? Bring Robbie, if that'd make it easier."

"Go," Kate urged. "We'll be there soon."

A short while later, Kate and Robbie cantered their horses into the thicket. Sam stepped out of some brush to greet them. Robbie exclaimed, "Sam, you look wonderful, like you've slept all night and not ridden instead!"

He hugged both the young women, then devoured his breakfast and coffee. "It's all still warm, and the coffee's hot! Thank you. It's very good."

Kate replied, "We rode fast to get here and kept the coffee in a jug."

"How's Ev doing, Kate?"

"Still in Nashville, still doing what he's been doing, minding a post office."

"You and Robbie are doing great things. I've heard from Jay Brown and Billy Moore."

"The latest recruits from the Rutherford Rifles for Coleman's Scouts. I see them from time to time."

"Do you ever see Coleman?"

"Maybe I have, maybe I haven't. I still don't know what he looks like."

"And that's good for you two and Coleman."

At that point Robbie excused herself. "It's such a beautiful morning, I want to walk among the wildflowers."

"She wants to give us a little time alone," Kate explained and laughed.

As Robbie disappeared into the long grass and thickets, Kate moved to Sam and held him close. "When will this all be over?"

"When the Yankees let us be. When there're no Yankees left to fight."

"Enough talk of fighting," Kate whispered. They passionately kissed.

An hour later Robbie returned and the three engaged in pleasant conversations about things other than war. Kate's two younger brothers brought dinner and the day continued without thoughts of war, death or espionage.

Late in the afternoon, Kate and Robbie prepared to depart. Sam placed a slip of paper in Kate's hand. "It's a list of things I need in Nashville. Can you go in tomorrow and get back here with them by tomorrow night?"

Kate looked at Robbie. "We're old hands at this, aren't we Robbie?"

"It all works fine as long as Kate stays on the good side of the generals."

"Be careful," Sam admonished.

"It's you who takes the real risks. We're never under suspicion," Kate replied.

The next morning, Monday, Sam's younger brother Oscar brought breakfast to Sam in the thicket. He found his brother sound asleep with his head resting upon a grapevine for a pillow. A snap of a branch under Oscar's foot brought Sam instantly to his feet, pistol drawn and cocked. Upon recognizing Oscar he smiled and warned, "Be careful who you're sneaking up on. You're lucky I look before I shoot."

Oscar handed Sam his food and offered, "Kate and Robbie left this morning by buggy for Nashville. I expect they'll be back here by sundown."

Sam agreed. "Nine miles each way, time to load and other things. Should put them here about dusk."

"I wish I could be with you," Oscar complained, "if not a scout like you and John, at least in the infantry."

"John was wounded early in the war. He could've been killed. I've been wounded twice. There's no glory in war, Oscar. Your mother and father want to see you grow to be a man. So do I."

Toward dusk Kate and Robbie rolled into the thicket. Kate gave several packets to Sam. "Eleven newspapers, mail, maps, and the personal items you requested for General Bragg, descriptions of Union fortifications at Nashville and Pulaski and a detailing of upcoming plans of Union forces."

"Thanks. I'll be leaving straight away." He took the packets, stuffed them in a large pouch on his steel-gray horse and turned to Kate.

She looked up at him with misty eyes and urged, "Please be careful, I'm having bad thoughts"

"I'll be all right, Kate, I know how to do my job." Then he smiled and patted his animal beside him. "And I've got a good horse."

After a quick embrace, the girls rolled off in their buggy, and Sam mounted his gray to ride south. He rode southwest from Nolensville to the area of Mt. Pleasant. On Tuesday night he traveled a dark path directly into a patrol of Union cavalry, headed by a Captain Naron, also known as Chickasaw.

The captain cried out to the solitary figure, "Halt and dismount!"

Sam wheeled his mount and dug in his spurs. The gray bounded away. The cavalry gave chase. Sam quickly outdistanced them in the dark. Then,

252 / Three Paths to Glory

on impulse, he stopped, turned his horse around, leaned low and said into the animal's ear, "Let's show 'em what we can do, boy!"

He raced back into the approaching cavalry and slapped their horses in the face as he flew through them like a fired cannon ball back down the road whence he had started. The confused, shocked Yankees couldn't catch him.

Sam continued his travels unmolested on Wednesday. But on Thursday, November 19, he encountered a seedy-looking man in a cheap suit riding an old horse down the road. It was Captain Shaw, E. Coleman.

"Captain Shaw," Sam asked, "what's happening?"

"Do you have what Bragg needs in Chattanooga?"

Sam slapped his pouch, "Right here."

"Good, I'll write my report and send it with you. Josh Brown and Billy Moore are in the area and have other dispatches. You men are doing fine work. You really are the eyes and ears of the Confederacy in Tennessee. Where are you going?"

"To Dixie."

"Could you cross below Decatur?"

"I don't think so."

"It's the best way to get there. I need you to carry something for me."

"All right, if it's not heavy. Where are you going now, Captain?"

"Not to Chattanooga. We'll spend the night up ahead at Carter's place."

Throughout Thursday the men kept to themselves most of the day in the house of W.T. Carter, near Campbellsville. They talked about the siege in Chattanooga, scout activities, and prospects for success. Sam went to bed early while Shaw worked late into the night on his report for Bragg.

On Friday morning, they parted company. Sam left before daybreak wearing his gray uniform under his dyed Union topcoat. As he swung onto his saddle, he briefly noted the boots Kate gave him. *Holding up well,* he thought. Then he smoothed his mustache, assuring himself it was still filling out. He put his papers in different places—his saddle bags instead of just in the packets.

Trotting south from Campbellsville he was glad the lady of the house had fed him a good breakfast: eggs, bacon, and biscuits. "Better than camp fare, that's for sure," he mumbled to his horse.

About mid-day, having traveled nearly thirty miles and being only a few miles from the Tennessee-Alabama line, Sam pulled to the side of Lamb's Ferry Road just below Minor Hill to rest. He tied his horse to a tree, found an inviting looking plum tree and settled down to rest.

Two men rode up wearing Confederate uniforms. Sam stood to greet them. The first said, "You're unattached. And in uniform. Private Farrar," he asked the other rider, "what do you think about a man in uniform away from the army?"

"Well, Private King, I'd suppose he's a deserter. We could just shoot him here or conscript him to join the army by order of Colonel Cooper for the Confederate Service."

Sam spoke up, "I'm in the service of General Bragg's army. I'm bearing dispatches for the general. Here's my pass," he showed the pass authorized by Bragg and signed by E. Coleman.

Farrar glanced at the pass and put it in his pocket.

Sam continued, "If that's not good enough, I'll show you something else."

"I won't recognize anything you show me. You're coming with us."

When about two miles from Pulaski, Tennessee, headquarters of Union General Dodge, Sam realized he wasn't being taken to a Confederate camp, but rather a Union stronghold. He was being led by Union soldiers, not Confederate. Sam rode between his two captors and suddenly put his spurs to his horse in an effort to escape. King reached down and grabbed his horse's bridle, wrenching the animal to a stop.

Farrar leveled his pistol at Sam's head. "Settle down, boy. We're taking you to meet General Dodge."

Chattanooga

NOVEMBER 1863

ONCE THE CRACKER LINE had been opened, Bragg tried to close it by sending Longstreet to attack at Wauhatchie. The assault was a comedy of errors by both sides. Hooker had not adequately deployed his defense, and Longstreet failed to send an adequate number of men to the right place on the Union position, failing to commit his whole force.

Bragg was livid, especially for failing to capitalize on the Union mistakes. He termed the effort, "ill-conceived, ill-planned and poorly coordinated, resulting in a shambles."

Open supply line meant his siege of Chattanooga was over.

Several options were now on the table. Bragg considered retreating, assaulting the Union position at Chattanooga, waiting for Grant to attack, moving around the Union right flank or moving around Grant's left.

In a council of war on November 3rd, he outlined his decision. "Gentlemen, a couple weeks ago I was prepared to send General Jackson and General Stevenson around Grant's left and take on Burnside at Knoxville.

"Upon advice from President Davis, I'm changing the plan. Pete," he said to Longstreet, "the president wants you in Virginia. Knoxville's on the way. You'll deal with Burnside. He controls the Knoxville-to-Chattanooga railroad. We have only the Atlanta line open. We need both to adequately supply this army."

Cheatham asked, "Is it wise to divide our army? We're already outnumbered."

"We have a strong defensive position. We control the heights. When Grant comes, we'll be ready."

"What about Sherman?" Longstreet asked.

"He's still on the way from Vicksburg, I'm sure he's being sent to Knoxville and not here. Once you move on Knoxville, Grant will have to send him there. That means the main Union offensive on us will come at Lookout Mountain on our left flank. General Stevenson, I'm placing you in charge of defenses there."

"Sir," Breckinridge complained, "you've given me the center of Missionary Ridge. That's a five-mile front. I've got 16,000 men. It's damn near impossible."

General Patton Anderson joined in. "I have defenses on the western edge of the ridge. Following its twists and curves, it's over two miles long. That's nearly twice as long as the number of bayonets in the division could adequately defend."

"They'll come on our left," Bragg repeated. "We will move brigades and divisions as needed."

Longstreet asked, "What's cavalry saying about Union troop movements?"

"My cavalry is dispatched. I haven't heard anything from them in days."

* * *

ON NOVEMBER 14TH Grant met with General Orlan Smith and George Thomas to develop a plan of assault on Confederate positions on Missionary Ridge and Lookout Mountain. They met at Grant's Chattanooga headquarters. He said, "Explain it to me. Remember I've got to run this by Sherman when he gets here."

Smith nodded. "Sherman's Corps will use our newly improved roads to pass north of Chattanooga. They won't be able to see him from Lookout Mountain."

Thomas interrupted. "Bragg won't know if Sherman's going to Knoxville or Chattanooga."

Smith said, "I'll assemble every available boat and pontoon to allow Sherman's corps to cross the Tennessee River near the mouth of the South Chickamauga Creek and hit Bragg's right flank at Missionary Ridge."

"If it works," Thomas continued, "we'll control both railroad lines that supply their army and force Bragg to withdraw. My men will keep the Confederate center busy on Missionary Ridge. Hooker will take Lookout Mountain."

Smith added, "From there Hooker'll take Bragg's left flank, continue on to Rossville and cut off their path of retreat to the south."

Grant looked pensive, then spoke slowly. "I like the plan. Not sure about Hooker though. He messed up at Wauhatchie. Sherman'll be here tonight."

That evening Grant and Sherman reviewed the plan. Sherman announced, "I've looked over the ground you want me to assault on the end of Missionary Ridge. I can have it by nine in the morning the day you want me to attack."

"How far out is your army?"

"It'll be a week before my first brigades get here."

"I hope they're moving with all speed. Pressure is coming from Washington. They want Bragg beaten right here and soon. I'm cancelling the part of the plan that puts Hooker moving on Lookout Mountain. I want all we've got hitting them on their right flank, and that means Hooker too."

On November 21st the first of Sherman's brigades crossed at Brown's Ferry and marched northeast. Bragg, sure they were going to Knoxville, the next day ordered Cleburne to remove his 11,000 men from his defense line and to report to Chickamauga Station for transport by rail to Knoxville.

On November 23rd Grant's chief of staff, John Rawlins reported to his general, "I just received word Cleburne has pulled back from Missionary Ridge. Confederate deserters claim the whole army's pulling back."

"Can it be?" Grant wondered. "Is Bragg's whole army going to reinforce Longstreet at Knoxville?"

"We need to ascertain their intentions, sir."

"Have Thomas send a division into the center. After rebel strength is determined, they're to fall back." Grant scribbled the order on a piece of paper and instructed Rawlins to bring it to Thomas.

Thomas ordered his division under General Thomas Wood to move forward from the Union center in a reconnaissance in force. In their front, about 2,000 yards to the east was a rise of ground about a hundred feet high. Missionary Ridge was beyond. The knob became the Union objective.

With Sheridan's division lined up on the right and Howard's corps on the left, 20,000 soldiers aligned in near-precise formation. At 1:30 p.m. 14,000 swept across the plain toward the rise—Orchard Knob. The surprised Confederates there numbered six hundred. They managed one volley, then were overrun.

Grant and Thomas watched the attack, then issued another order to Wood. "Do not fall back. Entrench and hold your position."

Both sides readjusted plans. Bragg, facing a Union assault, feared his center was vulnerable and called back troops within a day's march of Chattanooga. Cleburne's men, boarding a train at Chickamauga Station were told to return immediately to Missionary Ridge. Bragg transferred troops from Lookout Mountain to Tunnel Hill on his right flank and gave command to General Hardee.

The left Confederate flank would be under General Carter Stevenson, the center commanded by John Breckinridge. Breckinridge was ordered to fortify Missionary Ridge. He consulted Patton Anderson and William Bate.

"Bragg's finally getting around to building defenses on the ridge. We will, but I'm unsure as to the best location."

Anderson suggested, "The base of the ridge is best. Build rifle pits. We shouldn't even let them get close to going up."

Bate countered, "From the ridge we can fire down at the Yankees. It'd be like shooting fish in a barrel."

Breckinridge considered. "Both options have merit. So we'll do both. Divide your divisions. Put half at the base in rifle pits and half on the crest."

Grant was also forced to make a change in plans. Sherman's pontoon bridge at Brown's Ferry had torn apart after only three of his divisions had passed over. General Peter Osterhaus, with a division, was stranded in Lookout Valley.

"Cump, can you complete your mission with three divisions?" Grant asked.

Cump said he could. Grant said, "Then we'll attack Lookout Mountain. Osterhaus's over there and can join Hooker. It should relieve pressure on you. It starts tomorrow. You'll move across the river and hit their right flank at Tunnel Hill."

"It will be done, General."

On the morning of November 24th Sherman's three divisions began to transport across the Tennessee River. The crossing took much longer than expected, most of the day. Meanwhile, Joe Hooker put his plan in action. Stevenson and his command were on the summit of Lookout Mountain.

The mountain had a pathway, called the bench, running the length of the precipice about halfway up. Some Confederates were on the bench. At the base of the north end was Craven House. The rebel line stretched from there along the mountain. Hooker had 10,000 men poised to attack.

At 8:30 a.m. the first Union troops, the XII Corps under General John Geary, crossed Lookout Creek in front of the mountain. His orders: "to assault Lookout Mountain, march down the valley and sweep every rebel from it."

While other divisions stalled at the creek, Geary swept northeast along the base of the mountain and swept Confederate General Edward Walthall's badly outnumbered brigade back to the Craven House.

On top of the mountain, Confederate defenders found they were of little help intervening in the battle raging on the cliffs below. As Geary's forces plowed ahead, the stalled divisions crossed the creek and joined the battle. Confederate General John Moore brought up his brigade to fight Geary but was repulsed.

Artillery fire from Chattanooga blasted the bench, making it an untenable position for rebel marksmen. The fight moved up the mountainside. By 3:00 p.m. thick fog and mist enveloped the mountain.

The ground they fought on was rough, with ravines and dense forest. Boulders and rocks littered the mountainside, making it difficult to traverse.

Both sides blazed away blindly throughout the foggy afternoon. Halfway up the mountain was shrouded. On the ground, in Chattanooga the 2nd Minnesota waited in reserve. Clint Cilley stood with Judson Bishop and watched. "I can't see anything, Colonel, we have to follow the battle by sound."

"It's a battle above the clouds. They're moving up the mountain. They'll have to abandon their position by nightfall."

"I just got word from General Thomas. Sherman's finally crossed the river and is attacking the north end of the ridge. He's near victory there."

"Then we'll have both flanks by tonight. We'll be chasing rebs south tomorrow."

The fog lifted in the darkness and the progress of the battle could be traced by the bright flashes from muskets. About midnight a lunar eclipse darkened the battlefield and Bragg's men on Lookout Mountain moved onto Missionary Ridge where Bragg consolidated his forces.

Reports on success to the north had been premature. On the Confederate right flank things didn't go as smoothly as Sherman planned. After finally crossing the river and engaging in battle, he found the hill he had captured was not connected to Missionary Ridge. It was Goat Hill. The well-fortified Tunnel Hill on Missionary Ridge still lay before him.

That night Bragg consulted his two Corps commanders. Hardee urged a retreat, but Breckinridge was determined to fight it out from a strong position on Missionary Ridge. Bragg sided with Breckinridge, and the stage was set for the next day as Confederate forces all shifted to the ridge.

The Battle for Missionary Ridge

N THE NIGHT of November 24th Grant met with Sherman, Thomas and Hooker on Orchard Knob, his headquarters during the battle. "So, Cump, you captured the wrong hill. What is your situation?"

"I had faulty intelligence. I didn't know of a completely separate rise before the ridge. Now we're on Billy Goat Hill. Across a deep ravine we face Cleburne, who has the well-fortified Tunnel Hill on the northernmost end of the ridge."

Grant announced, "We'll make changes for tomorrow. I want a double envelopment by you from the north, Hooker from the south. General Thomas, you'll advance in the center after Sherman and Hooker reach the ridge."

Sherman asked, "When do you want the attacks to begin?"

"You'll advance as soon as it's light, and your simultaneous attacks will be in cooperation. Your command will either carry the rifle pits or ridge directly in front of them or move left, as the presence of the enemy may require."

"General," Thomas asked, "I need support on my flank. Can General Hooker cross the valley and demonstrate against Bragg's left flank at Rossville Gap?"

"I'm looking for Bragg to divert attention from Sherman by demonstrating near Lookout Mountain. Call on him if you need him."

Throughout the morning of the 25th, Sherman launched multiple direct assaults against Cleburne's line on Tunnel Hill. Only three Union brigades were committed by Sherman and stiff resistance by the rebels stopped them.

Just west of the southern end of the ridge, Hooker was slowed for hours by burned bridges on Chattanooga Creek. Grant stood on Orchard Knob with Thomas. "Pap, are you ready to go? It's 3:30 and nothing's happening on the flanks. The plan's in danger of falling apart. I want you to move forward as instructed. Attack the lower works. Don't climb the ridge."

"General, these men were at Chickamauga. Some fought bravely there and stood with me on Snodgrass Hill. But the ignominy of our defeat overshadowed their heroism. They've had to endure taunts and ridicule from Sherman's and Hooker's men who weren't even there. My men are ready."

"Then advance, General."

The 2nd Minnesota had been held half a mile south of Fort Negley. On the 23rd they'd been issued three days' rations and one hundred rounds of ammunition. At noon on Wednesday, the 25th, they marched to the left, a mile beyond and took position as Palmer's XIV Corps, Baird's Division, Van Derveer's brigade.

Colonel George was again on leave for health reasons. Judson Bishop led the regiment. In midafternoon Van Derveer's brigade, containing regiments from Indiana, Ohio, and Minnesota, advanced toward Missionary Ridge.

In front of the deployed forward line was an open field. The ground sloped toward a narrow creek, then gradually rose for about a quarter mile to the crest of a secondary ridge parallel to and about a mile from the base of Missionary Ridge.

Clint Cilley was back with his regiment for the battle. He stood alongside Lieutenant Harry Couse waiting for the order to advance. Clint advised, "Looks like log breastworks with infantry behind them on the low ridge."

"You're right, Captain, but it's the far ridge has most of their defenses. Look, on the crest are more breastworks and artillery batteries. They've got two guns each spaced at intervals along the line. They can sweep us with direct and crossfire the whole space between the ridges. When we get by them, it's another three to four hundred yards to Missionary Ridge and more guns."

"Well, Captain, at least the ground slopes down not up and we'll be in trees. There'll be some cover."

Clint squinted. "They've cut some trees down to slow us and get us tangled."

"And then," Couse added, "it's up the ridge."

The ridge itself rose with a gradual slope, becoming increasingly abrupt as the top grew closer, reaching a height of five to six hundred feet.

Rincie DeGrave stood in line next to Aaron Doty, fingering a blue kerchief in his left hand. "Watchcha got?" Doty asked.

"That blond girl in Chicago, Jenny Murphy. I think that's her name. She gave me this to remember her by. I remember. I was gonna give it back on the way home. But I got a funny feelin'. If I don't make it. Give it to Jenny, will you?"

"I recall the girl, but don't be silly, Rincie. You'll make it. We all will."

"Jest in case, Aaron, tell her I remembered."

"Sure, Rincie, but I won't need to. You'll tell her yerself."

Bishop came across the line in front of his regiment. "Colonel Van Derveer's order, men! Our entire brigade will march upon the first line of breastworks. We're to seize and occupy them if at all possible. If they drive us back, we're to fall in on our brigade. I know you'll do us proud!"

Cilley addressed Company C, "Hold your fire. Move steadily forward until we take the breastworks. Then defend it with all you've got. Fix bayonets!"

At 3:40 p.m. 23,000 veterans of the Battle of Chickamauga stepped off toward the ridge. Their line was two and one-half miles long and six rows deep.

With bayonets glittering in the afternoon sun, the whole front line advanced. As soon as the blue-clad soldiers emerged from the woods rifle fire blazed from both ridges and from the artillery on Missionary Ridge. Cannon fire erupted with the sound and fury of a thousand thunderclaps. The top of the ridge glowed in a sheet of flame and smoke.

In the face of shot and shell, with lead missiles zinging all around, the Minnesotans silently and steadily advanced. Shells ripped up the ground all around them and rebels blazed away with cannon and rifle. The 2nd Minnesota crossed the creek and went up the slope. Within about a hundred paces from the breastworks, the determined Minnesota soldiers cheered, then dashed headlong at the defenses before them. The rebels broke and ran into their camp behind them. They took cover behind stumps and huts and opened up rapid fire as the Minnesotans gained control of the breastworks.

Indiana, Ohio and Minnesota boys let loose a murderous volley from the breastwork, and the Confederate soldiers broke and ran, scrambling up the ridge.

Aaron Doty stood next to Rincie DeGrave on the captured breastwork. He turned and said, "See, Rincie, that wasn't so bad, was it?"

Rincie looked at his friend, his hand over his chest. Blood oozed between his fingers. Slowly he crumpled, dead by the time Doty reached him.

Aaron took the blue kerchief from his friend's pocket and softly wiped Rincie's face with it, then pocketed it before turning to face the enemy.

The brigade was in a precarious spot. On the Confederate side, the breastwork was chest high. On the Union side it was only knee high. Shot and shell rained down. The men had no cover. Officers pleaded for direction.

Bishop shouted at Baird, "This is a deathtrap. We can't stay here!" The general was hesitant, then reasoned, "The fire's murderous if we stay put, or if we run back. Those guns can't hit us if we get close to the ridge. They can't aim straight down."

Van Deveer noted, "Some men are already moving forward on their own."

Baird decided, "Let them all go up the ridge. Give the order."

Clint shouted at his men, "We're going in again! It's confusing, I know. Follow the colors however you can. Where it gets steep, it'll be every man for himself regardless of regiment!"

The regiment ascended from the breastworks, each man struggling through entanglements of brush and downed trees left by the rebels. A lethal blast of musketry mowed soldiers down like fresh cut grass. The battalions formed triangular shapes with their flags in the apex. Every time a flag holder fell, another man rushed in to take it up.

As they hit the steepest part of the slope, the regiments intermingled. Artillery fire blasted down largely went over the attackers. The rebel gunners were having trouble sighting their cannon down the steep sides of the ridge.

Below, on Orchard Knob, Grant was furious. "I didn't order a charge up the ridge! Thomas, what's going on here? Who ordered those men up the ridge?"

"I don't know. I didn't."

Grant turned to General Gordon Granger, "Did you order them up?"

"They went without orders. When those fellows get goin', hell can't stop 'em!"

The men began to cry, "Chicakamauga! Chickamauga!" as they twisted, climbed and scrambled up the ridge. The climb became steep. Handholds were necessary. The Union soldiers charged ahead as rapidly as possible. Then, overcome with fatigue, they'd find haven behind a rock or tree, rest and charge again.

They pushed fleeing rebels ahead of them until they reached the crest of the hill. After a final rest, the blue-clad warriors made a final rush into murderous fire. They swarmed over another set of breastworks and charged the defenders.

Confederates broke and ran, leaving their artillery. Then the rebels regrouped and made a desperate counterattack. The crowd of soldiers, a blending of all regiments, met the attack with a mass charge. After a few minutes of vicious hand-to-hand fighting, the ridge was cleared. The Confederates ran off the back side.

The captured artillery was trained on the fleeing rebels, but in the fading sunlight they escaped. The fighting ceased. The ascent up the ridge had taken twenty minutes. It seemed like an eternity.

* * *

THROUGHOUT THE DAY, Sherman battered away on the north end with little success. Hooker managed to get though Rossville Gap. Breckinridge had ridden to the southern end of Missionary Ridge to organize against Hooker but was too late and rushed north when he heard ferocious gunfire there. Again he was too late. The collapse of the center of his line spelled certain defeat for Bragg and his beaten army hurried south off the backside of the ridge.

On Orchard Knob Grant was elated but perplexed. "Pap, I wish I could say our victory was the result of great generalship, but I'm afraid individual heroism, bad tactics by Bragg and luck played a bigger role. Their cannons were placed on the crown of the ridge not at the military crest. Lower down they could have sighted their guns to get better shots. That high up their angle was wrong."

"Sheridan's giving chase, General Grant."

"I hope we can catch them and finish Bragg off."

Discovering he was alone in the pursuit, Sheridan called off the chase. Grant later sent Hooker's force out to run down Bragg.

Much of Bragg's army boarded trains at Chickamauga Station and headed south. But Tennessee troops under Cleburne were left to burn the town and destroy anything of value that couldn't be carried away.

It was heartbreaking for starving soldiers doing rear guard duty to have to destroy food and supplies. They took with them what they could, including hard tack and sides of bacon hanging from the points of bayonets.

Being the rear guard of a retreating army could be trying and hazardous. They'd move short distances, look back, move again and look back. Sometimes Yankees would get close enough to fire a volley, so it was returned by Confederates.

On November 27th, in northern Georgia, at Ringgold Gap, Cleburne's forces surprised Hooker's pursuing army and thwarted Grant's attempt to destroy Bragg's army. The Army of Tennessee escaped south leaving almost all of Tennessee in Union hands.

December 1st found the Rutherford Rifles in Dalton, Georgia, where they constructed winter quarters and recuperated from their recent battles. There they re-enlisted for the duration of the war.

The Trial of Sam Davis

ARRAR AND KING hauled Sam into Pulaski, Tennessee, and brought
him before the head of Union Special Forces in the area. Levi Naron
was a large block of a man. His thick dark hair touched his collar in
back and flopped over his ears. A heavy black beard covered half his face.

His service alias was "Captain Chickasaw" and he was the leader of the
Chickasaw Scouts, the Union's answer to Coleman. Naron was an unlikely
choice for this position. Born in Georgia, late of Mississippi for the past
twenty-one years and a slave owner, he was also an ardent Unionist, which
led to his moving to Illinois and joining the Union army.

The two privates dressed in their gray uniforms brought their prisoner
into Naron's office after dark on November 20th. "Another one?" Naron
stated. "It's been a busy day. Kansas cavalry brought in three more earlier.
This one looks like he just left his mommy. I'm surprised he's got that fuzz
on his upper lip. Is it real?"

"It's real. Did you find anything on 'em? The other three?" Farrar asked.

"Nope, they were clean. They work for Coleman though, I'd bet on it."

"Well," Farrar continued, "this one ain't so clean. The more we keep
lookin' the more we keep findin'."

"Oh . . . ?" Naron's interest heightened. "Like what?"

King held up a packet. "Newspapers, Union fortifications in Nashville,
Union troop movements and more."

"So, boy, are you one of Coleman's spies?"

"I'm a courier."

"What's yer name?"

"Sam Davis."

"What can you tell me about what you're carryin'?"

"I'm Sam Davis, and I'm a courier."

"This isn't getting anywhere. Let's go see General Dodge."

264

The two privates and Naron walked across the compound to the head-quarters of General Grenville Dodge, head of intelligence gathering for the Western District of the Union Army. In his mid-thirties with a full dark beard and neatly combed short hair, Dodge had been informed that "a well-organized and disciplined corps of scouts and spies existed within my lines." One of these corps was Coleman's, operating east of Pulaski.

"I have a spy, General," Naron announced.

"Courier," Sam corrected.

Naron put the packets and papers on Dodge's desk. The general perused them quickly. Looking up at Sam, Dodge smiled. "You're a well-formed, pleasant-looking young man, devoted to your cause I'm sure."

"I'm wearing a Confederate uniform, sir."

"Yes, but a Union soldier's overcoat. Some might say you are trying to pass as a Union soldier, as a spy would."

"It's dyed brown. That should remove suspicion of intent to pass as a spy."

Dodge smiled again, "And a well-spoken young man. However, you have items here that are problematic for you. Things a spy might have."

"I'm not a spy."

"All right, let's assume you're a messenger. You're still in big trouble here. There could be serious consequences. Is there anything you want to tell me?"

"No, sir."

"Captain Naron, take this boy to the Giles County Jail. We'll talk more later." He looked at his watch. "It's eight o'clock now."

Farrar and King escorted Sam to the jail. There were two cells. One had three men in it, the other one. Sam's eyes barely flickered in recognition as he passed the first cell. The three men in it were scouts Josh Brown, Billy Moore, and the E. Coleman the federals were seeking, Henry Shaw.

"Hiya boy," the middle-aged man in the cell greeted. "Name's Smith. What big crime did you do?"

"I've committed no crime," Sam replied.

"That's Yankees fer ya!" the man exclaimed. "Don't need reasons. They kin throw ya in jail fer writing notes or jes tellin' folks things. That what you did?"

"I don't want to talk about it, Mr. Smith."

"What's wrong with a little talk, our neighbors here ain't neighborly either."

Shaw called over, "Our new friend is quite talkative. It can get tiresome."

Smith glared at Shaw and then smiled at Sam, "We might as well git ta know each other a little. We might be together fer a while."

"Really, Mr. Smith, I'm sorry, but I don't want to talk."

Smith kept trying to initiate conversation with Sam, then the other three. He laughed, cajoled but could get no substantive response to anything he said.

Three hours later guards came and took Smith away. Sam looked over at Shaw, who shook his head and placed his finger over his lips. Then he mouthed, "Informer," and pointed at Smith.

A little later they came and took Sam. He found himself before General Dodge once again. Sam met Naron, who was leaving the office as Sam entered.

"Mr. Davis, it seems you're still a mystery to us."

"General, sir, you have my pass. You see I'm attached to General Bragg."

"And to E. Coleman. That's who I'm really interested in."

"I worked as a scout and courier for him."

"I want to know where he is."

"I won't tell you."

"Listen, young man, you're in a tight spot. I've gone over the evidence against you." He pointed to the packets still on his desk. "There's more than enough here to convict you as a spy."

"I'm a courier, a messenger. That's all."

"You are a spy. Do you know what's done to spies."

"They hang."

"You're a promising young man. I'm sure you have a bright future awaiting you when this war's over. Don't throw your life away over this, over a lost cause."

"I have nothing to say, sir."

"Think about it overnight."

Sam went back to his cell. Shaw and his two scouts shared looks of concern with him, but the captain again put his finger to his lips. There'd be no talking between them. Sam slept fitfully on the hard cot. He thought of home and Kate and wished he'd never stopped under that plum tree.

The next morning they came for Sam again and brought him before General Dodge for a third conference. This time there was no smile from Dodge. He was crisp and to the point. "Come with me into my private office." They went into a small room, devoid of any clerks or other personnel. Dodge sat behind a small desk and Sam stood before him. "Young man, the charge against you is very serious. Have you considered anything I said last night?"

"I listened to you, and I appreciate your concerns. Nothing's changed. I will say nothing more than I have. I'm dressed in uniform. I have a pass, and I'm not a spy."

Dodge was firm. "From what we found on your person, you are a spy. You had accurate information in regard to my army. I must know where you received this information."

Sam remained silent.

"Mr. Davis," Dodge tried again, "you'll hang. There's no chance for you unless you tell me from where you got this information."

"General Dodge," Sam relayed, "I know the danger of my situation. I'm willing to take the consequences. I know I'll have to die, but I won't tell where I got the information. There's no power on earth that can make me. I'm doing my duty as a soldier. I do so feeling I'm doing my duty to God and my country."

"Sam," Dodge earnestly pleaded, "help me to spare your life. Give me something, anything. You're a young man of the highest character and integrity. I don't want you to die over this."

"General, it's useless to talk to me. You can court martial me, or do anything else you like, but I will not betray the trust imposed on me. But I do sincerely thank you for the interest you've shown in me."

Dodge sighed, "Your trial will be in two days."

Sam was taken back to his cell where he spoke to the others for the first time. "Day after tomorrow I'm to be tried for a spy."

Two charges were filed against Sam Davis. On November 23rd he stood before a tribunal of three Union officers to answer to them. A court official read each count: "Charge number one: Being a Spy. Specification: That Samuel Davis of Coleman Scouts in the service of the so-called Confederate States did come within the line of the United States forces in Middle Tennessee for the purpose of secretly gaining information concerning these forces and conveying the same to the enemy and was arrested within the said lines on or about November 20, 1863. This in Giles County, Tennessee."

The chief officer asked, "How say you?"

Sam stood and firmly replied, "Not guilty."

The court official continued, "Charge 2: Being a carrier of mail communications and information from within the lines of the U.S. Army to persons in arms against the government. Specification: In this that one Samuel Davis, on or about November 20th, 1863, was arrested in Giles County, Tennessee. Engaged in carrying mails and information from within the lines of the United State Forces to persons in arms against the United States Government."

The chief office again asked, "How say you?"

Sam stood and replied, "Guilty."

The trial consumed the next two days. Farrar, King and Naron, as Chickasaw, all testified. The circumstances of Sam's capture, his attire and the contents of his packets were all discussed. Sam's refusal to offer any information about who his associates were and what he was doing sealed his fate.

Sam was allowed to read a statement in which he stated that he met Coleman on the road and was given packets to deliver and that he was given a pass authorized by General Bragg.

The courtroom was cleared for deliberation. It didn't take long. The court was reconvened and the verdict read: "The said Samuel Davis of Coleman's Scouts in the Service of the so-called Confederate States be hung by the neck until he is dead. Two-thirds of the Commission concurring in the sentence."

The sentence was ordered to be carried out Friday, November 27, in Pulaski.

After his sentence, Sam was brought back to the jail and put in a cell. Thursday, the next morning, Josh Brown and Henry Shaw were ordered to get ready, for they were going to be removed to the courthouse in the public square about a hundred feet from the jail.

Just as they were eating breakfast Sam was brought in bound by handcuffs. Josh handed him a piece of meat. Sam mouthed, "Where's Moore?"

Josh looked down and whispered, "Jumped out a second floor window last night. Got away, I guess."

Sam munched on the meat with two hands. "Thank you," he said softly.

Both Shaw and Brown clasped Sam's hand and bade him good bye. Shaw whispered, "Thank you," before both were taken away to the courthouse. The guard was doubled around the jail.

Sam spent most of the day in thought and silent contemplation as he considered what was, what might have been and what still could be. A local bank cashier and a Methodist preacher, who was also a Union officer, were given permission to visit Sam to offer spiritual comfort.

They found Sam sitting in darkness on the floor. It was too dark for them to read to Sam and his features were indistinct. Pastor Teter asked, "Son, are you at peace with the Lord?"

Sam looked up at them, tears streaming down his cheeks, and replied, "I don't fear death, but it makes me mad to think I'm to die as a spy. I'm not a spy!"

"You don't want to go to the Lord with anger in your heart."

The three then prayed together and as the visitors left another arrived. Chaplain James Young was a federal chaplain for the 81st Ohio Infantry. Young offered Sam comfort. The pastor asked gently, "Is there anything you wish to have known?"

"Just what I've said all along. I'm not a spy, I was in your lines on other business. I never opened the letter from Coleman to Bragg, and I don't know what was in it."

"God will judge, he knows what was in your heart."

"Chaplain, there's a song my mother always sings, it's a favorite of mine. Would you sing it with me?"

"Surely, what is it?"

"'On Jordan's Stormy Banks I Stand.'"

Sam and Young sang together. The boy's voice became animated as he came to the chorus.

I am bound for the Promised Land, I am bound for the Promised Land
O who will come and go with me? I am bound for the Promised Land.

"Chaplain," Sam asked when they were done singing, "would you stay here all night and pray for me at my execution?"

"Sam, I can't stay. I'm not a well man and my health won't permit it. But I'll pray for you tomorrow."

As Young stood to leave Sam picked up his overcoat and handed it to him. "Something to remember me by," he said.

During the night by the light of a single candle Sam wrote:

> *Dear Mother,*
> *Oh, how painful it is to write to you. I have got to die tomorrow morning—to be hung by the federals. Mother do not grieve for me. I must bid you good-bye forevermore—Mother, I do not hate to die. Give my love to all.*   *Your dear Son, Sam*

Then he continued with three other missives:

> *Mother, tell the children all to be good, I wish I could see all of you once more, but I will never, never no more.*

> *Mother and Father,*
> *Do not forget me. Think of me when I am dead, but do not grieve for me, it will not do any good.*

> *Father,*
> *You can send after my remains if you want to do so, they will be*
> *at Pulaski, Tenn. I will leave some things too with the hotel keeper*
> *for you.*   *Pulaski is in Giles Co. Tenn.*
>   *South of Columbia*

The morning of November 27th was bright and warm. Blue skies draped over Pulaski like a giant canopy. Assembly sounded and soldiers gathered and marched into town. On the brow of a hill to the left of the road stood a rough gallows.

Sam was alone in the early morning. All other prisoners were in the courthouse. Chaplain Young entered the cell and prayed with Sam again. Sam was dressed with his black broad-brimmed hat on his head, his gray Confederate uniform and his boots—the gifts from Kate. They had been cut up by Union soldiers looking for secrets, but he still wore them.

The condemned man handed his watch, letters written to his parents, buttons from his uniform, and a little book he had written in. About 9:30 the distant sound of drums, muffled at first and gradually louder sounded down the road.

Sam smiled in spite of everything. "They're playing the Dead March."

A few minutes later guards came to get Sam to take him to the waiting wagon and escort. Sam was seated upon a coffin in the rear of the open wagon as it rolled to the nearby gallows. Young sat next to him dressed in his blue uniform.

The procession consisted of the thirty-member band and the military escort.

From their courthouse confinement Shaw and Brown watched from the window. Sam saw them, stood from the coffin and saluted as the procession passed by. Shaw turned to Brown, his eyes welling with tears, and said, "If Davis tells, we'll all be hung, but he won't tell."

As Sam sat on his coffin Captain Chickasaw rode up. He dismounted, walked to Sam, placed his hand on his shoulder, and offered, "We'll give you a horse, rations, and set you on your way. All you have to do is tell us E. Coleman's whereabouts. His capture is a military necessity."

Indignantly Sam replied, "If I had a thousand lives, I'd lose them all here and now before I'd betray my friends or the confidence of my informer."

Thousands gathered around the square to watch. Once at the gallows Sam stepped from the wagon and sat upon a bench at the foot of the scaffold. Captain Armstrong, the Provost Marshall, stood waiting.

Sam asked, "How long do I have?"

"About fifteen minutes."

"What's been happening in the war?"

"Your army's just been pushed off of Missionary Ridge at Chattanooga. General Bragg's in full retreat south."

"That's too bad. I guess the boys'll have to fight the battles without me."

Armstrong hesitated and took Sam's hand. "I regret very much having to do this. I feel I'd rather die myself than do what I have to do."

"I don't think hard of you. You're doing your duty."

Chickasaw looked up at Sam and pleaded again, "Save yourself!"

Sam turned to Armstrong, "I'm ready." With a quick, firm step he ascended the stairway to the gallows.

Chaplain Young prayed, "If a reprieve is not to be given on earth, may a higher, better, lasting one be given in heaven, where no war is known. May God bless our country. May sweet peace soon return again. May that time when war should no longer be waged come speedily. May God bless Sam Davis."

The multitude cried "Amen!"

Sam stooped while Armstrong drew a white cap over Sam's head. He adjusted the noose around the boy's neck and sprang the trap door. The brave men watching who had seen death and blood in the worst battles in the nation's history, men who hated rebels and the Confederacy, turned their backs in disgust and refused to watch Sam Davis die.

Only the anguished cry of a woman wrenched their hearts. Kate Patterson had arrived too late.

The Interlude

I N THE SPRING OF 1864 the 5th Minnesota Regiment finally became actively engaged in the war again. During the winter of 1863-1864 they spent much time at Big Black River with occasional sorties into the surrounding area. In February they reenlisted, almost the whole regiment, for another three years.

They were transferred from Sherman's XV Corps to Nathaniel Bank's XVI Corps in A.J. Smith's division. The 5th was now part of the Second Brigade, First Division, of the XVI Corps.

In the reorganization that followed, Jim McGrew became captain of Company B with Tom Gere and John Bishop lieutenants. They were ordered to report to Vicksburg by March 4th to board transports.

Still in their Black River camp, Colonel Hubbard inspected his regiment and conferred with his Company B officers. "Gentlemen, it appears we'll be transported south to the Red River. Banks is being diverted from a campaign on Mobile to occupy east Texas and control the Red River to cut Texas off from the rest of the Confederacy. We'll be part of it."

McGrew, an artilleryman at Fort Ridgely, smiled. "The men are ready, sir."

Gere asked, "Do you have any news from Minnesota? What about our other regiments?"

"I just received a letter from Colonel Marshall, the 7th will be coming south soon. He's says they're tired of fighting Indians. They spent last summer in Dakota Territory with the 6th and 10th. They've pushed the Sioux west. Sully and the 8th are going into the Territory again this summer to finish the job.

"The 8th was, and the 9th is now, on frontier duty, guarding western forts in Minnesota. Not many, but people are still being killed by Sioux in the western part of the state. So, some protection is needed. All of our Minnesota regiments are eager to join us in the fight here."

* * *

JIMMY DUNN SAT in camp with Will Hutchinson and Levi Carr. He opened a letter and read slowly. Then he looked up at his friends. "It's from Tim Pendergast, sergeant with the 2nd. Rincie DeGrave was killed at Missionary Ridge. You fellas knew him, didn't you?"

"From Preston, wasn't he?" Carr said.

"A good man, liked to laugh," Hutchinson remarked.

Jimmy sadly looked at his letter. "We've lost lotsa good men, going back to Redwood Ferry, Captain Marsh, all the others."

"And we keep on losin' more, Jimmy."

"Sure, Levi, and we've been out of the fight fer months here so we don't git shot."

"But sickness gits 'em," Levi responded. "They die just the same."

"We're movin' out now," Jimmy said. "That's good. We gotta end this war."

Will Hutchinson whittled a piece of wood and remarked, "The rebs can't hold on much longer. It's been near three years now. They've lost Tennessee, we beat 'em at Vicksburg and control the Mississippi. They can't fight much longer."

"But Will, all they need to do is hold on," Jimmy countered. "If they can stretch this thing out, people in the north'll get tired of it. They already are. What if Lincoln gets beat by a Copperhead in the next election? What then?"

"Then a lot of men will have fought and died fer nothin'."

"That's why we have to win," Levi explained. "That's why I'm ready to head to Louisiana with Old Whiskey Smith and why I'd like to see the other Minnesota boys git here ta help us."

"They'll be comin'," Jimmy said hopefully, "and we'll win this war."

* * *

IN DALTON, GEORGIA, at the camp of the 1st Tennessee, Tod Carter rode into the bivouac of Company I. They were in tatters, he noted, some like walking skeletons, hollow eyed, skin and bones. Charlie Miller, Joe Hall, and Marion McFarland were munching on a skimpy ration of cornmeal.

Charlie looked up at the young officer. "Git us some food, sir. This ain't even enuf ta make sloosh."

"Where's your captain, private?"

"Cap'n Ledbetter? Over there." Charlie pointed.

As Carter rode over and conferred with Ledbetter, Joe Hall spit into the fire and remarked, "So Bragg's gone. Now we git Joe Johnston."

Charlie morosely stared into the fire. "Nobuddy'll miss 'im. That's fer sure."

"What do ya know 'bout Johnston?" McFarland asked.

Charlie shook his head. "He's careful, takes his time, takes care of his men."

"Well, that's an improvement," Joe Hall muttered.

After Carter rode off, the captain called his company together. Sadly, he stood before them and announced, "I just got word, Sam Davis is dead. The Yankees hung him for being a spy."

In spite of facing death constantly and being battle-hardened, the men from Rutherford County were visibly saddened.

McFarland called out, "Sam weren't no spy. He was a scout."

Ledbetter replied, "Whatever he's called makes no difference. Sam was a good soldier and devoted to our cause. He paid for it with his life. We've lost good friends. We've had a lot of sad days. This is one of them."

Charlie Miller simply looked down and muttered, "Damn."

* * *

THE 2ND MINNESOTA went back to Chattanooga where they faced a decision. In the summer of 1864 their enlistments would be up. They were encouraged to reenlist with the carrot of a thirty-day leave.

On Christmas Day, 1863, eighty percent of the regiment reported to headquarters and reenlisted. They shipped off for Minnesota, where they were feted at banquets and honored for their glories at Tullahoma, Chickamauga, and Chattanooga.

Under the influence of Governor Stephen Miller, they received new Springfield rifles, new uniforms, and equipment and transportation east when their time was up.

On April 10th they rejoined their brigade at Ringgold, Georgia. Captain Cilley was still a staff officer with General Thomas. He brought news to Colonel Bishop, "Orders coming, Colonel. Just thought I'd let you know."

"Don't tell me, they're sending us back to Minnesota again?"

Clint laughed, "No the climate'll be warmer. You're going south. You're going to help General Sherman take Atlanta."

"What about you?"

"I'll be resigning, staying with General Thomas in Nashville. Grant's been named general-in-chief. Pap wants me to stay with him. I may be assigned to Schofield."

Bishop shook hands with Clint. "The teacher from Minnesota's moving right along."

There's still a lot of war to fight. May God be with you, Colonel."

Terms

Infantry Units
  Company: 100 men
  Regiment: 10 companies
  Brigade: 3 to 6 regiments
  Division: 2 to 6 Brigades
  Corps: 2 to 4 Divisions
  Army: 1 to 8 Corps
These numbers could vary depending upon the numbers of men available. Confederate and Union command structures might also vary in numbers.

Cavalry
  Troop: 100 men
  Regiment: 12 troops
  Brigade, Division and Corps
Initially, each Union cavalry regiment was assigned to an infantry division. The Confederates brigaded their cavalry together. The Union eventually adopted this organization as well. As the war progressed, both sides formed cavalry divisions. The North also formed cavalry corps, and the South later also adopted this innovation.

The basic unit of artillery is the battery, which has 4 to 6 guns, is commanded by a captain and has 4 lieutenants, 12 sergeants and corporals and 120 privates. It typically had 4 guns in the South and 6 guns in the North.

Military Terms
  Flank: the end or side of a military position
  Long Roll: a long, continuous drum roll that commanded a regiment to assemble
Abatis: A line of trees chopped down with their branches pointed out at the enemy.
Wheel: Change direction to the reverse flank.
Oblique: Crossing the battlefield in a diagonal line.

Load in Nine Times:
  1. Load
  2. Handle Cartridge
  3. Tear Cartridge
  4. Charge Cartridge
  5. Draw rammer
  6. Ram cartridge
  7. Return rammer
  8. Prime
  9. Shoulder arms

Sources

The Life of Billy Yank, Bell Irvin Wiley, Louisiana State University Press, 1987

The Life of Johnny Reb, Bell Irvin Wiley, Louisiana State University Press, 1987

The Story of a Regiment, Judson W. Bishop, Newell L. Chester, editor, North Star Press, St. Cloud, Mn. 2000

"Co. Aytch," Sam R. Watkins, Collier Books, Macmillian Publishing Company, New York, 1962

Minnesota In The Civil And Indian Wars 1861-1865 V1, The Board of Commissioners, Pioneer Press Company, St. Paul, Minn., 1891

Minnesota In The Civil and Indian Wars 1861-1865 V2, The Board of Commissioners, Pioneer Press Company, St. Paul, Minn. 1893

Recollections of the Sioux Massacre, Oscar Garret Wall, The Home Printery, Lake City, Minnesota, 1909

A Blaze of Glory, Jeff Shaara, Random House, New York, 2012

The Rutherford Rifles, Mabel Pittard, Rutherford County, Tennessee Historical Society, Murfreesboro, Tennessee, 1988

The Unsinkable Mary Kate, Marion Herndon Dunn, http://tennessee-scv.org/colemanscouts/unsinkable.htm

The Chatfield Boys and the Dakota War, by Joe Chase, Chatfield, Minnesota

Pvt. Samuel C. Davis, Thomas L. Russell, Fayetteville, Tennessee, 2010

http://en.wikipedia.org aided in the depictions of some of the Civil War battles presented.

Civil War maps attributed to Hal Jespersen, www.posix.com/CW

Church History from First Presbyterian Church, Florence, Alabama